WILLI

Leonida drew in a ragged breath as Sage gently framed her face between his hands and lifted her lips to his. Her world began spinning as his lips pressed on hers, so hungry, so demanding. This time she would not pull back. She could not deny herself this pleasure—no more than she could stop herself from breathing. She shivered when his hand cupped her breast through the clinging wet fabric of her chemise, her skin on fire from his touch. Leonida moaned as Sage's strong, gentle hand caressed the silky bareness of her inner thigh and coaxed her to join him....

Leonida was no longer a captive of the Navaho. She was no longer a prisoner of her fears. For now her passion burned through all barriers...now she was free to love in the...

Savage
NIGHTS

CASSIE EDWARDS

Savage NIGHTS

LEISURE BOOKS NEW YORK CITY

A LEISURE BOOK®

June 2007

Published by

Dorchester Publishing Co., Inc.
200 Madison Avenue
New York, NY 10016

ISBN-10: 0-8439-5883-9
ISBN-13: 978-0-8439-5883-6

The name "Leisure Books" and the stylized "L" with design are trademarks of Dorchester Publishing Co., Inc.

Printed in the United States of America.

Visit us on the web at www.dorchesterpub.com.

Savage
NIGHTS

1

Shall I love you like the wind, love,
That is so fierce and strong,
That sweeps all barriers from its path,
And recks not right or wrong?
     —R. W. RAYMOND

Fort Defiance, Arizona
June 1863

She looked out at the cliffs, painted with red and pur-
plish brown and luminous shadows. It was a country
that changed with the positions of the sun, a land of
narrow canyons, great mesas, and unending sand.
Deep-green pinyons and juniper bushes dotted the distant, arid hills.

Her straw bonnet shielding her face from the hot
rays of the sun, Leonida Branson strolled arm in arm
with her fiancé, General Harold Porter, before the
many colorful tents that had been erected in the shadows of the high walls of Fort Defiance. A band of
Navaho had come down from the mountains and
pitched their tents to trade with the soldiers and their
wives at the fort. With their skillful geometric weav-
ings the Navaho bartered for the white man's knives
with which to shear their sheep. They also wanted red
silk handkerchiefs to wear around their heads, silver
ornaments for their horses, and silver buttons for
themselves.

Many Pittsburgh wagons brought to the fort by those
skilled in trading with various Indian tribes were sit-

ting a short distance from the tents. Beneath their carefully stretched canvas tops were bolts of brightly colored calico, beads, ribbons, and lace.

With her delicate white-gloved hand Leonida swept the skirt of her blue silk dress up away from the dusty sand, yet she was scarcely aware of it. She was too taken by the beautiful displays of all sorts of jewelry and handwoven woolens ranging from small mats to blankets, rugs, and tapestries that lay spread on the ground before the tents, their Navaho owners proudly standing beside them.

Leonida smiled at the lovely Navaho women as she moved from tent to tent, searching for one in particular. Harold had told Leonida that this young woman's skills at making blankets had gained her a reputation that reached far and wide.

Harold's left arm was even now heavily laden with special yarns to give to the talented lady, in hopes that she would weave a lovely blanket from it to be one of his many wedding gifts for Leonida.

Leonida glanced over at Harold, who today had abandoned his usual uniform to impress upon her that he was more than just a soldier. He wore high-buffed black boots, a pair of dark breeches, and a white shirt that was ruffled at the sleeves and throat, with a sparkling diamond stickpin in the folds of his satin ascot.

Nearing forty, Harold was handsome, with golden, wavy hair, and eyes almost as golden, and a complexion unmarred by the hot sun of Arizona, or by a hard life in general. His had been a life handed to him on a silver platter, or so it seemed to Leonida, and his brash, arrogant personality bespoke of his having been spoiled as a child.

Wanting to find excuses for him because she had promised to marry him, she wanted to blame Harold's shortcomings on having been an only child. But she knew that was not a valid excuse for his arrogance. *She* was an only child, and she did not see herself as spoiled. She always looked at everyone as her equal, even the poorest people who begged for food on the street corners of San Francisco, where she had lived with her mother after her father left them. Leonida even went out of her way to help the needy, by handing out food and clothes to them from time to time, as well as sometimes finding them decent housing and paying for it from the allowance that both her mother and her father gave her.

This had all come to an instant halt when her mother died and Leonida was forced to live with her father at his military establishments.

A wave of sadness descended on her as she was catapulted back in time to another death. Her father's.

He had been dead for only four months, and the pain was still sharp. His death had seemed to imprison her in a trap from which she had not yet escaped: this engagement to Harold.

She had agreed to marry him only because her father had wanted it so badly. He had seen many possibilities in Harold, both as a military officer and eventually as a civilian. Harold had the money to make Leonida comfortable for the rest of her life.

Her father had wanted to make sure that his daughter was well cared for when he was no longer around, but Leonida knew that if he could see how Harold's arrogance, especially toward the Indians, had worsened, he surely would not have expected her to marry him. Since Harold had taken over her father's post at Fort Defiance, she could hardly stand being around him at all.

The chances of traveling back to San Francisco during this time of warring between the states seemed an impossible wish that could not be fulfilled. She had to bide her time until it was safe for her to travel alone.

"My dear, there she is," Harold said in his languid way. He nodded toward a tent where many blankets and other items were spread on the ground. "That's Pure Blossom. Many army officers like to have her blankets because they are so tightly woven they are practically waterproof." He smiled down at Leonida. "But my reasons for getting one for you is not so much for durability as for the loveliness of the blankets." He pointed at Pure Blossom and frowned. "I imagine that's all she's good at. Look at her, all bent up and out of shape and as frail as a dove. I imagine she spends her days weaving and dreaming of what life could be for her if she weren't so downright disgusting and pitiful-looking."

Leonida paled and her jaw went slack as she gazed up at him, aghast at his scorn for this unfortunate little Indian woman whose back was hunched, and whose fingers were gnarled with some sort of wasting-away disease.

"That's a horrible thing to say," she gasped. "Harold, have some compassion. It isn't her fault that nature has been cruel to her. Besides, she obviously possesses a sort of beauty. Just look at her face. There is such a serene innocence in her smile."

Leonida turned away from Harold and tried to forget his unfeeling remarks as they stepped into the shadows of the huge tent, where Pure Blossom stood over her beloved blankets and jewelry, her eyes filled with pride as she looked up at Leonida.

Leonida smiled warmly in return, her gaze sweeping over the Indian woman's beautiful clothes, jewelry, and hair. She had beautiful black hair that hung nearly to the ground and teeth so white that surely they out-shone the stars at night. Pure Blossom wore thick strings of turquoise and coral around her neck, over a bright-blue velveteen blouse. Her skirt was of bright calico, very long and full, and she wore moccasins with silver buttons.

"For trade?" she said in halting English as she gestured toward her wares. "Lovely? They please beautiful lady? You take?"

Pure Blossom's gaze fell upon the yarn across Harold's arm, and her eyes brightened. "You trade for the pretty yarn?" she asked anxiously.

Leonida only half heard Harold explain that the bright-colored Saxony and Zephyr yarns had been shipped from the East, and that he had not come to trade with her at all. Instead he was willing to pay her well to make a special blanket for his future bride.

Leonida's gaze had been arrested by a Navaho warrior who had stepped from the tent and now stood protectively at Pure Blossom's side, his muscular copper arms folded across his powerful chest.

Both his handsomeness and his intense dark eyes, which locked with hers, made Leonida's heartbeat quicken and caused a strange, mushy warmth at the pit of her stomach.

Even after living among so many soldiers, Leonida had never become infatuated with any of them. None had touched her heart, nor had they caused strange sensations within her. Not until now had she known how it felt to be attracted to a man—and this was not a soldier, or an ordinary man.

He was an Indian.

Her heart pounding, Leonida turned her back on the handsome warrior. Yet she had been so taken with him, she had noticed every detail about him.

He was a tall man with jet-black hair that he wore long and loose over his shoulders, with a red silk headband to keep it in place at his brow. He had flashing dark eyes, and a smooth bronze face with sculpted features.

Broad-shouldered and lean-hipped, he was breathtakingly, ruggedly handsome, dressed in a shirt of handwoven woolen cloth with a V-neck. His dyed buckskin trousers had silver buttons down the sides and were tied with woven garters. He wore silver-buttoned moccasins, a concha belt of round silver disks on leather, and a *ketoh,* a leather wrist guard with silver ornaments.

Leonida felt a sudden hush at her side that roused her from her trance. She blushed when she saw Harold's jaw tighten and anger flash in his eyes as his gaze slowly turned from her to the warrior. Leonida realized that Harold had seen her interest in the Navaho warrior and had become instantly jealous.

She smiled wanly as he again looked her way, glad that his attention was drawn back to the business at hand. But she could tell that he was rushing things along now to get her away from the Indian.

"You will weave the blanket for many *pesos,* money?" Harold asked, smiling smugly when Pure Blossom accepted the beautiful yarn and draped it across her arms.

"Yes, Pure Blossom will do this for you," she said, her eyes bright with excitement as she gazed down at the yarn. "It delights Pure Blossom to have the ready-made yarns. The yarn is so fine and even. The result will be a magnificent blanket for the lovely white woman's wedding. Pure Blossom will weave the yarn into a pattern of stripes and zigzags, and even some in the shape of diamonds."

She looked from Harold to Leonida. "I promise to have the blanket ready for you . . . when did you say?" she asked.

"In three months," Harold said stiffly, unnerved by the Navaho warrior's cold gaze. Harold had had few dealings with Sage, the young Navaho chief, but enough to know that he was the most stubborn of all the Indians in the area and that he had too much control. Harold had thought long ago that something had to be done about this powerful chief. He smiled to himself, knowing that things were in the works even now to make changes that would affect Sage.

"*Uke-he*, thank you," Pure Blossom said humbly, feeling the heat of her brother's eyes on her and knowing why. The Navaho rarely said thank you to anyone. Normally when a thank you was necessary, thanks were given by other means than humbling themselves by saying it.

Glad to be on their way, Harold placed a firm hand on Leonida's elbow. She eased away from him, though, and knelt down on a knee to admire a striking necklace among those laid out on a colorful blanket. He nervously moved his finger around his tight collar and shifted his feet. Then he did a slow burn as Sage knelt down opposite Leonida, his eyes intent on her.

"You see one that you especially like?" he asked, smiling.

Leonida's pulse raced. The Indian's deep, smooth voice reached into her heart like warm splashes of sunshine. To keep from making a fool of herself, she looked away from him, and again down at the beautiful necklace that had caught her eye.

"This one," she said, pointing to a string of hollow silver beads with a large crescent-shaped pendant ornament called a *Naja*. "It's so very pretty, unlike anything I have ever seen before."

Her face became hot with a blush, and she was embarrassed by the strange huskiness of her voice. This Indian had affected her much more deeply than she had realized. And she knew that she must hide her feelings. Not only from Harold, but also from the warrior. It was forbidden to have feelings for an Indian, especially the sort of sensations now troubling her.

Sage picked up the necklace and spread it out between his large, callused hands. "This is called a squash blossom necklace," he explained. "The floral design represents pomegranates, and the crescent at the bottom is to ward off the evil eye."

He paused to sweep his eyes slowly over Leonida. He was quite taken by the color of her hair, where wisps of her golden curls were revealed at the sides of her straw bonnet. He also admired the azure of her eyes, having seen such a beautiful color of blue only in the sky on the clearest of days.

Where her low-cut bodice revealed her porcelainlike skin, the swell of her breasts was smooth and creamy. While she had been standing with calm dignity, he had noticed how tall and willowy she was, a blond beauty.

If he allowed himself, he could have many feelings for this woman, most sensual.

"It is so beautiful," Leonida said, trying to draw the Navaho warrior's attention back to the necklace. She could hear Harold's hastened breathing, a sure sign that he was growing angry.

"Yes, it is a thing of beauty," Sage said thickly. "The Navaho call the crescent 'big snake,' the Navaho's name for the constellation Draco."

Before Leonida could rise, the Navaho warrior moved quickly behind her, placing the necklace around her neck. Having already been mesmerized by his smooth voice and dark eyes, she felt almost swallowed whole by her heartbeats when he touched the flesh of her neck with his fingers while fastening the necklace around it.

"It is yours," Sage said, placing a hand on her elbow and helping her to her feet. "Wear it as a token of gratitude for coming to my sister with your lovely yarns."

Red-faced, Harold stepped between them. Glaring at Sage, he yanked the necklace from Leonida's neck and flicked it onto the ground. "She needs no gifts from you," he growled. "The blanket is the only reason we have come here today, and your sister will get paid well for her services."

Leonida was stunned by Harold's sudden burst of jealousy. She half stumbled when he grabbed her hand and pulled her from the tent. Awkwardly she looked over her shoulder, feeling that an apology was needed. When she saw the warrior's cold contempt, she was stung to the core.

Then she turned away, ashamed and angry. The more Harold jerked her along beside him, the angrier she became. Suddenly she yanked herself free and stopped to glare at him. "Why did you have to behave so—so terribly about that necklace?" she said, her gloved hands doubled into tight fists at her sides. "You humiliated not only the Indian but also me. Was that necessary? Did you feel *that* threatened by the Indian's attentions toward me? You don't own me, Harold. Please quit acting as though you do."

Harold's eyebrows narrowed together into one line as he leaned down close to her face. "Don't you appreciate anything?" he snarled. "I'm paying a lot of money for that blanket. Would you rather I go back and get the yarn and forget it? Would you rather I didn't get you anything for your wedding gift?''

"I don't care what you do with anything," Leonida snapped, then stamped away from him.

He caught up with her immediately. "I'm sorry for upsetting you," he said, glad to be away from the Indian tents and walking toward the fort. "But, Leonida, I must warn you against being so easily swayed by the Indians. I'm being too trusting myself to believe that I will ever see anything made from the yarn I handed over to that crippled wench."

Leonida cringed at his reference to Pure Blossom as a "wench," but she now only wanted to get to the privacy of her house. "Who was that Indian warrior?" she asked cautiously. "It is obvious that you don't like him."

Setting his jaw tightly, Harold did not answer her right away, but he finally responded, knowing that he would have to sooner or later, anyhow. Leonida was not the sort to let anything get past her. Especially the name of a man with whom she was so obviously infatuated.

"Sage," he grumbled. "A Navaho chief." He glared over at her. "Pure Blossom is his sister."

"He's a chief," Leonida said to herself, still tingling inside from Sage's touch, his voice, and the way he had looked at her with his midnight-dark eyes.

The sound of hooves behind her drew her eyes around just in time to see Sage riding away on a magnificent chestnut stallion with a saddle of stamped leather. The silver ornaments hanging from his saddle flashed in the sun. For a brief moment he turned his head her way. When their eyes met, a silent promise seemed to be exchanged between them, yet she did not know why.

Shaken by her feelings, Leonida tried to focus her thoughts elsewhere. She stared at the fort as they approached it. The western side had a strong wall twelve feet high. Adobe rooms along the inside of the wall were used as officers' quarters and garrison headquarters. The north end wall was similar but shorter. The south wall was a barracks that contained the main entrance to the fort. The eastern wall, called the "long barracks," had a hospital at one end and an enclosure for cattle and horses behind it.

Stretching to the west and south was a green valley that wove toward widely separated mountain ridges. Through this valley flowed a river of sparkling blue waters. Unable to shake the Navaho chief from her mind, Leonida turned and watched him as he rode toward the river in the distance.

It was her keenest desire to follow him.

2

Does there within thy dimmest dreams
A possible future shine,
Wherein thy life could henceforth breathe,
Untouched, unshared by mine?
—ADELAIDE ANNE PROCTER

Candlelight was reflected in the many sparkling, long-stemmed wine glasses on her oak dining table. Around it sat many important men of the fort and the highly honored guest, Colonel Christopher "Kit" Carson.

From the instant Leonida entered the room and seated herself, she had felt out of place, for she was the only woman in attendance and the conversations quickly made her most uneasy and angrier by the moment.

Glancing downward, she toyed with her asparagus, then sipped her wine as she listened, avoiding occasional admiring glances from the men. One and all noticed her gown of rich, pale-blue satin, with a bodice that came to a point in front, emphasizing the magnificent swell of her breasts and the smallness of her corseted waist. Little puffed sleeves trimmed with a lace ruffle draped to her elbows. Her golden hair was combed back at the sides and held there with a slide, tumbling across her shoulders in loose ringlets.

Leonida knew that she should feel honored to be in the presence of the great Kit Carson, the man who had guided the "pathfinders" sent by the government to open the West. From 1842 to 1846 he had guided the Rocky Mountains expeditions of John Fremont, and the publication of Fremont's reports of the journey had brought widespread fame to Kit Carson. In the 1850s Kit had been an Indian agent at Taos, New Mexico, and then he had become involved in the Civil War.

Now, as he related why he had been sent to Fort Defiance, she could not help but form a dislike for him. He had been sent to this region with strict instructions to bring the marauding Navaho under control.

The way the discussion was going, all Navaho were being considered marauders, not just a few who wreaked havoc on the white settlers and even their neighboring Indian tribes.

The fact that Sage and his sweet sister Pure Blossom could be a target sent chills up and down Leonida's spine. Even Harold had seen that they were gentle. Yet she could feel Harold's eyes on her throughout this evening's discussion of the Navaho, knowing that he was recalling Sage's obvious interest in her. She knew that this alone could fuel Harold's agreement to do whatever needed to be done with the Navaho, and that realization made her detest him more than ever.

She did not offer any comments as the evening wore on, not even when they had all gone to the drawing room and were sharing smokes and drinks, again in her presence. Wanting to hear their final plans concerning the Navaho, she had purposely not excused herself to go to the privacy of her bedroom.

Sitting demurely in a plushly cushioned chair, with her hands folded on her lap, Leonida listened as Kit Carson resumed explaining in his soft-spoken manner the reasons why the Navaho's activities should be curtailed. She gazed over at Kit, a short and stocky, sandy-haired, ruddy-faced man, dressed in fringed doeskin.

From what she had read about him, he was a quiet, self-reliant mountain man from Kentucky, his body as tough as whang leather, and he could shoot the eye out of a racing jackrabbit, and rope and ride any wild horse on the prairie.

He was known for his high quality of character, steadfastness of purpose, absolute honesty, and his cool judgment in the face of seeming disaster. All of the fighting was just good fun to him, and he had been know to exist for days merely by chewing his buckskin leggings for food.

"With the buffalo rapidly disappearing, the Navaho are finding it easier to raid ranches than to hunt game on the land the settlers don't want," Harold offered in support of Kit's ideas about taking over full control of the Navaho. "The settlements and ranches are being raided. Caravans are being plundered, travelers killed. Kit, whatever you decide is best to stop this devastation will suit me fine."

Kit rose to his feet and began pacing, as everyone watched him. "For years I've been writing the Department of Indian Affairs about these problems, and now they are worsening," he said, kneading his chin, watching his feet as he paced. "I believe it would be best for the Indians and the white population alike if all Indians were placed on reservations and taught modern farming."

He stopped and began looking every man in the eye as he continued. "I've learned the language of the Navaho people and their legends, which have been handed down through hundreds of Indian generations," he said solemnly. "I've learned how the Navaho think and reason, and of their resentment against the white man's taking the game which they say has been put on the earth for the red man. I've always sympathized with the Navaho. I've even found friendship easy with them. But nevertheless, I now see the need to deal firmly with them. I've been sent to take control of all Navaho. As I see it, I have no other choice but to force them to join the Mescalero Indians at Fort Sumner.''

Stunned, Leonida was seized by a surge of dizziness. She gripped the arms of her chair and stared up at the scout, disbelieving what he had just said.

Without thinking, she stood up and looked Kit square in the eye. ''What you are planning to do is wrong,'' she said, lifting her chin defiantly. ''My acquaintance with many of the Navaho in this region has proven they are not a warring band. Why must they pay for the evil others do?''

There was a sudden hush in the room. The soldiers' stares attested to what they thought of women who boldly spoke their mind, especially to a man such as Kit Carson.

He started to speak, but Leonida did not give him the chance, knowing if she did not have her say now, she never would be given the chance again.

''Even the Indian agents have always been political appointees and know nothing of the Navahos' true needs,'' she said, her voice rising in anger. ''And now, because the cavalry has not been able to track down the true marauders, you will take your spite out on the innocent?''

Not giving anyone a chance to say anything back to her, Leonida spun around and left the drawing room. She wished now she hadn't allowed these men to congregate in her house. Since she had heard so much about the famous frontiersman who had done so much for their country, she had been honored to have him as her guest.

Upon her arrival at Fort Defiance two years ago to live with her father, he had built her this beautiful adobe hacienda with gardens and terraces, all of the comforts that she had been forced to leave behind in San Francisco upon the death of her mother. Her bedroom was all lace and flower designs, with carpets her bare feet sank into.

She had shared this lovely house with her father until his untimely death, caused by a scorpion's sting. And now Harold expected to share it with her. That she would never allow!

Almost blinded with rage, Leonida started to run from the house, but was stopped when Harold grabbed her by a wrist.

"What's got into you tonight?" he said, turning her to face him. "What's Kit Carson to think? You behaved like some wild thing someone might find lost in the desert. You've got to go back in there and apologize, Leonida, for me to keep face. Kit knows you and I are betrothed."

She wrenched herself free and placed her hands on her hips. "Now, isn't that a pity?" she said, her voice taunting. "You have to suffer a mite of humiliation while the Indians are going to have to lose all of their dignity."

"Damn it, Leonida, what you know about Indians could be put in the palm of your hand," he argued. "Just because you've been protected here at the fort and haven't seen what the Indians can do, you stand up for them? Or has that handsome Navaho chief turned your head, making you behave so unlike yourself tonight?"

"What justifies you and those men in there making decisions for the Navaho that will take their pride, dignity, and their freedom away?'' Leonida said, her voice breaking. ''You know you're wrong, Harold.''

''It is the only way to stop the marauding,'' he said, his voice calmer. ''Reservation life is not as bad as you think. The Indians are given a decent life—''

Leonida did not give him a chance to finish his sentence. ''If you agree to this unfair treatment of the Navaho, I won't marry you,'' she said icily. ''I'll return to San Francisco. I've friends there. I'll live among them and be much happier than living here with the likes of you.''

''I don't like being threatened,'' he growled, glaring at her.

''It is not a threat,'' she said, glaring back at him. ''It's a fact, Harold. A damn fact.''

His eyes wavered. He ran his fingers nervously through his hair. ''You're being foolish,'' he said thickly. ''Your future is with me. My God, woman, I am offering you a life of leisure. You can't turn your back on it.''

A hint of smugness crossed his face. ''And besides,'' he said, laughing sarcastically, ''you can't travel anywhere. The country is being torn apart by war.''

''Harold, the war between us could—'' she began stiffly. Then her tone softened. ''Harold, how can you ask that Navaho woman to make that blanket for me as a wedding gift in one breath, and then with your next, condemn her and her people to a reservation?''

She did not wait for any more of his excuses. She opened the door and stormed out of the house into a moonless night.

Her heart beating furiously, relieved that Harold had not followed her, Leonida saw a saddled horse reined to a nearby hitching post. She knew the horse was

Harold's, a large, very swift black mare. And that was what she needed now. A horse that would carry her far from the men who were planning the Navahos' fate. She would ride until she was exhausted, and then perhaps she could return to bed and sleep.

Not caring that traveling on horseback would ruin her beautiful dress, Leonida swung herself into the saddle. Ignoring the warning shouts of the sentries, she rode through the wide gate of the fort. At this moment she hated the sight of blue-coated soldiers.

Tears streamed from her eyes when she thought of her father and how handsome he had been in his uniform, and how he had ruled with such gentleness and caring toward the Indians. Surely he would turn over in his grave tonight if he knew what Kit Carson and the others were planning.

With the night air brushing her face in a warm caress, Leonida urged the black steed to a trot, occasionally broken by a short lope. She rode past the spot where the tents had been and onward toward the river, sad at the thought that she might never see Sage again. She flinched at the notion that he might be seized on his way back to the mountains and forced toward New Mexico, where he would live penned up like an animal.

When Leonida saw a fire throwing light into the sky up ahead, her fingers tightened involuntarily on the horse's reins, causing the horse to jerk sidewise. Then she reined her mount to a halt. This fire could mean many things. It could indicate white travelers, marauders, or . . . where Sage's tribe had stopped for the night before heading on toward the mountains.

The thought of Sage made her heartbeat quicken and her knees weaken strangely. She slid out of the saddle and walked the horse slowly toward the fire, where junipers and pines began thickening on all sides of her.

Suddenly something rustled to her right. She did not have time to think before Sage stepped out in front of her, his hands quickly taking her reins.

Time stood still. Leonida's heart did not seem to beat, nor was she aware of breathing. She was numb to everything but Sage's dark, penetrating eyes gazing into hers. At this moment she did not know whether to be afraid or entranced.

3

I ne'er was struck before that hour
With love so sudden and so sweet!
—JOHN CLARE

"You have come to the camp of the Navaho," Sage said, his voice flat. "Why have you? What have you to say that you did not say while the white man was making decisions for you?"

Leonida blushed and lowered her eyes, embarrassed by how it must have looked when Harold had treated her so crudely in front of the Navaho people. Surely Sage thought that Harold made all of her decisions for her.

She wanted to spill out an explanation, to make herself look better in the eyes of this handsome Indian chief, but she felt that it was best left unspoken, at least for now.

"The white woman has the courage to ride unescorted beneath the stars, yet does not find her voice to answer Sage?" he prodded, reaching out a hand to touch her arm ever so gently.

His voice, the way it changed from flatness to soft caring, made Leonida's insides melt, as well as her reserve. "I answer to no one," she blurted. "Today it might have appeared that I do. But in truth, since my parents' deaths, I have made all of the choices in my life. Perhaps they are not always the best, yet still I allow no one to speak for me."

"But today you did?" he persisted, in his mind's

eye seeing her humiliation when the white man had taken the necklace from her.

Leonida straightened her back and swallowed hard. "Today?" she murmured. "It all happened so quickly, I did not have time to think clearly."

She wanted to tell Sage that moments after he had ridden away on his beautiful chestnut stallion she had put Harold in his rightful place. She wanted to tell Sage that Harold would never humiliate her again like that. Soon she would stop this charade with Harold once and for all.

"Are you thinking, as you say, 'clearly enough' now?" Sage asked, his hand at her elbow urging her from her saddle. "You do not look as though you took much time to consider the clothes you would wear for a ride on horseback."

His gaze swept over her as she slipped down from her saddle, seeing her as nothing less than beautiful in her blue satin gown, the magnificence of her breasts swelling from the top of it. He wanted to reach his hands out to her golden hair and run his fingers through its long ringlets, but refrained. The art of restraint had been well taught him as a child.

"The haste with which I left the fort did not allow my changing into something more appropriate," she murmured, her cheeks heating up as she again felt his eyes roaming over her, stopping momentarily at her breasts. She had to wonder if he could see them heaving with the excitement of the moment.

She even wondered if he could hear her heart thundering wildly within her chest at being so close to this magnificently handsome man.

"This haste that you speak of," Sage said, "will you regret having stopped to have conversation with a Navaho chief?"

Leonida smiled uneasily up at him. There was an ache in her heart that she could not quell. As she peered into the eyes of this Navaho chief, she was seeing his defeat, his future stolen away from him, his freedom stifled, just as though he were a wild horse taken from the prairie, tamed, and then placed in a pen.

The thought made her look quickly away so that he would not see the anger and humiliation for him in the depths of her eyes or the tears that she was fighting back. She was glad that the cloak of night hid her anguish.

"You look away," Sage said, placing a finger on her chin and turning her eyes back to his. "Why do you?"

Leonida searched for the right words to say. "I—I feel suddenly awkward," she quickly explained. "You see, I had no set plans for any destination tonight. I just needed to get away from the fort, to ride my horse and get a breath of fresh air." She glanced at the campfire through the break in the trees, then smiled slowly up at Sage again. "I guess I should have seen the signs of the fire in the sky, which would have let me know of your campfire. But I didn't. I just happened onto your camp."

The clouds slid away from the moon, showing Leonida the disappointment in his face. Had he actually thought that she had come searching for him? In truth, perhaps she had, unconsciously.

"But now that I am here, I would love to stay and talk a while with you," she quickly added.

As he tethered her horse to a tree, Leonida looked over her shoulder at the campfire. "Perhaps we could join the others at your camp?" she murmured. "I would enjoy seeing your sister again."

To her surprise, Sage took her by an elbow and began ushering her in the opposite direction, away from the campsite. With parted lips and widened eyes she gazed up at him, half stumbling as he continued guiding her through the forest, stopping at a creek that spiraled like a silver snake in and about the trees.

"Sit," Sage said, nodding toward the ground. "No one will disturb us here."

Leonida's stomach did a strange sort of flip-flop, and her heart skipped a beat as he gently pushed her to the ground, then sat down beside her. She smoothed her wrinkled dress with a hand as she stretched her legs out before her, feeling strangely at ease with this Navaho chief, even though she had only met him that afternoon.

Yet she could hear her father's warnings flashing in her mind: not to trust so easily, always to be wary of Indians, no matter their reputation. Little was actually known of what made their minds work, and to most, they were still vicious, heartless savages.

Leonida's own relationships with the Navaho Indians of this area had proven that the bigoted white people were wrong about them. That they were going to be forced to live on a reservation was an injustice she wished that she could right. But she was only one person, and a woman. The voice of a woman carried no weight.

"It's quite beautiful here," Leonida murmured, breaking the silence. "I'm so glad to be here instead— instead of back at the fort."

She swallowed hard and momentarily closed her eyes, trying to blank out the anger that welled up inside her every time she recalled Kit Carson's words, that it would be best for the Indians to be placed on reservations, that he saw no other choice but to force the Navaho to join the Mescalero Indians at Fort Sumner.

"It is a place of peace," Sage said, leaning back on an elbow. As he stretched one long, lean leg out before him, the silver buttons on his trousers caught the rays of the moon in them. "But what Sage likes best of all is to sit on a knoll, watching the horses of my village feed, when others of my village like to sit down for smokes and gossip. Nature is where I would rather be than around a fire, speaking of others' private lives."

"I have never been one who enjoys gossip either," Leonida said, smiling over at him. What he had just said made her ever more aware of how wrong it would be to imprison such a man within the confines of a reservation.

He was a man who inhaled freedom as though it were the very air that he breathed. To take it away from him would be the same as snuffing life from him.

Yet there was nothing that she could do to change what was to happen. She would try to absorb every moment with Sage, for it just might be the last.

"I did not think that you would be the sort to meddle in others' affairs," Sage said, returning her smile.

Those words stung Leonida to the core, for as badly as she wanted to meddle this time, she could not. Her words were powerless among men like Kit Carson and General Harold Porter.

She blinked her eyes to keep tears from splashing from them, then peered up at the heavens. Starlight, pale and cold, silhouetted the ragged oaks that stood tall and statuesque over her. She listened and enjoyed the sound of the water cascading over the stairs of stones in the cool stream, the rich bass of bullfrogs, and the rasp of crickets.

"I so love this time of night," she murmured. "Just look at the stars. Aren't they beautiful?"

She turned her eyes away from the sky and peered into the darkness. "And just look at the fireflies," she said, sighing. "Their cold sparks are like the fires of miniature lanterns blinking off and on in the night."

She laughed softly and gazed over at Sage. "Now if it were midday, who could enjoy any of this?" she said. "There are always snakes to fear when the sun is high in the sky." She hugged herself with her arms and shuddered. "If there is anything that I detest, it's snakes."

Sage stared at her for a moment in silence, unnerving her, for suddenly his dark eyes seemed lit with fire. She relaxed when he began talking, friendly as before. She had thought that she had said something that had irritated him, yet was unable to touch on exactly what it might be.

"The Navaho have stories full of poetry and miracles about such things as you speak of tonight," Sage said, looking away from her. He began picking up pebbles, tossing them one by one into the creek. "The stories are told by the elders of the Navaho villages in the wintertime when the snakes are asleep."

He moved a hand to her cheek. "The desert country *is* full of snakes, poisonous and otherwise," he said softly. "But to the Navaho, snakes are the guardians of sacred lore and will punish those who treat it lightly."

Leonida's eyes widened and she swallowed hard.

"I did not know . . ." she murmured, strongly aware of his hand on her cheek, the heat of his flesh against hers. Feelings foreign to her began warming her through and through. "I'm sorry. I never meant to speak so unkindly of snakes. It's just that long ago, when I was a child, I was bitten by a rattler. I . . . almost died. A preacher was even brought to my bedside. He said many prayers to God before I began to recover." She was torn with feelings when he drew his hand away and again began tossing pebbles into the water. "I imagine you have a Great Spirit that you pray to?"

"In the Navaho religion, there is no identifiable deity who can be described as the Supreme Being or Great *Spirit*," Sage explained. "There are many powerful personages—Changing Woman, Sun, First Man and First Woman, Hero Twins, Monster Slayer, Born of Woman, and White Shell Woman."

Leonida's head swam as she tried to remember all of the names that he was giving her. She was quickly learning one of the main differences between her culture and Sage's, and knew that this was only the beginning.

"The primary purpose for Navaho ceremonials, or 'sings,' is to keep man in harmony with himself and the universe," Sage continued.

He laughed softly. "I see that what I have said confuses you," he said, moving to an erect sitting position. He wanted to reach out and take her hand yet refrained, afraid that it might frighten or offend her.

In due time, he kept telling himself, in due time he would know the taste of her lips and the touch of her flesh. For now, words were enough, at least until she knew that she could trust him, that he wasn't a "savage."

"Yes, I am confused," she said matter-of-factly. "Yet I understand that there are many differences between your customs and mine, and I accept that."

"Not only customs," Sage said, his voice drawn.

He rose to his feet and offered Leonida a hand, which she took and stood up beside him.

Her heart pounded when he kept her hand in his as they began walking slowly beside the creek, then headed back toward her horse.

"Sage's people see that white men are beginning to understand they did not mean to harm the Navaho," he said. "The whites have their own ideas of law, and they carry them out just as carefully as the Navaho. The two ways are different and cannot keep clashing. It is good to think that warring is a thing of the past, an ugly past filled with hatred and bigotry."

Leonida stiffened and did not offer a response. She knew that if she said anything now, it would come out all wrong. She did not want to be the one to bear sad tidings, knowing that he would find out soon enough. There was to be a meeting tomorrow at the fort, and he would be one of the many Indian chiefs in attendance.

There he would surely learn early enough the fate of his people.

"As you know, the language of the Navaho is not the only language used by my people today," Sage said as he stopped beside her horse and began smoothing his hand over its sleek brown mane. "Sage's English is clear enough, is it not? It was learned from trading with white people and also from Kit Carson, with whom Sage has shared many smokes many times in the past."

He turned to Leonida, pleased to be talking of his association with Kit Carson, not knowing that very man was planning a future for Sage's people that would drastically change his feelings for the "pathfinder."

"Kit Carson has been known to me for many moons now," he said, proudly squaring his shoulders. "Sage has watched Kit Carson lasso a wild horse and throw his rope with the sure aim of an arrow. Kit Carson was an agent for the Utes a few moons ago, and because he so well cared for them, they gave him the name 'Father Kit.' ''

He turned from Leonida and stared into the distance, thinking of tomorrow's meeting, when he would be clasping hands of friendship once again with Kit Carson. He turned smiling eyes down at Leonida again.

"When the sun sits high in the sky tomorrow, Sage and many other Indian leaders will speak of peace and harmony again with Kit Carson and the leaders at the fort," he said thickly. "We shall share many smokes. It will be a good time. Sage will then return to his home in the mountains content."

His eyes became shadowed as he leaned down closer to Leonida. "There will be one thing missing in my happiness," he said, gently touching her cheek with his callused fingers.

Leonida's heart seemed scarcely to be beating as she gazed up at him, his lips so close, his eyes so filled with something quite unfamiliar to her, yet seeming to reflect deep feelings for her. "What is that?" she asked, her voice breaking as she was forced to swallow quickly. Her motions were becoming overwhelmed with a delicious sort of languor.

"There is no one woman that I can call mine in my life," he said. "Without a woman, a man is not complete."

He leaned so close that his breath was warm on Leonida's lips. "The man you have chosen. Does your heart agree to this choice?" he asked in barely a whisper, yet it echoed over and over again within her, for she could tell that he was feeling much more than what he was saying.

And so was she.

She knew that it was useless to allow her feelings to go any further than this, for tomorrow he would hate all white people, her included.

"I don't know how to answer your question," she said, seemingly swallowed whole by her thunderous heartbeats.

She jumped with alarm when someone came upon them from behind. She wrenched herself away from Sage, then laughed softly and relaxed when she found sweet and frail Pure Blossom standing there, the squash blossom necklace held between her hands.

"Yours," Pure Blossom said, holding the necklace over toward Leonida. "Take. Please take and keep."

In her mind's eye Leonida was recalling the very instant when Harold had taken the necklace from her. It gave her much pleasure that she was being given a second chance to have it, *and* to defy him at the same time.

"It is so lovely," Leonida said as Pure Blossom draped it across her fingers, then stepped back, smiling from ear to ear.

Leonida turned to Sage. "I know that your sister speaks good enough English, but how can I say 'thank you' to her in Navaho?" she asked.

"Thank you is not usually spoken in words, but performed instead with deeds," Sage said, then smiled. "But you are not Navaho. You can say *Uke-he* to my sister."

Leonida turned back, smiling. "*Uke-he*, Pure Blossom," she murmured.

Flattered, Pure Blossom nodded, then ran back to the campsite and joined the others.

"Your sister is so sweet," Leonida said, admiring the necklace.

"All of my people are good," Sage said, then took the necklace from Leonida's hands and stepped behind her. Leonida could not help but tremble when his fingers touched her neck as he fastened the necklace.

When he stepped around in front of her again, his fingers now on her shoulders, Leonida's breath was stolen as he moved his lips toward hers, his dark eyes burning like fire. As his lips covered hers in a quivering, lingering kiss, everything within her seemed to blend into something sweet and wonderful.

Yet, fearing these tumultuous feelings, knowing that Sage would soon be gone, she wrenched herself free and quickly mounted her horse and rode away before he had a chance to ask her why.

Tears streamed down her cheeks, and she knew that she would never forget the hurtful questioning in his eyes as she rode away. It was as though she was the one who was going to betray him, or even that she may have already been guilty of it.

Her hair loose and flying in the wind, her silk dress hiked past her knees, Leonida bent low and rode hard out into the open, away from the creek, away from the wondrous, sweet sounds of night, and away from the man that she now knew she loved with all of her heart and soul.

"Why?" she cried to the heavens. "Why did I ever have to meet him? Why did I have to fall in love?"

Her heart seemed to drop to her feet when she caught sight of a horseman riding toward her in the distance.

"Harold," she gasped, drawing the reins tightly. As her horse skittered to a sudden stop, she tried to straighten her hair, and then her skirt, dreading the questions and even more the answers that she might have to give him.

While she tried to make herself more presentable, her fingers came in contact with the necklace, and she groaned.

"I will not allow him to remove it from my neck twice," she finally decided, lifting her chin stubbornly.

She gave him a cold look of defiance when he wheeled his horse to a stop beside hers.

"What is the meaning of this?" he said in a feral snarl, frowning at her. "Where the hell have you been? And look at you. You look like some wild thing, your hair all blown, your lovely dress all wrinkled and soiled."

She refused to tell him where she had been, or with whom, knowing that it was enough for him to know that she had fled because of what he was planning with Kit Carson and the others.

She saw him turn pale and his eyes widen with horror when he discovered the necklace around her neck. "My God, woman, isn't that the same necklace . . . ?" he said.

He reached a hand toward her to yank it off.

Leonida covered the necklace with her hand. She glared over at him. "Don't you dare," she threatened, then rode away from him, at least for the moment smiling triumphantly.

4

. . . the sunflower turns to her god when he sets,
The same look which she turned when he rose.
                                        —THOMAS MOORE

The mountain shapes were softer than the skies. Canyon wrens darted in and out of the mesquite, trilling their startling but melodious songs.

The smoke from the large outdoor fire curled skyward in the courtyard of the fort. Around it sat the many Indian leaders who had come to the fort for a council with Colonel Kit Carson and the leaders at the fort. Everyone was sitting in a wide circle around the fire, Leonida among them.

Dressed demurely in a plain cotton dress devoid of any trim, her hair drawn back with a ribbon, Leonida sat in silence, looking and absorbing, while a long-stemmed pipe was passed around the circle of men.

Leonida ignored the occasional angry glances that Harold sent her way; she had defied his orders to stay away from the meeting. She felt a trace of hope that the Indians would be given a choice of where they wanted to live instead of being automatically forced onto a reservation. She knew that the other Indians had been rounded up without notice and marched to the reservation, as the Apache had been forced to do. At least some semblance of respect was being shown the Navaho by first talking to them about it.

Also, she hoped to get to speak with Sage before he left, to apologize for her hasty retreat the night before.

She now regretted it, for she had not slept a wink all night, worrying about what he must think of her to allow a kiss, then to flee from it. She could not let them part forever without telling him that she had not meant to lead him on, that she had true feelings for him, though telling him was perhaps foolish.

Her heart pounding at the prospect of allowing herself another glance across the fire, Leonida lifted her eyes slowly. She could not stop the thrill that enveloped her when she gazed at length at Sage again. He was dressed in his finest clothes. A striped blanket was wrapped around his shoulders and belted at his waist. His deerskin moccasins reached to his knees, his tight breeches were slit down the side and edged with silver buttons shining in the sun. A red silk handkerchief was tied around his brow to hold his sleek black hair in place.

As he looked her way and she discovered that he seemed indifferent, she flinched and turned quickly away, shame overwhelming her.

Soon, unless the plans had changed, Sage's eyes would fill with feelings, those of hate and anger, directed toward her as well as Kit Carson and those responsible for the fate of his people, for she was white, as were they, soon to be Sage's enemies.

Fighting back tears of frustration, shame, and hurt, Leonida lifted her chin and stared ahead, not resting her gaze on any one thing. She crossed her legs on the ground before her and stiffened her arms, placing her palms on her knees, gripping them so hard that the flesh of her fingertips turned ghostly white. She swallowed hard and began dying a slow death inside when the conversations began and grew more heated as each moment passed.

Nothing was in the Indians' favor.

Leonida grimaced as she listened to the debate between the two factions of men, Kit Carson and Sage now the main speakers.

Kit's voice became measured and calculated.

Sage's became cold, his face grim with anger as he rose to his full height over the circle of men, towering over Kit, who moved over to stand next to him as their debate heated up even more.

Leonida smiled, somehow pleased that Sage was so much taller than Kit. It was a well-known fact that he was the runt of fourteen Carson children, and when he was sitting down he always tried to conceal his short legs.

"Damn it, Sage," Kit said in his soft-spoken way. "You know I've always been sympathetic to Indians. But now I've got to think of the settlers. The settlements and ranches are being raided. Caravans are being plundered. Travelers are being killed. To stop the raids, *all* Indians must be transferred out of the territory, even the Navaho."

"You know that the Navaho do not go to war as a whole nation," Sage said, angrily folding his arms across his powerful chest. "It is the renegades who raid. There is no central Navaho government, and the chiefs speak only for their tiny bands." He paused, then added more softly, "Sage has never wanted trouble with whites," he said solemnly. "Sage's heart has been good toward the whites. So has Sage's people's heart."

Kit Carson shifted his feet nervously and stroked his clean-shaven chin in contemplation before responding, the fringe of his buckskin shirt and breeches blowing in the gentle breeze. Then Kit placed a fist over his heart, as though to prove to Sage that his heart was good also.

"Sage, you know that not long ago I was an Indian agent at Taos when escaped convicts, thugs, and outlaws of every description were pouring into the West," he said softly. "There the laws were few and the enforcement agencies fewer. You know that then I was as determined to protect the Indians from the whites as to protect whites from Indians. When a white man injured an Indian, he had Kit Carson to deal with, and that dealing was sharp and to the point."

Harold, dressed in full uniform, got hurriedly to his feet and interrupted just as Sage was about to respond. With an even and impersonal voice, he stamped over to Kit's side and glared down at him. "Get on with it, damn it," he said. "We didn't come here to play footsie with the Indians. Tell them exactly why they have been brought here."

Harold peered up at the blazing sun and wiped beads of perspiration from his brow. He wiped his damp fingers on his breeches leg, glaring down at Kit again. "Damn it, Kit, why drag it out to ungodly lengths?" he said, his voice drawn. "I'd like to get out of this damn sun."

Kit's face became hot with anger as he glared back. "I've been brought here to handle this matter," he said icily. "And I will do it at my own pace and in my own way. If you don't approve, wire Washington about it. Until you get a response, though, and perhaps a replacement, I will deal with this problem as I see fit."

Harold's face tightened and his lips pursed angrily. He glared for a moment longer down at Kit, then swung around and moved in measured steps away from him, his eyes shifting momentarily to Leonida. He flinched when he found Leonida smiling devilishly up at him, having obviously enjoyed Kit's reprimanding him. His eyes narrowed as he paused long enough to stare at the Indian necklace that she wore so boldly around her neck.

There had been only one way—the damned Navaho leader. The thought of them being alone together made him grow cold inside with rage. He vowed to himself that never would it be allowed to happen again. He would marry Leonida now, even if he had to hold a gun to her head to get the words out of her. No Indian would humiliate him by taking his woman away from him.

Yet Harold had known for some time now that Leonida had changed her mind, that she was not planning to marry him. Ever since her father's death she had been biding her time until it became safe to travel again. She had promised to marry him only to please her father.

And now he was gone.

"What is that you have to say that has not yet been spoken today to Sage and the other leaders who have come to your fort, as requested, for council?" Sage asked, taking a step closer to Kit. Sage felt the eyes of all the Indian leaders on him, trusting that in the end he would make all wrongs right for them. He had been their spokesperson for many moons now and had achieved peace between them all and the white chief in Washington.

"As I said before, Sage," Kit said, "the raiding must not be allowed to go on. A new home has been provided for the Navaho. There will be land for grazing, good flat land for farming, and a big irrigation ditch."

As Sage's eyes narrowed with anger, Kit cleared his voice and continued. "It's time for this empty land to be turned into wheat fields and grazing grounds to produce food for the country,'' he said, his voice low now. ''So many Indians often do not produce but only use what the wild land gives. This is why they—why *you*—are being asked to make room for the settlers, who will use the land in the right way. It is the only way, Sage. Your people must move into reservation land called Indian Territory, in the country east of New Mexico.''

The sudden silence, the hush that washed over the group of Indians, made Leonida suck in a wild, horrified breath of air. She looked guardedly around her as the Indian leaders rose angrily to their feet. Though weaponless, they still looked threatening as they moved closer to the soldiers who had seemed to have come out of nowhere to make a wide circle around the council of men, their hands resting on their holstered pistols.

Her knees weak, Leonida pushed herself up from the ground and inched away from the Indians, her gaze never leaving Sage. Never had she seen anyone as controlled in his anger as he. She was proud of his ability to restrain himself from lashing out at those who were intent at imprisoning him and all of the Navaho people alike. She watched, breathlessly, as he began to speak, his voice calm and collected.

''What you say is wrong, is *hogay-gahn,* bad,'' Sage said. ''The white man does not stand alone in this problem. Our cattle as well as sheep are also being stolen. Find the renegades responsible, then peace will again be achieved between the Navaho and white people.''

''That is not the way it is to be,'' Kit said. ''It has been decided that all Navaho will settle on the reservation. There you will have a good life. I give you my word, Sage.'' He reached out a hand of friendship.

Sage's jaw tightened and he stiffened his back. He gestured with a hand toward the wide sweep of land that surrounded him. "*Tinishten,* as far as a man can see, the land belongs to the Navaho," he said. "The Navaho love their land. We have lived here for five hundred years or more. *E-do-tano,* no, the Navaho cannot leave this land. They will be here, *Sa-a-nari,* living forever, *ka-bike-hozhoni-bi,* happy evermore."

Tears flooded Leonida's eyes, her heart breaking as she listened to Sage's pleas. She knew they were falling on deaf ears. In her mind's eye, she imagined Pure Blossom weaving her blankets, so innocent and unthreatening, soon to be confined to land that was foreign to her.

In her mind's eye, she saw Sage sitting on a high knoll, watching his horse grazing peacefully, smoke spiraling from his fancy long-stemmed pipe.

She did not expect him or his sister ever to have such peaceful moments again.

Kit Carson started to speak, but Sage stopped him and continued his plea, his voice tight.

"The Navaho, who call themselves *Dineh,* meaning 'The People,' need lots of space," he said. "A great many Navaho are shepherds, and their flocks must have great areas in which to graze. Others are ranchers and farmers. They need space too. If placed on reservation, there won't be enough grass to feed the sheep and goats and cattle. The Navaho will become poor, *very* poor."

Kit lifted his chin and placed his hand on his holstered pistol. "I don't like this any more than you do," he said solemnly. "But what must be done must be done, and I hope it can be achieved in as peaceful a fashion as possible. Sage, if you and the others will surrender and promise to go to the reservation, you will have rations until you get started in your new life.'' He cleared his throat nervously, then added, ''You will travel to the reservation peacefully, or by force.''

There was another strained silence. The heat in Sage's look stung Leonida's heart as he gave her a quick glance. In his eyes was such hatred, such torment.

She covered her mouth with her hands as he stared down at Kit again and said a loud, determined ''*E-do-ta*,'' which she knew meant no.

Another Navaho leader appeared beside Sage. ''The Navaho nation is as powerful as whites,'' he said stiffly. ''They will stay and raise sheep. Now. *Always*. If war is needed, the Navaho will scatter like birds into the canyons and among the rocks until you come. Then we will kill, if forced to.''

Leonida's heart was scarcely beating as she watched Sage stoop to one knee before the fire, his disgust and disapproval of the white man's plans evident in his face. She gasped when Sage angrily picked up a handful of sand and tossed it into the fire, which was a way for the Navaho to show the extent of their anger. Then he rose to his full height to leave.

But just before he went, he gave Leonida a stern, then a wavering stare. He walked away at a slow, dignified pace, and the other leaders followed him.

Everything within Leonida made her want to run after Sage and apologize for the white people's inhumanity toward his people, but she knew that even she was now perhaps hated by him. She wiped tears from her eyes as Sage mounted his chestnut stallion and rode slowly away.

Then suddenly, with everyone following him, Sage

kicked his horse into a hard gallop, shrieking, *"Ei-yei."*

Harold hurried to Kit Carson's side. "Send the men after them," he shouted, his pistol drawn, taking aim at Sage's back. "Don't let them get away."

Kit placed a firm hand on Harold's firearm and lowered it to his side. "No, we're not going to do anything as hasty as that," he said, frowning. "We've got to give them a chance to think this through more carefully. They'll come around. They'll change their mind."

"And if they don't?" Harold said, slipping his pistol back into his holster.

Kit didn't answer, just gave him a grim, sad look.

The sound of the Navaho horses' hooves riding toward the mountains was like distant thunder, matching the vibrations of Leonida's pounding heart as she shielded her eyes with a hand and found Sage at the lead of those fleeing the injustices of the white man.

Sobbing, she picked up the hem of her skirt and ran away from the soldiers, who were now laughing and poking fun at the Indians.

5

Thou must give, or woo in vain!
So to thee—farewell!
—ANONYMOUS

After a night of little sleep, Leonida was woken with a start by a commotion outside. She sat up in bed and stared toward her bedroom window, wondering why there were so many excited voices, among them those of women and children.

Wiping sleep from her eyes, she crept out of bed. With the hem of her lacy nightgown sweeping around her ankles, she went to the window, drew back the sheer curtain, and looked outside. Her heartbeats quickened and her eyes widened as she watched the rush of women and children in the courtyard and saw the many trunks and travel bags being stacked on the board walkway where passengers usually waited for the stagecoach.

Scarcely breathing, Leonida watched the women and children coming together, anxiously awaiting the arrival of the stagecoach.

"There aren't that many of us women at the fort, and very few children, and it looks as though all but me are waiting for the stagecoach," Leonida whispered to herself. "Why?"

She spun around, her eyes even wider at the sudden thought that came to her. "Unless . . ." she murmured—but didn't stop to finish her thought.

Shedding her gown, she slipped into a floor-length

skirt and a comfortable drawstring white blouse. After putting on her shoes, she hurried to the door, stopping only long enough to grab a hairbrush from her dresser.

Brushing her hair with one hand, Leonida yanked the door open with the other and ran down the long corridor until she reached the officers' quarters at the far end of the building. Since Kit Carson's arrival, her father's office had once again been turned into the main officers' quarters of the fort.

Leonida resented this intrusion with a passion, even more now that she contemplated what might have happened to cause such a stir in the women and children to the point that they were waiting to flee the fort as soon as the stagecoach arrived this morning.

Leonida stopped just outside the door that led into the office. The voices inside were loud enough for her to hear what was being said. Putting her ear to the door, Leonida listened intently, growing cold inside the more she heard.

"The last of the women and children have been readied for travel," Harold said. "Except for Leonida. I'm not sure what to do about her. The other night she left like a wild thing bent for hell, and then I found her later wearing that damn Indian necklace again. It only proved one thing to me—that she met up with the Navaho chief again, and the thought disgusts me."

"She does seem to have a mind of her own," Kit said, chuckling.

"If her father were alive he wouldn't allow such behavior," Harold grumbled. "And by God, I'm not going to either. She's not going anywhere except to a preacher with me. Then I'm going to teach her some manners she's forgotten since her father's death.''

"I'd say you're asking for trouble you don't need," Kit warned. "You've enough on your hands with the Indians in this area, much less a woman who obviously hates your guts."

"She'll change her tune once she discovers she's the only woman left on the fort's premises," Harold said, laughing throatily.

"You're wrong to do that," Kit scolded. "Damn wrong."

"She's my woman," Harold said flatly. "I'll say what she is and is not to do around here."

Kit laughed sarcastically. "Seems she's shown you a time or two just how much she's *not* your woman."

"I'll pretend I didn't hear you say that," Harold grumbled. He paused, then said, "Are all of the women and children ready? The stagecoach should be rolling in any moment now."

"As far as I can tell," Kit said. "I hope we've assigned enough soldiers to their protection. It's one thing to send them away from this area because it's heating up with Indian troubles. It's another thing to send them right out into the hands *of* the Indians."

"I've assigned as many men as could be spared," Harold said. "We're right to send the women and children away. When I received the news of this latest raid, just last night, I knew that something had to be done. Last night was the last straw. None of those settlers were left alive. And now that Sage has been pointed out to be the leader of these renegades, he must die."

"We haven't got positive proof it was Sage," Kit

said in Sage's defense. "I know that he was angry as hell yesterday, but I assure you, he would not do anything as cold-blooded as what was reported to us today."

"Kit, damn it, I mean business," Harold stormed. "I'm going to stop these raids and killings once and for all. Kill all of the Navaho men, and take the women and children prisoners. They've been warned. They didn't listen."

"I just can't do what you are asking," Kit said somberly. "But I will round up the Navaho. For years I've been writing the Department of Indian Affairs about the Navaho being placed on reservations. At least now I'm being given the job of carrying out my own recommendation." He paused, then added, "And one thing for damn sure, I'm going to give Sage a chance to prove his innocence."

"I say to you, Kit Carson, that if Sage so much as looks like he's going to resist, shoot him dead," Harold said, his voice cold and impersonal.

Leonida's knees grew weak. Sage was being accused of raids. Had someone said that they had seen him? Had he been with her one minute, kissing her, and then killing innocent women and children in his next breath?

"No," Leonida whispered to herself. "Sage isn't the one. He couldn't be."

Then she recalled Harold's embittered words and his orders to kill Sage. Surely Kit Carson saw the reason for Harold's eagerness to see Sage killed: jealousy.

Her eyes wild, Leonida ran to a window and looked out again at the women and children who waited anxiously for the stagecoach. She could not believe that she had not been included. She could not believe that Harold had said all of those horrible things about her, and how he was going to force her into marrying *and* obeying him.

"That's what he thinks," she whispered harshly, anger swelling within her.

Harold's loud voice boomed through the closed door again. Leonida cringed when she heard him talking about how the Navaho women and children would be taken prisoners and forced to march to the reservation in New Mexico. If Sage resisted, he would kill him on the spot. The Navaho had had the chance to leave in peace.

Leonida abhorred what she heard, but knew that she could not say anything that would stop them. Also, she did not know where Sage's stronghold was, so she could not warn him. She had only one choice—to leave Harold and this dreadful fort along with the other women and children, no matter the risk.

Breathlessly Leonida hurried back to her room. She locked the door behind her, then went to the window and checked to see if the women and children were still there.

"Thank goodness," she murmured when she saw that they were. She watched the soldiers stirring up screens of dust as they prepared their horses for traveling. When a stagecoach rumbled into the courtyard and came to a stop beside the crowd of waiting passengers, fear gripped her heart. She didn't have much time. And even if she did escape from the house without Harold seeing her, how could she board the stagecoach without being caught?

Again she looked at the billowing dust from the horses, then at the stagecoach, partially hidden by the dust.

A thought came to her.

"That's how," she whispered. "*If* I hurry quickly enough."

She grabbed her travel bag and began cramming clothes into it, not stopping to fold them neatly. That would come later, when she was far from the clutches of General Harold Porter.

Once her bag was bulging with whatever she could get into it, Leonida started to go to her door, then stopped short when she remembered the necklace. Setting her bag down, she went to her dresser, opened the drawer, and took the necklace from it. She gazed into the mirror and secured the necklace around her neck, sighing when she recalled the two times that Sage had placed it there.

She could still feel the touch and the heat of his fingers. She closed her eyes, allowing herself to recall the thrill of his kiss.

Then she was jolted back to the present when again she heard the commotion outside her window. She did not have any time to waste.

It had not been her destiny to love Sage, nor had it been his to love her.

She went to her door and unlocked it. Scarcely breathing, she peeped around the corner. When she saw no activity in the corridor, she rushed from the room, through the parlor, and out the front door.

She was soon lost in the haze of dust and even had to feel her way across the courtyard. When she reached the stagecoach and found that she was the last to board, she threw her travel bag up to the driver and took only a moment to glance over her shoulder toward the house that her father had so lovingly shared with her.

Then with tears warming the corners of her eyes, she hastily boarded the stagecoach.

"Lord have mercy, Leonida," said Carole, the mother of a five-year-old son, as Leonida squeezed onto the seat with them and two other children and women fitted tightly together. "I was wondering when you were coming. I thought you weren't going to make it. The stagecoach should be leaving any time now."

"Yes, I know," Leonida said, giving Carole a wavering glance. Then she looked slowly around her at how many were squeezed in. Besides Carole's son, Trevor, who was snuggled onto his mother's lap, his eyes wide with fear, there were four other adults and five children, squashed into a space hardly big enough to breathe, much less move.

It was obvious that this flight was an act of desperation. The fear of Indians was quite evident in the depths of each of their eyes.

Leonida herself was not all that afraid, for she was too angry and disgusted with Harold to consider that she had as much reason to be afraid as those settlers whose lives had been snuffed out the previous evening.

And she knew that no matter how many soldiers escorted this stagecoach, if Indian renegades wanted to stop the stagecoach and murder everyone, they could.

"Leonida, are you afraid?"

A tiny voice brought her out of her deep, troubled thoughts. She looked down at Trevor and put a hand on his brow, smoothing a lock of raven-black hair out of his eyes.

"Am I afraid?" she said, gazing down into wide, dark eyes that reminded her of someone else's eyes in their darkness.

Sage.

Oh, if she could just forget that she had ever met him.

Her hand went to her throat, where the squash blossom necklace lay. As long as she had that necklace with her, she would always be reminded of Sage.

"Well, are you?" Trevor persisted, reaching a hand to Leonida's arm, giving it a slight shake. "Leonida? Tell me."

Leonida turned to Carole. "Can I hold him for a little while?" she asked, reaching out to Trevor.

Carole nodded and moved Trevor into Leonida's arms. Leonida snuggled the child close, even though she was already almost too hot to breathe. "Honey, let's not talk of being afraid," she murmured. "Let's make this story time instead. Would you like me to tell you and the other children stories to get your minds off your fears? My father was a master storyteller. I'd love to share some of his stories with you."

Carole smiled warmly over at Leonida, as did the rest of the mothers. All of the children chimed in at the same time, telling Leonida that they wanted to hear her stories. Leonida began telling the story of the frogs who ate too much bread and blew up like balloons and floated away, and the one about twin rabbits that had nothing better to do than to eat the flowers in the gardens in the cities; because of this habit they were turned into flowers themselves.

Leonida continued telling her special stories until the children had all drifted off into a sound sleep. Left awake were the mothers, within whose eyes lay the haunting fear not only of what lay before them but also of what they had left behind them—their beloved husbands, left to settle the differences between the whites and the redskins.

Leonida lifted Trevor over onto Carole's lap, then leaned her face closer to the window, trying to inhale a breath of fresh air. Her mind was not on any soldier; instead it was on the handsome Navaho chief whose life was soon to be turned topsy-turvy.

6

But I, grown shrewder, scan the skies
With a suspicious air—
—EMILY DICKINSON

Day lay golden along the top of the cliffs. Like a desert mirage, the canyon spread an emerald counterpane in the midst of an arid land. Irrigated by springs that swelled to a creek, the valley bloomed with willows and lofty cottonwoods. The canyon and the village of hogans nestled in the shadow of a colossal rampart of red rock wall.

Sage took the saddle and bridle off his stallion and began tying a thong about his animal's lower jaw, then stood with one hand on the horse's withers as he turned to welcome two of his most trusted scouts, riding hard toward him.

Something in Sage's heart told him that the scouts were bringing more bad news. It was in their eyes and the set of their jaws and the way they made such haste into the village. Sage was not sure that he was ready to be told anything else. He and his people had just arrived back at the stronghold, the journey from Fort Defiance a quiet one.

Although Sage and many other Navaho leaders had said they would not leave this land that had belonged to their ancestors, he knew that to stay meant death to many of his people. Kit Carson had become someone foreign to the Navaho. He had stopped being Sage's friend when he aligned himself with the other white leaders whose lives were fueled by greed and cold hearts toward all Indians.

As Sage's scouts wheeled their horses to a thundering, dust-flying halt, his thoughts returned fleetingly to the moment when he had held the lovely white woman in his arms. In that instant of passion he had forgotten everything but the woman.

But now, thinking back, she was to him like the peace that had once sealed hearts in friendship between himself and the white leaders.

Forever gone.

"What news have you brought me?" Sage asked, forcing his thoughts back to the present. "It is *hogaygahn*, bad?"

Spotted Feather stepped forward and placed a heavy hand on Sage's shoulder. "Yes, it is *hogaygahn*," he said. The silver buttons on his leggings flashed in the sun, his waist-length black hair fluttered in the breeze. "A lie was spread to those in charge at Ford Defiance, and to Kit Carson. It was said that you led a recent raid that killed many settlers. Because of this lie, and because the white leaders believed it to be true, the white pony soldiers have been ordered to round up our people, and to kill you if you resist."

Sage's heart began pumping wildly within his chest. His eyes flared with rage. "And so they go this far, do they?" he said between clenched teeth. "It is not enough that they have given the order that our land will no longer be ours. But now they will take it by force. Even kill me, while doing it?"

"Only if you resist," Spotted Feather said, lowering his hand from Sage's shoulder. "Only . . . if . . . you resist."

Black Thunder stepped forward, his dark eyes narrowing. "Let us gather together many Navaho and attack Fort Defiance," he growled. "Let us show them that they are wrong to go against us in such a way. Let us fight for our land to the death. That is the honorable way."

Sage nodded. "We will not go against the whole United States Army," he said. "But we will use a tactic used before that made the white leaders stop and take notice. Although the strategy is unpleasant to me, I see that we must blackmail the white leaders into changing their minds."

"Blackmail?" Spotted Feather said, arching an eyebrow. "Why do you plan blackmail? And how will this blackmail be carried out?"

"We will use white women and children as bargaining tools," Sage said, smiling slowly.

"And where do we get these captives?" Black Thunder asked, as he curved his fingers around a knife clasped at his waist. "Do we take scalps from some and leave them dying beneath the sun, to prove we have others as hostages?"

"No, no scalps," Sage said, his thoughts once again catapulting to Leonida and the beautiful color of her hair. It was as golden as the sun, and it gave him a feeling of foreboding to think even for a moment of seeing it hanging on a scalp pole.

"And no, no deaths," Sage said in a deep growl.

"Where do we get these captives?" Black Thunder persisted. "Do we raid the settlers' homesteads since we are already being accused of the atrocity anyway?"

"No," Sage said dryly. "We will not raid the homesteads to get our captives. We will go in search of a stagecoach. Those who journey aboard that sort of travel vehicle are usually related closely to those in charge at the fort. Those will make the best bargaining tools of all.''

''There are always military escorts,'' Spotted Feather said, leaning his face close to Sage's. ''Do we kill them?''

Sage glowered at Spotted Feather. ''Did you not hear me say there are to be no deaths?'' he snapped angrily. ''We will avoid killing at all costs. We kill only if forced to save our own lives.''

Sage gave his horse a fond pat, then walked away from it. He looked over his shoulder at his two scouts. ''Spread the word. Let us make haste in preparing ourselves. I will be waiting in the sweat lodge for my warriors.''

Hardly aware of anything around him, his mind so torn with feelings, Sage walked through his village, paying no heed to those who spoke to him from the doorways of their hogans or from the outdoor cook fires where many had gathered in the late afternoon. He was hardly even aware of the pleasant aroma of corn roasting over the large, communal outdoor fire, or of the sounds of the looms at work throughout his village. In his imagination he was experiencing an impossible dream that involved Leonida.

He was feeling her deeply within his heart.

He was tasting her.

His fingers were warm on her body, arousing her.

Oh, how he wanted her.

Oh, how he was missing her.

As he stepped up to the four-foot-high conical sweat lodge, many of his warriors were already assembling around it. He nodded to them, his mind now back where it belonged, on what was right for his people as a whole instead of just himself, a man who hungered for a woman.

Sage shed his clothes while Spotted Feather built a fire close to the sweat lodge and began heating stones in it. Sage had seen to it that the hut was made large enough to seat as many men as were required for warring, and each of them bent down and entered after he had stripped himself.

Wedged together in a wide circle inside the low, pitch-dark enclosure, the warriors sat with their legs crossed and their heads lowered. They were silent as Spotted Feather began shoveling hot coals into the lodge.

After enough rocks were piled in the center of the floor, Spotted Feather set a huge wooden vessel of water inside, removed all of his clothes, then crawled into the hut and sat down beside Sage.

Slowly and methodically, Spotted Feather began splashing water from the container onto the hot rocks. A wave of intense heat wafted around the inside of the hut, striking the warriors' bodies, causing them to sweat profusely. Some who got too hot sank their heads lower, between their legs.

"Han-e-ga! Han-e-ga!" rang out among the men each time water splashed on the rocks, meaning "good."

Then Sage began singing softly, *Naye-e sin,* the War Song. In earlier times it had been sung by the god Nayenezrani, the Slayer of the Anaye. Nayenezrani made the ancient war songs and gave them to the Navaho so that when they prepared for war the warriors could chant this song and then put the war feather in their hair. These feathers were very holy and were ornamented with turquoise. No woman or child could ever look upon them, lest the warrior, in battle, become like a child or a woman.

The war chant told how Nayenezrani hurled his enemies into the ground with the lightning, one after another. The four lightning strikes from him would go in all directions and then return, for lightning always looked as if it flashed out and then came back.

The other warriors joined Sage, singing—

>"Lo, the flint youth, he am I,
> The flint youth.
>Nayenezrani, lo, behold me, he am I.
> Lo, the flint youth, he am I,
>   The flint youth.
>Moccasins of black flint have I;
> Lo, the flint youth, he am I,
>   The flint youth.
>Leggings of black flint have I;
> *E-na*
>Tunic of black flint have I;
> *E-na*
>Bonnet of black flint have I;
> *E-na*
>Clearest, purest flint the heart
>Living strong within me—heart of flint;
> Lo, the flint youth, he am I,
>   *E-na*
>Now the zigzag lightnings four
> From me flash,
>Striking and returning,
> From me flash;
>Lo, the flint youth, he am I,
>   *E-na*, the Flint Youth,
>There where'er the lightnings strike,

Into the ground they hurl the foe—
Ancient folk with evil charms,
     E-na.

After singing and taking the sweat bath, they
left the lodge and dived into the river to cleanse
themselves, then banded together as they dressed
in their finest warring gear. They put on war shirts
made of the thickest buckskin obtainable. Since Sage
was their chief and the wealthiest of them all, he
used four thicknesses of buckskin, glued together
with sticky gum from leaves of the prickly pear
cactus.

The shirts were made in the poncho style, but sewed
up the sides, with the sleeves to the elbow in one piece
with the shirt. The garment was tight around the neck
and laced down the front. Warriors wrapped themselves in striped blankets belted around the waist, their
deerskin moccasins reaching to the knees, their tight
breeches edged with silver buttons and slit down the
sides.

Before they left, they ate dried yucca, for its sugar
gave them energy.

Some carrying lances made of hard oak with han-
dles three to six feet long and painted various colors
and decorated with eagle feathers, others carrying
bows and arrows and rifles, the warriors left the village on their handsome mounts.

Sage felt displaced. Never had he expected to have
to go against the white pony soldiers for any reason.
Especially not now, for he did not want to think that
Leonida might be harmed. At this moment in time,
her heart was pure toward the Navaho. But how would
she feel once she discovered that he was capable of

abducting innocent women and children? He despaired to himself.

He sighed heavily, knowing that he must restrain himself from ever thinking about her again or caring what she thought about anything.

She was now as much his enemy as Kit Carson was.

7

A creature might forget to weep, who bore
Thy comfort long, and lose thy love thereby.
—ELIZABETH BARRETT BROWNING

After a full night in the stagecoach, having stopped only long enough at daybreak for everyone to see to their personal needs in the privacy of the bushes, and for everyone to partake of a quick meal of cold beans and beef jerky, Leonida was now squeezed back inside, among the whining children, long tired of hearing stories, and their mothers, who had ran out of ways to please them.

It was midday, the sun was pouring down from the sky in a beating heat, the worst of it seemingly trapped inside the stagecoach.

Leonida fanned herself with one hand as perspiration trickled down her face. She drew her drawstring blouse partially away from her chest, where perspiration was beading up in the valley of her breasts. As she held the blouse away from her skin, she blew down the front of it, receiving at least a moment's relief.

Feeling lucky to be sitting beside a window, Leonida leaned her face over close to it, flinching when the driver of the stagecoach drew back his whip and uncoiled it, snapping it like a fusillade of rifle fire.

Chains clanked. Axles groaned. The horses strained in their harnesses as the stagecoach moved along on its way in a great cloud of dust. The driver whistled softly through his teeth while the military escorts kept a steady pace beside, in front of, and behind the stage-coach.

Trying to ignore the complaining children, Leonida settled herself as comfortably as possible against the back of the seat again. Once again fanning herself with her hand, she closed her eyes and became lost in thought. Always her thoughts returned to Sage. It gave her an empty feeling at the pit of her stomach to realize that she would never see him again.

Leonida recalled something her father had said long ago before they had moved to Fort Defiance, that among all Indian tribes, the Navaho were the most difficult to control. After arriving at Fort Defiance, though, he had come to understand that the Navaho, except for a few renegades, were a gentle, caring people who kept to themselves, leaving the whites alone.

She bit her lower lip as she thought of her father and how he would have handled this situation. If he had been alive, there would have been more bargaining with the Navaho, instead of just giving them an ultimatum. Even Harold and Kit Carson understood the dangers, or they wouldn't have sent the women and children of the fort to find temporary shelter and safety elsewhere.

As the stagecoach rounded a clump of thorn bushes in a flurry of dust, pitching Leonida forward, her eyes flew open wildly. She grabbed for the door and steadied herself. Then she gasped when she heard the sudden shrieks of Indians and gunfire approaching the stagecoach from behind.

Leonida's heartbeat quickened at the thought of an Indian massacre. Panic had seized the women and children, and they screamed and clutched at one another. Leonida turned from them and leaned her head out of the window just in time to see a long Indian lance pierce the arm of one of the soldiers, and she watched as gunfire felled others.

The Indians came into view, riding like the wind, their backs level with their horses? Gritty dust rose from the trail in clouds, blocking the sight of the other Indians. But Leonida could still hear their murderous cries, and the screams of the soldiers as they fell from their horses.

Then the dust cleared somewhat, and Leonida paled when she recognized Sage among the Indians, pouring leather into his horse, advancing closer and closer to the stagecoach. She was shocked and disappointed that Sage was taking part in this dreadful raid. All along she had seen him as a peace-loving man, incapable of violence such as this.

She gasped as Sage raised his rifle and aimed at the stagecoach, leveling the gun on the driver. She was glad when he didn't shoot immediately but shouted to the driver to stop, at least giving him a chance.

She inhaled a deep breath when the driver did stop the stagecoach. Not only did he throw down his arms but the soldiers who were not wounded stopped their horses and dropped their weapons to the ground, soon thrusting their hands into the air, giving up the fight to the Navaho.

From the shadows of the stagecoach Leonida watched Sage closely as he rode up close and drew a tight rein. Sage ordered the driver down, then his gaze moved to the door.

"All passengers step to the ground," he shouted, motioning with the barrel of his rifle toward the door. "One by one, leave the stagecoach. Quickly!"

Leonida's trembling fingers reached for the door latch.

"Quickly!" Sage said, this time more impatiently.

With the children crowding in behind her, crying, and the women sobbing, Leonida slowly opened the door. The moment she moved out of the shadows and Sage got his first glimpse of her, she heard him gasp. As she stepped out, she looked up. Their eyes momentarily locked. But Leonida could not continue looking at him, for she was torn with too many feelings about him right now.

There were several wounded soldiers lying on the ground, groaning with pain. It was hard to believe that Sage had led an attack that had caused such suffering. And even though she perhaps understood that he had to retaliate in some way to prove a point to Kit Carson and Harold, she could not condone such violence.

A finger on her chin, turning her eyes upward, made Leonida's pulse race, for she knew whose finger it was. Sage's.

He had dismounted and come to her, singling her out from the others to speak to. It was going to be hard for her to treat him coldly, while her insides warmed with his mere presence.

"You are with these women and children," Sage said, forcing her to look at him. "Why are you?"

Leonida defied him with a set stare and a tight jaw. A part of her wanted to fling herself into his arms and apologize for his having to resort to this way of life. Yet she kept reminding herself that she did not know this man at all. Perhaps he *had* been responsible for some of the other raids. This one had seemed easy for him, as though practiced many times.

"You too are now Sage's enemy?" Sage said, fighting to keep his voice cold and impersonal. "This is why you travel away from Sage? You see him as criminal? As renegade?"

Leonida could not keep her silence any longer.

There were too many things to be explained. "Haven't you proven today that you are both?" she said. She placed her hands on her hips. "If you were innocent of all crimes, you wouldn't be here now, with those men lying wounded. If you were innocent before, you certainly aren't now. You are rightfully the hunted one now, Sage. I have no choice now but to see you as you truly are. An unruly renegade."

Sage took his hand from her chin. He motioned with a nod of his head toward the soldiers whose wounds were being looked after by his warriors. "If things were different, this would not be of my choosing," he said thickly. "It is not something long planned. Only one sunrise ago did I know that this must be done. Only then did I have to scheme ways to turn the tide back in my favor. Taking hostages is the only way. Surely you can see that."

"No, I can't see how maiming and stealing can solve anything," Leonida said, dropping her arms slowly to her side. In truth she saw his point, but she still could not condone his tactics. And he still had not proven to her that he had not been one of those murderous, thieving renegades all along.

"It is the *only* way," Sage said, then walked away from her.

Leonida edged back to stand among the other women and the clinging, sobbing children. When Trevor took her hand and looked up at her with fearful eyes, she reached down and lifted him up into her arms and held him tightly to her breast, still watching Sage as he went from one wounded man to the other, saying words of comfort to them. To her amazement, the soldiers responded in kind, their hands momentarily locking with Sage's as they smiled up at him.

Then Leonida was filled with horror when some of

Sage's warriors yanked the other soldiers and the stagecoach driver over to the wagon and tied them one by one to the four wheels, until they were a crowded jumble of flesh and faces massed together.

Sage came back to the women and children. His gaze moved slowly over them, then stopped at Leonida. He grabbed Trevor away from her and put him with the other children. "You will ride with me," he flatly ordered her.

He shifted his eyes to the other women and the children. "We are taking you all to our stronghold in the mountains," he said solemnly. "All but Leonida will walk."

He motioned with his rifle. "Go," he commanded stiffly. "Start walking. We will soon follow on horses."

Terrified, the women and children stumbled away, clutching each other and sobbing. Leonida dared Sage with a set stare. "I'm no better than they," she said icily. "I won't ride while they walk."

She hurried after them. She was aware of Sage's eyes on her, angry and hot, and she was aware when he mounted his horse and began riding toward her.

She walked more quickly, so fast that she passed up some of the other women in her haste to put as much distance between herself and Sage as she could.

Then her breath was stolen when Sage reached down and grabbed her around the waist, yanking her onto his saddle in front of him.

"Let me down," Leonida cried, trying to pry his arms from around her waist with her fingers. "Sage, I don't want to be on your horse with you. Let me down."

"*E-do-ta,* no," Sage said, his hold on her not weakening. "I did not intend for you to be a part of my vengeance. You will not suffer for it more than I can help.''

''If you don't want me to be a part of it, then let me go,'' Leonida said, unable to control the sensual feelings that looking into his eyes caused.

''For many reasons Sage cannot do that,'' he mumbled, wheeling his horse around, then leading it into a soft trot behind the frightened women and children. ''You will go with me to my stronghold. There you will stay.''

Leonida's lips parted in a slight gasp. ''Do you mean that I am to be your captive forever?'' she finally managed to say in a stammer. ''The others will be captives forever also?''

Sage did not respond. He just gave her a look that she could not define.

8

I strove to hate,
But vainly strove.
—GEORGE LYTTELTON

Aspens and fields of wildflowers brightened the wayside as the trail began to climb gradually into the mountains. Leonida noticed that Sage's horse would turn, stop, or start at the mere pressure of his foot. The silver ornaments jingled on the horse's bridle. They flashed brightly in the sun, reflecting into Leonida's eyes as she sat much too close to the man that she had so many torn feelings about. Yet she had given up struggling with him long ago, knowing that he was as determined to hold her there as she had been to be set free.

Glancing ahead at the women and children stumbling along the trail, dread filled her. What could Sage be planning for these innocent women and children? Even herself?

Licking her parched lips, which had been baked the whole afternoon, Leonida glanced over her shoulder at Sage. He looked past her, his jaw tight, his eyes cold. But she could not hold her silence any longer. They had not stopped once since they had left the stagecoach. There had been no water offered or moments of rest. She was afraid that if they went any farther, those moving on foot might drop, not only from exhaustion but from thirst as well.

"Sage, when are we going to stop?" Leonida

blurted out, her voice raspy from her thirst. "Have mercy on those who are walking. The children. The women. They must have a chance to rest. And they are in dire need of water."

She regretted having not said something earlier, for the moment she asked, Sage drew his reins and motioned his warriors to stop. He gave his warriors commands in Navaho, then rode up to the women and children and told them to make a turn to the right.

"I will take you to a wet place where cattails can be found, pulled, and eaten raw," he said. "This will quench your thirst even more than water. It will sustain you much longer once we move again farther into the mountains, toward my stronghold."

Leonida's heart cried out to the children, especially Trevor. He looked in worse condition than all the rest. His eyes were scarcely open and his mother had to keep pulling him up as he would slowly crumple toward the ground. Leonida understood why Carole did not lift the child up into her arms. She was too weak herself to carry the burden of another.

Leonida turned to Sage. "Let me walk with the others," she pleaded. She nodded toward Trevor. "I can carry the child. I doubt he can go much farther on his own. Please allow me to help him, Sage. What should it matter to you that I do?"

Sage peered into her eyes, finding it more and more difficult to look at her as his captive. It was still hard for him to comprehend that she had been in the stagecoach. Seeing her there had brought many feelings to assail him.

But most prominent of all was the fact that she was traveling on that stagecoach away from him—which meant that she had not cared enough for him to stay.

This he could never understand.

He had felt so much in her kiss.

He had read so much in her eyes.

Yet another thought had come to him, one that pleased him. If she had been leaving Fort Defiance, she had also been leaving the man that she had planned to marry.

"May I?" Leonida pleaded.

Sage's heart pounded as he gazed into Leonida's eyes, seeing within them more than a pleading for the child. He could see that she was battling her feelings for him. Perhaps she was recalling their kiss, and the message that the kiss had sung to her heart.

If she searched her heart and thoughts carefully, he knew she would discover that she still had the feelings for him that had surfaced when he had held her and kissed her.

Yes, he thought to himself, if anything good at all came from the stagecoach attack, it was that it had led him to her, as though it had been their destiny.

"You may go to the child," Sage said, loosening his arm around her waist. With his other arm he helped her down from the horse, her eyes having not yet left him.

"I learned from you how to say thank you in Navaho," Leonida murmured. "*Uke-he*, Sage. Thank you from the bottom of my heart."

Sage nodded stiffly, then watched with a deep love for her as she went to the small boy and lifted him gently into her arms. It was at this moment that he knew that he had been right to choose her to be his future wife. There, standing before him, was how she would be in the future as she would hold *their* child with such compassion and tenderness.

Humming a lullaby, Leonida cradled Trevor in her arms and slowly rocked him back and forth. When he managed a smile, then lay his cheek back against her bosom, she knew that he was going to be all right.

"Leonida, thank you for helping," Carole said, eyeing Trevor with wavering eyes. "I'm so weak. I—I just couldn't lift him."

Carole looked over at Sage bitterly. "That Indian will pay," she hissed. "Once Kit Carson finds out what he's done, he'll come and shoot him. Or better yet, hang him. He deserves no pity, that one."

A deep sadness overwhelmed Leonida, torn between how she should feel about Sage and how she actually did feel. Had he, in truth, been responsible for more than this one raid? Did he have placed in a sacred place in his hogan many white men's scalps, perhaps even those of women and children . . . ?

She closed her eyes to such a horrendous thought and began following Sage. Trevor lay limply in her arms and fell into a sound sleep. When they reached the shade of cottonwood trees and the splash of a waterfall as it careened down the walls of a high butte, everyone ran to the river and fell to their knees, splashing water into their mouths and onto their faces.

Leonida moved carefully to the water's edge with Trevor. Carole took the child from her arms and lay him down beneath a tree. After she ripped a portion of her skirt away, she soaked it, then began bathing her son's face and squeezing water over his tiny lips.

Leonida was not aware of Sage behind her until he placed a hand on her shoulder, causing her to turn with a start. "Eat the meat of the cattail," he said, handing her a cattail spike that had been stripped of its tightly packed outer flowers. "This will quench your thirst." He held a yucca plant in his other hand, as well as a leather pouch of food. "Once your thirst is quenched, you can feed on other offerings that I give you."

"No, thank you," Leonida said stiffly, pretending that which she did not feel. "I will drink what everyone else drinks, and if they aren't given food, nor will I eat."

At almost the same moment, her eyes widened as she watched Sage's warriors mingle with the women and children, sharing food from their leather pouches. The dried wild seeds, some jerked beef meat mixed with tallow, and the fruit of the yucca were consumed quickly, followed by deeper gulps of water.

Sage walked away from Leonida with his offering of food. "You can rest for a while and then we will move onward," he said, looking from woman to woman, then from child to child. "We will not stop again until we are safely within the folds of the mountain."

Leonida was deeply touched by Sage's generosity. Everyone's needs were being seen to, and even the warriors seemed to have relaxed. They were more like Leonida had first seen them at the fort, standing outside their tents with their wares to trade. They did not seem like renegades at all, except that she had seen them shoot to kill and force those taken from the stagecoach into captivity.

Her stomach's sudden growling, so loud that surely even the fish in the stream heard it, made Leonida forget everything but her hunger and her thirst. She eyed the pouch of food in Sage's hand, and the fruit of the yucca, which looked like a short, fat banana. Her throat was so parched that she could hardly swallow. She glanced over at the stream, then went quickly to the water. Kneeling down beside it, she began scooping large handfuls of water up to her lips, and the water trickled down the back of her throat so quickly that she began to choke and gag.

Embarrassed, she rose to her feet and cleared her

throat one more time. When Sage came to her with a concerned look on his face, she turned her eyes away, not wanting him to sense her feelings for him.

"You are being foolish," Sage said. He forced the pouch of food into her hand and then the fruit of the yucca. "I will share my food with you. You eat. *Now*. You have heard me say that we will not stop again until we are in the mountains. Only moments ago you had strength enough for both you *and* the child. Later, after much more travel, you will see that because you did not eat when told to, you will have to depend on someone else's strength, as did the child yours."

He leaned down, closer to her face. "I would be more than glad to lend you a helping hand should you need it," he said softly. "But would you accept it as readily as the child accepted help from you? I doubt it. Your trust in me is gone. Is it not?"

"How could I trust you now, after what you did?" Leonida said, eyeing the pouch hungrily. She looked slowly up at Sage. "You injured the soldiers. Isn't that reason enough not to trust you?"

"Did you not notice that none of the soldiers were mortally wounded?" Sage said stiffly. "The aim of Sage and his warriors is accurate. Had I wanted dead soldiers, they would be dead. I chose *not* to kill, only to maim."

Leonida's mouth opened in a gasp; now she realized that it was true. None of the soldiers had been killed.

Sage continued before she could offer a response. "And you know that I would never hurt you," he said. "Trust me, Leonida. What I have done is the only way for the Navaho. My people's future is dim because of Kit Carson and the other white leaders. They would not listen to reason peacefully. I was forced into using means other than that which my father taught me. He was a peaceful Navaho. So was I until today. This is the first time Sage has ever lifted a firearm against the white pony soldiers. I hope it will be the last.''

"How can you expect it to be the last time, when you know that the soldiers are even now hunting for you?'' Leonida asked. "Sage, no matter what you say, I cannot condone what you have done today.''

Sage took her by an elbow and urged her to sit beside the stream. "In time, you will follow my reasoning for everything,'' he said. He nodded toward the food pouch. "Open. Let us share equally.''

She didn't have to be told again. Her stomach ached so terribly, she opened the pouch and broke the long strip of jerked deer meat in two and handed half to Sage. Between bites of tasteless deer meat and dried, wild seeds, she enjoyed the sweetness of the fat fruit of the yucca.

Sage ate along with her, his mind on what lay ahead. "It is important to reach my stronghold before word has spread too far of what my warriors and I have done,'' he said suddenly. "Once we are there, no one can find Sage and his people, or his captives. It is well hidden from the soldiers. Only a few neighboring Indians with whom the Navaho trade even know where it is located.''

"It will take you quite a long time to get there if you continue forcing the women and children to travel on foot,'' Leonida said guardedly. "Especially if they have to travel the narrow paths of the mountainsides.''

As she took her last bite of food, she gave Sage a half glance, hoping that what she had said had planted an idea in his head. The government had always given the officers' families more than adequate housing, clothing, and food to satisfy them. This had made them weak.

"You are right," Sage said, nodding. "The captives will now all travel on horseback with my warriors."

Leonida was stunned that he had agreed to her suggestion. A warm feeling swam through her: Sage was changing back into the gentle, caring person that she had known at first. It would be so easy to forget everything but the good about him.

"Once we are safely at my stronghold I will send a scout to Fort Defiance with word of the ambush and my intentions," Sage said, gently taking the empty pouch from Leonida and folding it in fourths.

"What are your intentions?" she asked. "How long do you plan to hold everyone captive?"

She paled when he did not answer.

9

The clearest spring, the shadiest grove;—
Tell me, my heart, if this be love?
                                    —GEORGE LYTTELTON

The long ride, the hot sun and scorching wind, weighed on Leonida. Combined with the lack of sleep, the discomfort made her limbs sluggish and her eyes heavy. Her head bobbed as she forced herself not to lean back and rest against Sage's powerful chest. It was enough that she had to ride with him at all, constantly battling her feelings for him, let alone having to ride on into the long night without any sleep or rest from the grueling journey on horseback. She had long since forgotten the others, who were as fatigued as she, for it was taking all of her own willpower and concentration not to give in to her exhaustion.

The morning sun had been welcomed, for she hoped it would reveal that they were approaching Sage's stronghold. Yet Leonida saw that they were still traveling a small footpath at the side of a mountain, this only occasionally leveling out into a valley wide and green with grass.

With a heavy sigh, Leonida looked around, trying to focus her attention on her surroundings to keep herself awake. They were riding down a slope of bald rock into another valley. Here and there were fragments of petrified trees. They were of all colors. Some were dull, others reflected like marble, their many shades made more brilliant by the clear sunlight.

They followed a winding path under firs, and then they rode into another narrow canyon. Leonida was relieved to get a reprieve from the sun in this strip of mid-morning shade, the air cool and pleasant on her face and arms.

For warmth through the long, cold night of travel on horseback, Leonida had worn a poncho, a shoulder blanket with a hole in the center for the head. She had ignored Sage when he had first offered it to her, but it had not taken much shivering for her to agree to wear his generous offering. Yet she had shoved his arm away as he had tried to draw her back against him, to share his body warmth with her.

She had known the dangers.

As the horses topped a brush-covered ridge, Leonida blinked her sleep-heavy eyes and discovered a little green meadow in a pocket of the canyon. A grove of young quaking aspens reached into the meadow. Beyond them, half a dozen fat elk were grazing.

"There you see fresh meat for dinner," Sage said, breaking the silence. He reined his horse to a stop and held up a fist as a silent command to his warriors to draw their own mounts to a halt.

Leonida's shoulders slumped forward. Her eyes slowly closed, feeling the wondrous lethargy of sleep momentarily claim her.

Then her eyes flew open wildly when she felt herself being taken off the horse and into powerful arms. She looked up into Sage's handsome face as he carried her toward the shade of the trees, to which the other women and the children were being herded.

Leonida wanted to yank herself free of Sage's arms, but it felt too wonderful to be held so gently. She could not help herself when she lay her cheek against his chest, her eyes closing again, snatching another moment of sleep before she felt herself being lowered to the ground.

Not wanting to wake up, she snuggled onto her side on a thick carpet of moss and sighed when he covered her with the poncho that she had worn through the night. Soon she felt a small body creep next to her and snuggle against her bosom—Trevor had missed their camaraderie. Leonida put an arm around the boy's tiny waist and drew him closer against her, opening her eyes only enough to see Carole stretched out beneath the next tree, oblivious to everything, her sleep so sound, so deep.

The sound of gunfire a short distance away made Leonida flinch; then once again she drifted off into a merciful void of sleep. Dreams soon replaced reality. She was riding on Sage's chestnut stallion with him, her hair blowing in the wind, her arms willingly wrapped around his waist. She was feeling content. She had never felt so loved. When Sage turned and gazed at her, his eyes dark with feelings for her, her insides thrilled. She lay her head on his bare, muscular back, reveling in this wondrous moment as they rode toward his village, where she was going to become his wife. She had already found paradise in his arms as he had taught her ways of loving a man. She was eager to bear his children.

Then a shot rang out in her dream, changing it into a nightmare as she watched Sage's body jerk when a bullet pierced his heart. Harold Porter came riding out of the brush, laughing, with his rifle barrel smoking.

Leonida was aware of someone screaming, then she felt someone's gentle hand on her shoulder, shaking her, awakening her, and realized it had been her own scream.

Bolting to a sitting position, perspiration lacing her

brow and her heart pounding, Leonida gazed anxiously into Sage's midnight-dark eyes. Without thinking, she reached a hand up to his face as he leaned down over her.

"It was a dream?" she murmured, her voice drawn. "It was just a terrible dream?"

"Yes, a dream," Sage said thickly, her gentle hand on his face showing him more than she dared to confess aloud to him—that she did care.

She realized that she was displaying too much affection for Sage in front of the other women, who were staring at her, and jerked her hand away. She gazed down at Trevor, who was also closely scrutinizing her. She drew him within her arms and gave him a hug, glad to have him to take the focus of attention away from herself.

"Did I frighten you, honey?" she asked softly, stroking his back through his cotton shirt.

Trevor nodded and clung to her. "Don't scream again," he murmured. "It scares me too much." Then he leaned away from her, and tears came to his eyes. "I'm hungry. My belly hurts."

Carole crawled over and sat down beside Leonida. There were deep, dark circles beneath Carole's eyes, and her breathing seemed shallow. Some strange sort of rattle came from her lungs, and each breath took much effort. This alarmed Leonida.

"This woman needs to eat," she said dryly to Sage. "You shouldn't have made us wait so long."

"You were told the need to get higher in these mountains," he explained softly. "Not only for my benefit but also for yours. While you are traveling with me and my warriors, you are in as much danger from the gunfire of the white pony soldiers as are the Navaho. Traveling without stopping was the only way. Now we are at a safe distance from those who might shoot at us. We can stop often to rest and eat.''

Leonida became aware of the wonderful fragrance of meat cooking over open flames. She realized how long she had been asleep. Long enough for an animal to have been slain, skinned, and cooked. Her gaze followed the aroma and caught the sight of a large hunk of meat roasting brown over the campfire, its juices dripping into the flames, sizzling tantalizingly.

Carole reached for Leonida's hand, drawing her attention back. "I've got something that needs to be said," Carole said, her voice thin. "You can't totally blame the Indian chief for my condition. There is more than hunger that makes me weak. I—I never confessed my illness to anyone. Not even my husband. I had planned to, then . . . then . . . my husband was shot on one of the recent Indian raids. I had no one else. I was hoping that someone would have mercy on my Trevor once I worsened. Leonida, perhaps you can . . . ?''

"What are you saying?" Leonida asked.

"I'm dying," Carole said, tears rushing from her eyes. "It's a lung disease. There is no hope. Do you think you could look after Trevor? He's such a dear boy and—and as you know, he has become quite attached to you.''

Leonida's heart despaired at the news of Carole's illness, and she was torn with conflicting feelings about the sick woman's request. She glanced at Trevor, who was looking ever so trustingly into her eyes, and then at Sage, who was removing the meat from the spit over the fire. She suddenly realized how short life was and how one must take from it what he or she could.

Putting an arm around Carole's frail shoulders, Leonida drew her into her embrace. "I'm so sorry," she whispered. ''Yes, I'll see to Trevor's welfare. He's so dear. How could I say no?''

''Thank you,'' Carole murmured, holding back torrents of tears. ''God bless you.''

Carole went to Trevor and sat down beside him, then took him onto her lap, cuddling him close. Leonida watched, filled with many tumultuous emotions. She did not know how long Carole had, and she did not want to ask. Knowing that she was dying was bad enough.

Again she gazed at Sage, wondering how he would feel about her mothering Trevor? Would Sage want him as well if Sage and Leonida were ever free to commit themselves to one another?

Realizing where her thoughts had taken her, and feeling foolish for it, Leonida started to look away, but when Sage turned to her with a large chunk of meat, she forgot everything but the hunger gnawing away at the pit of her stomach. She didn't hesitate. She accepted the meat and sank her teeth into it. She gobbled it down hungrily, watching as everyone else joined in the feast until there were only stripped bones lying on the ground beside the fire. The bones were carried far away from the camp and discarded.

Everyone took turns going to the river to splash water onto their faces and take deep, refreshing drinks.

By then the sun was low in the sky. Leonida watched Sage anxiously, afraid that he was going to command his warriors to ready their horses for travel again. But to her relief, he instead went to his stallion and removed a roll of blankets from behind the saddle. He began unrolling them close to the campfire, and gave Leonida occasional questioning glances. Her heart began to pound. Was he going to force her to sleep with him, as he had forced her to travel with him on his stallion?

The thought sent a sensual thrill coursing through her veins, yet she knew that she couldn't. She could not be that close, so intimately close to his hard, muscular body, without dying inside with need of his lips and hands, although this was something new to her, had only become a part of her after having met this handsome Navaho chief.

Leonida looked slowly around the camp, seeing that the other Navaho warriors were spreading blankets. Then Sage turned and locked eyes with her.

"Tonight we sleep. Tonight you will be *warm*," Sage said, gesturing toward the blankets with an outstretched hand. "You will share blankets with Sage."

A blush heated Leonida's cheeks. "No, thank you," she murmured. "I'll do just fine sleeping by myself beside the fire."

"The flames of the fire lose their warmth as they turn to embers," Sage said flatly. He went to Leonida, took her by an elbow, and led her toward his blankets. "You sleep beside Sage, whose heat never dies."

Leonida's pulse was racing maddeningly. She stumbled as she gazed over her shoulder at the women who were staring, aghast, at this order that had been given her. She watched the Indian warriors settle down onto their blankets, some already snoring.

That did it. It was obvious that she was to be the only captive who would have blankets for warmth tonight, and she could not stand for that.

The others, especially Carole, needed protection from the chilly dampness of this mountain valley.

She jerked sharply to be set free. "I absolutely refuse to sleep with you between your blankets, especially if the women and children have none with which to keep warm tonight," she fumed, daring Sage with an angry stare. "Give the women and children blankets. I will fuss no more about where I must sleep or with whom."

Sage glowered at her, then shouted to his warriors, waking them, telling them to give half their blankets to the captives. There was much grumbling of dissatisfaction, but being the dutiful warriors they were, they did as Sage ordered and soon everyone, including the women and children, was settled in beside the fire beneath a blanket.

Sage stood over his blankets with his arms folded across his chest and his feet spread wide. He gave Leonida a silent stare, then went to her and took her hand and led her down beside him beneath the blankets.

Her heart thumped wildly as she lay with her back to him, wondering what to expect next from the handsome chief.

She was surprised when he did not attempt approaching her in any way sexually. Instead he was soon fast asleep behind her.

Sighing heavily, Leonida relaxed and closed her eyes, quickly welcoming the soft cocoon of sleep herself.

Harold shoved his chair back and rose hastily from behind his desk when he heard a commotion out in the courtyard. His lips parted and his eyes widened as he saw the stagecoach that had taken the wives and children from the fort. Driving alongside it were horses, upon them several wounded soldiers.

A quick shuffling of feet and harsh breathing behind him caused Harold to turn around and come eye to eye with Lieutenant Nelson, who came red-faced and sweaty into the office. The lieutenant saluted, then began talking so fast that Harold could hardly understand him.

"Slow down, Maverick," Harold said, placing a firm hand on the man's thick shoulder. "I'm as anxious to hear what happened as you are to tell it. Now start in again. Say it slow and easy like. Tell me who ambushed the stagecoach."

Lieutenant Nelson, one of the soldiers who had been tied to the wagon wheel and who had been rescued by some soldiers who had just happened along and found the ambushed stagecoach, told everything—how it had happened from beginning to end.

Harold jerked his hand away and threw his hands into the air in a frenzy. "Sage?" he shouted. "I knew he was nothing but a savage. Damn him. Damn him to hell and back."

"I'm not sure it can all be blamed on Sage," Lieutenant Nelson, who was one of the soldiers sympathetic with the plight of the Navaho, said. "One of our soldiers shot first. Who's to say why Sage was approaching the stagecoach? Perhaps it was just another attempt at peace talks with us."

"Several men are wounded, aren't they?" Harold shouted, leaning his face close to Lieutenant Nelson's. "Others are wounded, aren't they? That's all I need to know about what the Navaho chief's intentions were. We're trying to find him and string him up to the tallest tree we can find. Let his people view him and see what it means to go against the United States cavalry."

Nervously running his fingers through his thick head of red hair, the lieutenant's eyes wavered as he broke the further news to Harold, the news that would really throw him into a frenzy. "Are you aware, sir, that your fiancée was on that stagecoach with the other women?'' he said guardedly. He had heard through the grapevine before the departure of the stagecoach that Leonida was to be the only woman *not* to go and why.

"What . . . ?'' Harold said, grabbing the corner of the desk to steady himself.

"Leonida apparently boarded the stagecoach just before it left,'' Lieutenant Nelson said even more guardedly. "Sir, she's among those that Sage and his warriors have taken captive.''

Harold slumped into his chair and held his head in his hands. "Lord, this gets worse by the minute,'' he said somberly. "Leonida. My Leonida. She's being held captive? That damn savage renegade. Wait until I get my hands on him. He won't get away with this. He probably ambushed the stagecoach just to get Leonida.''

"But, sir, you act surprised that she's gone,'' Lieutenant Nelson said, raising an eyebrow. "Sir, she's been gone for two days now. Didn't you even know it?''

"I thought she was in her room, pouting,'' Harold grumbled, his face reddening as he looked slowly up at the lieutenant. "I figured that she'd heard that the other women and children had left and . . . and was being stubborn about confronting me about it. I guess I was wrong.''

"I'd say so, sir,'' Lieutenant Nelson said, grinning nervously down at the general.

Harold bolted from his chair. "Well, don't just stand there,'' he shouted. "Gather together as many men as you can and get out there searching for Sage and his captives. Don't come back until you have some word as to their whereabouts.''

Kit Carson ambled into the office, his shoulders slouched. He sank into a chair. "It's a waste of time to send anyone after Sage,'' he said, his voice flat. "He's had enough time to get into the mountains, too close to his stronghold now for anyone to find them. We've got to wait and see what his next move is.''

"But Leonida . . . ?'' Harold whined. "She's with them,''

Kit Carson nodded. "Yeah, I know,'' he mumbled.

Harold turned on his heel, stomped to the window, and looked at the mountains in the distance. In the dusk they were streaked with opaque purple shadows. Leonida was in those shadows somewhere with Sage. The knowledge tore at his heart.

"Go after them, anyhow,'' Harold blurted as he sent a determined glare Kit Carson's way. "No matter how long it takes, find Sage.''

He paused, then hissed, "And damn it, let's have no more pussyfooting around. Kill the bastard.''

10

Why so pale and wan, fond lover?
Pr'y thee, why so pale?
                        —SIR JOHN SUCKLING

A gentle hand on her cheek awakened Leonida. She
blinked her eyes open, realizing that she had slept the
entire night through. It was early dawn, and soft grays
were buried in the cliffs. The walls of the canyon
loomed soft with wells of coolness. The world seemed
a secret place, one of peace.

Sage bent down low so Leonida could see him,
and she quickly drew her blanket more snugly to her
chin. Glancing around, she realized that she and Sage
were the only ones awake. She could not help but
fear what he might be wanting of her before the others awakened . . .

"Come," Sage said, taking the blanket from her.
"It is time to bathe. We will bathe together."

Her face hot with blush, Leonida jerked the blanket
away from him and covered herself with it again. "We
most certainly will not," she said in a harsh whisper.

Sage sighed heavily and stared at her, then in one
motion swept her and her blanket into his arms and
carried her away from the campsite, toward a shining
stream a short distance away.

Leonida kicked and squirmed and pounded his chest
with her fists. "Let me down," she said, trying to
keep her voice from awakening the others. "I absolutely refuse to take a bath with you. Why would you
even expect me to?"

"There is much between us that you are fighting," Sage grumbled, frowning down at her as she stopped pummeling his chest. "We will bathe, talk, and settle our differences before we travel onward. The journey will become less strained for both of us."

"The journey is only strained because you are constantly forcing me to do things I don't wish to do," Leonida said, inhaling unsteadily. In his arms she was weakening in her defense against him. He troubled her so, in all ways sensual. If he kissed her, oh, but how she would be lost to him, to his desires, to his demands.

She was thankful that he could not read her thoughts, even though sometimes she wondered if he just might be able to do exactly that. Although he still expected her to be betrothed to another man, he was obviously pursuing her affections.

He would do that only if he realized that she cared for him instead of Harold.

"After today I will not have to force you to do anything," Sage said. "After today, you will no longer think of the other man in your life. He will become as the fleeting wind."

"You are so confident of this, are you?" Leonida said, her heart pounding. She feared what he had planned in the next moments, yet anticipated it all the same.

She expected him to kiss her.

She expected him to hold her.

She knew that she would allow it.

Both became silent as he carried her farther and farther away from the campsite. They were a part of the intimate hour of dawn. The air was fresh and cool, and smelled sweetly of wildflowers just opening their faces to the first light of the sun rising from behind the mountains.

Sage carried Leonida until he came to a huge, thundering waterfall that tumbled over a high peak above them. The ground was carpeted in green, the grass thick and soft beneath Leonida's bare feet as Sage lowered her from his arms. She clung to the blanket, embarrassed as he began undressing before her, shocked at his boldness.

Although in awe of his muscular copper body, she had to turn her eyes away, her pulse racing. She had just seen a man totally nude for the first time in her life. Seeing the part of his anatomy that she had only heard women whispering about had made a strange sort of thrill shoot through her, and she was ashamed of such wanton feelings.

She flinched when she heard the splash of water, yet was relieved to know that he had dived into the river, thankfully hiding his body from her wide, wondering eyes.

Knowing that it was now safe, Leonida turned slowly around. Fear gripped the pit of her stomach when she did not see Sage anywhere in the river. A sudden thought came to her that made her knees grow weak: perhaps he had hit his head on rocks at the bottom of the river and had been knocked unconscious.

When his head popped to the surface, she could not deny the relief that flooded her. That alone revealed to her just how much she did care.

The reprieve from her anger at him did not last long. She blanched when he shouted something to her, another order that she most definitely refused to follow.

Sage treaded water and gazed up at Leonida, admiring her spunk, her fire. He smiled, then gave her the same command a second time. ''Unclothe yourself and come into the water to bathe with Sage,'' he shouted, seeing that her stubbornness did not wane as she clutched the blanket around herself and stared angrily back at him.

''I shall not,'' she shouted back. ''And you cannot make me.''

''Oh?'' Sage said. With long and masterful strokes, he began swimming toward shore.

Leonida looked frantically around, feeling a desperate need to flee and hide from him, yet afraid to budge. He had carried her far from the campsite. Who knew what lurked out there?

Sage began climbing from the river, water surging from his lovely copper body. Leonida's breath caught at the sight of him. It was so captivating, she could not deny how her insides were melting. So taken by him, Leonida was locked in a strange sort of trance. As he moved toward her, his muscles flexing, his nakedness so blatantly beautiful, Leonida swallowed hard, her eyes following his every movement.

Then she looked up into his eyes, her heart beating so loudly she felt as though she might faint.

And then the spell was broken when he grabbed the blanket from her and began undressing her.

Again she struggled and tried to get away, only to become weakened and breathless in the process.

Seeing that her struggles were futile, Leonida stood stiffly before him as he tossed aside all her garments except for her petticoat. ''Why are you doing this?'' she asked, her voice quavering. Although her body was still covered, she tried to hide her breasts beneath her crossed arms, and she tried to cross her legs to cover that most intimate place at the juncture of her thighs that she feared might be visible through the thin gauze of her undergarment.

Sage refused to answer her. Words would come later, after she realized that what he asked of her this morning, before everyone else arose for a full day of travel, was right. Their closeness was needed to make everything in her heart and mind turn to a clear understanding of why he had gone against the white people.

To him it was very important that, above all else, she understand. It was their destiny to be together, as kindred spirits instead of enemies.

It was their destiny to be man and wife, their hearts locked into a mutual respect and loving forever.

And he would make her understand, even join him against those who were threatening the Navaho's existence.

Yes, for him, the man she would love, she would do this.

"Sage, it's so *cold*," Leonida said, the crisp air brushing against her body.

"The water is warm in comparison," Sage said, quickly sweeping her up into his arms. "You will welcome its caress on your body."

Leonida's eyes widened as she looked from Sage down to the water, then up at Sage again. "Please don't," she said, clinging to his neck. "I don't want to . . ."

Again her pleas fell on deaf ears. She choked back a scream as he let her ever so casually roll out of his arms. She kicked frantically and swung her arms in the air as she plummeted downward.

As she entered the water, she stiffened her legs and closed her eyes and felt herself plunging deeper and deeper. Then when she began paddling her feet, she stopped her descent and pushed herself back to the surface.

Infuriated, coughing, and wiping her drenched,

clinging hair out of her eyes, Leonida glared at Sage.
When he dived into the river, she made a quick turn
and began swimming in the opposite direction. Her
petticoat kept getting tangled around her legs, making
it impossible to pick up speed, and then her breath
caught in her throat when something else became even
more of a threat. She began battling the motion of a
whirlpool that was sucking her beneath the great splash
of the waterfall.

Floundering, fighting to keep her head above the
water, Leonida screamed between swallowing great
gulps of water. "Help me!" she cried as her head
went under. Then she bobbed back up to the surface,
which took all the effort she could muster. "Sage, help
. . . me . . . !"

She saw a great blur of black as another vicious spin
of the whirlpool pulled her under. Leonida stared with
wide eyes through the hazy water at the fish swimming
past, and then . . . and then . . .

She breathed in a great gust of air as Sage grabbed
her by the waist and tugged her upward. Surfacing beside her, he drew her into his embrace and held her
there until she was breathing more easily, then swam
her to safety on a ledge hidden behind the falls.

Shivering and coughing, her eyes and throat burning
from the water, Leonida welcomed his comforting
arms around her as he held her close. She lay her head
on his chest, still heaving from exhaustion. "*Uke-he*,
thank you," she murmured, twining an arm around
his neck. "For a moment I thought . . . I thought that
I was going to drown."

"Not with Sage so close," he said thickly, leaning
her partially away from him, weaving his fingers
through her thick golden hair, spreading it away from

her entrancing face. "Never would I let anything happen to you. Surely you know that."

"Yet you take me captive so easily?" Leonida murmured, searching his eyes, melting inside from his closeness.

"Do you think I knew you were aboard that stagecoach?" he said, tracing her chin with a fingertip. "Do you think I would have ambushed it had I known I was placing you in danger?"

"You should not have placed anyone's life in danger," Leonida fussed, now knowing for certain that he had not planned just to steal *her* away. She was torn in her feelings about that. She had felt honored, in a way, that he might have cared enough for her to go to any lengths to stop her flight from Fort Defiance, and *him*.

"The white leaders should not have placed the Navahos' lives in danger," Sage said, slowly drawing her into his embrace again. "Then not everyone's life would have been altered. Yet weren't our lives altered the moment we spoke that first word to one another? Did you not feel the magic being spun between us? Did you not feel the energy flowing between us, as though we were one heartbeat—one soul? Let us explore those feelings. Let me show you the extent of mine for you. Show me the extent of yours for Sage."

Leonida drew in a ragged breath as he gently framed her face between his hands and lifted her lips to his. Her whole world seemed to begin spinning as his mouth bore down upon hers, so hungry, so demanding, awakening her to an ecstasy she had never experienced before. The first kiss they had shared had been filled with wonder and rapture, but it had been too short-lived.

This time she could not pull away. She had dreamed

of this moment, of the thrill of being held and kissed by him again. She would not deny herself the pleasure anymore than she would stop herself from breathing.

Sweet currents of warmth spread through her, and she twined her arms around his neck and clung to him as he lowered her to the shelf of rock beneath the falls, ignoring the occasional sprays of water and the coldness of the rock pressing on her back.

Sage leaned over her, his mouth never leaving her lips, and she shivered with passion when she felt his hand cup one of her breasts through the clinging wet material of her petticoat. She moaned and leaned into his hand as he began kneading her breast, the nipple hardening from the fires that his fingers seemed to be igniting. The heat spread as Sage's hand trailed downward, soon gathering the petticoat between his fingers and shifting the wet garment upward . . . upward . . . upward.

Leonida sucked in a wild gasp of pleasure when she felt his first touch at the center of her passion. She drew her lips away and closed her eyes in ecstasy as his fingers began caressing her, arousing her to blissful feelings.

When his mouth found her lips again and his tongue flicked between them, tongues meeting, tip to tip, she began running her hands over his bare flesh, thrilling at the feel of his taut muscles, and then dared to move her fingers lower, breathless at the thought of touching his manhood. Could she give him the same sort of pleasure that he was giving her by the mere caress of her fingers?

Then she drew her head away and closed her eyes, shame filling her at where her thoughts had taken her. She began shoving at Sage's chest, but he grabbed her wrists and held them as he began caressing her passion's center with his manhood, his eyes dark and passion-filled as he gazed down at her.

Leonida's eyes widened as she felt his manhood begin to twitch and grow against her flesh. Her heart was thundering wildly from these feelings that she seemed to have no control over.

"Sage, please . . ." Leonida said with her last trace of reason. "Let's stop now, or . . ."

"Or else Sage might take you to paradise and back?" he said huskily. "Or Sage might prove to you the extent of your love for this Navaho chief?"

"I'm so confused," Leonida murmured. "I want you, yet I do not want to be forced. I want it to be beautiful, Sage."

He released her wrists and held his hands out away from her. "You are no longer being forced to do anything," he said. "Rise and leave if you wish. Sage will even give you a horse to return to Fort Defiance. You are captive no more. In truth, Sage is the captive—to your heart. I will love you always, even if only in my midnight dreams."

Leonida scarcely breathed, understanding what he was doing and why. She had just won her freedom. Yet she could not find it in her heart to leave. She saw no future now without Sage, and she would have to come to terms, somehow, with what he had done. The ambush had been wrong, yet . . . She suddenly realized that had she been in his place, she would more than likely have taken the same road as he.

"You are free to leave," Sage said, moving away from her.

Leonida watched him begin to walk away beneath the thundering falls, then moved quickly to her feet and went to him and grabbed his hand. "Don't go," she said. "I love you, Sage. Oh, how I love you."

When he turned to her, his eyelids heavy with passion, she twined a leg around one of his, moaning as she felt her swollen, throbbing center come into contact with his flesh as her petticoat scooted up her leg. Closing her eyes, Leonida began rubbing herself against him, becoming dizzy with the pleasure.

Feeling that part of her moving against his flesh drove Sage almost out of his mind. He wrapped his arms around her and helped anchor her to him as she continued moving herself on him.

But afraid that she was nearing that point of no return when pleasure would seize her like explosions of fire, he placed his hand on her waist and lifted her away from him.

Her face hot with a sensual blush, Leonida smiled up at Sage, her whole body seeming to be one consuming, throbbing heartbeat. "Make love to me," she whispered, reaching a hand to his manhood.

She watched his eyes become glassy with pleasure as she moved her fingers on him, herself mystified by that part of him that seemed so hot and alive. She watched his expression as he closed his eyes and moaned, the ecstasy seemingly mounting the more she moved her fingers.

When his body stiffened, and he jerked quickly away from her, she questioned him with her eyes.

"We will ride the wings of eagles together," he said huskily. "Not apart."

His hands moved to the hem of her petticoat and gathered it into his fingers. Slowly he lifted it away from her. Tossing it aside, he gazed with pleasure at her slim, curvaceous body. His hands began traveling over her, following the path of his eyes, first touching and kneading her breasts, then moving lower, across her flat tummy, lower still to that golden floss of hair between her legs.

When he again found her center of passion, this time he slowly thrust a finger within her. He gazed down at her as he explored and found that tight membrane within that proved that she was a virgin.

"You are willing to become mine today, totally?" he asked, his voice low. "You will be my woman, forever?"

Anxious and afraid, Leonida could manage only a quick nod, giving her approval. What happened next was quite a surprise to her. Her eyes widened and she cried out when he thrust his finger quickly deeper into her, causing her a moment of pain. She gasped when he withdrew his fingers and she saw blood on their tips.

"Oh, Lord," she whispered, covering her mouth with a hand. "Why am I bleeding? What did you do?"

"I prepared you for lovemaking," Sage said, leaning his bloody fingers out into the waterfall and washing them. "Now it will be easier for you. You will not have to suffer pain at the moment you should be experiencing rapture."

He gave her no further cause to wonder about this. His fingers reached up to entwine her hair and he drew her close. His mouth forced her lips open as his kiss grew more passionate.

She was filled with strange, wondrous desires, acutely aware of his body as he leaned against her while leading her down onto the slab of rock again. As he leaned over her, one of his knees parted her thighs. He surrounded her with his hard, muscular arms, pressing her against him as his lips moved from her lips to a taut, pink-tipped breast. She threw her head back in ecstasy as his tongue swept around her nipple and his teeth nipped at its throbbing point.

And then once again his mouth bore down upon her lips, causing threads of excitement to weave through her heart. She clung to him, then sighed deeply and moaned with intense pleasure when she felt him thrust his manhood deeply within her. As he held her close, he began his masterful, rhythmic strokes that sent her soaring above herself, seemingly separate from that person she had always known. Never had she felt such bliss, such joy. She clung to him and rocked, allowing herself to enjoy this wild, sensuous pleasure.

Sage yearned to find that final plateau that would send his heart leaping, and he felt the urgency building as he moved within her. Surges of warmth swam through his body, causing a wondrous tingling from his head to the tip of his toes.

Becoming breathless with pleasure, he leaned his mouth away from her lips and lay his cheek on her heaving bosom. Tremors cascaded down his back, and he caught his breath when he felt the familiar rush of ecstasy claim him. He held her tight as his body spasmed into hers, smiling amid his pleasure when he felt her body explode with rapture to match his own.

Taking from each other that which they both gave willingly, they clung together a moment longer after the passion was totally spent. Then Sage rolled away from her, lying on his side next to her. His hands touched her, almost as though she were a precious flower. Then he turned her and drew her into the warmth of his body.

"You fill my heart with gladness," he whispered, caressing her back with gentle fingers. "It is easy to forget the sadness in the world while with you. You are like a soft ray of sunshine, warming me through and through.''

"You showed me such gentleness," Leonida whispered back, softly touching his face. She brushed his lips with a kiss. "My darling, you are everything to me. Everything."

"Sage will make things right for you," he said, leaning away from her, gazing at her with a deep devotion in his eyes. "We will be man and wife. Soon."

"I already feel as though I am your wife," Leonida murmured, moving into his arms, hugging him. "Today you and I committed ourselves fully to each other. There will never be another man or woman in either of our lives. Our moments shared within one another's arms will be solely ours alone to enjoy. We could not be more married than that, do you think?"

"I will never have enough of you," Sage murmured, placing a finger on her chin, bringing her eyes up to meet his. "Never."

His mouth bore down upon her lips in a bruising, lingering kiss, then he broke away from her. "Although my body cries out to have you again this moment, time does not allow it," he said as he rose to his feet. He reached for a hand, which she gave to him. "Come. We must return to our clothes, and then to the campsite. We will eat, then once again move more deeply into the mountains. Soon you will see my stronghold and meet all of my people. Pure Blossom will welcome you with eager arms, I am sure."

They kissed again, and then Leonida slipped her wet petticoat over her head. Together they moved to the edge of the ledge and dived into the river below. When Leonida splashed back to the surface, her face became hot with a blush. One of Sage's warriors had appeared, looking anxious.

Sage bobbed to the surface beside Leonida. He treaded water as he gazed questioningly up at Spotted Eagle, the trusted scout that he had sent back to keep an eye on the trail behind them.

"What is it?" Sage shouted, still treading water. "What have you found that is of so much importance you come to interfere in my private affairs of the morning?"

"Kit Carson and the white pony soldiers have left Fort Defiance in search of you and the captives," the scout said, clamping a hand on a knife sheathed at his waist. The fringes of his buckskin breeches and shirt blew in the gentle breeze.

Sage swam to shore and climbed from the water. He turned and offered Leonida a hand which she refused.

"I won't leave the water until the warrior leaves," she said stubbornly, covering her breasts with her arms as she found a steady footing on the gravel bottom of the river.

Sage turned to Spotted Eagle. "Go to the camp and warn everyone that it is time to move onward," he said. "I will soon be there to give direct orders."

Spotted Eagle gave Leonida a lingering, questioning glance, then nodded to Sage and turned and left.

Her knees still trembling from the ecstasy that she had discovered within Sage's arms, Leonida climbed from the water and bashfully, hurriedly, dressed.

Just as she turned to leave, Sage grabbed her by the wrist and swung her around to face him. "Do not forget our promises," he said huskily. "Our bodies spoke of promises, as did our lips, and hearts. I love you, white woman. You love me. From this day forth, do not turn your eyes shyly away from me. What we shared is ours forever. And we will share much, much more. Nothing will stand in the way of our future happiness. Nothing.''

He paused, then added, ''Not even Kit Carson. And especially not General Harold Porter.''

She flung herself into his arms and clung to him. She closed her eyes, trying to block out all thoughts of fears and doubts.

There was only now.

11

The winds of heaven mix forever,
With a sweet emotion.
—SHELLEY

Traveling through the deep canyons that gashed the high plateau and the steep gullies that snaked along the mountainside, everyone was now on foot. The warriors were leading their horses in a fatiguing, scrambling climb in and out of ribbons of shadows, through the narrow, dark gorges, everyone following, the children crying as they clung to their mothers.

Having stopped seldom and eaten little once the steeper climb had begun, Leonida forced herself to move onward beside Sage. She was tired and stiff, in awe of his toughness, yet she reminded herself that he was an imperious warrior accustomed to all sorts of inconveniences in life, now even having to flee the wrath of the white man.

Her hair blowing in wisps around her face, Leonida brushed it aside and glanced over at Sage. Although she was constantly aware of what he was inflicting on these women and children who lagged along behind her, she could not help but sympathize with his plight. His whole future was in jeopardy. How could she not worry about him?

She was now a part *of* his future.

Her gaze swept up over the red rock that met a flawless, turquoise sky. Touched by the sunlight, the rock became dull orange and buff with flecks of gold. She jumped with a start when a protesting raven croaked at the passing entourage from her nest, close by on the side of the cliff.

They traveled onward through narrow passages of warm rock. The sun was fading in the sky. The shadows were lengthening. Fatigue was setting in on Leonida rapidly. She was glad when Sage stopped and turned to everyone as they reached a table of rock that stretched out into clumps of junipers and pinyon pines, and where dark, dusty-green grass reached to a cliff that overlooked a valley far below.

"We will stop for the night here," Sage announced, giving Leonida a quick glance, knowing that she was worn out yet had not lodged even one complaint. "Tomorrow we will arrive at the Navaho stronghold. There we will await the decision of the white leaders, whether or not they will cooperate so that you can all return to your loved ones."

Sage moved closer to Leonida. He smoothed some locks of hair from her eyes as she gazed over at him.

"Soon you all *will* be returned to your people," he said, looking from woman to child. "It was never my intention to keep you as captives forever. I have not enjoyed inflicting suffering upon you. In time, I hope you will understand why I was forced to do this. As for tonight, try to rest. Tomorrow is the fiercest climb of all to reach the final destination of our journey."

Sage paused, then added, "You *will* return to those who love and miss you," he said more determinedly. "But first I must use you to ensure my own people's future."

There was a strained silence, and then the women sought the softest clusters of grass and sat down upon them. The children were soon lying in their laps, asleep in their arms.

Leonida gave Carole and Trevor a worried look. Carole was already fast asleep, her cheeks sunken and pale, her breathing shallow. Trevor was snuggled up next to her, unaware of his mother's weakness, taking from her what he could, while he could. Perhaps he could sense that his mother did not have much longer on this earth.

As several warriors efficiently got a campfire going, others left the campsite to hunt for the evening meal.

Placing her hands at the small of her back, Leonida strolled away from everyone and went to the farthest edge of the cliff and sat down upon it. Out of everyone's view, she leaned her knees against her chest. As she gazed below, something caught her attention. She gasped and leaned closer, to get a better look. There was enough evening light left to see something that awed her.

"And so you see that which belongs to my people that is so necessary for their survival?" Sage said as he came to sit down beside her.

Leonida looked up quickly. She had not heard his approach. She had been too caught up in looking at the vast fields of peach trees in the valley far below her, as well as fields of corn, beans and squash, and many merino sheep with their thick, curly wool.

Also, she had seen a small hogan, apparently for the man who saw to the sheep and the fields of fruit and vegetables.

"I could hardly believe my eyes when I first looked down and saw all of those things in the valley," Leonida said, her eyes wide. "Why, Sage, it's like a miracle that you can have all of that way out here where there is more rock than grass. And peaches? My Lord, it's like some sort of miracle that you could grow peaches at all, much less in such abundance.''

"It took much time to get this land prepared for planting, and to get it cultivated enough to grow the necessities of my people," he said. "I regret that it cannot be closer to my stronghold. Much is left to chance to leave it so vulnerable to those who might discover it and realize its importance to my people. Without it my people would perish. Far up in the mountain, at my stronghold, there is no way to grow the foods of my people. It is gathered below and carried up the mountain trails.''

"And no one knows it is there?" Leonida asked as she once again gazed at the vastness of the crops and the great flock of sheep.

"Besides the Navaho, there is one tribe of Indians who know," Sage said, frowning. "A small band of Kiowa. They know, also, of the stronghold. But they find trade with my people too valuable ever to tell any of my enemies of these secrets.''

"If Kit Carson ever found out . . ." Leonida said, her words trailing off.

"Yes, it would be a quick way to exterminate my people without ever firing a shot against them," Sage mumbled. He leaned closer to Leonida. "It is good that you care so deeply about the welfare of Sage and his people. And I know that you do. It is in your eyes and your voice. My woman, tonight we will sleep here, away from everyone. Tonight we will love again. All cares and fears will be cast aside within our hearts and minds, at least for that moment we will be within each other's arms. My woman, tell me you anxiously await that moment to be with your Navaho chief again? Tell me now, Leonida. Whisper it into my ear. Let me carry your voice within my heart until we are together again after the others are asleep.''

Leonida moved to her knees and leaned into his embrace, her lips brushing his right ear. "I love you," she whispered. "I can hardly wait to show you how much. My heart is pounding now with the thought of it. My entire being is crying out for you, my handsome Navaho chief. Kiss me now, Sage."

Sage placed his hands at Leonida's waist. He lifted her up until her legs straddled his waist and her dress was hiked up past her thighs, then sat down again. His pulse was racing as he placed the bulge in his breeches where she was spread open to the hardness of his touch. He thrust himself more tightly against her and could feel a shiver of passion soar through her.

Leonida lowered her mouth to his lips. She twined her fingers through his shoulder-length hair and drew his lips more firmly against hers. Her whole body tremored as they kissed passionately.

So breathless with the kiss and with the ecstasy flowing through her veins, she wasn't sure if she could wait until the darkness gave them cover.

The evening fled quickly by, baths in a nearby stream and eating taking up the time. Leonida became more worried about Carole, making her hesitate for a moment before accompanying Sage away from the campsite, to their own little lovers' nest on the cliff that seemingly overlooked the world. She helped Carole bathe Trevor and get him ready for bed. She helped Carole with her own bath, having found that Carole was even weaker than she had realized. Every movement seemed an effort for her now.

Leonida fussed over being afraid to leave Carole, but she encouraged it. She had even whispered to

Leonida that she understood and approved of her feelings for the handsome chief. She herself now understood Sage's reasons for having taken the captives.

Carole even went as far as asking Leonida not to blame Sage should she not make it back to the fort alive. Perhaps Sage had even done her a favor, for Trevor and Leonida had formed a special bond while on this journey to the Navaho's mountain stronghold. Carole said that she could now die in peace, since Leonida would be there for Trevor.

Smelling fresh and clean from her bath in the cool stream, her hair finally dry after being washed in the shallow depths of the water, Leonida walked beside Sage toward the cliff. She did not feel awkward that everyone had seen their departure together. She felt no shame, though she realized that they must know why she and Sage sought refuge away from the others. At this moment in time, the love she felt for Sage pressed so sweetly against her heart, she felt dizzied by it.

Being with him, anticipating what they would soon share, was making her forget her worries for Carole and her concerns for Trevor should anything happen to his mother. Although Leonida had promised to care for him, she was not his mother. She was not so sure he could adapt that easily.

"You are so quiet," Sage said, reaching down to take Leonida's hand in his. "What troubles you?"

His flesh against hers made Leonida tingle from head to toe. She was engulfed with gloriously passionate feelings that made her reluctant to talk about anything that troubled her. For the moment there was only Sage. He was the center of her universe, now and forevermore. She wanted nothing to enter this precious center, to spoil their private moments together.

"It's nothing," Leonida said quickly, smiling softly up at him. "Truly, it's nothing."

"It is good to see you smile," Sage said, leaning down to brush a kiss across her lips as they stopped within an arm's length of the cliff. "Your smile encompasses the stars, the moon, the wind. I feel the touch of your smile deeply within my soul. It stirs me into needing you. My woman, I need you now."

Leonida's heart pounded as he stepped away from her and spread a luxurious sheepskin across the ground. Gently he placed an arm around her waist and laid her down. As he knelt over her, Leonida reached up and twined her arms around his neck, bringing him down closer to her. She flicked her tongue across his lips, sighing when his tongue came out and met hers.

"Remove my clothes," he said huskily, moving to his knees before her.

Leonida rose to her knees and while her heart thumped wildly, she removed his bright-red velveteen headband and laid it aside.

Sage held his arms out as Leonida began unbuttoning his shirt. When it was completely opened, Leonida reached her trembling hands to his smooth, hairless chest and ran her fingers over the mounds of his muscles, reveling in the mere touch of him.

Recalling how wonderful it felt for him to touch the nipples of her breasts, Leonida leaned closer and flicked her tongue around one of his, eliciting a moan of pleasure from him as she then nipped one of the hard peaks with her teeth.

When he twined his fingers through her hair and urged her head lower, she ran her tongue along his flesh, loving the taste of him. His stomach quivered as she moved her tongue over it.

Moving ahead of her tongue, she unfastened his breeches and began lowering them over his hips. Her eyes widened and her heart skipped a beat when his manhood sprang into sight. He was well aroused, and when Sage urged her mouth toward him, her breath seemed to catch in her throat, not knowing for sure if what he asked of her was right. She was not educated in ways of making love. But the strange sort of thrill that she was getting at just the mere thought of touching her tongue to him made her think that this was surely all right.

"It is something a woman does for a man if she loves him enough," Sage said huskily at the thought of the pleasure that awaited him. "It is something beautiful between a man and a woman. You love Sage in this way. Sage will then return the love to you in the same way."

Leonida's eyebrows raised, unsure of how a man could give her pleasure in this sort of way. Yet just the thought of something seemingly so forbidden made her knees grow weak and her heart soar with anticipation.

Closing her eyes, she placed her fingers on each side of his hardness. Then slowly, in a testing fashion, she flicked her tongue over the very tip of him. When he placed his fingers at her shoulders and sank them into her flesh as he groaned with deep pleasure, she thought no more of whether or not she should be doing this. She was happy to do something that gave her beloved such pleasure. She wanted to prove to him in many ways the extent of her love for him.

Leonida loved him in this fashion until he urged her away from him, his breathing harsh and guarded. She let his hands guide her in what to do next. First he tossed his breeches aside, and then quickly disrobed her.

"Lie down," Sage said, gently urging her down on the sheepskin again, the moon silvering her body. "The pleasure will be so intense, you will feel as though you are flying on wings of an eagle."

Leonida lay as though in a dream beneath Sage as he knelt over her, his hands and tongue moving, touching, and caressing her every secret place. She tossed her head from side to side, biting her lower lip to keep herself from crying out with pleasure as his tongue flicked over the center of her passion, making wonderful splashes of pleasure swim through her.

"Sage," she murmured, reaching down to urge his head away. "It is *too* wonderful. Please stop. I want you to make love to me in . . . the other way. I want you to fill me with your hardness. I want to feel it. I want to give back to you, as you give to me. Please? Let us fly on wings together."

Sage leaned down over her. He took her wrists and put them above her head and held them there. His lips moved from breast to breast, inflicting more pleasure. His mouth rose to her lips and he kissed her long and hard, while below he thrust his throbbing manhood within her.

Experiencing the wonders of how he did fill her, Leonida sighed against his lips. Lifting her legs, she wrapped them around him and moved with him, meeting every one of his thrusts with a bold upthrust of her hips, not wanting to miss an inch of him as he pushed himself into her, over and over again.

Again he moved his lips from her mouth. This time he pressed his cheek against one of her breasts and closed his eyes as his pleasure mounted. Each stroke promised more. The air was heavy with the inevitability of pleasure. He made sure that his thickness brushed rhythmically against her throbbing center, wanting her to feel all of the miracles of love, from moment to moment. He could feel the white heat building within him, traveling in flashes through his body. He held her fingers tightly above her head. He kissed the hollow of her throat as she held her head back, sighing.

Leonida gave herself up to the wild splendor of the moment. She could feel it growing within her, building to something beautiful again. Desire raged and washed over her, and when he began trembling inside her, she felt the same surge of splendor as he, her entire body warming with it as she went over the edge into bliss with him.

Afterward, they lay in one another's arms. His hands moved slowly over her body, stopping to cup one of her breasts. "You are my woman," he whispered huskily. "Never again the white man's."

"I never was his, not *ever*," Leonida whispered back, her hand moving caressingly down his back, stopping at his powerful buttocks. "The marriage had been arranged by my father. I will never understand why I allowed it. I never loved Harold Porter. Never."

"That is good to know," Sage said, rolling away from her. He stroked her breast, then rolled his fingers around its nipple, causing it to harden into an even harder peak. "He was not a man I would think any woman could love. He is not a likable man. He is *hogay-gahn,* bad."

"I doubt if he ever finds a woman who was as tolerant of him as I was," Leonida murmured, sighing with pleasure as his tongue took the place of his fingers on her nipple. "Sage, what you are doing to me."

"*Daltso-hozhoni,* all is beautiful when I am with you," he whispered, then once again showed her exactly why she had made the right choice of men.

He sent her soaring again with splendor as his tongue skillfully awakened her to many special ways of being loved.

As she lay there, her mind spinning with pleasure, she not only loved him, she adored him.

12

Suffer herself to be desired,
And not blush so, to be admired:
—EDMUND WALLER

Smooth hues of pale pink spread across the sky. Hawks soared overhead, shrieking their strange cry, awakening Leonida. She blinked her eyes open and discovered that she was still in Sage's arms. She wasn't so amazed that she had slept with him the full night through again, but she was in awe of where they had spent the night.

Her eyes widened when she discovered just how close they were to the edge of the cliff, realizing that should they have rolled away from each other very far during the night, they might have plummeted to the valley below. Then she became aware of the strength of Sage's arm around her waist and realized that he had thought of the danger and had kept her locked close to him to avoid it.

She gazed up at him, studying him in his sleep, overwhelmed again by his handsomeness, his skin a copper sheen in the morning light, his face so peaceful and rested while asleep, momentarily unburdened of the trials of daily life.

Wriggling free of his tight embrace, Leonida moved closer to his face. Framing it with her hands, she kissed the lids of his eyes, his bold nose, the high cheekbones, and then his sculpted, beautiful lips. Her lips trembled as her kiss deepened, then rapture swept through her when she felt Sage's arms locking her to him, his lips responding in a crushing kiss, his body pressed against her as he turned her so that she now lay beneath him.

As his hands worked their way up the skirt of her dress, Leonida felt dizziness claim her, wanting him as badly as she had the previous night. She moved her hands down from his face, across his bare chest, and lower still, and dared to touch his manhood through the sleek velveteen fabric of his breeches. He was as aroused as she. As his kiss and his probing fingers became more demanding, she began moving her hand over his hardness, eliciting a lazy sigh from deep within him.

But too soon this was brought to a halt when they heard the sound of a child crying in the distance, back where the others had slept at the camp.

"We will continue later," Sage said, brushing a kiss across her lips. "Tonight. We will have total privacy in my hogan. Tonight Sage will love you as never before." He gave her throbbing center another caress with his fingers, then pulled the skirt of her dress down and helped her to her feet.

Her face red and her knees trembling from the passion that had been aroused in her, Leonida half stumbled as she began walking quickly beside Sage down the steep grade that led to the campsite. The cries were louder now, and she could hear excited voices and other people crying, mainly the women of the camp. As Leonida and Sage came closer to the camp, she looked intently ahead, then grew numb inside when she discovered Trevor leaning over Carole, his deep sobs lifting to the heavens.

"Carole," Leonida whispered. "Oh, Lord, something has happened to Carole."

She tried not to blame herself for anything that might have happened, or feel shame for having been with Sage in such a wondrous way when it may have occurred. But if Carole was dead, Leonida wondered if she could help but blame herself.

She broke into a mad run, and when she reached Carole's side, she fell to her knees. Leonida stifled a cry behind her hand when she found Carole gasping for breath. Trevor was overwrought with fright as his mother clasped his hand hard, her eyes wild.

"Carole, oh, Carole, I'm so sorry," Leonida said, gently touching her cheek. She recoiled and withdrew the hand quickly when she found just how cold Carole's flesh was.

Leonida gave Sage a troubled glance when he came to rest on his haunches beside her, his own hand testing the feel of Carole's face.

When Sage slowly drew his hand away and gave Leonida a slow shake of the head, meaning that Carole was not going to make it, Leonida swallowed a growing lump in her throat. She had to find courage enough to face the next few moments. It was necessary for her to keep her composure.

A little boy would soon depend on her.

"Leonida?" Carole whispered, her voice scarcely a scratch of a sound as she turned and gazed up at her. "Lean close. I've . . . something . . . to say."

Willing the tears not to fall from her eyes, Leonida leaned her face down close to Carole's. "What is it?" she murmured, her voice breaking. "Tell me."

Carole reached a trembling hand to Leonida's and gripped it softly. "Trevor," she whispered, stopping to hack a painful-sounding cough. "You promised to care for him. Please love him as though he were your own."

Sniffling, tears near, Leonida replied, nodding, "I shall." Her heart ached with the torment of the moment.

Carole slowly closed her eyes and sucked in a shallow breath, then looked up at Leonida again. "Do not cast blame," she said, again coughing fitfully. "It is a blessing to die. The . . . pain is . . . unbearable. Teach Trevor not to cast blame either, upon the Navaho chief. He has done me a favor if traveling up the mountainside has hastened my death. If I had put a gun to my brow, God would not . . . have allowed me to . . . enter Heaven. Now I look forward . . . to . . . the opened gates of Heaven, finally . . . at . . . peace."

Leonida could not hold back the tears any longer. They gushed from her eyes in warm torrents against her cheeks. Before she had the chance to say anything else, Carole was dead.

Trevor wailed and threw himself upon his mother. Sage rose to his feet, took the child away from his mother, and held him tightly as he walked him away from the death scene. He took him to the cliff and showed him the wonders of the valley below, trying to draw his attention from the truth of the moment—that he no longer had a mother.

"Do you see the sheep, Trevor?" Sage asked, pointing to a flock of sheep running down a hillside, three goats leading them, and a small dog barking alongside. Behind came a Navaho brave, carrying a tall, curved stick. "The sheep were named 'churros' by the Spanish. See how they are so long-legged? They are thin and light with long legs and coarse, smooth wool, often brown. Do you see how some have four horns? Do you not think they are strange-looking with so many horns?"

Trevor finally stopped wailing. He wiped his nose

and sniffled as he leaned away from Sage to take a better look. "They are funny animals," he said softly. Then he turned to Sage, his eyes wide. "You have a pretty animal. Your horse. I like it."

Sage smiled down at him. "You like horses?" he said.

"It would be fun to have one of my own," Trevor said, again wiping his nose with the back of his hand. He cast his eyes downward. "I will never have a horse. I don't even have a father or mother now."

Sage drew Trevor into his embrace again and held him close, feeling a sudden bonding with this small, innocent child. Sage felt in part responsible for his mother's death. He would spend a lifetime making it up to the child. If Leonida had agreed to raise the child as her own, then the child would be Sage's as well.

"You will have a horse," Sage said, gazing down into Trevor's dark eyes. "One day you will own many. You will be raised in the tradition of the Navaho, as a Navaho."

Trevor's eyes widened and his lips parted in a pleasurable gasp. "I have played Indian and soldier before," he said. "I was always the Indian. Now I will be one for real? I will one day fight the soldiers for real? That will be fun."

Sage frowned down at Trevor. "*E-do-ta,* no. Warring is never fun," he said. "It is not a game that one plays for fun. When soldiers and Navaho shoot at one another, it is not with toy firearms. They shoot real bullets and fire real arrows. They kill. They maim. Never want to go to war with anyone, unless you are forced to."

"You will soon be forced to fight the soldiers from Fort Defiance?" Trevor asked innocently enough.

"*E-do-ta,* no. I would hope that it would be prevented," Sage mumbled, not wanting to be forced to explain to Trevor that he, the small child that he was, was one of the pawns in this real war game with the white pony soldiers.

In time, Sage knew, Trevor would understand how it had happened, and why, if fighting did break out between his people and the soldiers. And Sage expected that it might, now that Kit Carson and the soldiers had left Fort Defiance to search for him and the captives. Sage's only hope was that they would not find his stronghold.

"We must go back and see to your mother's burial," Sage said, his voice guarded as he gazed down at the child in his arms. He expected another outburst of tears, but to his amazement, and growing pride, the child seemed to be accepting his loss like a man. He saw in Trevor many possibilities. He seemed the sort that could be taught well the ways of the Navaho.

Trevor nodded.

Sage carried him back to the campsite. Leonida met them and lovingly took Trevor in her arms. "Sage, there is too much rock to dig a grave for Carole," she whispered so that Trevor would not hear.

"We will place her as we place our own to those whose deaths come to them in the mountains," Sage said. He gazed over at Carole, and then looked over his shoulder at the very spot where he and Leonida had found such love and peace within each other's arms. It was a place of sweet fragrances, soft winds, and sunshine. At night the stars and moon would caress Carole as she began her long journey to her land of the hereafter.

Yes, Sage concluded to himself. It was a place where

this kind woman could rest in peace as she waited to join those who had passed away before her.

"The Navaho do not touch the corpses of their own people, and never those of outsiders," Sage said, looking around at the mournful women. "Come together, women, and carry your dead to the cliff yonder. There she will rest in peace until eternity."

Leonida went and stood dutifully beside Carole, looking at the other women, one by one, until they received her silent message that they must follow her lead. Not saying anything, the women went to Carole and lifted her gently into their arms and began carrying her toward the cliff, everyone solemnly following.

After Carole was placed on the soft bed of grass, Leonida moved to her knees beside her, beckoned for Trevor to climb on her lap, and then quoted remembered scriptures from the Bible over his mother.

Everyone gazed at Sage as he then sang a song of his people over Carole, touching everyone's heart with the gentleness of his voice and the translation of the words as he then sang it in the English tongue.

"Yonder in the north there is singing in the lake," he sang softly. "Cloud maidens dance on the shore. There we take our being.

"Yonder in the north cloud beings rise. They ascend into cloud blossoms. There we take our being.

"Yonder in the north rain stands over the land.

"Yonder in the north stands forth at twilight the arc of a rainbow.

"There we have our being.

"*Haijiash-iye-beasdje*, there beneath the sunrise we have our being."

Tears streamed from Leonida's eyes. She had never loved Sage any more than she did at this moment.

* * *

It was a fatiguing, scrambling climb, alleviated by the increasing growth of jack pine and spruce. Winded and hungry, Leonida sighed with relief when she realized that Sage's stronghold was finally in view. Holding Trevor's hand tightly, she followed a winding path under firs. The horses were being led by the warriors. Beside them the cliff fell away over a hundred feet. Below, the world was red in late sunlight, the distant hills streaked with purple, the opaque shadows like deep holes in the world.

Though her knees would scarcely hold her up any longer, Leonida continued placing one foot before the other. Trevor's whines and his sluggish steps made her feel guilty that she could not carry him, but she was finding it difficult enough to hold herself up under such fatigue, much less carry a child. And Sage was too busy keeping his horse at bay along this narrow passageway to be able to help her.

"*Tsanti-hogani-la-lo,* yonder the hogan," Sage suddenly said beside her.

Leonida sighed. Before her, shimmering in the heat, were many little groups of domed hogans built on a rock terrace and nestled against moderately high cliffs, with black spots of doorways that watched the canyon.

As she moved closer and could see more of the village, she noticed one especially tall building, two or three stories high, and decided that it was a watchtower. On the top of the building she could see a platform where sentinels stood. She could envision the Navaho fighters rolling stones down upon approaching enemies from that strategic position.

Leonida followed Sage from the narrow path onto a wide stretch of rock that led into the village. From this vantage point she could see some families cooking outdoors and eating under a roof of brush held up by posts to keep the sun off. Sheepskins with the wool side down were spread for tablecloths, and she could see that each member of the families dipped into one big dish with his own spoon.

"You see much about my people already," Sage said, handing the reins of his horse to a young brave as he came running from the village with eager eyes.

Sage nodded to the boy to take the horse away, and Trevor seemed to come to sudden attention at the sight of the youngster, who seemed no less than his own age.

"Yes, and I'm intrigued," Leonida said, her insides tightening with a fear she did not want to feel when the attention of the villagers soon turned toward them. Some were already running toward them, shouting a welcome to Sage and the warriors; others were more cautious upon seeing all of the white captives. They stopped and watched Leonida guardedly when they saw Sage's attentiveness to her. They stood and waited for them to advance farther into the village.

Leonida tried to pretend that she didn't notice how apprehensive Sage's people were toward her. "Your houses are all different," she said, sensing more and more eyes following her approach.

"The hogan, the traditional Navaho house made of mud and logs, is more than just a place to eat and sleep," Sage explained softly. "It is a gift of the gods and as such occupies a place in the sacred world."

Trevor tripped and fell to the ground. Sage just as quickly leaned down and swept him up into his arms, carrying him as people parted to make a path for them.

Sensing Leonida's uneasiness, Sage continued talking softly to her to steady her nerves. "The hogan is round and symbolic of the sun, and its doors always face east to greet the rising Father Sun, one of the

most revered of the Navaho deities,'' he said. ''After
a new hogan is completed, it is consecrated with a
Blessing Way ritual in which the Holy People are asked
to 'let this place be happy.' If a hogan is struck by
lightning, it is bewitched and deserted. Thick, win-
dowless walls keep out much of the heat in summer
and make rooms warm in winter.''

Leonida's eyes widened when Sage grabbed her hand
and stopped her. ''This dwelling is Sage's,'' he said,
nodding toward one of the largest hogans. ''We will
go inside. You will acquaint yourself with your new
way of living. Later you will become acquainted with
my people.''

Glad to be given the opportunity to get away from
the staring eyes of the Navaho people, Leonida willingly moved toward the small opening in the hogan
that was the door. She went inside with Sage, surprised to find that the hogan was adequate in size, with
two rooms leading off from the main one.

Once inside, she found that the light filtered in
mainly from the smoke hole in the center of the domed
roof overhead, and there was a fire that was burning
brightly near the center of the room, where a round
pit was edged with stones.

Quickly she took in the scene. There were saddles,
cooking utensils, dried Indian corn, and a loom and
blankets hanging on the walls, a loom frame hanging
over the door, and, on the other side, an anvil. Around
the fire were more kitchen utensils, made of wood,
clay, and basketry. There were four smooth sticks, tied
together with strips of yucca leaves, which were used
to stir soup.

Also there was a hearth brush, a bundle of stiff
spikes from the narrow-leafed yucca, or beargrass.
This was tied near the middle, with the butt end all at

one end, the spiky ones at the other. The stiff butt ends served as a broom to sweep the hearth and floor; the spiky ends made a hairbrush.

The hogan was neat and cozy, the adobe walls and clay floors clean, smelling pleasantly of the sweet aroma of the yucca leaf.

"It is to your liking?" Sage said. Trevor too was at her side, clinging to her skirt as he gazed slowly around at what was most strange to him.

"I think it's lovely," Leonida murmured, turning a smiling face to him. "Although I have been lucky to live with luxuries, since my father was a wealthy cavalry officer, I find this home much more suitable than most settlers' homes that I've seen."

She spun around and clasped her fingers together before her. "And it's so clean," she sighed. She eyed a thick cushion of blankets spread out before the fire. Her weary bones ached to go and sit down on them, but this thought was brushed aside when a familiar voice spoke up behind her.

"Sage, you bring white woman and child into your hogan?" Pure Blossom said as she stepped in. Then her lips parted in a gasp when she recognized Leonida. "It is you?"

Puzzled, Pure Blossom turned back to her brother, the hump in her back twisting strangely as she peered up into his eyes. "There are others outside," she murmured. "What have you done, Sage? Are these people your captives? Are they? Is Leonida?"

She turned questioningly to Trevor. "Is this your son, Leonida?" she murmured. "I thought the blanket I was weaving for you was for a wedding. And you already have a son? I do not understand."

Leonida took Trevor's hand and urged him toward Pure Blossom. "This is Trevor," she said softly.

"Trevor's mother is dead. I am going to raise him now, as though he were my own."

Leonida gave Trevor a gentle shove, pushing him closer to Pure Blossom, realizing that his hesitation stemmed from her deformity, a difference that made her outwardly ugly.

Pure Blossom's smile faded when she saw the fear in Trevor's eyes. Yet she was glad that it was not disgust as he stared at the hump on her back. "Pure Blossom glad to know you," she said, offering a frail hand.

Trevor bolted behind Leonida, then slowly peered around her with wide, wondering eyes.

Trying to hide the pain that his response inflicted, Pure Blossom went to Leonida and gave her a gentle hug. "My brother has not told me the reasons you and others are here, but I welcome you," she said softly.

She eased from Leonida's arms and turned back to Sage. "Is she captive?" she asked, this time more determined.

"No, she is not a captive now, nor has she ever been," Sage said. "But the others? Yes, they are the prisoners of the Navaho. For now they are captives. Soon they will be freed. Until then, Pure Blossom, go to the women of our village and ask them to share their blankets, food, and drinking water with the women and children. Tell the young braves to build lean-tos for the captives so they can be comfortable while they are forced to live away from their loved ones. They will become as one with our people while they are in the village of the Navaho."

Pure Blossom nodded and left, after giving Leonida a quick smile over her shoulder.

Touched by his concern for the other women and children, Leonida went to Sage and twined her arms around his neck. "*Uke-he*, thank you," she murmured.

Trevor came to them and nudged them apart, his little arms reaching up to Leonida for her to pick him up. Leonida laughed softly and swept him up into her arms. Sage watched for a moment, then swallowed them both in his arms.

"I did not intend to find a family to bring home to my hogan when I planned the ambush on the stagecoach," he said, smiling from Leonida to Trevor. "But it seems destiny made it so."

He stepped away from them and Leonida saw a sudden sadness as he leaned down to stare into the slow burning flames of the fire. She put Trevor on the floor and leaned down on her knees beside Sage. "What is it?" she asked, placing a hand on his cheek. "What are you thinking about that pains you so?"

"The mention of family," Sage said thickly, gazing slowly over at her. "Pure Blossom is all that is left of Sage's family. Our parents died long ago in an attack by renegades when our village was elsewhere, away from these mountains. It will be good to fill my hogan with family again. Pure Blossom prefers to live alone, where she can fill her own hogan with her looms and what is required to make her fancy blankets."

Trevor scooted onto Sage's lap and wrapped his small arm around Sage's neck. "Can I call you daddy?" Trevor asked, snuggling close.

Neither Sage nor Leonida had expected Trevor's quick acceptance. They exchanged glances and then Sage said, "Yes, my son, it would please me to be called father." One of his arms reached out for Leonida and brought her close. "Here is a child who has been given to us,'' he said. ''Let us, together, bring him to manhood.''

Leonida's eyes misted with deep emotion as Sage pressed his lips to hers, ever so gently, yet with much, much meaning.

13

Before I trust my fate to thee,
Or place my hand in thine,
Question thy soul tonight for me.
    —ADELAIDE ANNE PROCTER

The light was soft in the bedroom from the shimmering shadows of the fire in the outer, larger room. Leonida knelt beside a narrow platform, where Trevor now slept peacefully on thick, soft pelts, after she had sung him to sleep with sweet lullabys.

Sage had stayed at Leonida's side until Trevor had been almost asleep, and then he had joined the other Navaho warriors and elders to have council beside a roaring fire outside.

Before Trevor had gotten too drowsy with sleep, Sage had told him that soon Trevor's bow and arrows and other objects that were important to the making of a young brave would be there with him in his room.

"Have dreams of angels, my little brave," Leonida whispered as she smoothed a colorful blanket up to Trevor's chin.

She ran her fingers through his raven hair, choked up with feelings that already grew within her heart, then kissed his brow. "I'm going to do my best, Trevor, to make life good for you," she whispered as she rose slowly to her feet. She stood a moment longer looking down at the small, trusting child. "But I can never take the place of your mother. I know that."

Not wanting to get caught up in thoughts of Carole's death, Leonida spun around and left the room. She turned and stared at the room that Sage had said would be theirs. Trevor slept in the room that had once been Pure Blossom's.

She had been amazed to find a hogan with three rooms, yet she suspected that most important Navaho leaders had the same. Wondering about the room where the man she loved slept, she crept into it and stopped to stare down at the sleeping platform, much larger than in the other room. It was piled even higher with thick pelts.

Her heart seemed to skip a beat when she spotted the distinct impression of Sage's body outlined in the pelts, where it had been pressed while he had last slept there. Her pulse racing, Leonida went to the sleeping platform and gently lay down on the very spot where her beloved had been. Strangely, she did not feel like an intruder. It was as though she truly belonged, had been there before in bed with him, sharing a wild splendor with him.

Closing her eyes, she envisioned Sage there with her now, feeling his hands on her breasts, warming them as he rolled his fingers over her nipples.

She did not have to concentrate hard to feel the passion of his kiss.

She felt the warmth of his embrace.

When she heard soft voices coming from the outer room, Leonida was jolted back to reality. Her face red with embarrassment over where her thoughts had taken her, Leonida sprang from the bed and walked cautiously to the outer room, then stopped, in awe of what she found.

Running her fingers through her hair, straightening it, she smiled awkwardly at two young braves who were pouring water into a copper tub they had brought for her.

"White woman take bath," one of the youngsters said, smiling toothlessly up at Leonida, new teeth just barely showing at the base of his gums.

"Why, thank you," Leonida said, dropping her hands to her sides. She leaned closer, questioning with her eyes the suds that were floating on the water.

"Yucca," one of the braves said, as though having read her thoughts. "Suds from the yucca plant. It will make your hair and skin smell sweet and feel soft."

"How nice," Leonida said, smiling at the young man.

Then her eyes widened when a young maiden brought a lovely red velveteen skirt and a cotton blouse designed with stripes and zigzags into the hogan and laid them at her feet. She fled from the hogan without a glance up at Leonida.

"Sage," one of the young braves said. "The water and clothes are gifts from Sage."

Leonida blushed as the two boys smiled knowingly at her. These boys seemed to know that she was more to Sage than a mere stranger sharing his hogan and bed, she thought to herself. She wondered just how much he *had* told them, for the two youngsters giggled and whispered to each other as they made a quick exit, leaving her standing over the tub, staring blankly after them.

But the lure of the sudsy water, and the temptation of the fresh, clean clothes soon caused her to forget everything else. Finally a true bath again.

Hastily shedding her clothes, Leonida stepped gingerly into the tub and found it comfortably warm, surprised that those who had prepared the water for her had been thoughtful enough to warm it over the outdoor fire.

Sinking lower into the water, resting her head against

the rounded edges of the tub, she sighed and closed her eyes, enjoying the feel of the water and the soft suds against her flesh before actually bathing. No bath water had ever felt as good. Not even the water back at the fort into which she had poured full bottles of bubble bath.

This water seemed to mysteriously relax her tired and aching bones. The suds were making her skin so soft. Her hands slid effortlessly over her arms as she washed herself with them, and along the swells of her breasts.

Her skin now clean and satiny soft, she lowered her hair into the water and gave it a scrubbing.

Completely relaxed, and feeling sparkling clean, Leonida climbed from the water. Dripping wet, she looked around for a towel. Finding none, she backed close to the fire and began turning slowly around, letting the heat dry her.

Afterward, she lay on the mats beside the fire, not feeling it necessary to get dressed yet. Trevor was sound asleep. Sage was still in council. She was enjoying lying beside the fire, her hair spread out, drying. Slowly her eyes drifted closed and she welcomed sleep as it came to her in gentle folds of black.

Then the sound of someone singing outside the hogan awakened her. She listened as several songs were sung by several different voices. She leaned up on an elbow with a start, recognizing the newest voice.

"Sage," she whispered, her eyes wide. "My Lord, it's Sage." She listened intently, marveling again at how beautifully he sang, as she had before when he had sung over Carole's grave.

Not wanting to take the time to dress but not wanting to miss seeing him as he was singing either, Leonida rose to her feet and looked around. There, a luxurious rabbit-fur blanket, woven from long strips of cottontail pelt.

Hurrying to it, she wrapped it around her shoulders, then crept outside. She stood in the shadows where no one could see her, yet she had a full view of those who were in council a few feet away, the huge bonfire lighting up their faces enough for her to find Sage among the warriors and elders.

She was finding out Sage's true devotion to his horse, perhaps *any* mighty, powerful steed of the mountains, as he sang a song about horses, almost meditatively:

How joyous his neigh!
Lo, the Turquoise Horse of Johano-ai,
How joyous his neigh,
There on precious hides outspread standeth he;
How joyous his neigh.
There on tips of fair fresh flowers feedeth he;
How joyous his neigh.
There of mingled waters holy drinketh he;
How joyous his neigh.
There he spurneth dust of glittering grains;
How joyous his neigh,
There in mist of sacred pollen hidden, all hidden he;
How joyous his neigh.
There his offspring may grow and thrive for evermore,
How joyous his neigh!

Each warrior took his turn singing about that which was most important to him. Leonida listened raptly, seeing these men as gentle, even beautiful.

Her gaze locked on Sage, loving him so much it made a slow ache burn at the center of her desire for him. She wanted to beckon him to her, yet she did nothing to disturb these moments with his companions, which seemed to have so much meaning.

The singing ceased and the warriors began eating

and talking. An elderly gentleman served some of the warriors boiled mutton from a large black pot, and corn, with a chunk of tough white bread. Others were reaching into clay bowls which rested on the ground before them, for handfuls of mush made of wild seeds.

As they ate leisurely, all eyes became drawn to Sage as he began talking. Although Leonida felt as though she were intruding on their private affairs, she could not help but stay there and listen. Sage's voice always mesmerized her.

At first she listened mainly to be hearing his voice, cherishing the sound of it, as though he were talking to her, touching her heart with his words. And at first she saw nothing troublesome in what he was saying, but as he spoke with a more cold and angry tone, this coldness seemed to touch her with a warning.

Anger soon replaced all her other feelings as Sage said what seemed to be the opposite of all that he had promised her. He began ordering many sentries to their posts in the canyon. Then he chose a warrior to send word to those soldiers who were searching for their stronghold that if they wanted the women and children returned to them alive, they must return to Fort Defiance and leave Sage and his people in peace.

Otherwise, one by one, the captives would die.

Leonida covered her mouth with a hand to stifle a gasp. Sage had promised the captives that no harm would come to them. And now he was saying that they would die if Kit Carson and the other white leaders did not cooperate with his demands. She had to wonder what other lies he had told her.

She felt betrayed.

Completely drained of feeling, Leonida turned to flee back inside the hogan. As she turned, her feet got tangled in the rabbit fur blanket, causing her to fall clumsily to the ground. When she landed, she cried out with pain, then stiffened when she realized that suddenly there was silence behind her. She had been discovered.

The blanket had shifted in the fall and now lay spread over only part of her body. Leonida blushed and quickly reached for it, gathering it around her as she got slowly to her feet. When she lifted her eyes, she gasped; Sage was gazing down at her questioningly.

Leonida felt a tremor in the pit of her stomach, and not from the feelings that had forced her to flee back inside the hogan. Again her strong passion for Sage replaced all other feelings, which should make her hate him.

She fought her passion with all of her might. She gave Sage a last lingering stare of defiance, then turned and fled from him, panting hard when she found momentary refuge inside the hogan.

But it was only a brief reprieve from the confrontation that she knew she must have with Sage.

How could she even think of forgiving him? she despaired to herself.

Why did her body also betray her?

Her heart pounded like claps of thunder as he entered the hogan and came to her, his fingers brushing the rabbit fur wrap away from her.

His dark eyes burned along her flesh as his gaze raked over her. "You came to listen at the council?" he grumbled. "Why did you feel it necessary to listen to what was being said? Most women are now warming the blankets for their men. I expected no less from you."

"Ha, I would guess not," Leonida said, lifting her chin haughtily. She reached down and pulled the fur around her again. "Just like you expect so much more from me, like me believing the lies that you have fed me from the moment we first met. I heard what you said tonight about killing the women and children. Sage, earlier, more than once, you promised they would be set free. You promised! Everyone believed you, including me. I feel betrayed. So will the others."

She glanced toward the room where Trevor slept so trustingly, then looked back at Sage. "And what of Trevor?" she said, her voice breaking. "Was all that you did for him pretense? Has this all been a game with you? You said that you loved me. Was that also a part of your ploy to, in the end, get what you wanted from Kit Carson and the other white leaders?"

She lowered her eyes. "I feel used," she said, almost choking on the words.

Firm fingers closed on Leonida's shoulders, causing her to wince and look up quickly.

"Your trust in Sage is too weak," he said, gripping her tightly, the fur blanket the only thing that saved her tender flesh from the full pressure of his fingers. "How can that be? Did you not understand that my warnings and threats were a strategy only, to get what I must to save the future of my people? It is sad that you chose to see only what you wanted to see, and to hear only what you wanted to hear. What Sage says to you, Sage means. What Sage promised the women and children, he meant! Now tell me, my woman, that you do not believe me. Tell me that you do not feel shame for doubting this man who loves you with every heartbeat."

Tears welled up in Leonida's eyes. She was engulfed by shame, knowing that she had been wrong to doubt him. She wished that she could withdraw all that she had said to him and start anew.

Wrenching herself free from his grip, she flung herself into his arms. "I'm sorry," she whispered, clinging tightly to him, oblivious of the fur blanket having slipped away from her body again. She closed her eyes and hugged him tightly. "Tell me you forgive me. Truly, I'm so very, very sorry for all that I said."

His hands trembling, Sage wrapped her in his muscular arms, his fingers splayed across her bare buttocks as he drew her even closer. "There is no need for forgiveness," he said, burying his nose into the sweet depths of her hair. "It is enough that you now accept that when Sage gives his word it is kept. I will release the children and women at my first opportunity, hopefully after Kit Carson and the other white leaders have righted everything for my Navaho people. And never fret again over their welfare. They will never be harmed at the hands of the Navaho."

He drew his face away from her hair. "The women and children will become as one with my people while they are here," he said, smiling softly down at her. Then he frowned. "Now you see that it is not wise to stand and listen to those who are in council. Words can be misinterpreted. It is best to leave the counciling to the men." He glanced over at the door that led into his bedroom, then smiled slowly at Leonida. "You have not warmed my blankets. Do you not realize that the hastening hours of night in the mountains bring with them cold temperatures?"

Leonida gave him a soft, teasing smile. "Perhaps we could warm the blankets together?" she murmured, shivering sensually when he began moving one of his hands slowly over her bare flesh, stopping to cup, then knead a breast. She sucked in a wild breath of pleasure when his other hand moved across her tummy, stopping at the flowering of the golden, curly tendrils at the juncture of her thighs, slowly yet knowingly caressing her there.

She closed her eyes and threw her head back. His lips kissed their way down from the hollow of her throat and soon suckled the stiff peak of the breast that he had just kneaded into a soft, throbbing nub of pleasure. The pit of her stomach grew queasy with rapture as he then kissed his way farther down, stopping where his fingers had so aroused her. When he bent on a knee before her and she realized what he was about to do, she opened her eyes wide and gazed over at the door to the room where Trevor slept.

"We're not alone," she whispered, nodding toward Trevor's bedroom. "Remember?"

Sage rose to his feet and swept her up into his arms. "You will not put me off that easily," he said, chuckling. He floated a kiss across her lips, then carried her into his bedroom. "Moments ago you doubted my love for you. After tonight, never will you doubt anything I say or do again."

He laid her on his sleeping platform, then knelt over her. She sighed languorously when his lips found her hot, moist place and he began pleasuring her again with his lips, tongue, and hands, soon sending her into a spiral of ecstasy.

She had never felt so alive, or so needed, as now.

Her body was turning to liquid, with a lethargic feeling of floating.

Soon he raised his head. As he peered down at Leonida with passion-heavy lids, she began undressing him, slowly and methodically. When he was finally naked and she saw his arousal, she bent on a knee before him and as he stood on the floor, with his legs widespread and his hands on his hips, her fingers surrounded his manhood.

She gazed up at him and noticed that his head was thrown back, that his eyes were closed, and then she began moving her hand on him. When he uttered a groan and she realized the intense pleasure she was giving him, she fisted him even more tightly and moved her hand more rhythmically on him.

She watched him grow even larger within her hand, and she became in awe of the size of him all over again.

Trembling hands on her head urged her away from him. Allowing him to lead her in which way to make love again, she followed him to the bed, stretching out on her back on the soft pelts.

Sage moved over her, his hard, taut body and his smooth copper skin against hers. As their stomachs touched, and her breasts pressed into his powerful chest, she placed her fingers on the nape of his neck and brought his lips to hers.

Her stomach churned wildly as she became lost in the kiss and the wondrous way his manhood was so magnificently filling her after entering her with one insistent thrust.

Her whole body quivered as he began his rhythmic strokes within her and his kisses became more demanding, even savage.

She responded to the heated thrusting of his pelvis, his strokes speeding up, and moving deeper, deeper. She lifted her legs and wrapped them around his hips, opening herself wider, her hips responding in a rhythmic movement, matching his.

His mouth moved from her lips and her blood surged in a wild thrill when his tongue began circling one of her nipples, burning into her skin, it seemed, the heat of passion that was growing so intensely within her. He rolled her nipple with his tongue, over and over again, drawing a lingering sigh from deeply within.

Surprising her, he suddenly lay still above her. He framed her face between his hands and looked down at her, his eyes glazed over with passion. "My woman, you have become the center of all my thinking," he said huskily. "I have never loved before as I love you. We must marry soon."

Clinging around his neck, Leonida's eyes filled with joyous tears. "Yes, oh, yes," she whispered. "Soon. I find such joy within your arms, oh, so much joy. I love you, Sage. I want to be your woman, forever and ever. I want to be your *wife.*"

Sage smiled broadly, then brought his lips down upon hers in a crushing kiss. His body began moving more quickly, and soon they spasmed together, their bodies rocking and swaying together gloriously.

Afterward, Sage rolled away from Leonida. She turned on her side to face him, and placed a cheek on his heaving chest. "What brought me from the hogan was you, darling, when you were singing a song about your horse," she said, gazing up at him. "It was so lovely. You had said something earlier about songs and their importance to your people. You also said that you would explain this meaning to me. I would love to hear it now, darling. I want to know everything about you and your people. I want to feel one with them soon."

Sage placed an arm around her and drew her closer. "The Hozhonji songs have been given to the Navaho by the gods," he said softly. "They are songs of peace and of blessings. They protect the people against all evil. We sing a Hozhonji song to purify or bless ourselves, or others."

He turned and faced her, one arm draped over her

side. "The Navaho sing as white men say their prayers," he further explained. "The Navaho hero, Nayenezrani, is like the white man's Bible hero David. By our Holy Ones were the songs made, even as the Bible was made by holy people."

Leonida thought back to how impressed she had been by the singing of not only Sage but the others as well. She had been listening to traditional songs which had been learned and handed down through generations. The quiet, monotonous quality of the chant had seemed heightened by Sage's concentration as he had sang; with closed eyes, he had seemed to bend his every thought upon his singing.

"You sang of your horse," she suddenly blurted out. "Is he sacred to you, Sage? Is he something holy?"

"A horse comes second only to a man's woman," Sage said, then drew her against him and smothered her lips with his mouth, stifling any further conversation.

14

There we will sit upon the rocks,
By shallow rivers, to whose falls
Melodious birds sing madrigals.
—MARLOWE

The sound of someone softly weeping awakened
Leonida from her restful sleep. She tensed and listened more closely. When she did not hear the sobbing
any longer, she thought perhaps she had been dreaming. There had been enough sadness of late to cause
such nightmares.

Yawning, Leonida wiped her eyes, somewhat dis-
oriented as she looked slowly around her. When her
gaze fell on Sage, sleeping so soundly beside her, remembrances of their lovemaking washed over her. She
felt nothing even akin to shame over having given herself to this handsome headman before wedding vows
were spoken. Deep within her heart, where she always
separated right from wrong, Leonida knew that loving
Sage so freely was not wrong. She could never allow
herself to think that it was, for never would they have
the opportunity to stand before a minister. His Navaho
marriage ceremony would have to do, and she accepted this without reservation.

Leonida's eyes widened and she sat up quickly when
she heard the soft sobbing again. This time she realized that it most definitely was real, and she knew
without a doubt who was crying.

Trevor!

Leonida bolted from the sleeping platform. She

looked around her for her clothes, and then she remembered having come to this bedroom naked. The skirt and blouse that had been brought to her were still in the outer room.

Sage awakened and gazed up at Leonida, his eyes feasting on her nakedness, instantly desiring her. Then he tensed as he heard the soft sobbing coming from the other bedroom. "Trevor?" he said, moving quickly from the bed. "He cries?"

Leonida turned away, blushing over being nude in a man's presence. Then she forgot her inhibitions, knowing that this was not just any man. No one could know her body any better than Sage, perhaps not even herself.

"Sage, it *is* Trevor," she said, her voice anxious. "He's missing his mother. And he's probably frightened after waking up in strange surroundings. I must go to him."

She gestured with a hand toward the door. "But my clothes are in the other room," she said, watching Sage step quickly into his velveteen breeches. "I can't go out there naked. I'm afraid Trevor would see me from his room."

His breeches secured at his waist, Sage rushed from the room and soon returned with the skirt and blouse, and also soft moccasins that Pure Blossom had brought.

"I will go to him," he said. "Come when you are dressed."

Leonida nodded and began hurrying into the clothes. She admired Sage's attentiveness to Trevor, yet could see that it was partially because he was feeling guilty over Carole's death. Perhaps he felt more responsible for Trevor now than even Leonida did. If so, they could come together to make a wonderful life for Trevor, if . . .

"If Kit Carson and Harold don't find Sage's stronghold and ruin everything," she said, frowning as she tied the drawstrings of the brightly colored blouse together in front. She recalled the steep climb to get to the stronghold. That made it almost unaccessible. Yet Sage had worried about the Navaho crops way down below in a valley, quite accessible to outsiders. Those crops were the lifeblood of the Navaho. Kit Carson was clever enough to realize that if he burned the crops, he would starve those who depended on them.

Hers and Trevor's future with Sage might become questionable if they were all forced to flee the stronghold. And even though Sage's intentions were pure toward the captive women and children, if he was enraged enough, he might have cause to forget his promises.

Leonida suddenly realized that Trevor had stopped sobbing. Weaving her fingers through her hair to straighten its tangles, Leonida hurried into Trevor's bedroom, stopping, breathless at the sight that she came upon. Trevor was in Sage's arms. Sage was rocking the child back and forth, singing to him the song of his horse again. Trevor now emitted only an occasional sob, resting his fat cheek against Sage's chest.

Touched by the tender scene, Leonida felt tears coming to her eyes. She watched a moment longer, then went to stand beside Sage. The only light in the room was the soft glow from the dying embers in the fire pit in the outer room, but it was enough to see that Trevor's cheeks and nose were rosy from crying. And when he held his arms out to her, she gladly took him and cuddled him close.

"I want my mommy," he said, again softly crying.

A deep sob wracked his tiny body. "Take me to my mommy."

Leonida and Sage exchanged quick glances. Sage then walked gingerly from the room, leaving Leonida with Trevor to explain.

After a lengthy discussion, with Trevor listening intently, he reached up and gave Leonida a big hug.

"You will be my mommy now," he said, a delayed sob causing his body to shudder, then grow still. "Sage will be my father. That will make my real mommy happy?"

"As she looks down from heaven, I am sure she approves of what she has seen this morning," Leonida said, caressing his tiny back through his white cotton shirt. "She has seen not only me loving you, but also Sage. I'm sure she is smiling down at you even now, Trevor. Can you give her a smile back?"

Wiping a desultory tear from one of his eyes, Trevor looked heavenward and smiled, then looked at Leonida for approval. "Was that smile big enough?" he asked softly. "Did she see it, do you think?"

"She saw it and she liked it," Leonida said, carrying him to the outer room. As she set him on his feet, she noticed that Sage had put fresh wood on the fire and was gone. She had to wonder why he had left without telling her first. And where had he gone so early in the morning? She did not hear any commotion outside. And as she peered at the smoke hole in the ceiling, she realized why. She could see that it was just barely daylight.

Trevor had gone to the copper tub, where the suds still floated atop the water. She smiled to herself as he started picking at the bubbles with his fingers, giggling as they burst and splashed onto his hand. She was recalling how much she had enjoyed the bath and thought that perhaps Trevor might enjoy one as well. She went to the tub and studied the water. It seemed clean enough, with only her having bathed in it.

She then eyed Trevor. She became suddenly bashful at the thought of undressing the little man and bathing him. Perhaps she might wait and see if Sage would do the honors.

But Trevor was taking care of the chore himself. He was undressing eagerly and was soon standing naked before her.

"Water?" he said, holding his arms out to her. "Will you put me in the water? I want to play with the bubbles."

Laughing softly, seeing that she had worried for naught about this little boy feeling uncomfortable in her presence with his clothes off, Leonida put her hands beneath his armpits and lifted him up into the tub. He squealed as he settled down into the water, which was cold to his tender flesh.

A noise behind her drew Leonida quickly around. Sage came up to her and smiled devilishly down at her, then went and knelt down beside the tub of water and playfully sprinkled some water over Trevor's head.

"My son, there is something special for you outside the hogan," Sage said, caressing Trevor's back. "Let us get you out of the water so that you can see what Sage has brought for you."

Leonida glanced toward the hogan door, then down at Sage. She was dying to know what he was talking about, so grateful that he was finding time for her and Trevor at this time when his mind was surely filled with worries of his stronghold being discovered and concern for the future of his people.

Sage lifted Trevor out of the water and stood him beside the fire, which was now blazing. Sage dried

Trevor off with a towel made from soft doeskin and helped him into his clothes. "You will soon wear only clothes of the Navaho," Sage said. "Though your skin is white, in your heart and actions, you will be Navaho."

Twining her fingers together behind her, Leonida watched Sage pampering this child as though he were his own. Sage brushed Trevor's shoulder-length hair with the short, tight end of a brush made from a sheaf of straw and dry grass. She stepped closer, watching Sage pull Trevor's hair back and tie it in a *chongo,* a bundle of hair at the nape of the neck.

"Now you look part Navaho," Sage said, laughing softly as he rose to his full height, towering over Trevor, who looked devotedly up at him, smiling broadly.

"Take me to see the surprise now," Trevor said, lifting a hand to Sage to be held. He glanced over at Leonida, lifting his other hand to her.

Smiling down at him, touched by this child's innocence and sweetness, Leonida took his hand, and they went outside.

In the shadows of early morning, Trevor moved slowly toward the brown-spotted palomino pony whose dark-brown eyes were looking trustingly at the child. Reaching a hand out, he gently touched the pony's nose, then squealed when the pony nuzzled his hand playfully.

"The pony is yours," Sage said, going to lift Trevor onto the back of the animal. "Forever it is yours. You will grow into the saddle that I will give you. The pony will know you always by your touch and smell. You will become as one when you ride with the wind beneath the sun, moon, and stars."

Sage took one of Trevor's hands and placed it on the pony's mane. "Familiarize yourself with him, my son," he said. "Give him a name. Never will he be called by anything else."

Trevor's eyes became as wide as silver dollars as he began lovingly stroking the pony's mane. He looked trustingly over at Sage and revealed his choice of names for his pony. "Can I call him Spottie?" he asked. "I once had a doggie named Spottie but he ran away."

"Spottie is a good name," Sage said, nodding his approval. He lifted Trevor down from the pony as Pure Blossom came walking toward them, carrying a steaming pot of food.

Leonida hurried to her and eased the pot from her frail hands. "Let me help you with that," she murmured, Pure Blossom smiling up at Leonida from her awkward, tw sted position.

Leonida inhaled the wondrous fragrance of the food in the pot. "Who is the lucky one that gets this for breakfast?" she teased, in awe that Pure Blossom would have been up so early in the morning preparing food. She glanced down into the pot. It contained meat from the backbone of a yearling calf boiled with corn. Never had she smelled anything as delicious, yet she knew that it was only because she was so hungry. Right now anything would smell and taste good.

"I prepared food for you, Sage, and the child," Pure Blossom said, pulling a round, rubbery loaf of bread from a deep, large pocket of her skirt. "Soon I will teach you how to cook the food of the Navaho. Until then you eat what I prepare. Does that please you, Leonida?"

"Yes, that pleases me very much," Leonida said. Her smile faded as she took a closer look at Pure Blossom and noticed that her usual pallor was even worse today and her eyes were sunk in.

"Are you all right, Pure Blossom?" Leonida asked as they all turned to enter the hogan. She was glad when Sage took the heavy pot from her and took it inside, Trevor trailing devotedly behind him.

"Pure Blossom never feels good," Pure Blossom said, shrugging.

Just before entering the hogan, Leonida put a hand on her brow and was relieved that Pure Blossom did not show any signs of having a temperature.

"If you start to feel worse, be sure to tell me or Sage," Leonida said, placing a gentle hand on Pure Blossom's frail face. "We want to make sure nothing happens to you. You're special, Pure Blossom. So very, very special."

Pure Blossom blushed and ducked her head, then followed Leonida into the hogan.

Once inside, as they were all getting settled on the mats around the fire, Pure Blossom reached a hand to Leonida's arm. "You like Navaho clothes and moccasins?" she asked, her eyes shining. "They made by my own hands."

"I like them very much," Leonida said, smiling over at her. "I do appreciate having them. Thank you."

"The blanket your white pony soldier paid for should be finished soon," Pure Blossom said. An awkward silence fell, and Sage scowled at her.

Pure Blossom looked shyly from her brother to Leonida. "You do not want the blanket?" she innocently asked. "The white pony soldier paid well for it. Should I send it to him by a Navaho messenger?"

"Burn the blanket," Sage said. "It was intended for a wedding between the white man and my woman. There is to be a wedding, but not the one planned by the white man. The marriage ceremony will be performed in our village between Sage and Leonida, and Sage does not have to offer gifts paid for by the white man. Sage's gifts will be from Sage.''

Leonida smiled weakly over at Pure Blossom as she gaped openly at her. Leonida had to wonder if Pure Blossom approved or disapproved. It was important to Leonida that she be accepted first by Sage's sister. The acceptance of the rest of the people would, she hoped, follow shortly after.

She sighed with relief when Pure Blossom leaned over and gave her a big hug.

''Pure Blossom has always wanted a sister,'' she murmured. ''Even that your skin is white does not matter. You have proven that you have the heart and soul of a Navaho.''

Sage smiled, then moved in front of the fire and the large pot of food hanging from a spit over it. ''It is time to bless the hogan, and then we eat,'' he said, drawing Leonida and Pure Blossom apart.

Trevor got on his knees and crawled to Sage. His eyes were large as he watched Sage sprinkle white cornmeal and then white powder made from prayer sticks into the fire.

Then everyone enjoyed the breakfast, the time spent in eating and talking cheerfully. Afterwards, Sage took Trevor to introduce him to other children of his same age, while Pure Blossom took Leonida to her hogan and showed her how she wove yarn into blankets and other wearing apparel, then how to make bread, the Navaho delicacy. Leonida watched as Pure Blossom spread with her hands a thin batter of blue-corn meal on a smoking-hot griddle, allowed it to bake a few seconds, then lifted it off. Pure Blossom told her that it took years of practice to smear the batter onto the griddle without burning one's fingers. She bragged that her stone griddle was one of her most treasured possessions, having been handed down for generations.

After several batches of bread had been made, Leonida ate some of it, and found that she didn't like the taste as much as the smell.

The day passed quickly. Trevor was ready to go to bed even before the sun set behind the mountain. It was a day of Leonida's being introduced to Sage's people and accepted by them for they accepted everything of their leader's choice, even if his choice of a wife was a white woman.

Leonida hated the reaction of the white women, who stood aside with their children, obviously appalled by Leonida's decision to marry the Navaho chief.

At dusk she walked arm in arm with Sage away from the village of hogans, finding refuge behind the oaks and the currant bushes that grew in a niche of red rock like the folds of a giant curtain.

They continued walking, not saying anything, just enjoying one another's company. Behind a lofty fir was a cleft that opened at shoulder height into transparent shadow. The footholds were worn to velvety roundness, and it was hard for Leonida to keep her footing.

But she did not mind the challenge, for here she was finding it so beautiful—the soft, gray stone, dark shadows, green coolness, and sweet smell of dampness. No breeze stirred. No details could be seen in the cliffs, only the silhouette of a river of mountains in the distance against the sky.

Sage gave Leonida's hand a gentle jerk, stopping her. Swinging her around, he pulled her against his hard body. His heart thumped wildly as she gazed up at him with adoration in her eyes. He reached his hands up to her hair and gently pushed his fingers through her silken tresses, then placed a hand at the nape of her neck and brought her lips to his. His mouth trembled against hers, his tongue flicking between her lips, touching her tongue, tip to tip with his.

Leonida splayed her fingers against his chest, then moved her fingers lower until she had managed to get his shirttail out from the encumbrance of his breeches. Slowly her fingers worked with the buttons of his shirt, then spread the shirt open and placed her trembling fingers on the magnificence of his chest.

Sage stepped back a fraction, giving her space to work at removing the rest of his clothes, and when he was naked, he gave her a lingering kiss as his fingers worked at disrobing her.

After they were both naked, he led her beneath a rock overhang, where there was a thick bed of moss. Pressing his body against hers, he led her down so that her back lay against the soft cushion of moss. She was not even aware of the air becoming cooler as night came on. Sage was blanketing her with his body, his hands warm as he softly kneaded first one breast and then the other.

Leonida hungrily strained her body up against Sage's when one of his hands went to the center of her passion and began caressing her, readying her for the ultimate pleasure. She moaned throatily when he leaned down and flicked his tongue around one of her nipples, causing a fierce, fevered heat to spread through her like wildfire. Needing him, wanting him so badly, she opened herself to him, almost choking on a cry of bliss when he understood her message and entered her with one deep thrust, which seemed to reach clear up into her heart.

Rhythmically he moved within her as she rocked with him, thrusting her pelvis. She was becoming delirious with sensation as desire washed over her, his thrusts becoming faster and more determined, his lips everywhere, it seemed, kissing, his tongue lapping.

Sage felt pleasure spreading within him, tremors of ecstasy cascading down his back. He kissed Leonida again, his mouth urgent and eager. Their flesh seemed to fuse, their bodies sucking at each other. He was nearing that moment of sensual shock, feeling it growing within him, spreading, growing, then bursting forth, as though great, flashing rays of sunshine had been set off inside his brain.

His hands moved to her buttocks and cupped them, forcing her hips to his, crushing her against him, pressing himself endlessly deeper.

And then he gave himself up to the shuddering in his loins, flooding her womb with his seed, smiling as she strained her hips up at him, crying out at her own fulfillment.

Afterward, their bodies subsided together, exhausted. They lay there for some time with her stroking his smooth copper back. Sage caressed one of her breasts, then leaned over and sucked the nipple between his teeth, softly chewing on it, his tongue flicking around it.

Leonida closed her eyes in ecstasy. "If you don't stop, we'll spend all night here," she said. In response, his hands moved down her body, his fingers soon touching the center of her desire again, softly caressing it.

Sighing, Leonida moved with him as he turned her around so that she lay on top of him, her breasts crushed against his chest. Her hair tumbled down, surrounding his face, as she moved her mouth to his lips and urged them apart, soon touching her tongue to his.

She gasped and threw her head back when she felt him thrust himself into her again. Her heart pounded and she bit her lower lip as the same wild splendor captured her.

Sage clasped his fingers to her breasts, and she moved to a sitting position atop him so that he could more easily fill her with his hardness. Once more they entered that realm of total bliss, forgetting what might happen tomorrow, only relishing the moment, as though it were their last.

15

Is there within thy heart a need
That mine cannot fulfill?
One chord that any other hand
Could better wake or still?
—ADELAIDE ANNE PROCTER

The fire was burning low and soft in the fire pit. The aroma of food lay pleasantly in the air. Sitting beside the fire on mats, Leonida filled Trevor's bowl again with corn mush. She patted his head affectionately as she replaced the black pot of food on a hook over the fire, marveling at how Pure Blossom could come and go with her offerings of food without Leonida hearing her. Leonida was surprised that Pure Blossom could keep going when she so obviously showed signs of being progressively ill with some mysterious disease. Leonida feared the morning that she might awake and hear that Pure Blossom had passed away in her sleep.

Shuddering at the thought, hoping that she was wrong about Pure Blossom's state of health, Leonida forced herself to think of other things. Her gaze shifted toward the door of the hogan. When she had awakened this morning, Sage had been gone already, without even a word.

"I want to go out and see my pony," Trevor said, bringing Leonida out of her reverie. "Please? Can I? I want to show him to the other children."

Leonida swept him into her arms and gave him a hug. "Yes, darling," she murmured. "You go outside and see your pony. But don't go far. There are cliffs everywhere. Stay within the village.''

"I will," Trevor said, easing out of her arms. He scrambled to his feet and left the hogan at a run.

Leonida stared at the door blankly for a moment, knowing that she should feel grateful for so many things, but the weight of the world seemed to be on her shoulders this morning and she was finding it almost impossible to shake the feeling.

She could not help but wonder how close Kit Carson might be to finding Sage's stronghold. And what Harold's rage at finding her taken captive might lead him to do? Then there was the welfare of the rest of the captives, even though they had been given shelter and food enough to make them comfortable. She only wished that they could be set free soon and returned to their loved ones.

Sighing heavily, Leonida picked up Trevor's empty bowl and her own, which was still half full, and started to go outside to wash them in the basin just outside the door. She stopped in midstep and stared as Pure Blossom came into the hogan, her arms loaded down with clothes. At one glance Leonida saw that these were much different than the ones she had been given before. These were made of doeskin, so pure white they resembled the fluffy soft clouds one could see in the sky on sweet mornings of spring in San Francisco. Her eyes widened as she discovered also that the beadwork on the clothes was brilliantly pretty in design.

"It is good that you have eaten already," Pure Blossom said, going to Leonida, smiling up at her from her awkwardly twisted stance. "You must prepare for the ceremony. You must prepare Trevor. It is a special day, Leonida. There will be much laughter and gaiety.''

"There will?" Leonida asked. She lay the bowls beside the fire again, then accepted the soft clothes as Pure Blossom laid them across her outstretched arms. "Why is there to be a celebration? I am sure your people are worrying about too much now to celebrate anything."

"When their chief marries, there is cause to forget troubles, at least for that day of the ceremony," Pure Blossom said, smiling broadly.

Leonida's eyes widened and she felt the rush of heat to her cheeks. "Marries?" she gasped, stunned. "Sage? He is going to marry . . . ?"

"Beautiful Leonida," Pure Blossom said, nodding eagerly. "He is marrying you. Did he not tell you? He is preparing for the celebration even now. He is even showing Trevor how to decorate his pony. Then Trevor will come to the hogan and get dressed in his Navaho attire. No more will he wear the clothes of a little white boy."

Leonida's head was spinning. Sage had left early to prepare for their marriage ceremony.

Soon they would become man and wife.

Pure Blossom laid Trevor's Indian attire across Leonida's arms. Leonida stared down at the briefness of the garment, recognizing it to be a breechclout.

She looked quickly up again, wonder in her eyes at the thought of Trevor wearing such a garment, especially when there were still other white children in the village who might poke fun at him.

"I don't know," she murmured, again staring at the scant garment. "Trevor might not want to wear the breechclout."

"For Sage, he must," Pure Blossom said softly. She placed a gentle hand on Leonida's shoulder. "Do not worry about what others might think or do. Think only of Sage and what pleases him. That is also how Trevor must react to his new attire."

Leonida silently nodded. She watched Pure Blossom turn and walk shakily away, the frail maiden seeming even weaker today, yet filled with no less spirit and sweetness than before. Whatever was slowly draining her of life did not seem to weigh heavily on her heart. She seemed to be accepting it, as she had always accepted the fate of being different in appearance from everyone else.

"*Uke-he,*" Leonida said quickly before Pure Blossom left the hogan.

The maiden stopped and smiled back at Leonida, then went on outside.

She lay Trevor's breechclout aside, staring at it doubtfully only a moment longer, and then she knelt on the mats and spread out her white doeskin dress, entranced by its loveliness. The edges of the long sleeves and the hem of the skirt were fringed. The beads were soft pinks, blues, and turquoises, shaped like flowers. The new moccasins that Pure Blossom had brought with the dress were beaded to match, and a beaded headband was also there to be worn at her brow. She would not only be marrying a Navaho today, she would in a sense become one herself.

"It is lovely enough?"

Sage's voice behind her sent a thrill through Leonida's veins. She could not move to her feet quickly enough. She went to him and flung herself into his arms. "Why didn't you tell me?" she asked excitedly. She gazed up at him, marveling anew at his handsomeness. "Darling, you knew last night that we were going to be married today and you did not tell me. Why?"

"I saw no need," he said, slipping his fingers

through her hair. "Is it not best this way? Is not the surprise worth everything?"

Leonida giggled, then hugged him tightly as she lay her cheek against his bare chest. "Yes, I believe so," she said, closing her eyes. "Oh, darling, I do love you so much."

"Our path of happiness will no longer be beset with ambushes. We *will* be married, and it will be in a beautiful way," Sage said, lovingly stroking her back. "The gods will marry us."

He framed her face between his hands and lowered his lips to hers. He gave her a kiss of reverence, of forever.

16

I love thee to the depth and breadth and height
My soul can reach.
                        —ELIZABETH BARRETT BROWNING

The sun was down. The streaming, wavering flames
of torches stuck in the ground in the midst of the village made a golden glow in the blue dusk. The beat
of a lone drum and several rattles resounded in the air,
supplying the music for the various dances being displayed for those who participated in the marriage celebration.

Feeling like a princess in a storybook, dressed so
beautifully in her Indian dress and so filled with love
for Sage that she ached with the heady sweetness of
it, Leonida sat on a soft pelt spread on a platform with
her beloved, amid Sage's people.

A great outdoor fire usually marked a wedding celebration, but to avoid drawing attention to those who
might be at the foot of the mountain tonight, only gray,
dark, and cold ashes lay in the center of the circle of
Navaho, who were stiffly and quietly awaiting the moment when their chief would become one with a
woman not of their skin coloring.

Leonida was trying not to let the people's indifferent
attitude toward her spoil her special day. She could
often feel them glaring at her, and she herself was
aware of how the Indian costume accentuated her
whiteness.

She was even trying to understand why none of the

captives had chosen to leave their dwellings for the marriage ceremony. If she glanced toward the lean-tos where they were living until they were set free, she could catch an occasional glimpse of a woman, or perhaps a child with eager eyes, staring out at Trevor, who was running and playing with the young Indian braves of his same age, now dressed as one of them.

Leonida feared that Trevor's attire had been the final insult as far as the women had been concerned. She doubted now that they would ever forgive her, even though she saw herself that there was truly nothing to forgive. If they had loved as she loved Sage, they also would have followed their heart and given themselves totally to the man with a commitment for a life of loving and caring for him.

Although various dancers continued entertaining in the midst of the crowd, Trevor was having footraces with the young Navaho braves. Leonida turned and watched, marveling not only at how comfortable and accepting of his scant Indian attire Trevor seemed but also at his speed for such a young boy.

Leonida turned to Sage and touched his face gently, silently urging him to watch the youth of his village at their games. Sage followed her bidding and set his attention on Trevor. He had not seen such speed in a child in years. Strange how pride seemed to swell within him at the sight, he thought to himself, at this moment, feeling so like a father who saw the gifts of a son. Sage's eyes gleamed as he turned to Leonida and leaned his face down close to hers.

"He will no longer be called Trevor," he whispered to her. "He has earned the name Woodii, which means 'runner' in Navaho. When we speak of Runner, we speak of Trevor. Is that something you can accept?

That he will no longer carry the name of a white boy around with him?''

Leonida did not speak right away, stunned to silence by Sage's further acceptance of Trevor—he thought enough of him to give him a Navaho name. And she no longer was suspicious of his reasons for showing such affection toward the orphan. Sage no longer had to do anything to persuade her to accept him as her husband. She was only moments away from becoming his wife. His feelings toward Trevor were sincere.

Filled with emotions too numerous to separate and define, Leonida leaned into Sage's embrace, placing her cheek on his chest, which was bare today, as was his whole body except for the briefest of breechclouts.

''Yes, I can accept your decision to call Trevor 'Runner,' '' she murmured. ''I think it is wonderful that you are so involved with the child that you would give him a Navaho name.''

''He is our son, is he not?'' Sage said, placing his fingers on Leonida's shoulders to push her slightly away from him so that their eyes could meet. ''He will know this in all ways Navaho.''

A squeal behind them drew their attention back to the boys at play. Leonida sucked in a breath of delight when she found that one of the other white boys had joined the fun, Adam Jones.

Leonida shifted her gaze to Sally, Adam's mother. She had left her lean-to and was watching the children at play. When Sally moved her eyes to Leonida and smiled at her, Leonida sighed with gratefulness. She returned the smile, knowing that if Sally's anger had waned, so would that of the other women. She seemed to be a leader among women, so well liked that no one could refuse her anything.

''All will soon be right again between you and your

friends," Sage said, taking Leonida's hand and lovingly squeezing it. "They are allowing themselves to relax and see that I meant them no harm. As each day progresses, they must realize it draws them closer to freedom. Soon they will walk among those who love them again and look back upon this experience as something not evil but as a learning experience—learning from it the wrong of the white man toward the Navaho and what those wrongs are forcing *upon* the Navaho. How could they not walk away from our village with this in their hearts and souls—that their people have wronged my people and will continue to do so, I am sure, until there is no breath left in any Navaho or any white and the world becomes barren of either?"

His words, his prediction of doom between both races of people, caused Leonida to shudder. She looked up into Sage's dark eyes, seeing so much torment and pain, even now, on his wedding day.

"I'm sorry for so much," she murmured. "If only I could help in some way. But I am only one person, only a woman, powerless against those who are making plans against the Navaho. If only I were a man . . ."

Sage was pleased at the way she looked in her Navaho attire. Even the headband was right for her. His gaze swept lower, seeing the swell of her breasts beneath the soft doeskin of her dress; his loins turned to fire when he thought of touching them again. Never could there be anything as soft as her breasts.

His lips trembled into a smile. "You are too much woman ever to wish to be a man," he said, chuckling low. "There are many men in the world, but only one woman. You, white woman. You. And you are mine."

Choked with the happiness that he was bringing her,

his words like magic to her ears, Leonida sniffed back the urge to cry. But the crowd stirred, and people suddenly started clapping in time with the music and singing. A young man, hardly any older than Runner, had emerged from the crowd. Alone, he began dancing gracefully as the audience watched appreciatively. He wore a breechclout, moccasins, and a horsehair roach and feather on his head. His thumping moccasins raised clouds of dust. His head bobbed. His knees reached almost to his chest as he bent them in his dance. When he whirled around, the women of the village shouted bravo, and the men grunted loud exclamations of pride.

Then he was joined by many other children. They danced all together, or by turns, without fixed order, laughing joyously.

Leonida scarcely breathed as she saw one of the young braves coaxing Runner to join them. She covered her mouth with her hand as Runner moved among the dancers, himself laughing and carrying on as he mimicked the dancers.

Sage leaned closer to her. "Perhaps his name should be Dancer instead of Runner?" he whispered, chuckling softly. "This child already stands out from the others as special."

This statement made Leonida a bit uneasy. She leaned close to Sage. "Does this bother you?" she whispered. "That he is performing so well, making your young braves look less skilled in the eyes of their mothers and fathers? Will this cause jealousy to grow against Trevor?"

"My people admire fortitude in anyone, no matter what their skin coloring," Sage whispered back. "From childhood on, it is taught to be the best among those of your acquaintance. Each child strives for this.

As they watch Runner, they will strive even harder. Challenges make men of boys. Winners become warriors more quickly than others. It is good to have Runner here to teach the others that they must work harder to become the best of those their same age. Yes, it is good that they are seeing this white boy as better. They will understand when they see the persistence of white men such as Kit Carson, how he might have risen above the others in his own challenges. They will work harder to fight off such challengers in the future, when they are men.''

Leonida shuddered at the mention of Kit Carson, who was ready to stop at nothing to take Sage's freedom from him and place him in the confines of a reservation. Soon she would be Sage's wife. This meant that she also might be doomed to a reservation.

The thought terrified her, yet then she reminded herself that when one loved as strongly as she did, she could live anywhere with her beloved. She would do everything within her power to make life more bearable for the man she loved.

Leonida and Sage's attention were drawn to his people. Everyone had become lighthearted and accepting of their chief's marriage to a ''captive.'' The young braves had ceased their dancing, and singers had stepped forth to sing to the bridal couple, making her melt with relief that perhaps she might be accepted into their hearts after all. She had to believe their change in attitude was somehow linked with Trevor and the young Navaho braves' acceptance of him. Children could always touch people's hearts when nothing else would.

Leonida smiled from one to the other, filled with joy. The celebrating went on for some time, until the skies were carpeted with black and the stars were like tiny twinkling beacons in the sky.

Soon the singers went back and sat down among the others. Everything became quiet as Pure Blossom appeared before Sage and Leonida, spreading a rug on the ground in front of them.

Sage turned to Leonida. He smiled as he took her hands, then helped her from the platform. She followed him to the rug and sat down beside him on it.

"My sister, bring the medicine basket to us," Sage said, smiling up at his sister, yet noticing her extreme pallor. She was walking slowly, as though each step might be her last. He felt helpless, knowing that everything had been done for her as a child to make her stronger and to rid her of her afflictions. There was nothing else to do now but watch her slowly fade away.

Not wanting to think further about the sadness of his sister, Sage turned his gaze to Leonida. He had wanted to do everything possible to make this wedding ceremony beautiful for his woman. She must be of prime importance today, her welfare the only thing filling his thoughts and heart.

"What is a medicine basket?" Leonida whispered.

"It is part of the ceremony that makes you my wife," he said, gently touching her cheek with his hand.

Leonida smiled weakly at him, wondering about a wedding ceremony that included "medicine baskets." But she did not have time to question Sage further. Pure Blossom came to them with a basket filled with corn mush that she had prepared for the ceremony.

Leonida did not question anything else. She just followed Sage's lead, doing what he asked her to do.

Sage divided the mush in four directions.

Now he was praying for them.

Now they were ceremonially partaking of the yellow corn.

Then Leonida sat spellbound as Sage began singing to her solemnly.

First he sang in Navaho, then translated the words so that she could understand . . .

> Now Hastyeyalti
> And Hastyehogan
>   Meeting, joining one another.
> And the white corn
> And the yellow corn,
>   Meeting, joining one another.
> *Ka-sa-a narai,*
>   Life that never passeth,
> *Ka-bike-hozhoni-ye,*
>   Happiness-of-all-things,
>   Meeting, joining one another.
> Now all is beautiful,
> All is beautiful,
> All is beautiful, indeed.

She was touched deeply by his song and the endearing look in his eyes as he gazed at her, and tears streamed down her cheeks. She flung herself into his arms and hugged him tightly, then thrilled when he said softly in her ear: "You are now my wife. The ceremony is complete."

Everyone swarmed around them. Sage helped Leonida to her feet. She accepted hugs and kisses, and was touched deeply when Sally came and gave her a heartfelt hug.

"I shall talk to the others," Sally said, standing back from Leonida and holding her hands. "It's been hard to understand, all of this between you and the Indian. But I see such happiness in your eyes. How can I question that? Please stay happy. And may God be with us all should Kit Carson arrive intent on killing Sage and his people. I fear Kit now more than any Indian.''

Choked with emotion, Leonida could only nod and hug Sally again. When Trevor came to her and tugged the skirt of her dress, Leonida broke away from Sally and knelt down to give him a big hug.

''You said that I would be staying the night with Pure Blossom,'' Trevor said, wriggling from Leonida's arms. ''Can Adam stay there with me? Can two other boys? We promise not to bother Pure Blossom. We'll be quiet.''

Leonida glanced up at Sally, realizing that she had heard Trevor's request. She saw a reserve in Sally's nervous smile, but was glad when she gave a nod of approval. Leonida had to wonder if Sally would be so eager to approve if she knew that Sage had assigned Trevor an Indian name.

Soon everyone was scattered in all directions, going to their own hogans. Sage was leading Leonida through the night, to the cliff that she now knew so well. He had wrapped her in a rabbit-fur cloak and was holding her snugly against his side as they reached the summit of the cliff where the world was basking in night's silence.

''My wife,'' Sage said, testing the words on his lips again, as though finding them hard to believe. ''You are now my wife. My heart is singing with the knowing.''

He turned to her and put his hands at her waist. Gently he drew her into his embrace and gave her a kiss that made her head swim and her knees grow weak. When he reached up and brushed the cloak from her shoulders, she was not conscious of the damp mountain air. She was too consumed with the fires being ignited within her by her husband's kisses and the caresses of his hands as his fingers went to her breasts, kneading them through the soft doeskin of her dress.

Lost heart and soul to this adorable man, Leonida began running her hands over his powerful chest, reveling in the mere touch of him. Lower her fingers wandered, and she smiled to herself when his stomach muscles quivered as she touched him ever so lightly when seeking out the fabric of his breechclout. When she had been held against him, she had felt his arousal even through her dress, and it made her seek out that part of him now, to touch, to caress.

When she finally reached his breechclout, she did not stop her exploring. Her heart pounding, she slipped her hand inside it, hearing Sage's gasp of pleasure against her lips as she soon wrapped her fingers around his throbbing member, moving them on him slowly, ever so slowly.

Sage slid his mouth from her lips and kissed the hollow of her throat, becoming mindless from her skillful ways of pleasuring him. He smiled to himself, realizing that he had taught her well. Even now, as she stopped long enough to slip his breechclout down his thighs, he knew what to expect next from her.

But he did not want that sort of pleasuring just yet. He wanted to touch her all over, feel the heat of her passion rise as he caressed her body with his tongue and fingers. Then he would accept her lips on him, wherever and however she wanted to pleasure him. Now it was *her* turn to be awakened fully to how much he truly loved her—would always love her.

With the urging of his hands, Leonida stepped away. Her pulse began to race as he slowly disrobed her, his hands reacquainting themselves with her newly revealed flesh a portion at a time, enjoying teasing her. He could see the rapture building in her eyes, and in the way her breasts heaved, as he finally bared them to his feasting eyes.

Leaving the dress resting around her hips, Sage cupped her breasts in his hands, letting their weight rest within his palms. His thumbs circled the nipples, causing Leonida to close her eyes and sigh.

When Sage knelt over and touched his tongue to one of the nipples, he drew a groan of ecstasy. Leonida placed her fingers at the nape of his neck and urged his lips even lower, her whole body pounding as if it were one large heartbeat, with that which she was encouraging him to do.

He answered her plea by slipping her dress down to the ground. Then he knelt before her, gaining access to the center of her passion. Spreading her soft down of hair apart, he touched his tip slowly to her swollen nub, sending a shiver up and down Leonida's spine. She urged him even closer to her and sighed languorously when he complied and gave her a loving so intense, she felt as though she might faint.

Just as she almost soared into the clouds with the intense pleasure he was giving her, he placed his hands on her waist and drew her down on her knees before him.

Pulling her to him, he kissed her with a feverish heat, his every nerve ending raw with the building passion. He removed her headband and tossed it aside, then twined his fingers through her hair and held her lips tightly against his. Back onto the cushion of the rabbit-fur cloak he urged her, soon spreading himself atop her.

Their bodies strained together hungrily as he sought entrance with his throbbing member. He sucked in a wild breath and eased his lips from hers as he thrust himself deeply into her and began his smooth, even strokes, her rhythm matching his as she lifted her hips to meet him.

Leonida could not keep her hands off him. Her heart thudded within her; she felt growing sensations that left her breathless. She smoothed her fingers over his back, and down to his buttocks, and then around so that she could get an occasional feel of his manhood.

When he stopped suddenly, she gazed up at him with a silent question, then followed his bidding when he urged her to move to her hands and knees. She shuddered with desire when he entered her again from this position, his hands reaching down and around, kneading and teasing her taut breasts.

A delicious tingling heat was spreading within Leonida as he molded her even closer to him from behind, making it so that he could fill her more deeply with the wondrous, continuing thrusts.

Just when she came close to the height of the languorous feelings that spilled through her when she reached the ultimate splendor, Sage withdrew from her.

Leonida turned again, to stretch out on her back, wondering why he had stopped.

And then she knew.

He straddled her so that she could give him the pleasure that he had denied her earlier. She leaned up on an elbow and loved him with her lips and mouth until she realized it was enough. She knew by the reactions of his body, and by the way he was moaning so pleasurably, it was time for them to find paradise together.

Sage moved over her and parted her legs with a knee. The fires of his passion became known quickly to Leonida as he plunged deep within her and his mouth closed hard upon hers. She placed her fingers on the nape of his neck, urging his lips closer. She wrapped her legs around his waist, locking them together at the ankles, riding him as his strokes sped deeper, deeper.

His steel arms enfolded her. She could feel his hunger. It matched hers. She was almost beyond coherent thought. The euphoria filling her was more than ever before, so wonderful, so beautiful. She was floating, floating.

Sage's senses were reeling as he continued to move his lean, sinewy buttocks. He buried his face next to her neck when he felt the pleasure mounting. His fingers bit into her shoulders as licking flames swept through him, igniting the blaze that fired his passions. His whole body quivered when he felt release so close.

He kissed her again, this time softly, her lips parting as his tongue probed. Then everything seemed to explode within him, sending great splashes of warmth throughout him. The sensations seemed to be searing his heart, his very soul, matching Leonida's own passion as she clung to him, her body shaking against his.

Afterward, Sage rolled onto his back beside her. His chest was heaving. His breath was coming in short gasps.

Leonida felt drugged with passion, her chest heaving from the aftermath of what seemed impossible, intense pleasure.

She turned to Sage and kissed him, her mouth soft and passionate against his. He lifted her atop him and urged her to lie down on him, reveling in the touch of her soft body and large breasts against his.

"I will never get enough of you," he said huskily, his dark eyes hazy with passion. "My wife, you will desire your husband as much?"

"Always," Leonida whispered.

Her breath was stolen when he put his hands on her waist and hurriedly placed her on the soft cloak again and rose over her. She closed her eyes in rapture as he entered her, overwhelming her again with his skillful, torrid ways of loving her.

17

Where'er she speaks,
My ravished ear no other voice than hers can hear.
—GEORGE LYTTELTON

Leonida had not known the toll it had been taking on Pure Blossom to cook her daily meals and generously share them with Leonida, Sage, and Runner. Not until today.

Even though Pure Blossom had insisted on cooking the meals before, she had sent word that she could not prepare any meals today, that she was not feeling well enough.

Leonida was kneeling beside the fire in her hogan, feeling awkward as she stirred the large pot of stew that she was preparing for the evening meal. Sweat poured down her face in silver streamers, and her hair hung loose and damp across her shoulders. Even as well as she was, she felt the strength draining from her body as the heat from the fire combined with the heat beating down upon her from the sun-drenched domed roof of the hogan.

Guilt plagued her for having allowed Pure Blossom to prepare the meals. But she kept reminding herself that Pure Blossom had insisted. Sage and Leonida had allowed it only because they agreed that this made her feel happy and useful.

Resting the wooden spoon in the pot, Leonida put her hands on her aching back and rose slowly to her feet. Besides cooking, she was learning other ways of being a Navaho wife. She carried water from the creek daily, as well as gathered wood wherever she could find it. She had not allowed Runner to accompany her, always fearing the cliffs and the danger they posed to a small child who did not know the meaning of the word "danger."

Fanning herself with her hand, Leonida moved away from the fire and went into the bedroom she and Sage shared. Her heart pounded even now at the remembrance of his lips and hands caressing her to heights of joyous bliss she had never thought possible. She wished that he were here now to rekindle their love-making of only a short while ago, before Runner awakened and came into their room, his stomach growling from hunger.

Wiping his eyes sleepily, Runner had looked so innocent and sweet as he waited for them to stir from their bed. Sage had playfully pulled him into the bed with them, and Runner had been oblivious that they were naked. Sage said it was best to allow him to see their nudity as a natural way of life, to see nothing in it that might embarrass him.

A sound of scampering feet and giggling drew Leonida from her thoughts. She spun around just in time to see Runner and Adam come into the bedroom. Runner's eyes were dancing as he gazed up at her.

"See Adam?" Runner said, smiling broadly. "Pure Blossom made him a breechclout. Does he not look Navaho now, like me?"

Stunned, fearing Sally's reaction, Leonida gasped, then knelt down before Runner and Adam and placed a hand on Runner's shoulder. "Honey, I know that Pure Blossom meant well," she murmured. "But I don't think that Adam's mother . . ."

"No, Adam's mother does *not* approve," Sally said,

bursting into the hogan, her face red with anger. "I saw Adam running toward your hogan dressed—dressed as a savage."

Sally grabbed Adam's hand and jerked him away from Runner's side, then up into her arms as she turned to stamp away. "I was wrong, Leonida, to offer you my friendship again," she said across her shoulder, her voice breaking. "You might want to turn Trevor into a savage. But never will I allow you to even get near my son again."

Adam was crying as he was carried from the hogan. Runner went to Leonida and wrapped his arms around her legs, his tears pooling in wet spots on her blue velveteen skirt. "She's mean," he wailed. "She's mean. I'm no savage. Go and tell her I'm no savage."

Although Leonida expected no less of a reaction from Sally, she still found it hard to accept. She wove her fingers through Runner's thick black hair, then bent down and lifted him into her arms. As he straddled her with his legs, his arms clinging to her neck, he continued to sob against her bosom.

"I'm sorry that had to happen, darling," Leonida murmured, rocking him back and forth. "You aren't a savage, nor is Adam just because he wears a breech-clout. Nor is your new daddy a savage. That word is ugly, Runner. Never should it be used in the same breath as Sage. He is more civilized than most whites I have known."

"My new name is savage, though?" Runner said, leaning back and gazing with red and swollen eyes up at Leonida. He wiped his nose with the back of his hand. "Some of the other children who were my friends while I lived at the fort called my name savage when they heard that Sage had assigned me a Navaho name.'' His lips curved into a pout. ''I want to be called Trevor again.''

Leonida was torn. Here was a child having to adjust to the loss of a mother, as well as many other new things all at once.

Yet she saw the importance in his not giving in to those who wrongly tormented him. In truth, Leonida felt that perhaps the children were jealous of the special attention that Runner was getting in the Indian village. Jealousy fired much ugliness among people, children as well as adults. It was up to her to make sure that Runner knew the difference between jealousy and sincere feelings and learned how to react to both when confronted by them.

''Darling, I think your new name is beautiful, and I don't think you should toss it away just because of what a few children said to you about it,'' she tried to explain, placing a gentle hand on his cheek. ''Do you think Sage's name is savage?''

''No,'' Runner said, sniffling. His trusting eyes gazed into Leonida's. ''I like his name. It is Navaho like my name, Runner? It is not a savage name?''

''I like his name also,'' Leonida said, smiling at him. ''And yes, it is Navaho. Now you tell *me*. Do you think it is a savage name?''

''No,'' Runner said, his eyes innocently wide.

''Nor is your name, Runner,'' Leonida said matter-of-factly. She drew him close and hugged him. ''Now let's not hear any more talk about not wanting a new name, or about the word 'savage.' Run on outside. There are plenty of other children that you can play with if Sally keeps Adam in his lean-to.''

As Leonida put Runner on the floor, her gaze stopped at the breechclout. She saw it as nothing short of precious in the way it fit his tiny body. And his skin was becoming tanned, soon perhaps to be the same shade of copper as the skin of the other Navaho children.

She so badly wanted life to be fair to him. He had lost so much already, and at such a young age. She hoped that Sally would see the wrong in her behavior today. Runner was just a child.

"I wish I could play with Adam," Runner said, taking Leonida's hand as they left the bedroom. He looked trustingly up at her. "Do you think I'll be able to play with him again? He likes me. I know he likes me."

Leonida walked Runner on to the door, then knelt down before him. She put her hands on each side of his face and drew his lips to hers. She gave him a kiss, then drew him into her arms again. "Yes, Adam likes you," she murmured. "And I'm sure he'll play with you again. But not today, honey. Play with the other children today."

Runner nodded, then eased away from Leonida and left the hogan.

Leonida sighed as she got back to her feet. She eyed the steaming stew, realizing that it needed stirring again. As she went and knelt before the fire, she was not aware that someone entered the hogan. She jumped with a start when a movement beside her revealed that she was not alone.

Dropping the spoon into the stew, Leonida scrambled to her feet. She sighed and smiled down at Pure Blossom, who stood with her arms filled with freshly made bread.

"Pure Blossom, you weren't supposed to be working over a hot stove today," Leonida scolded, glancing from the bread up at Sage's sister. Her cheeks were sunken. Her eyes were dark pits. "You were supposed to be resting. It's extraordinarily hot today. Even I feel weakened from the heat."

Pure Blossom leaned shakily toward the floor and placed the bread beside the fire. "Pure Blossom happy cooking and weaving," she said softly.

Leonida placed her arm around Pure Blossom's waist and helped her back to a standing position.

"Pure Blossom same as dead if she does not do what makes her happy," Pure Blossom said, breathing hard. "Please not fuss over me. Please?"

Sighing, Leonida nodded. "All right," she said. "I promise not to fuss over you. But please try not to do so much, especially in this sort of heat."

"I promise," Pure Blossom said, giggling. She coughed into a cupped hand, then turned toward the door. "Now Pure Blossom goes home and rests."

When she teetered, momentarily losing her balance, Leonida went to her rescue. She placed an arm around Pure Blossom's tiny waist and steadied her. "I'm going to walk you home," she said in a determined voice. "I'm going to see to it that you get into bed."

"You are fussing over Pure Blossom again," she said, smiling up at Leonida.

"Yes, I guess I am," Leonida said, returning the smile. "And I see that you are allowing it this time."

"Yes, it is easy to," Pure Blossom said, getting more winded the more she struggled to walk. She leaned into Leonida's willing embrace as they stepped out into the blinding sunshine of late afternoon.

Then they both stopped and stared at the approaching Indians on horseback. Leonida realized quickly that they were not Navaho. "Pure Blossom, who are they?" she asked as Sage and several of his warriors left an outdoor council to greet the mounted visitors. "What tribe are they from? How did they know to find the stronghold so easily?"

Pure Blossom twisted her face into a frown. "They

are Kiowa,'' she said, her voice practically a hiss. ''They come and trade for our blankets and wool from our sheep, and even fruits from our gardens. They are few in number now, and they hide also from the wrath of the white man's pony soldiers. The chief of this small band of Kiowa is Chief Four Fingers, a man I have despised since the death of my parents.''

''He's responsible?'' Leonida whispered back, her eyes following the chief, who was leading the others closer to Sage and his waiting warriors.

''All we knew was that renegades killed our parents, but Pure Blossom suspects Four Fingers is somehow responsible,'' she said sourly. ''He brought their bodies to the village. He said other renegades killed them.''

''Why would you not believe him?'' Leonida asked, watching the hefty, middle-aged Kiowa chief dismount. He suddenly turned to her, closely scrutinizing her. A chill crossed her flesh, and she felt as though he was undressing her with his eyes. Although he was a handsome man, Leonida felt nothing for him except a keen fear. His eyes were not friendly. They were cold and guarded even as he turned away and reached a hand of friendship out for Sage to accept.

''So often he is known to be a man of forked tongue,'' Pure Blossom said. ''He has found only a measure of friendship with the Navaho since the white settlers came to this land that once belonged solely to the Indians. My brother, Sage, saw it was wise to keep alliances with other tribes of Indians in case war broke out between the whites and our people. In numbers the whites might be defeated. The Kiowa added to that number. So they are important now, but only until their alliance is no longer needed. Then my brother will send them away, enemies again.''

"They were once the Navaho's enemy?"

"Yes, and it has never been an easy or trusting peace."

Leonida was surprised when Pure Blossom wrenched herself away and began walking boldly, and with much more energy than she had had moments ago, toward the assemblage of Indians.

"Come," Pure Blossom said over her shoulder. "We join the council. Sister and wife of Chief Sage are allowed."

Leonida hesitated for a moment, unsure that she should, or even wanted to, then she rushed ahead and walked beside Pure Blossom. Her gaze never left Chief Four Fingers as Sage offered him a seat on a spread blanket in a gesture of friendship. When the Kiowa chief crossed his legs and then placed his hands on his knees, her eyes widened as she stared at his left hand. Its thumb was missing.

"How did he lose his thumb?" Leonida whispered, leaning closer to Pure Blossom so she would be the only one to hear.

"His story is that it happened as a child," Pure Blossom whispered back, "when he tried to free an imprisoned raccoon that had gotten ensnared in a white man's steel trap."

She cast a bitter look toward Leonida. "It is one of his forked tongue tales," she hissed. "I am sure he got it in a cowardly act, not a courageous one. It is impossible for Pure Blossom to see anything about him that is likable—or trusting. I have warned my brother to guard his words carefully while talking to the Kiowa chief."

They had reached the blanket. Leonida felt out of place as the Kiowa and Navaho warriors turned their eyes to her and Pure Blossom.

But following Pure Blossom's lead, she sat down on the blanket; Sage's sister gave her the spot beside Sage, on his right side. The Kiowa chief was on Sage's left. When he leaned out and stared directly into Leonida's eyes, she felt a foreboding in the pit of her stomach.

She looked quickly away from him, afraid, herself trusting him no more than Pure Blossom did. It was there in his eyes, the way they gleamed, that he was untrustworthy.

"You are aware that the white pony soldiers, led by Kit Carson, are perhaps dangerously close?" Sage said, trying to draw Chief Four Fingers's attention away from Leonida. Sage wished that Pure Blossom had not joined the council this time, bringing Leonida into the center of attention also. Yet he was glad to see Pure Blossom showing revived energy. It gave him hope that perhaps her end might be delayed.

He understood just how little his sister trusted the Kiowa chief. Little did she know that he trusted Four Fingers even less. He was just tolerating the Kiowa chief because it was best to have him as an ally at this time instead of an enemy. Sage would even ride beside Four Fingers if it meant ridding this land of the white pony soldiers. Only time would tell which was most necessary—tolerating the Kiowa chief or the white pony soldiers.

"We have seen Kit Carson and the white pony soldiers searching the land," Four Fingers said, turning his attention to Sage. "We rode quickly into hiding. Is it you he seeks? It was rumored that you walked away from the council you were having with Kit Carson and the others at the fort."

He puffed his bare chest out proudly. "Four Fingers did not go to council," he said smugly. "The humiliating words of the white man did not enter my ears and touch my heart. They did not reach as far as the mountains where I have my stronghold. There I stayed, minding my own business, leaving the white man to wonder how he can force this powerful Kiowa chief out of hiding." He chuckled low. "And so it is now that they are looking for you instead of Chief Four Fingers. Did it not prove who was the most wise between chiefs?"

Sage's jaw tightened and his eyes flashed in anger. "You speak loosely to this chief with whom you have come to trade," he said flatly. "Let us get it behind us so that you can return to your tepee and I can return to my hogan. The day is waning. I have other pleasures awaiting me than being with a chief whose words tire me."

They discussed trading, making bargains between themselves that suited both tribes of Indians well enough. And when Sage thought it was over and had risen to his full height, even having helped his sister and wife up from the blanket, he was stopped dead when Chief Four Fingers said: "This white woman, she is your slave? She is one of the captives that I heard you took from a stagecoach? She is pretty. I will pay much for her. She will make a delightful love slave."

Lightheadedness swept through Leonida at the Kiowa's words. She reached for Sage and clung to him, glad when he felt her distress and placed a comforting, possessive arm around her waist, to steady her against his side.

"This woman you speak of is my wife," Sage said, glaring at Chief Four Fingers. "Do not speak of her again to me." He gave Leonida a comforting glance, then turned to the Kiowa chief again. "Your horses are now loaded with the supplies you have traded for. It is best that you leave.''

Chief Four Fingers stepped around Sage and took it upon himself to touch Leonida's hair, sighing at its utter softness, and then he gazed into her eyes again, giving her a slow, sure smile.

Then he turned abruptly and left.

Sage held Leonida close until they could no longer see the Kiowa descending the mountainside.

''I'm frightened,'' Leonida said, trembling. ''Did you see the way he looked at me? He does not seem the sort to take no for an answer.''

''Chief Four Fingers needs the alliance of the Navaho too much to do anything foolish that might harm their peace,'' Sage said, swinging her around so that he could hold her in his arms. ''Do not fret so. While you are in my village, among my people, nothing will happen to you.'' He looked in all directions, then into Leonida's eyes again. ''My sentries are posted well. They would let no one get past them, especially Chief Four Fingers, if he is caught sneaking about.''

A sudden soft cry next to them drew them apart. Leonida stifled a scream behind her hand when she discovered that Pure Blossom had fainted and lay sprawled out on the blanket, looking more dead than alive.

Sage fell to his knees beside Pure Blossom and whisked her slight form up into his arms. ''I will take her to her hogan,'' he said across his shoulder to Leonida. ''Go to ours. I will return when my sister awakens. Stay in the hogan, my woman. You will be safe there.''

The fact that he was ordering her to stay in the hogan made Leonida realize that he did not trust that she was safe from Chief Four Fingers all that much, either.

The thought of Four Fingers even getting near her, much less touching her, made shivers of dread envelop her.

"Let me go with you," she pleaded, hurrying after him. "Perhaps I can help."

"You must be at the hogan for Runner," Sage said, again over his shoulder. "He was among the children moments ago, watching the council. He is probably in our hogan now, awaiting your return. We do not want to give him cause to become frightened. Go to him. Stay with him."

Realizing that Sage was right, Leonida stopped and watched him carry Pure Blossom into her hogan, then turned and headed hurriedly toward hers. She glanced all around her, seeing the shadows deepening as the sun sank behind the high cliffs around the village.

Again she shivered, hurrying toward the hogan. She would be counting the minutes with her every heartbeat until Sage returned to her and she could find a safe refuge within his powerful arms.

18

How small a part of time they share,
That are so wondrous, sweet and fair.
—EDMUND WALLER

Runner smelled clean from his bath as Leonida bent over him and drew a soft blanket up to his chin. She then kissed his brow and smoothed his black hair back from his face. "How sweet you are," she whispered, touched by how he had listened so intently to her latest bedtime tale. She knew that soon she would have to start teaching him more than made-up tales. Since he would never have the opportunity to go to school, she would be responsible for giving him an education. Having been fortunate enough to have a thorough education herself, she knew even more than the fundamentals of English, mathematics, and . . .

A noise in the outer room catapulted Leonida's thoughts elsewhere. "Sage," she whispered. "Finally, he's returned home."

Anxious to find out how Pure Blossom was, she turned and walked briskly from Runner's room, but stopped abruptly and gasped when she discovered Chief Four Fingers and two of his warriors.

Leonida's knees grew rubbery and a scream froze in her throat when a third Kiowa warrior stepped up behind her and clasped his fingers around her mouth, his other arm grabbing her tightly around her waist.

Fear gripped her heart. She was too stunned to think

straight, and then suddenly something seemed to snap inside her brain, releasing her from her fears. Finding the courage and strength to fight back, she pulled on the man's hand that covered her mouth but couldn't budge it. She grabbed and pulled at the arm locked around her waist. She kicked at him, but nothing caused him to loosen his hold on her.

Knowing that she was wasting her energy, which she might need later in her attempts to escape, Leonida stopped struggling and glared at Chief Four Fingers as he moved stealthily toward her. Her heart was pounding at the thought that perhaps the whole village was at the mercy of his warriors, the fear that perhaps even now Sage lay dead.

The thought sickened her, yet she bravely held her chin up, her eyes looking unwaveringly into the Kiowa chief's. She reminded herself that she had not heard any gunfire in the village or any commotion which might mean that the Navaho people had been taken by surprise in their sleep.

This gave her hope that perhaps she was the only victim tonight.

Her heart skipped a beat when she remembered Runner asleep in the next room. Should he awaken and come into the outer room to see what was happening, surely the Kiowa would kill him for his interference.

"No one denies Chief Four Fingers anything," the Kiowa chief said. He held a rifle in one hand, and with his free hand he traced the outline of one of Leonida's breasts with a forefinger, causing her to shudder with distaste. "Four Fingers wants a white woman slave? He takes her."

Four Fingers stepped back from Leonida, smiling devilishly at her, and in what seemed a flash, she was gagged with a bright neckerchief and wrapped in the rabbit-fur cloak that had cushioned her back while Sage made love to her. A Kiowa warrior secured it around her with long strings of animal-hide rope.

Totally disabled by the cloak, Leonida could not fight back when she was lifted onto the shoulder of one of the warriors and carried like a bundle of potatoes toward the door. The last thing she saw in the hogan was the squash blossom necklace which had broken and fallen from her neck during her struggles.

And then she was outside. She strained her neck to look around to see if anyone else was being taken hostage. Seeing no one, she knew that Chief Four Fingers had dared to enter Sage's village only for her. She had to wonder why the sentries had not stopped the silent midnight invasion. Sage had placed several in strategic places. It seemed impossible that the Kiowa warriors could have gotten past them.

As she was carried hurriedly into the shadows of the hogans, she peered anxiously toward Pure Blossom's hogan, knowing that Sage must still be there. Tears of frustration stung her eyes as she was then carried on away from the village. Soon she saw the outlines of horses and other warriors just ahead of her.

Then spirals of despair swam through her when beneath the light of the moon she could see more than one Navaho sentry lying dead, arrows piercing their backs. Now she understood how the Kiowa could have gotten away with the abduction. They had killed everyone who had gotten in the way.

As she was laid over the back of a horse and secured there with a rope, Leonida realized that Chief Four Fingers did not want an alliance with Sage and his people any longer, or he would not risk losing it over the abduction of a woman.

Now tied onto the horse, hanging over its back, Leonida found her head spinning, the blood flowing quickly to it. When the horse began traveling down the steep incline, a keen dizziness overcame Leonida.

She soon drifted off into a black void of nothingness.

Sage felt hopeful for his sister again when her breathing became easier and more even. Finally she lay on her platform, sleeping soundly. He stayed on his knees a moment longer and watched Pure Blossom sleeping, remembering her when she was a small child, even then battling all sorts of ailments. His mother had told him that it did not appear that Pure Blossom's health would ever be strong and had warned him even then that she might not live past three years.

"My sweet sister, you fooled them all," he whispered, stroking her cool brow with his fingers. "Even now you tease death and are victorious. Perhaps you will live to see my children? Little one, that would make your brother happy."

When she emitted a shaky sigh and turned to lie on her side in a fetal position, Sage made sure the blankets were still fully covering her, drawing them up over her, smoothing them out just beneath her chin.

"I think I can leave you now," he whispered as he rose to his full height next to the sleeping platform. "My wife has been without her husband long enough. When the sun replaces the moon in the sky I shall return and check on you again."

Anxious to be with Leonida, always desiring her as though it were their first moments together, Sage left Pure Blossom's hogan and hastened his steps until he entered his own dwelling. A soft fire was burning in the fire pit as he walked past it. He stopped and looked into Runner's room, smiling when he found that the child was fast asleep.

Stopping just outside his bedroom door, he stepped out of his breechclout and moccasins. He smiled down at himself, seeing how aroused he had become at only thinking of her. Perhaps he would awaken her and let her see how he hungered for her even at this midnight hour. Surely she would want him as much.

His loins on fire with desire, Sage walked on into his bedroom, having decided that he must awaken her. He could not wait until morning to quench his passions.

When Sage looked over at the empty sleeping platform, he stopped short. Where was she?

Not believing she could be gone, Sage rushed to the sleeping platform and gazed down at it with wide, worried eyes. Then he spun around and raced back to the outer room, looking frantically around him.

He stopped when he discovered the squash blossom necklace on the mats beside the fire. His pulse racing, he swept the necklace up from the floor and spread it out between his fingers, inspecting it. His eyes locked on the break, and he realized that only a struggle would have caused such a break. Leonida had not just wandered away from the hogan.

She had been abducted!

He dropped the necklace to the floor and began pacing in agitation. "Who would do this?" he growled, his fists tight at his sides.

He recalled the time when Harold had grabbed the necklace from Leonida and had forbidden her to wear it. Seeing the broken necklace reminded him that the white man just might do anything to get Leonida back, perhaps even risk entering the village alone to achieve his foolish goal.

"But he knows not where the village is," he said, kneading his brow feverishly.

He stopped and his jaw tightened. "Chief Four Fingers," he said, his teeth clenched. "He desired her. Has he risked everything to have her?"

A rush of feet in the hogan made Sage spin around to see who had entered, hoping it was Leonida. Instead he saw two breathless Navaho warriors standing there, their eyes filled with anguish.

"What brings you to my hogan this late?" Sage asked, fearing the answer.

"All of our sentries have been slain," Spotted Feather said in a rush of words. "It was time for change in sentries. All those who went to relieve the others found death on the mountain. They are all dead, Sage. All of them had Kiowa arrows in their backs."

Sage was taken aback by this news. Despair and anger fused within him. He shook his head back and forth, not wanting to envision his friends all dead, or wanting to think that his beloved was now in the hands of those who betrayed him.

"My wife has been abducted," he said, turning to grab his clothes. He hurried into his breechclout and moccasins, then yanked his rifle from where he had leaned it against the wall. "Gather together many warriors. We must go after Four Fingers. He is responsible for this."

"It is such an unwise thing to do," Black Thunder

GET UP TO
4 FREE BOOKS!

You can have the best romance delivered to your door for less than what you'd pay in a bookstore or online. Sign up for one of our book clubs today, and we'll send you **FREE* BOOKS** just for trying it out...**with no obligation to buy, ever!**

HISTORICAL ROMANCE BOOK CLUB

Travel from the Scottish Highlands to the American West, the decadent ballrooms of Regency England to Viking ships. Your shipments will include authors such as CONNIE MASON, CASSIE EDWARDS, LYNSAY SANDS, LEIGH GREENWOOD, and many, many more.

LOVE SPELL BOOK CLUB

Bring a little magic into your life with the romances of Love Spell—fun contemporaries, paranormals, time-travels, futuristics, and more. Your shipments will include authors such as KATIE MACALISTER, SUSAN GRANT, NINA BANGS, SANDRA HILL, and more.

As a book club member you also receive the following special benefits:

- **30% OFF all orders through our website & telecenter!**
  (Plus, you still get 1 book FREE for every 5 books you buy!)
- **Exclusive access to special discounts!**
- **Convenient home delivery and 10 days to return any books you don't want to keep.**

There is no minimum number of books to buy, and you may cancel membership at any time. See back to sign up!

*Please include $2.00 for shipping and handling.

YES! ☐

Sign me up for the **Historical Romance Book Club** and send my TWO FREE BOOKS! If I choose to stay in the club, I will pay only $8.50* each month, a savings of $5.48!

YES! ☐

Sign me up for the **Love Spell Book Club** and send my TWO FREE BOOKS! If I choose to stay in the club, I will pay only $8.50* each month, a savings of $5.48!

NAME: _____

ADDRESS: _____

_____

TELEPHONE: _____

E-MAIL: _____

☐ **I WANT TO PAY BY CREDIT CARD.**

☐ VISA   ☐ MasterCard   ☐ DISCOVER

ACCOUNT #: _____

EXPIRATION DATE: _____

SIGNATURE: _____

Send this card along with $2.00 shipping & handling for each club you wish to join, to:

Romance Book Clubs
1 Mechanic Street
Norwalk, CT 06850-3431

Or fax (must include credit card information!) to: 610.995.9274.
You can also sign up online at www.dorchesterpub.com.

*Plus $2.00 for shipping. Offer open to residents of the U.S. and Canada only.
Canadian residents please call 1.800.481.9191 for pricing information.

If under 18, a parent or guardian must sign. Terms, prices and conditions subject to change. Subscription subject
to acceptance. Dorchester Publishing reserves the right to reject any order or cancel any subscription.

JOIN NOW!

said, walking from the hogan with Sage and Spotted Feather. "And all for a woman? I see her as special also, Sage, but to destroy peace over her? It is not something I will ever understand."

Sage turned to his warriors. He clasped his hands on Black Thunder's shoulders. "It is not hard to see why he chanced all for my woman," he said, his voice drawn. "First, I denied her to him. Second, he realizes that Kit Carson and the white pony soldiers are near, and perhaps he thinks our time of camaraderie has been outlived. He has taken my woman and will ride even farther than the mountains. He is fleeing life as he has always known it, believing it is gone anyhow. He no longer sees a need for an alliance with the Navaho. Taking my woman was a way to throw sand in my face to say that he is no longer my friend and ally, but as before, my archenemy."

"He is foolish," Spotted Feather mumbled, and Black Thunder nodded in agreement. "Never can he outrun the Navaho."

"Yes, that is so," Sage said. "We will overcome them soon. But we must be cautious in how we approach them. Getting my wife back is more important than how many Kiowa we kill."

Sage's thoughts went to those warriors who had been killed. He ordered Spotted Feather to take others with him to return the dead to the stronghold.

Black Thunder rushed away to awaken many other warriors.

Once he saw that his orders were being carried out, Sage stamped away toward the corral. It was hard to control the rage that was searing his insides, yet for his woman he had to keep a level head.

Her survival depended on him.

And he would not allow himself to think that the

Kiowa chief would take the time to stop to ravage his woman. He would keep thinking that her body would be left pure, to be touched only by her husband.

19

Singing and loving—all come back together.
—COLERIDGE

With his bow slung over his left shoulder, his wildcat quiver of arrows poisoned with rattlesnake blood secured at his right, and his rifle sheathed at the side of his horse, Sage was ready to travel. He was not taking the time to share war songs with his warriors, or even to dress in his thick buckskin war shirt. He had stopped only to eat dried yucca for energy. Haste was of the essence, for the longer he tarried, the farther his wife was being carried away from him.

He was already riding through his village when a thought struck him. He brought his horse to a stop, his warriors following his lead, when he remembered Runner all alone in his hogan. If he awakened and found no one there, he would become alarmed and feel as though he were orphaned all over again.

Sage quickly explained to his warriors, then urged his horse into a hard gallop until he reached his hogan. Dismounting in a bound, he gazed over at Pure Blossom's dwelling. Most people of the village had been awakened by the noise of the departing warriors. All but Pure Blossom. He looked at her hogan but still saw no signs of her at the door, and he did not think it wise to awaken her. She needed the rest. And she was not well enough now to look after a young boy full of spirit and spunk.

"Then who?" Sage mumbled to himself, staring at the door of his hogan.

"You've returned because you are worried about Trevor?"

The gentle, friendly voice behind Sage made him turn around with a start. He was stunned when he found who it was. His jaw tightened and his eyes narrowed. Because of prejudice, this woman had turned her back a second time to his wife. She had also refused Runner a friendship with Adam—Runner, who was innocent in every way.

And now she was showing concern? Somehow he did not trust her.

"Yes, I have returned because of my son, and I do not have time to talk with you," Sage grumbled.

Sally lowered her eyes, then lifted them stubbornly up again. "I know you have no time to waste," she said hurriedly. "That's why I came to you. I am offering to watch Trevor for you while you go and search for Leonida." She swallowed hard. "I feel terrible about what has happened. Terrible."

"And so you should," Sage scolded. He looked past her at his waiting warriors, then put a hand to her shoulder. "I accept your offer. Watch over this boy I now call my son." He lowered his hand from her shoulder and leaned down into Sally's face. "But never call him Trevor again. He carries with him a Navaho name because he is the son *of* a Navaho."

He straightened his back slowly, his eyes watching her expression for signs that meant that he still could not trust her.

But she showed no visible signs of resistance. She seemed accepting now of Runner's new lot in life, and perhaps even of this man who now called himself the boy's father.

"Please go on," Sally said, smoothing her hands down the front of her dress. "I promise to look closely after Runner and call him by the name you've chosen for him."

Sage nodded, placed a hand of friendship on her shoulder again, then left in a run toward his stallion. He mounted his horse in one leap and rode away, his men soon following after him.

When they reached narrow mountain passages, Sage risked everything by not stopping to walk the horse to safer footings. His stallion knew the way. His steed's hooves stayed firm on the narrow, slippery path until once again they reached a stretch of stone that was wider and safer.

Determined to catch up with Four Fingers, Sage gave his horse no rest. He pushed him farther and farther, and his stallion seemed to understand the desperation of its master in the way it galloped steadfastly onward, snorting white clouds of air from its flaring nostrils.

Crouching low on his horse, Sage raced through the twilight of morning as it became evident in the lightening skies overhead. He knew that they should be reaching the base of the mountain now, and he feared finding Kit Carson somewhere close by.

Yet Sage could not let this worry stop him. The life of his woman was at stake. If he allowed anything to happen to her, his future would be gray and lifeless. So would it be the same for his people. Without his woman at his side, he would no longer be the leader they needed to keep their lives meaningful.

When flat land stretched out before him, shadowed by the hazy morning light, Sage rode onward. He knew of a place where Chief Four Fingers might have stopped to rest and eat, a place that Sage had so often used himself before tackling the steep sides of the mountain to get to his stronghold. It was another canyon, only a short ride away, where a waterfall splashed and fish were in abundance in a mountain stream. If Four Fingers had been at all careless or had misjudged the amount of time it would take Sage and his warriors to follow, then Sage was in luck.

His pulse raced, hoping that Four Fingers had not yet had the chance to touch Leonida.

If so, Sage would make Four Fingers' death agonizingly slow.

Four Fingers would beg for the poison arrow to be shot into his heart.

Leonida was only slightly aware that her horse stopped. She was still drifting in and out of consciousness, her head pounding from having been forced to hang low for so many hours. She looked dazedly over at a Kiowa warrior as he came and untied the ropes that held her on the horse's back. She sighed with relief when he laid her on the ground, even though she was fearful of what might happen to her next.

She was fully awake now.

She glared up at Four Fingers as he came and stood over her, his legs outstretched, his fists on his hips. The gag was removed from her lips, and another warrior untied the rope that held the hot, clinging rabbit fur against her body. When that also fell away from her, and her pores were allowed to breathe again, and she had inhaled enough breath to give a reprieve to her throat, Leonida tried to scamper to her feet, then fell clumsily back to the ground, weak from having been tied so awkwardly on the horse for so long.

"Your legs will become strong again," Chief Four Fingers said, sinking to his haunches before Leonida. He reached a hand toward her, chuckling when she raised a hand and knocked his away. "The white woman is not only beautiful, but she also has spirit. This is perhaps why Sage chose you over women of his own coloring to be his wife? Does your spirit exceed that of women of Sage's village? Has it been put to a true test?"

"I will tell you nothing," Leonida said, her throat parched from the need of water.

"That matters not to me," Four Fingers said, shrugging. "Words from a white woman are foolish and unimportant. And as for testing, once you are among the Kiowa women, they will test you plenty."

He grabbed her wrists and held them immobile as he lowered his lips toward hers. "Now? Let Chief Four Fingers test your ability to kiss," he said huskily. "After your strength has returned, your skills at love-making will be thoroughly tested by Four Fingers, and then by those of my warriors who desire to see how a white woman might compare with a Kiowa squaw, in all ways sexual."

His threats made Leonida shiver. She was going to be used by many men? If Sage ever found her, she would not be fit ever again to be his wife. She would be too defiled, perhaps even ripped apart.

As Four Fingers' lips covered hers, she struggled to get free but found him too strong. She could not budge him.

As his kiss deepened, she tried to blank out the moment, pretending it was not happening. Tears streamed from her eyes as he lowered her to the ground. One of his hands now held her wrists together over her head, and his other hand moved up her velveteen skirt. When his hand covered her womanhood and pressed down against it, his middle finger seeking entrance inside her, she wanted to die. She tried to kick her feet but realized now that they were being held down by warriors on each side of her. They were forcing her legs farther apart, making her more accessible to Four Fingers' probings.

When two other warriors came to kneel on the ground on each side of her head, each one taking one of her hands and holding it on the ground, she stiffened and readied herself for the assault that was near. She wrenched her lips from Four Fingers' mouth and turned away, trembling with fear when his free hand swept up her blouse and cupped one of her breasts, his thumb circling the nipple.

After this was all finished, she vowed, she would find a way to steal a knife.

She would kill Four Fingers first, and then herself.

For now she would concentrate on the peaceful sound of the water splashing down from the waterfall.

She would concentrate on the smell of the wildflowers that dotted the banks of the stream.

She would imagine herself somewhere else, floating, free and pure again, and held in the protective embrace of Sage's powerful arms.

Suddenly her eyes opened wide. Four Fingers jumped away from her. The warriors who had been holding her immobile were all running toward their horses, left watering at the stream.

"Sage!" the sentries shouted as they came running into the camp. "Sage has been spotted. He brings more warriors than we have to fight him off! We must flee! Now!"

Hope filled Leonida in warm splashes, and tears streamed from her eyes.

Sage.

Wonderful Sage.

He was going to rescue her.

But she had to help him. She had to get away from the Kiowa before they had a chance to grab her and put her on one of their horses.

No matter how hard she tried to get up, though, her knees buckled from weakness and she fell back to the ground, breathless. Desperate to get away from the Kiowa, she began crawling toward a nearby boulder.

As she did, she kept looking guardedly behind her, waiting to be discovered. But the Kiowa seemed to have forgotten her. They hurriedly mounted their horses and rode away.

As Sage came into the camp, he got a last glimpse of the fleeing Kiowa. Anger grabbing at his pounding heart, he urged his horse into a faster gallop.

His hands strung his bow without conscious willing. The arrow leaped to the string almost by itself. His hands and arms worked methodically together.

He drew the arrow to the head and released. The twang of the bow echoed and the arrow soared through the air. Pride seized Sage when he saw the arrow pierce the back of a Kiowa warrior, and he strung his bow again as he raced onward, another Kiowa warrior in sight.

Leonida pulled herself up against the rock, steadying her back against it, panic racing through her as she saw Sage and his warriors rush on past her without having seen her.

"Sage!" she screamed, stumbling after the rush of the mounted warriors.

To her, the world seemed a roar of hooves, the Navaho leaning forward over their horse's necks, their mouths wide, shouting "E-e-e-e."

Again Leonida screamed Sage's name, her arms outstretched before her. "Please, Sage," she cried. "Oh, darling, it is I, Leonida. Please hear me."

Above the staccato of the horse's hooves, Sage heard his name being called. And then he recognized the voice.

He whipped his head to the side and saw Leonida stumbling along in the path of the swirling dust.

Swinging his bow back in place across his shoulder, he wheeled his horse around. He raised his fist in the air, stopping his warriors. There was no longer any need to follow the Kiowa. Now that he had found his woman safe and sound, he must make haste to hide in the folds of his mountain again.

After his warriors had drawn their steeds to a halt, Sage rode on past them. When he reached Leonida he stopped and dismounted, quickly drawing her into his arms.

"Sage, oh, Sage," Leonida whispered, clinging to him and sobbing. "I feared I would never see you again. Thank the Lord you found me."

He held her close, yet he had seen the disarray of her clothes. He ran his fingers through her tangled hair. "They did not touch you wrongly, did they?" he asked, his voice breaking.

"No," she murmured, almost choking on another sob at the thought that he had arrived just in time. She did not tell him that, not wanting to kindle his rage any more. It was enough now that he was there and she was safe again in his arms.

"I will take you home," Sage said, whisking her up into his arms, carrying her toward his horse.

She looked adoringly up at him, so grateful that he was hers—her husband.

20

I break all slighter bonds, nor feel
A shadow of regret.
—ADELAIDE ANNE PROCTER

Having dozed comfortably snuggled in Sage's arms on his stallion on the return home, Leonida did not even awaken when Sage drew his horse to a halt, then dismounted, lifting her into his arms again, and carried her into their hogan.

The fire had gone out in the fire pit, and daylight had turned to night again. Sage felt his way through the hogan until he reached their bedroom. He then gently laid Leonida on their sleeping platform. He bent low over her and kissed her brow, then drew a blanket up over her.

Sage reluctantly left her side to go to the outer room to build a fire. Bending on one knee, he began laying twigs on the cold ashes of the fire pit, and once he had them lit, he placed thicker logs across the flames. Settling back on a soft mat, he stared at the fire, broodingly. His jaw tightened at the thought of having allowed Four Fingers to escape.

Stealing a man's wife was a crime punishable by death. One day Sage would see that this punishment was carried out.

"Sage? Darling?"

Leonida's voice behind him drew Sage from his troubled thoughts. Pushing himself up from the floor to go to her, Sage was suddenly startled when Leonida emitted an ear-splitting scream. His eyes were wild as he rushed toward Runner's bedroom.

He was moved deeply by what he found.

Leonida was on her knees, her arms stretched across Runner's bed, her fingers clawing at his blankets.

"He's gone," she wailed. She turned woefully toward Sage. "Why didn't you tell me that he also was abducted?"

Sage went to her and knelt down beside her. Placing his hands on her waist, he drew her to her feet before him, then eased her into his arms, gently hugging her. "Darling, our son was not taken captive," he said as he ran his fingers through her golden hair. "He is with Sally. She offered to watch over him while I was gone searching for you."

He could feel her muscles relax, yet she still clung to him. "Darling," he murmured, "you have nothing to fear now. You are safe. Runner is safe. Put all fears from your heart. Do you not feel the protection of my arms? Never will I allow another man near you. You must trust this promise."

Leonida swallowed hard. She forced a smile, not wanting Sage to know that it would take some time for her to get over the trauma of the near rape. It *was* wonderful to be back in Sage's arms, yet she knew that even his promises could not totally protect her. She had thought that she was safe from all harm earlier, and hadn't the Kiowa warriors taken her so easily?

"You know that I trust you," she murmured, hoping to sound convincing enough. "And I know that your promises are spoken from the bottom of your heart, as are all of your words spoken to me. I love you, Sage, for loving me so much. I love you for coming after me when I thought that I might never see you again."

He placed a gentle finger to her lips, silencing further words. "A thank-you is not necessary for everything I do or say."

"It is that I am just so grateful," Leonida murmured as his finger slipped from her mouth. Her heart thumped wildly as Sage lowered his lips toward hers. "I do love you so . . ."

Her words faded as his mouth covered hers with a deep kiss. She twined her arms around his neck as he lifted her into his arms and began carrying her out of Runner's bedroom. She trembled with ecstasy when one of his hands slipped around and cupped her breast. Then she tensed when she suddenly recalled other hands on her breasts, and how she had been forced to spread her legs, unwillingly submitting to Chief Four Fingers' probing fingers and hands.

Tears swelled in her eyes at these ugly remembrances and she drew her lips from Sage, turning her head away from him, one of her hands brushing his away from her breast. Somehow she could not help but feel contaminated. How could she ever feel the joyous bliss she had felt before with Sage?

Sage's eyes widened and his insides tightened as he gazed down at her. She was refusing his kiss. She had even brushed his hand from her breast, which she had never done before.

It meant only one thing. The Kiowa had touched her. They had, in a sense, branded her. She might never be the same.

Not wanting to allow these memories to continue, Sage carried Leonida to their sleeping platform and lay her gently on it. He knew the importance of making love to her now. If he waited, she might dwell too much on the ugliness of having been touched wrongly by the Kiowa, and forget the beauty she had shared with her husband.

She had already told him that she had not been raped. In that respect, she was still pure. But it was the touching, the fondling, that he now was almost certain she had been forced to endure at the hands of the Kiowa.

This he must erase from her mind, as though it had never happened.

Sage stood over Leonida and removed his clothes and moccasins. And although she looked wildly up at him and stiffened when he began undressing her, nothing would stop him.

He must make love to her now.

Leonida shivered at the cold air of the hogan against her bare flesh. She hugged herself with her arms, covering her breasts, which seemed lifeless now that she allowed herself to remember that the enemy had touched them. She guardedly watched Sage as he came to the sleeping platform with her, finding it hard to understand why he would force lovemaking on her at such a time. He knew that she did not want to do it. Was he going to force her to scream at him, and tell him why?

"Sage," she murmured, brushing his hand aside as he placed it on the bare flesh of her hip. "Please don't. I'm too tired. I . . . I need to rest."

"My woman, tomorrow might be too late for you," Sage said, determinedly putting his hand back on her hip, his fingers softly stroking her tender flesh as they moved inch by inch around to where the center of her passion lay. "You must allow me to make love to you tonight so that you can forget that which makes you draw away from me. Tonight my loving you will make tomorrow come with pleasant memories, not those that are soiled by the Kiowa.''

He moved over her, spreading her legs with a knee. His one hand was now stroking her throbbing center, his other gently kneading a breast. He smiled to himself when its nipple hardened and strained against the palm of his hand. She was awakened to her feelings for him again. He was succeeding at arousing her!

Both of his hands cupped her breasts. He leaned lower against her, the touch of her breasts against his chest momentarily stealing his breath away.

Leonida could not fight the euphoria that was claiming her, so glad that her breasts were responding to the wonders of his touch. When his swollen shaft began probing at the juncture of her thighs, she willingly opened herself to him.

She gasped with pleasure when he lunged his hardness inside her and he began his rhythmic thrusts. Her body responded, as her hips lifted and fell, meeting him stroke by stroke.

She twined her fingers through his thick black hair and urged his lips to hers. When he kissed her, she returned the kiss in a frenzy. Tears of joy streamed from her eyes. She was so glad that the wild splendor was still there while she was being loved by her husband.

Slowly the remembrances of those ugly moments with the Kiowa were fading away.

Pleasure was spreading in warm splashes through Sage. He knew by her response that his plan had worked, and that she was lost in ecstasy now, instead of doubts and fears about being with a man again sexually.

He moved his mouth from her lips and swept his

tongue around one of her nipples, drawing a gurgling sound of delight from the depths of her throat.

He suckled the nipple and tongued it again, then lay his cheek on her magnificent bosom, the fire raging higher and higher within his loins. He was near to experiencing the height of pleasure with his woman again, and he felt blessed. The gods were still favoring them as a couple.

Leonida wrapped her legs around his waist, locking her ankles together in an effort to draw him even more deeply into her. She closed her eyes in rapture, feeling how he so wonderfully filled her. In and out he moved, each time reaching more deeply, each time stroking her with more ambition and heat.

She placed her fingers on his buttocks, unknowingly digging her fingernails into his flesh as the pleasure spread . . . and spread . . . and spread.

She tossed her head and moaned as the height of pleasure was finally reached. She clung to his rock hardness as his body shook and quivered into hers, accepting the spilling of his seed as it splashed into the depths of her womanhood.

A child.

She hoped that tonight they had made a child, a brother or sister to Runner.

Afterwards, they lay snuggled together. Leonida was stroking his perspiration-laced back. "I know that you have told me not to thank you for anything," she whispered. "But, darling, I can't help but thank you for what you did tonight. I understand why you were determined that we make love."

He whisked her into his arms and gave her a kiss filled with heat, his body arching against hers as he drew her against him. Again he plunged himself into her. This time she responded without any hesitation, or with any thought of why she had ever shied away from him even for a moment.

Having succumbed to the need for sleep, Chief Four Fingers and his warriors had stopped and were now sleeping soundly in a canyon, unaware that they had been surrounded by soldiers. When the chief felt the nudge of a rifle barrel in his back, he awakened with a start, then slowly turned and looked up and saw Kit Carson standing over him. A soldier beside him held a rifle aimed at the Kiowa chief.

A commotion drew his gaze away. He scowled when he discovered his sentries being herded into the camp at gunpoint, their hands raised high into the air.

"Got a mite careless, didn't you, Chief?" Kit said, chuckling low as Chief Four Fingers emitted a growl of anger. "I've had a hell of a time finding the Navaho. *You've* just handed yourself over to us on a silver platter, it seems. That's not like you, Four Fingers. I'd have thought you'd be the last Indian this easy to find. But it's about time. I've wanted the Kiowa no less than the Navaho. Once you're all rounded up neat like, I expect the settlers will be able to sleep at night without their fingers wrapped around the barrel of a shotgun."

"Get to your feet, Injun," Lieutenant Nelson ordered Four Fingers. "You've a long way to travel to get to the reservation. You might as well get started now while the sun is low in the morning sky. You'll be wishin' for the shade of a canyon again soon enough."

Chief Four Fingers moved slowly to his feet, looking guardedly around him, then glared down at Kit Carson. "Let us have council between us," he said, his voice devoid of emotion. "There is information Four Fingers can trade with you in exchange for Four

Fingers' freedom. My band of Kiowa is less in number than Sage's Navaho. Would you not rather capture them instead?''

Carson looked up at Four Fingers. ''It is my intention to place the Kiowa *and* the Navaho on reservations,'' he said blandly. ''It is not my intention to make a bargain with one for the other. So, no council this time.'' He motioned with his head toward the other herded-up Kiowa. ''Join the others. As of today, your rank is no greater than those others who will walk the many miles with you to the reservation in New Mexico.''

Chief Four Fingers' eyes narrowed. He leaned down closer to Kit Carson's face. ''The white woman who is now married to the Navaho Sage is not worth bargaining over?'' he hissed. ''Chief Four Fingers can direct you to Sage's stronghold, where this woman and other white captives are being held. Is not that information worth the release of us few Kiowa? What harm can we wreak on the white pony soldiers in comparison to what Sage has already done? Give your word that I and my warriors can ride freely onward, then I give my word to you that I will give you accurate directions to Sage's stronghold.''

Carson's eyes widened with interest. He kneaded his chin, his eyes locked with the Kiowa chief's. ''You say that Leonida is now Sage's wife?'' he asked, confused by this bit of news. ''How do you know this?''

''Chief Four Fingers trades with Sage,'' he said. ''I sought to trade for the beautiful white woman. Sage refused. He called her his wife. She spoke nothing against his declaration. So she is his wife.''

''You say you saw her,'' Carson said, inhaling a quivering sigh. ''That means you do know where Sage's stronghold is.''

Chief Four Fingers nodded. "That is so," he said, folding his arms across his chest. "I will give you directions. You will give me and my warriors freedom. Do you not think it is a fair enough exchange?"

Carson's eyes shifted, staring at the chief's hand on which he displayed only four fingers. Then he looked slowly up at the chief again. "I vowed long ago that if I ever caught up with you, I would hang you," he said. "Severing a finger from your hand was not enough vengeance for me for what you did so long ago against me. Although I have not written about it in my journals, and it is not something I have broadcasted for the world to know, my marriage to a lovely Indian maiden lasted only long enough for you to steal her away, rape her, and then leave her dying at my doorstep. I caught up with you after she told me who had done this to her, but it was a cursed day for me when you escaped after having only the one finger cut from your hand. I had meant for you to lose your fingers first, then suffer long and hard before I cut out your heart."

"That was long ago when we both were young and foolish," Four Fingers said, again unemotionally. "I had not yet been assigned my adult name. Because of you, I was appointed the name Four Fingers because it defined so well my appearance to those who would come across me on outings. So you see, white man who disfigured this Indian, at the age of twelve winters this act I am guilty of came as a careless prank of a youth trying to look big in the eyes of the older warriors. This was a challenge I could not say no to. If so, I would have been viewed as a woman in the eyes of the older warriors. I was next in line to be chief. I could not be labeled a 'woman' and be a chief in the same lifetime."

"Yes, I know all of that," Kit Carson said, his voice sounding exhausted.

"And you also know the worth of my information today about Sage's stronghold," Chief Four Fingers urged. "Forget the past transgressions of this Kiowa chief. This is today. Sage could be yours today. Is he not worth many times over one Kiowa chief and his few warriors?"

"Yes, it is true that you are worthless to me, except dead," Kit grumbled. "But right now you *are* more valuable to me alive." He leaned on his rifle, shaking his head at being forced into a decision that he did not like. But he had to put the women and children first.

"Tell me where Sage's stronghold is, and by God, I give my word that you can ride free," Kit said, inhaling a deep breath. "But you'd best ride hard and get hidden again, for once I am through with Sage, I'll be looking for you. The next time nothing anyone says will keep me from finally avenging the death of my beautiful Indian bride. Now, damn it, Four Fingers, draw me a map in the sand, then get the hell out of my sight."

Four Fingers knelt down beside Kit. He accepted a stick from a soldier and started drawing the directions to Sage's stronghold in the sand, then stopped, startled when Kit placed a firm hand on his wrist.

"You'd better be leading me to the right place," Kit drawled threateningly. "If not, Four Fingers, you'll have hell to pay once my men and I catch up with you again."

"Sage means nothing to me," Four Fingers reassured. He jerked his wrist free and began drawing again. "Except dead."

Once the map was completed and Kit Carson recognized the mountain, he was stunned. He had ridden past it many times. Not once had he seen the glint of a rifle barrel, or any sign of sentries on the cliffs, keeping watch. He looked suspiciously over at Four Fingers. "You are certain this is the mountain?" he questioned.

Four Fingers rose to his full height. He turned and pointed toward the purple haze of Sage's mountain in the distance. "Yonder, one half day's ride away, you will come to Sage's mountain," he said sternly. "There you will find peach trees, many fields of crops, and grazing sheep in a canyon at the foot of Sage's mountain." He turned to Kit. "Once there, it is up to you to decide how to reach Sage's stronghold. Chief Four Fingers can only do so much. Your pony soldiers must do the rest—if you wish badly enough to take Sage prisoner."

Kit Carson stepped back and allowed Four Fingers to walk away from him. He watched as the Kiowa chief mounted his horse, then rode away, his chin held high.

Kit hurriedly mounted and gave the orders to the soldiers. They rode long and hard, and when evening was drawing nigh, with its dark and brooding shadows across the land, Kit was finally at the base of the mountain.

Moving onward, Kit soon found the vast peach orchards, the fields, the grazing sheep. High above this valley was the true encampment of the Navaho.

Upon further investigation, Kit discovered it would be impossible to travel the paths that led so high up, into the Navaho camp, without being picked off one by one by the Navaho sentries. The straight cliff walls rose more than a thousand feet above the valley floor. Two hundred feet above the narrow valley floor, the Navaho had their permanent fortifications, which could not be reached by rifle or cannon fire. From these they could rain down arrows and heavy boulders on an invading enemy.

Kit studied his options and came to the conclusion that the only way to dislodge the Indians was to starve them out. He quickly decided to institute a "scorched earth" policy. He would burn the crops, destroy the orchards, and kill or capture the sheep.

As Kit saw it, it was not his business to kill the Navaho, but simply to move them. He would go about doing this in a way that would save the most lives. Instead of hunting down the Navaho any further, especially Sage, he would make them come to him.

He would make Sage give up his captives.

Kit turned to the soldiers. He raised his rifle in the air. "Go to work destroying, burning, and taking . . . !" he shouted.

21

We vowed we would never—no never forget,
And those vows at the time were consoling.
                              —MRS. CRAWFORD

Leonida was washing the wooden dishes in a basin of
water just outside her hogan door, glad that Pure Blossom had felt well enough to eat her morning meal.
Leonida already had food cooking for the noon meal,
having learned quickly that it was best to prepare meals
early in the morning instead of during the heat of the
day. On this mountaintop the sun was more intense,
and even the brisk breezes were not able to alleviate
the heat that it created.

"I will be in council with the elders the remainder
of the morning," Sage said as he stepped out of the
hogan, attired only in his breechclout and moccasins.
"Runner is at Adam's?"

Leonida turned to Sage, warming through and
through with the remembrances of what they had
shared throughout the entire night, it seemed.

"Yes," she murmured, drying her hands on the tail
end of her skirt. "He came home long enough to give
me a big hug, then ran back to Adam's lean-to. Sally
has changed. Not only is she allowing Runner in her
lean-to but she also allows several other young Navaho
braves. The braves are teaching Runner and Adam
some games."

She glanced up at the glaring sun, wiping a bead of
perspiration from her brow with the back of her hand.

"Those boys have the right idea," she said, laughing softly. She gave Sage a teasing smile. "Perhaps I will join them in their fun and games instead of working so hard."

Sage placed his hands at her waist and drew her against him and kissed her.

Leonida wrenched herself away from him, her face flooding with color as she looked guardedly from side to side. "Sage, not out here for everyone to see," she murmured. She then looked up at him, slowly smiling. "I'm not saying I don't want you to kiss me. I would even invite you back inside our hogan—that is, if you wish to postpone your council meeting until later."

"Your suggestion is tempting," Sage said, his eyes twinkling down into hers.

"Fire! Fire below!"

Those words, and the desperation in the voice of the Navaho sentry, sent spirals of chills up Leonida's spine.

She glanced quickly up at Sage, seeing fear in his eyes and knowing that the threat today was real, perhaps explosive.

Sage stiffened, knowing that fire was almost as bad an enemy as Chief Four Fingers, and now Kit Carson and his soldiers.

Fire could wipe out the entire crop of the Navaho. Fire could kill their sheep. Without those things his people could not survive.

Breaking away from Leonida, Sage met several of his warriors and ran with them through the village toward a cliff where they could look down upon the valley below. They saw wisps of smoke rising. Sage knew that the tall grass and brush surrounding the orchard, garden, and grazing pastures of the sheep were as dry as tinder, and a breeze was rising. In the freshening morning breeze, the whole valley could quickly become a raging bonfire.

Leonida broke into a mad run and caught up with Sage. "How could a fire get started?" she asked, breathless as she walked briskly to his side. "There has been no lightning. And it is midmorning. In the valley dew should still be on the grass."

"An enemy would start the fire purposefully to ruin the Navaho," Sage answered back, glaring down at Leonida. "There is only one enemy who knew where to set the fires. That is Four Fingers. I was wrong to allow him to escape my vengeance. Now he has gotten his, over the Navaho."

"I feel responsible!" Leonida cried, finding it hard to keep up with Sage as he stamped on toward the cliff. "Four Fingers wouldn't have become this bitter with you had it not been for his interest in me. I wish that I had stayed hidden from him when he came to trade with you. I should have known to. The moment he looked at me I knew what to expect from him. I shouldn't have lingered so that his interest in me would not soar to such ungodly heights."

Sage frowned at her. "Never blame yourself for what others do," he growled. "Your heart and your intentions are pure."

"I never meant anyone harm," Leonida said softly. "Especially you."

"Wait for me," Runner cried, running after Leonida and Sage. "I want to see. Let me see."

Sage's full attention was on the smoke billowing up past the cliff just ahead. He broke into a faster run as Leonida stopped and waited for Runner. Even though the child was almost too large for her to carry, she swept him into her arms.

A coldness seemed to seize Leonida's heart when

she saw more dark billows of smoke rise into the sky from the valley below. In her mind's eye she was remembering the peach trees in the valley, and the rich pastures, and large fields of corn, beans, and squash.

She was recalling the animals, both goats and sheep alike, that had grazed on the abundance of spring-fed grasses in the valley. These animals were surely now either dead or captured by the enemy.

It sickened her when she came to stand at Sage's side and peered over the ledge at the devastation below.

Everything was on fire.

There was a stiff breeze blowing. The brush in the thicket was powder-dry, and as it burned it set the tall grass afire. Flames were leaping high, the breeze sweeping them straight into the midst of the thicket. Animals were scattering, and then Leonida saw something else.

Soldiers.

She gasped. Even from this high vantage point she could recognize Kit Carson among those who were still setting fires along the valley, while others were beginning to round up the animals, herding them away from the fire.

"Kit Carson," Leonida gasped, her voice drawn. She looked quickly up at Sage. "Do you see? It's Kit Carson. It isn't Chief Four Fingers. Kit Carson found your stronghold."

Sage was watching the destruction, his muscles tight, knowing that there was nothing that could be done to stop the devastation below. It had begun too quickly for his warriors to go down the steep sides and paths of the mountain to kill the white pony soldiers. He could tell that Kit Carson had methodically scouted both sides of the canyon and had stationed soldiers to cut off the escape of the Navaho from any side exits. He was not trying to keep his troops concealed but was letting the Navaho see what he was doing. He knew that the Navaho were too high up on the buttes to be able to shoot and kill the soldiers.

Sage knew that Kit Carson was not clever enough to have found the stronghold of the Navaho. He had been led there by someone who knew where it was—and who hated Sage and his people. There was only one man: Chief Four Fingers.

Sage's hands tightened into fists at his sides, as he vowed revenge.

For now, there was only one thing to do. He would most definitely not bow down to defeat. He would go elsewhere and begin a new life.

Those who believed in him would follow. Those who did not would surrender to Kit Carson and allow themselves to be placed on a reservation where men became children again in their hearts, minds, and souls.

"Sage?" Leonida said, stepping closer to him. "Darling, you didn't answer me. What are we going to do?"

Sage turned to her, his eyes no less proud and confident than before he had seen the devastation below. "We are powerless against the fire," he said. "But I know an escape route on the back side of the mountain. I know another canyon, untouched and undiscovered by the white man. I will take my people there. Kit Carson will not have informants this time to lead him to the Navaho. Only I know of this place. I have kept it a secret within my heart just in case of such a tragedy as today's."

"Then you aren't devastated, darling, over this?" Leonida murmured, weaving her fingers through Runner's thick hair as he stared down at the fire below.

"What Kit Carson has done today is an act against all humanity, not just the Navaho," Sage said, his jaw tightening even harder. "It is a coward's act that destroys food, animals, and land. He thinks this will force us out, to beg for mercy at his feet? He is wrong. *He* is the one who will be *forced*—forced to live with his decisions today. The Navaho will be elsewhere, planting new crops. Somehow we will also find sheep to fill the fertile valleys of our new home. It will take time, but it will be done. My people will never have cause to lose hope in their future. Not as long as I am there to chart it."

Runner began coughing and rubbing his eyes. "I don't like the smoke," he whined. "Take me away from here."

Sage put an arm around Leonida's waist and led her away from the cliff. His warriors followed, their expressions drawn, some even looking as though they had lost not only crops and animals but also hope.

Leonida felt drawn to them as never before, wanting to be able to help them in their time of hardship and loss. But she couldn't find the words to say to them, and she thought perhaps that was best. Her skin was white. Those who were destroying the Navaho's crops and animals were white. The Navaho just might decide that she was at fault somehow, because of her presence in their village.

They might look to her as a bad omen—as bad luck.

As they entered the village, Leonida eased Runner from her arms and watched as he joined the silent group of children. Everyone had left their hogans, stopping to stand in a circle in the center of the village, around Sage and Leonida.

Leonida looked slowly around her, feeling out of place as the Navaho were standing so quietly, gazing only at Sage, looking desperately to their chief for guidance. She was glad when he once again placed a comforting arm around her waist, as though he sensed her uneasiness.

"My people, this is a day we shall look back upon with much anguish in our hearts," Sage finally said, his voice booming above the silence of the crowd. "But it is not the end of the Navaho. It is a beginning. It is a new beginning for those who put trust in me. Those who feel as though we have failed and do not want to try any longer—those who wish to surrender to the white man's ways—*go*! Go to them. Those who don't wish to submit to the white man's ways *ever,* flee with me to a place far away, known only by me. Live in peace and harmony with me and my family there! Those who wish to surrender to the white pony soldiers, go now without looking back. Those who wish to travel with me, go to your hogans and pack up your belongings. But make the load light on your horses. It is a dangerous path down the back side of the mountain to get us free of the white men. Make haste. We leave soon."

Leonida clung to Sage, scarcely breathing, as several of his people walked lifelessly away, their heads hung, toward the paths that led downward, to Kit Carson. It was apparent that they had given up—that they did not believe that such a place as Sage had described existed.

She watched as others rushed into their hogans, readying themselves for this new land of promise.

"Pure Blossom," Sage said, his tone worried. "I must find a way to travel with Pure Blossom so that she will be comfortable. The paths are narrow. It will be hard to travel with a travois. But that is the only way."

Sage turned to Leonida and framed her face between his hands. "I vow to you, my wife, that this is only the beginning of our happiness," he said. "No white man is going to win against Sage now or ever."

He sealed the promise with a kiss.

Leonida clung to him, yet she was so afraid, she felt sick to her stomach.

When he drew away from her and they started walking toward their hogan, another thought came to Leonida. She grabbed his arm and stopped him. "Darling, what about the captives?" she asked. "Are they going with us, or are you going to set them free and allow them to join Kit Carson? You did promise their release."

Sage glowered down at her. "Yes, I promised their release," he said, his voice flat. "But that was before Kit Carson decided to destroy all that is precious to the Navaho. So now Sage will keep that which is precious to those soldiers who have set the fires and who have stolen the Navaho animals. The captives will accompany us down the back side of the mountain. Those who live through the dangerous ordeal may be released at a later date. Those who die, die . . ."

Leonida paled at the tone of his voice. Never had she heard it so filled with hatred. She thought it best to say nothing against his decision, for deep down inside herself she understood.

Kit Carson paced back and forth, his hands clasped behind him, and watched the flames roar through the tall grasses. He flinched when he heard the scream of another animal dying amid the fire; he had not been able to save them all, as he had planned. A Navaho sheepherder stood by, blackened by the smoke, his eyes dull and empty as he stared in space.

"Damn it, Sage," Kit mumbled to himself, wiping beads of perspiration from his brow. "Why'd you force me to do this? Why?"

He stopped in his tracks when one of his soldiers began shouting, saying that some of the Navaho people had been seen on the paths, coming down from the mountain. It was obvious that they were surrendering.

Kit Carson mounted his horse and rode through the smoke and flames, up to the paths where there was clear passage. He maneuvered the steep, winding paths until he reached the first group of Navaho.

Swinging himself out of his saddle, nervously twining the reins around his fingers, he met the approach of the Navaho. "You are now my prisoners," he said stiffly, nodding at one of the soldiers who had accompanied him up the mountainside to place ropes around each of their waists so that they could walk in single file the rest of the way down the mountain. The fire was abating. The smoke was thinning. By the time they reached the charred valley, the fire should be completely out.

Kit Carson looked from one Navaho to the other. "Did your chief release the white captives?" he questioned. "Are they coming down behind you? Where's Sage? Is he also surrendering?"

He became disgruntled when no one offered a response. He could see that they remained loyal to their leader even though they had lost their freedom as they had always known it.

Kit Carson stared up at the high cliff overhead. He no longer saw any Navaho looking down from it. In fact, he saw no activity whatsoever.

Kit shook his head slowly and slipped back into his saddle. He was not going to walk into any of Sage's traps. If he had to, he would camp out at the base of the mountain until Sage and the remainder of his people were starved out.

He regretted that Leonida was among those who were being forced to follow the orders of the powerful Navaho chief. He knew that General Harold Porter would not take this news civilly in the least.

22

Keep thee today,
Tomorrow, forever.
—EMERSON

Pure Blossom was safely on a travois, wrapped snugly in pelts to keep her from rolling off the traveling apparatus. Horses and mules were loaded down with the personal belongings of the Navaho. Some preferred to walk. Others chose to ride on horseback down the narrow paths. Leonida was on horseback, Runner on the saddle before her, tied to her with a rope that reached around each of their waists.

Tumultuous emotions flooded Leonida as she watched Sage take one last walk through his village while everyone waited for him to give the order to start. She wanted to go to him, to be with him in his time of sorrow, yet it seemed inappropriate at this time. It was a private mourning of sorts for her husband, having to leave his home behind because of the cruel, insensitive plans of white men. At this moment Leonida was ashamed of her heritage. To see such innocence taken away from such a beloved band of Indians tore at her heart. Would it never end? This constant choice of destroying the lives of innocent Indians to make things better for white people?

Her eyes widening, Leonida wondered why Sage had called many of his warriors to his side as he gazed down into the valley below, where occasional belches of smoke still rose from the destroyed crops. Her back stiffened when each of Sage's warriors picked up torches that she had not noticed lying at the edge of the cliff. She gasped as the torches were lit, then tossed down the sides of the mountain, igniting all of the trees and grass that clung to the sides of the mountain, setting them all ablaze. The fires were fanned by the breeze, and a mile-wide line of flames soon swept down the sides of the mountain like a giant scythe.

Sage and his warriors hurried to their horses. Sage mounted his close beside Leonida's. Before they left, she reached to grab his arm. "Why did you set the fire?" she asked, wishing that she could remove the pain in his eyes.

"It is a fire wall of sorts," Sage said, his voice emotionless. "We will escape behind the cover of the dense smoke that rolls ahead of the flames. Also, it is to give Kit Carson cause to wonder about the fate of our village. It is best to draw him to the village rather than to us. By the time he reaches my stronghold, we will be long gone, safe from the man who was once a friend, now turned tyrant."

The long, dangerous march down the back side of the mountain began. Leonida kept a close watch on the one side of her, where the sides of the mountain dropped off sharply. She clutched the reins hard, feeling as though she were scarcely breathing. Runner sat stiffly in front of her, his steady gaze on the cliff, his eyes wide as silver dollars.

Sage headed the travelers. Pure Blossom's travois was attached to the horse of a warrior who traveled just behind Leonida. Occasionally, when Leonida felt it was safe, she would cast a worried glance back at

Pure Blossom. From this vantage point she could not see her face, to see how she was faring.

Leonida turned her eyes back to the path, smiling. Of late, she had sat at Pure Blossom's bedside, holding her hand, making up one story after another, feeling rewarded for her efforts when Pure Blossom would emit a soft laugh and give one of her warm smiles. Leonida hoped that she could give her the same sort of pleasure for many, many more months.

They moved relentlessly onward, through the tangled brush and occasionally across a wider span of ground, with trees and creeks alongside the path.

Again, then, they traveled on a narrow, slippery, winding path, the air filled with the fragrance of wildflowers that grew strangely from the sides of the mountain, in yellows, reds, and pinks.

As the day began to wane and the air became brisk, they arrived at the base of the mountain, the halfway point of their travels to their final destination.

Sage drew his reins tautly and gazed about him. He knew this land well, for he had studied it many times, charting it out with his mind, in case a speedy escape from his stronghold was required.

He knew where to make camp for the night, where everyone could be safe. It would take only a short while to get there. They could even build a campfire to prepare their evening meal and to give them warmth during the night.

Raising his hand, he gave the silent order to travel onward, to follow his lead. He flashed Leonida a smile over his shoulder, then edged his horse back to ride beside hers. "We will make camp soon," he said, noticing the weariness in her eyes. "We will be safe. As soon as tomorrow we will be building hogans at our new stronghold."

He glanced down at Runner, who was fast asleep, turned so that he could cuddle against Leonida's bosom. Seeing the awkwardness of the rope that still bound Runner to Leonida, and seeing no more need of it, Sage leaned over, untied the knot, and jerked the rope over to himself, dropping it into his saddle bag at the side of his horse.

"I'm worried about Pure Blossom," Leonida said, giving the travois a troubled glance. "I haven't checked on her because Runner fell asleep in my arms. I did not want to awaken him." She laughed softly, stroking her fingers through his tousled black hair. "If he is as tired as I am, the poor child might even sleep a full week."

Sage reached a hand to Leonida's cheek and softly caressed it, then fell back to ride alongside the travois. When Pure Blossom gave him an easy smile, everything within him warmed. "My sister, we shall be arriving soon where we can make a safe camp," he said, returning her smile. "You are well enough?"

"I am weary of being secured to this dreadful travois," she murmured. "But, yes, my brother, I am well enough."

Sage flinched somewhat to hear the weakness of his sister's voice, which proved the lie that she was telling her brother to keep him from worrying. He wanted to jump from his horse and gather his sister into his arms.

He was not even sure that she would live long enough to see the paradise of their new village. This time it would not be atop a mountain, where the weather changed from morning to night, from scorching to freezing.

Yes, he was traveling to another mountain to seek

refuge, but this time his people would live in its shadows, in a wide, fertile canyon, instead of on it.

There, where he had explored so often, were trees in abundance, for shade and firewood, and mountain-fed streams to water the gardens and his people.

Birds filled the air with their melodies, and flowers spread their heady fragrance far and wide.

The grass was thick and tall, perfect for the sheep and goats that he would one day acquire, even if stealing them was the only way. Whatever his people needed for survival, he would supply, even if he, too, was added to the list of renegades that rode the land at the midnight hour.

Sage's heart pained him when Pure Blossom closed her eyes and fell immediately into a deep sleep. He blinked back tears as he studied her paleness and her gaunt features. She was so frail, it seemed that even a slight breeze might blow her away if she was not secured to the travois. Too soon now, he would be saying his final good-bye to his sister.

Sage nudged his horse with his heels and rode away from her, and even past Leonida. He had sent several sentries on ahead to keep watch, even though he felt it was unnecessary. He had traveled this land many times before, alone, and never had he seen signs of people, red- or white-skinned alike. He had watched the wild animals at play, their footprints the only tracks left in the dirt and along the damp ground beside the streams.

Yes, he felt confident in his decision to bring his people to this land, uncharted, he believed, by anyone but him. It was shrouded by thick trees, and clinging vines ran back and forth across the ground, popping and snapping in two as the horses rode across them. Sage's spine stiffened when he got a faint whiff of smoke. His fingers tightened on his reins and stopped any further advance. He knew that all traces of smoke from the mountain and the valley below it, far away from where Sage and his people were now traveling, should have been left behind long ago. He had not smelled smoke since they had reached the halfway point down the backside of the mountain. And the winds were still as evening fell in deep pools of purple around him.

The smoke was coming from somewhere close by, instead of far, far behind him.

Sage's warriors milled around him just as his scouts came riding toward them. Leonida scarcely breathed, afraid, yet not sure of what. The way Sage was acting, they were no longer alone in this wilderness. And she, too, now smelled the smoke. She also could read the expressions on the scouts' faces and knew that possible trouble lay ahead.

She held Trevor closely to her bosom and listened to the conversation between Sage and the scouts, frustrated when they sometimes used more Navaho language than her own.

But she heard enough to know that intruders were near, and not just anyone—Chief Four Fingers.

''Chief Four Fingers abandoned camp just as we spied him through the trees ahead of us,'' Spotted Feather said, his eyes wild. ''They did not see us. They rode off in the opposite direction.''

A feeling of hopelessness swam through Sage, dashing his hopes of finding shelter for his people after all. If Four Fingers was making camp close by, it surely meant that he had also traveled on land that until now Sage had thought was a paradise in its secrecy.

"And so the Kiowa stand in the way of our peace again," he mumbled, looking up at his scouts.

"We did not pursue Four Fingers," Black Thunder said in a tone of apology. "We were too few in number."

Spotted Feather intervened. "And we did not think it wise to draw attention to ourselves, with our people only a short distance behind us," he said. "It is imperative to keep our people safe, even at the cost of allowing Four Fingers to escape again."

"And you were right," Sage mumbled. He glanced over his shoulder at the anxious faces, not only of his people but of the white captives as well. He was beginning to regret ever having taken hostages. He must discard the captive women and children at the first opportunity.

He looked slowly around, into the stretches of trees ahead of him. For now, he must find a safe refuge for everyone, so that he could be free to go and search for Four Fingers one last time. If the Kiowa was near, he could destroy all of the Navaho's future.

"What must we do?" Spotted Feather asked wearily.

"We will get our people comfortably safe and then we will go and search out Four Fingers . . . and kill him," Sage said in a low growl.

When he heard a low gasp behind him, he turned and met Leonida's frightened stare. She knew the dangers in going against Chief Four Fingers and his Kiowa warriors at this time. If Sage and his warriors were overtaken in a surprise ambush by the Kiowa, *then* what of the future of the Navaho?

But he saw no other way than to take the gamble. No one but the Navaho could ever be allowed to know of this special place that Sage was taking his people to. It troubled him that perhaps Chief Four Fingers already knew. There was no recourse except to silence the Kiowa chieftain once and for all.

Putting Leonida's fear out of his mind, Sage motioned to his people to follow him again as he led his stallion at a soft trot into the beckoning, purple twilight of evening.

23

Let no false pity
Spare the blow—
—ADELAIDE ANNE PROCTER

The moon was high as Sage finally decided on a spot
for a campsite for his people. The children were restless, some weeping from exhaustion. The women
moved listlessly about, spreading blankets across the
dew-dampened ground and digging among their belongings for food for their families.

Since Chief Four Fingers and his warriors were in
the vicinity, Sage refused to allow a campfire. His
people were forced to eat cold provisions and to sleep
without the comfort of a fire to warm them through
the long, cool night.

As Leonida gently lay Runner on a blanket that Sage
had spread for her, the child awakened, yawning and
rubbing his eyes.

"Are we there yet?" he asked, leaning on one elbow. "Are we where we will have a new home?"

Sage knelt down and ran his fingers through Runner's thick hair. "We are at a temporary shelter," he
said. "Tomorrow we will move onward. We will arrive at a place you will learn to call your home."

Runner shivered. "I'm cold," he whined, gazing
questioningly up at Sage. "There is no fire. Why is
there no fire?"

"It is not safe to throw off the light of a fire into
the heavens to be seen by our enemies," Sage grum-

bled, grabbing another blanket and wrapping it around Runner's tiny shoulders. "Tonight the blankets alone must warm you."

"I shall keep you warm, sweetie," Leonida said, sitting down beside Runner. Sage lifted the child onto her lap, smoothing the blanket back around his shoulders as it fell down away from him.

As Runner cuddled against Leonida, she gazed up at Sage, frowning. "Must you leave us?" she murmured. "Surely Chief Four Fingers is far gone by now, so far you will never be able to catch up with him. Let us trust that he is, Sage, and go on with our lives as we have planned."

"Our plans were altered the moment I smelled the smoke and discovered it was from a temporary camp of the Kiowa," he said. "Four Fingers knows too much about this land that I foolishly thought was my own secret. There is not enough room for both the Kiowa and the Navaho on this land, nor can I risk that Four Fingers may find our new village once it is established."

He paused and put a gentle hand on Leonida's cheek. "Or we will always be looking over our shoulders wondering which rock or tree he is hiding behind," he said thickly. "Or which moment one of his arrows will find the hearts of those we love."

He rose to his feet and placed his fists on his hips. "Once and for all I must rid our lives of all obstacles," he said flatly, looking down at her.

"But that's impossible," Leonida said, easing Runner from her lap. She made sure he was wrapped securely in the blanket, then rose to her feet. She put a hand on Sage's arm. "Darling, besides Chief Four Fingers, there is Kit Carson and . . ."

"This I know," Sage said, his eyes flashing. "He,

too, will vanish from our lives. Soon I will guarantee
that to you."

Leonida paled at the thought of his coming face to
face with Kit Carson, which meant that he would also
be facing the soldiers from Fort Defiance. She started
to risk his anger by arguing with him, but he was already walking stiffly away from her.

She hugged herself with her arms, staring at him,
loving him and fearing for him in the same heartbeat.
In the spill of the moonlight's silver rays, he looked
so magnificently noble as he went to his horse and
quickly swung himself into the saddle. One thing that
she was grateful for was that he had taken the time to
dress in trousers and shirt of goatskin and tall moccasins of deer hide, instead of his usual scanty breechclout. At least he would be shielded against the colder
breezes as he rode hard across the land toward danger.

Leonida looked nervously past him at the many
Navaho warriors awaiting Sage's command to follow
him into the forest, in search of their enemies. Every
warrior was mounted on a fine war horse, and the
gleam of the moon glittered threateningly on the steel
of their rifles. As Sage whirled his horse and galloped
away, his warriors wheeled their horses and swung
their rifles above their heads, following his lead.

"My belly hurts," Runner whined. "I'm hungry."

Leonida turned around and looked down at him,
glad that she had something to do to busy her hands
and her heart while Sage was out there somewhere
risking his life for the freedom of his people.

As she reached for their travel bag, in which was
food enough to last them several more days, she
glanced over at Pure Blossom, asleep close by on a
blanket. Leonida wasn't sure if she should awaken her
so that she could share the cold, late meal with her

and Runner, or if she should allow her to sleep. Rest sometimes was as important as food for those who were ill.

Leonida chose to let her sleep. When she awakened, there would be time enough to eat. It seemed that food had lost its importance for Pure Blossom these past few days. Sleep seemed of prime importance, and perhaps that was a blessing for someone who was facing imminent death.

Taking one of the last peaches, Leonida placed it on a wooden platter and split it in half. She plucked the pit out and carefully put it in a leather pouch. It, along with many other seeds, was being saved as the last of the peaches were eaten, to be planted later, so that another orchard might be allowed to prosper for the Navaho at their newly established stronghold.

After the seed was securely in the pouch and back inside the travel bag, Leonida gave Runner half of the juicy fruit.

Before eating her half, she looked slowly around at the others. When she found Sally and Adam on a blanket on the far side of the group, she smiled to herself, for they had been seen to as though they were as important as the Navaho. They were eating beef jerky, and a peach split in half rested in a wooden bowl beside Sally.

A thrill of sorts spread through Leonida as she watched Sally place the seed from her peach in a leather pouch, obviously also thinking of the Navaho's needs in the future, showing that she was willing to do her part.

She turned her attention back to Runner as he swallowed the last of his peach and put his small hand on her arm, shaking it.

"I'd like more, please?" he said softly, his eyes looking trustingly into Leonida's.

Leonida knew there weren't that many left, and she wanted to spread out the pleasure of having them to eat for several more days. She glanced down at her uneaten half of the peach, then looked at Runner again.

Without hesitation, she scooted the dish toward him. She smiled as he grabbed the peach half from the dish and began taking eager bites from it, the juice rolling down his chin in pink streamers.

Leonida searched inside the travel bag and chose a piece of beef jerky for her meal, trying to forget the peach and how she had thought of eating it all day while traveling. Her mouth had even watered while she broke the peach in half, as though she were already able to taste the sweetness, the juiciness soon to quench her thirst.

"That was good," Runner said, gulping down the last bite. He wiped his face with the back of a hand. "Now can I go and get Adam? Will you tell us stories?"

"Yes, go and bring whoever you wish to hear my stories," Leonida said, but she grabbed one of his hands before he could leave. She gave Pure Blossom another troubled glance, then said sternly, "But you tell the boys that they must sit quietly and not say a word. They can't even laugh. We don't want to do anything to disturb Pure Blossom. Do you understand?"

"I understand," Runner said anxiously, then wrenched his hand free and left in a mad run toward Adam.

Before Runner returned with the eager children, Leonida took a moment to lift her eyes to the heavens with a soft prayer that might help Sage in the moments of trial that awaited him. She prayed that she be given strength to accept what might happen these next few hours to her husband.

Dawn was just breaking along the horizon when Sage caught sight of a fire up ahead, beside the shine of a river. He brought his horse to a shuddering stop, quickly dismounted, and secured the reins on the ground beneath the weight of a large rock. Then he nodded to his warriors to follow him as he began moving stealthily toward the camp ahead. His hand clutched his rifle, his eyes narrowed with hatred as he crept closer and closer.

Then he stopped, puzzled by the paucity of horses grazing at the riverbank. There were only four, which meant that there were only four riders.

Where were the rest if this camp was Four Fingers and his warriors?

If it wasn't Four Fingers, then who . . . ?

Motioning with his hand for his men to spread out and surround the camp, Sage began moving again, his moccasined feet making not even a shuffling sound in the sand beneath them. He frowned up at a red-winged hawk as it began soaring in the air in slow circles above the campfire, its screeches piercing the morning silence.

Then a rattler slithered into view, shaking its rattle at Sage, threatening him at this moment more than those who were only footsteps away with rifles lying at their sides.

A knife suddenly hissed through the air and sliced the head of the rattler off before it had time to strike at Sage.

Sage smiled over his shoulder at Spotted Feather,

glad that he had chosen to stay close behind instead of going in another direction.

Sage nodded a silent thank-you, then continued moving stealthily onward until he was close enough to the sleeping men to realize for certain that he had not found Chief Four Fingers. Yet these were four of his warriors, who surely had separated from Four Fingers to continue scouting the area.

Anger and disappointment fused into one single explosive emotion within Sage. As his men moved in on all sides of the sleeping Kiowa, he inched his way toward them.

Then, as though with one heartbeat, the Navaho raced into the camp, and before the Kiowa understood what was happening, they were captured and tied together with one rope.

"Four Fingers," Sage growled, leaning down into their faces. "Tell me where I can find Four Fingers."

None of the Kiowa offered a response. They stood with their shoulders squared and their lips tightly pursed, eyeing Sage with contempt.

Sage nodded at Black Thunder. "Release one of them," he said, his voice tight. "Release the one who is called Red Bonnet."

Red Bonnet was set free. He was shoved over, to stand in front of Sage.

"Tell me where I can find your chief or you will suffer for your silence," Sage ordered, handing his rifle to Black Thunder and yanking his knife from its sheath at his right side. "Count your fingers. You now see five? Soon it will be four, and then three."

Red Bonnet glared at Sage, unmoved by the threat.

Sage jerked one of the Kiowa's hands out and held it out before him. Sage raised the knife, unflinching. But just as he was ready to set the sharp blade to Red

Bonnet's flesh, one of the others spoke up, stopping the planned torture.

"He is gone far away," the Kiowa said, his voice anxious as he watched the steadiness of Sage's knife. "We separated from him. We go our way. He goes his. He threatens your peace no longer. Nor do we. Allow us to leave. We will ride away and not look back. I vow to you that this is true."

Sage eased his knife to his side, studying the Kiowa's expression, trying to tell if he told the truth. What the Kiowa said did seem logical. Usually scouts did not leave in groups of four, especially if the band of Indians was so small in number anyway. Sending so many away weakened their defenses too much should an enemy suddenly appear along their path of travel.

"It is true," Red Bonnet said thickly, sweat pearling on his brow as he watched Sage's knife. "Let us ride free. We tell no one about you. You see, I understand that you are fleeing your stronghold. Four Fingers told Kit Carson where to find your stronghold. He did this to gain more freedom for himself from the white people. Kit Carson agreed. He allowed Four Fingers to go on his way. It was a short time later that Four Fingers sent us all away from him in groups of four, to find a life of our own. That is what I desire. To live in peace. If that is what you also seek, so be it."

"Which way did Four Fingers go to seek his new path of life?" Sage asked guardedly. He sighed with relief when Red Bonnet pointed in the direction opposite from Sage's planned destination.

Sage went to the three Kiowa who were tied together. He untied them and frowned at each of them. "You are allowed to go, but should you decide to go back on your word and I find you anywhere near my people, you will learn the most grueling ways of slow death imaginable," he warned.

Going to his stallion, Sage swung himself into the saddle. He took his rifle as Black Thunder handed it to him. He gripped it tightly with one hand, and with the other snapped the reins and sent his horse into a hard gallop away from the campsite. As much as he tried, he could not feel at peace with the decision that he had just made. As much as he tried, he could not see Chief Four Fingers giving up all that easily to the white pony soldiers—not even Kit Carson.

"Kit Carson," he whispered to himself. "He is next. He must make promises that I *can* believe."

He rode back in the direction of his camp even though tomorrow he would search for Kit Carson's. First he must make sure that enough warriors were left to protect his people in their temporary camp. If Four Fingers did decide to seek him and his people out, especially now that he must know they were no longer at the stronghold, his warriors would be ready for him.

24

When from the frowning east,
A sudden gust of adverse fate is blowing. . . .
—ELLA WHEELER WILCOX

The day had dragged along. Restless, Leonida had paced often as she watched for Sage's return. When the sun began sinking behind the mountains and Sage and his warriors still had not arrived, Leonida could not help but think that they had met with disaster.

Hardly able to bear her thoughts, she focused them elsewhere. Going to Pure Blossom and sitting down beside her, she took Pure Blossom's hand in hers. Sage's sister was struggling to keep awake, also worrying about Sage, but her eyes drifted shut more often than not.

"I'm sorry about the blanket Sage won't allow you to have," Pure Blossom said, as she rolled over on her side. "It is finished. And I did not burn it as my brother ordered me to. It is among my belongings. When I die, it is yours. Tell my brother that it is a special gift from me, *not* the white man. As it keeps you warm nights, always think of Pure Blossom."

"Don't talk about dying," Leonida scolded softly. "Soon you will be stronger. When we reach this land of promise that Sage is taking us to, you will become strong again. Sage will build you a lovely hogan. You will set up your looms inside it beside a fire and while away your days making lovely blankets and shawls to share with your people."

"It is a pleasant thought," Pure Blossom sighed, her voice silent. "That would make Sage happy, I know. All I have ever wanted was to make my brother happy. My body betrays my hopes and wishes for my brother. But soon it will be over. Pure Blossom will no longer be a bother."

Her words stung Leonida's heart. It did not seem possible to lose two friends almost at once. First Carole, who had died of a lung ailment, and now Pure Blossom, whose body had not developed fully as she had progressed from a child to a woman.

Yet both friends had accepted death so easily, more than it was possible for Leonida. The thought of Pure Blossom dying made a sick sort of feeling swim at the pit of Leonida's stomach. This reminded her again to worry about Sage.

She looked into the darkening shadows of night, searching for movement. She listened intently, hoping to hear the sound of horses approaching. But she was not blessed with either seeing or hearing anyone approaching.

"My brother?" Pure Blossom murmured, her fingers tightening around Leonida's. "He has been gone too long. I fear for him. What if Kit Carson found him?" Her voice broke with emotion. "We would never know. No one knows where we are, except perhaps Four Fingers. He would not come to spread the word of Sage's capture. If he came, it would be to destroy the Navaho, or to take the Navaho as his slaves."

Knowing that worrying was not good for Pure Blossom, Leonida tried to reassure her that Sage would be all right. "He will be arriving soon," Leonida said. She slipped Pure Blossom's hand beneath the blankets. The chill breeze of evening was already spreading across the land, the dew sparkling like miniature diamonds on the tips of the grass.

"I must get Runner ready for bed," Leonida said, bending to kiss Pure Blossom's cheek. She then leaned away from her. "Did you have enough to eat? You have scarcely been touching your food."

"I require less each day," Pure Blossom said, smiling weakly up at Leonida. "Go to Runner. Give him a kiss. He is such a fine boy. It is easy to see why Sage has accepted him so eagerly as his son."

"Yes, Runner is special," Leonida said, pushing herself up from the blankets. "Sleep well, Pure Blossom. Upon tomorrow's dawning, I know that Sage will be with us again. Keep that thought and carry it with you into your dreams."

Pure Blossom nodded, then slowly drifted off again into the protective cocoon of sleep.

Having already eaten the evening meal and finding it too hard to function once night had dropped its black cloak over the camp, Leonida started to search for Runner but was surprised to find him already snuggled in his blankets, fast asleep.

Leonida knelt down beside him and caressed his brow. "My child, you played so hard today," she whispered. "You simply wore yourself out." She frowned. "But that is good. You did not even notice how long Sage has been gone. If you had, you would be as worried as I am. Ah, my child, how you would feel the loss if anything happened to Sage. You do love him. Oh, how you do love him."

She did not want to slip between the blankets herself just yet, knowing that her mind would not rest enough from her worries for her to sleep. Leonida took one of her blankets, wrapped it around her shoulders, and moved away from the camp, where more were asleep now than awake. She strolled through the forest, stopping at the stream that snaked beneath the stars.

Sighing, she spread the blanket on the ground, then sat down on it, gazing heavenward. The moon was being elusive tonight. First it was there, and then it was behind a fluff of clouds. In the distance she could see lightning forking in zigzags across the sky, followed by a rumble of thunder.

"That's all we need," she grumbled to herself. "A storm. Without protection, everyone would get soaked. In the night air, many would catch a cold. Lord, haven't we had enough to contend with? Please keep the storm in the distant hills."

Suddenly her spine stiffened. She bolted to her feet and turned to stare across an open meadow. "Horses," she said, her heart thumping almost as loudly as the hoofbeats fast approaching.

She began running when she finally saw the horses coming toward her. She stopped and squinted into the night, trying to see the lead rider. But with the night so dark, she could see only shadows and the outline of the riders.

Fear suddenly grabbed at her heart. What if it was someone besides Sage and his warriors? Frantic, Leonida looked around her for cover but found nothing.

Then she gazed at the riders again and a sigh of relief coursed through her when she could finally see the face of the lead rider.

"Sage," she whispered as joy spilled over within her.

Then she began running toward the riders.

"Sage," she cried, waving at him with both hands. "Oh, darling, it *is* you. You are all right."

When Sage spied Leonida, he broke free from the

others and rode hard toward her. When he reached her, he wheeled his horse to a halt. Bending over, he pulled her up onto the horse with him. As she clung to him, her arms twining around his neck, they kissed in a frenzy.

"I was so afraid for you," Leonida whispered as they drew apart. She touched his face, as though to make sure he was truly there. "You were gone for so long." She looked over his shoulder, counting the warriors who were now drawing their mounts to a halt behind Sage. They were all there.

"We did not find him," Sage said, as though reading her thoughts. "Four Fingers eluded us again."

"All of this time and you did not achieve your goal?" Leonida said softly. She lay her cheek on his chest, the goatskin fabric soft against her flesh. "I'm sorry, darling. I know how important it was for you to find Four Fingers. Now he will always be a threat to you and your people."

"Perhaps not," Sage said. "We came upon four of his warriors who are no longer in alliance with him. They told us that Four Fingers ordered his warriors to disband, to find another life separate from his."

"You believed them?" Leonida said, raising an eyebrow.

"I never want to believe the word of any Kiowa," Sage grumbled. "But for now, I will accept it as truth."

"Then we can travel onward to our original destination?" Leonida asked.

"Not quite yet," Sage said, gazing down at Leonida, realizing how disappointed she was by the way her eyes wavered.

"What do you mean?" she asked, fearing the answer.

"At this time, I have done all that can be done about Four Fingers," he said, his voice drawn. "But I have yet to settle things with Kit Carson. I will stay the night with you and my people, then tomorrow, at break of dawn, I must travel again, away from you. I alone will go after Kit Carson. It is an itch that must be scratched, then healed!"

"Do you mean that you are going to abduct Kit Carson?" Leonida gasped, paling.

"It is the only way," Sage said, his jaw tight.

"No," Leonida said in a moan. "You mustn't. Kit Carson is always surrounded by many soldiers. It will be impossible to get past them. And if by chance you do, what will you do once you have him? You know that he will never give in to any of your demands."

"It is not something I would gamble with," Sage said stiffly. "If he is abducted and brought back to be among my people, you will see who is in charge then and who will give in to demands and who will not."

He framed her face between his hands. "Do not have such little faith in your husband," he said.

"I'm sorry," she murmured. "But it is not because I doubt you, or have little faith in you. It is because I love you so much. I don't want anything to happen to you."

"My woman, you worry needlessly," Sage said, then kissed her. "But it is good to have a wife whose devotion and caring is so unwavering."

Sage's warriors rode up on each side of him, waiting for instructions. They all already knew of his plans to search for Kit Carson alone. That was the only possible way to get past the soldiers. One person, especially one who moved as stealthily as Sage, could abduct him.

Many warriors would draw too much attention.

"Go on to the camp," Sage ordered his warriors. "I will spend time with my wife, then come to camp myself. I alone must explain to our people why it is necessary for me to leave them again before we venture onward to our new home. I must explain to them the need to rid our lives, once and for all, of the threats of the white pony soldiers led by Kit Carson."

The warriors nodded and rode onward.

"I left my blanket beside the stream," Leonida murmured as Sage sank his heels into the flanks of his horse, riding onward at a soft lope.

"Take me to it," Sage said, reveling in this moment, with her snuggled close, her breasts pressed against him. For a while she would be the only thing on his mind. Later, he would think about the dangers of riding into the white men's camp—if, indeed, he could even find their camp—while they were on their way back to Fort Defiance with their Navaho prisoners.

"How is Pure Blossom faring?" he suddenly said, realizing it was impossible to think only of his wife.

"She is growing gradually weaker, yet today she took broth almost eagerly," Leonida said, pointing as the stream came into view. "My blanket is over there."

"We shall make use of it," he said huskily.

"We shall sleep there?" Leonida teased, smiling up at him.

He drew his steed to a halt. He slid easily from the saddle, then reached for Leonida. She moved into his arms, and when her feet touched the ground, she clung to him, her fingers at the nape of his neck, urging his lips to hers.

Their kiss was feverish with desire. Leonida leaned into his embrace, feeling the heat of his passion as he pressed his manhood against her. Even through the fabric of her skirt, she could feel how large he was in his arousal.

She slipped a hand between them and stroked his throbbing member through his breeches. His husky groan quivered against her lips, urging her onward.

With trembling fingers she crept to the waist of his breeches and began lowering them. As they finally fell around his ankles, leaving himself fully accessible to her, she wrapped her fingers around him and began moving her hand in rhythmic up and down strokes.

The pleasure mounting, stealing his breath away, Sage placed his hands at her waist and began lowering her to the blanket, yet giving her room to still maneuver her hand on him.

His head spun, and afraid that he was reaching that plateau of heightened passion too soon, he eased her hand from him.

"It is better used elsewhere," he said, lifting her skirt and lowering her undergarment in one quick movement. "Woman, open yourself to me. Let me love you."

A delicious languor stole over Leonida as he entered her and began his rhythmic thrusts. His eager mouth came to hers and forced her lips apart, his tongue touching hers as he kissed her.

Surrendering herself, Leonida trembled beneath his touch as he lifted her blouse, his hands soon claiming her breasts, enfolding them within his fingers. He kneaded her breasts, his thumbs lightly caressing the nipples.

Happiness bubbled from deep within, and she shook with building sensations when Sage slipped his mouth from her lips, his tongue now moving maddeningly in circles over her breasts, while his hands traveled lower, teasing and stroking the supple lines of her body.

His eyes glazed with desire, Sage stopped his strokes within her and drew back far enough to be able to look at her as the moon crept out from behind a cloud, silvering her body with its splash of light.

"You are more beautiful than the loveliest of butterflies," he said huskily. He ran his hands up and down her fiery flesh, then stroked the center of her passion between her thighs. "You are softer than the petal of a rose." He kissed the hollow of her throat, drawing a hungry sigh deeply from within her. "You taste sweeter than honey found in a bee's hideaway."

He buried his throbbing hardness deeply inside her, kissing her hungrily as he filled her over and over again with his swollen, aching need of her. His senses yearned for the promise her body was offering him. He locked his arms around her and drew her closer, her body responding as her hips moved in sinuous hollows against his hunger.

Leonida's heart was pounding as surges of warmth flooded through her body. Her whole universe seemed to be spinning, the sensation rising up and flooding her whole body.

As his kiss deepened, she drifted and floated, then gave herself up to the bliss of the moment as she went over the edge into ecstasy, his body thrusting wildly into hers, proving that he had just followed her there.

Afterward, they dressed without many words between them, having been thrust too soon back into the troubles of the real world. Sage took his horse's reins and led him toward the camp, Leonida beside him.

"Tomorrow will come too quickly," she murmured, giving Sage a downcast glance. "I don't want to say good-bye again. Each time I do, I fear it might be the last."

Sage looked at her with a troubled expression. He knew full well that he might never return this time. What he was planning to do might even be considered tempting death.

25

My life and all seemed turned to clay.
—JOHN CLARE

Sage's search went well. Because Kit Carson's return to Fort Defiance was being slowed by the many Navaho people accompanying him, traveling on foot, they had not gotten far. Night had just fallen again, and the white pony soldiers' campfire, like a beacon in the night for Sage, had quickly drawn his keen attention.

Sage stopped far enough away so that his horse could not be heard if it whinnied. The rest of the way he was going by foot; the knife clutched in his right hand would be the quietest way to silence anyone who tried to stand in the way of this abduction.

The smell of cooked venison wafted through the air, teasing Sage's hunger, for he had not stopped to eat—nor would he stop to sleep, until he was among his people again, Kit Carson with him.

When he got close enough to the campsite to be able to distinguish faces, pain circled his heart at the sight of so many of his Navaho people who had unwisely chosen the life of a reservation over trusting their chief. As he watched the Navaho eat good portions of meat and drink from canteens of water, it appeared that they were being treated fairly enough. That somewhat alleviated his pain at no longer being an integral part of their lives.

Sage's gaze shifted, singling out Kit Carson from among the soldiers sitting away from the Navaho, closer to the fire. Kit was eating and talking, laughing when one of the soldiers told a raunchy joke.

This lighthearted side of Kit Carson reminded Sage of a time when he had called Kit a friend of the Indians. It had been good to ride with him, to challenge him with looped ropes and races on horseback.

Sage smiled grimly. No one had ever been able to outrope Kit Carson, and scarcely anyone ever won against him while racing horses.

Sage squatted on his haunches behind a thicket and rested his knife on a knee, forcing himself not to remember the good things about Kit Carson. At present, too much bad flooded his mind.

It was up to Sage to change that bad to good again.

Time seemed to move slowly, but finally everyone had finished eating, and all that was left to do was to move comfortably into their bedrolls. Sage watched guardedly as first one man and then another went into the brush to relieve themselves before retiring for the night.

He then watched the women take the children into the privacy of the bushes, aching inside when he realized that the young braves among the children would never experience the wonders of being a Navaho warrior, riding free across uncharted land. They might never feel the rush of the wind on their faces while on horseback or the feel of a lance clasped tightly in their hands.

"By living on a reservation, these young braves will lose everything that is naturally Navaho to them," he whispered to himself. "It is sad that they are not old enough to make their own decisions as to where they wish to live."

He circled a hand into a tight fist, and his eyes narrowed angrily. "It is sad that they will be raised to behave more like women than men!'' he hissed under his breath.

Soon everyone was settled in for the night. Sage watched slowly from bedroll to bedroll. The soldiers seemed to be asleep.

And then he eyed the two soldiers who had been chosen to keep watch. A smile crept onto his lips when he saw these men sit down and lean their backs against a tree, their heads soon bobbing as they fought off sleep.

Sage patiently waited, watching the soldiers, smiling again when he saw them sitting perfectly still now, their heads bowed. He watched the slow heaving of their shoulders, showing that they were sleeping soundly, hopefully soundly enough for Sage to get in and out of the camp without being detected.

Moving out of the thicket, Sage crept into the camp. Kit Carson was sleeping partially away from the others. He had stayed awake the longest, studying what seemed to be a map. Then he had folded the map, slipped it into his front shirt pocket, and crawled into his bedroll. Soon he was fast asleep.

His knife poised before him, ready for action should someone awaken and find him there, Sage moved stealthily around the soldiers, glad when he finally reached Kit Carson. Without hesitation he yanked a red handkerchief from his rear pocket.

Bending down beside Kit Carson, Sage momentarily lay his knife aside. Then as quickly as lightning strikes, he had Kit Carson gagged. The little man's eyes gleamed wildly as he peered up at Sage in the dim shadows of the campfire's glowing embers. Sage hurriedly picked up his knife and held it at Kit Carson's throat, giving him a message that Kit interpreted well enough—to do as he was told or be killed.

Sage rose slowly to his full height. Kit Carson got slowly to his feet also, careful not to stumble since the knife followed his every move. Scarcely breathing, Kit Carson walked easily and lightly through the camp as Sage led him with a firm grip on his arm, the cold blade of the knife still against the flesh of his throat.

When they were finally out of the camp, Sage took Kit to his horse. Kit hesitated before climbing into the saddle. He gave Sage and the knife a nervous look.

Sage understood this silent message. He lowered the knife, then nodded silently toward his saddle again.

Grumbling obscenities against the fabric of the neckerchief, Kit put his foot in the stirrup, then swung himself into the saddle.

Sage eased onto the horse behind his prisoner, took the reins into his hands, then sank his heels into the flanks of his stallion and rode in an easy lope away from the camp. When they were far enough away so that no one could hear the horse's hoofbeats, Sage urged his mount into a hard gallop across the land. When he saw Kit reach for the gag, Sage did nothing. He allowed it. He smiled, knowing that Kit Carson could shout and scream and curse all he wanted now, and no one but Sage would hear him.

They rode until the sunrise was splashing great orange-pink streaks across the heavens. Then Sage drew his steed to a whirling halt beside a coolly glowing river. He said nothing to Kit, just nonchalantly dismounted and led his horse to the water to get its fill.

Then Sage bent to a knee and scooped mouthfuls of water down his parched throat with his hands, not flinching when Kit Carson came and knelt down beside him. His angry words seemed to echo across the river and back again. "Do you honestly think you will get away with abducting me?'' Kit shouted, gesturing wildly with his hands. ''When the soldiers discover that I'm not at the camp, they'll come looking for me, and by God, Sage, you have to know they will find me.''

''Drink your fill of water now because we will not stop again until we reach the camp of the Navaho,'' Sage said flatly, giving Kit an indifferent stare. ''And if I must gag you again to silence you, I will. From this point on, your hands will be tied behind you and you will be blindfolded. It is not wise to allow you to see where you are going. That way you cannot return once I have set you free.''

''Ha!'' Kit said sarcastically. ''At least I am able to look forward to freedom again. But when, Sage? Why have you abducted me? What plans are you setting into motion with my abduction?''

''You still talk instead of drink?'' Sage said, frowning at Kit. He shrugged. ''That is your choice, but if you start begging for water later, this Navaho chief will ignore you.''

Sage's eyes danced, and a slow smile tugged at his lips when Kit uttered a sigh of frustrated annoyance, then began drinking from his cupped hands.

Sage got to his feet when he thought Kit had had time enough to quench his thirst. Surprising him, Sage suddenly grabbed his wrists and tied them together behind his back.

''You will live to regret this,'' Kit said, then gasped again and stiffened when Sage determinedly tied a bright red handkerchief around Kit's eyes.

''It is time to go now,'' Sage said, gripping one of Kit's elbows. He urged Kit up from the ground, turned, and led him to the horse. Sage fitted Kit's foot in the stirrup. "Your foot is in the stirrup. Push yourself up into the saddle as I help you."

"I feel like a damn idiot," Kit swore, his face red from his building rage. "Are you enjoying humiliating me?"

"Are you enjoying humiliating the Navaho by ordering them to live on a reservation?" Sage said, swinging himself onto his horse behind Kit. "The man you once were would never humiliate my people. The man you now are is someone I do not recognize."

Kit Carson had no rebuttal to snap back at Sage.

Sage laughed softly, seeing that Kit was finding it hard to stay in the saddle without the use of his hands. He slipped to one side, then righted himself, then began slipping to the other.

"Traveling with my hands tied like this, I'm going to break my neck before you get me to your camp," Kit said sourly. "Why must my wrists be tied?"

"It would be too tempting to you to remove the blindfold if your hands were free," Sage said. "I want silence now between us. When we reach my camp, then we can go into council. There is much to be said, but only that which benefits the Navaho, not Kit Carson."

"Like I said before, you won't get away with this," Kit said. Then he clamped his lips together tightly and concentrated on staying in the saddle. He couldn't wait until his soldiers were on Sage's trail.

Sage was drained of energy and his eyes were stinging with the need of sleep when he spied his camp through a break in the trees a short distance away. He had ridden relentlessly onward through the pulsating heat of the day, and it was now dusk, the shadows lengthening all around him. He welcomed the evening with its cooler temperatures. He could feel the perspiration finally drying on his face. He inhaled the sweetness of the fresh, cool air.

But most of all, he was anticipating seeing Leonida.

As he rode into his camp, Sage was greeted differently than usual. Everyone stood quietly by, staring at Kit Carson, the man they all now despised. They had always thought that he was invincible, incapable of ever being conquered by anyone.

Their gazes shifted, looking in admiration at their chief. Sage had proven to them again that he was perhaps the wisest and bravest of them all. He had done what no other man had ever done. He had taken Kit Carson prisoner. Pride shone in everyone's eyes as one by one the men began to shout Sage's praises, while the women broke into merry songs.

Sage drew his steed to a halt. As he dismounted, his eyes scanned the crowd for Leonida, yet still he did not see her. This gave him a strange sense of foreboding. Something must be seriously wrong for her not to have been among those greeting his return.

"Help me off this damn horse," Kit Carson growled, drawing Sage's attention back to him. "Take the damn blindfold off, Sage. Or do you plan to keep it on me the whole time I'm here?"

Sage turned to Kit. The man was so small that Sage was able to lift him bodily from the saddle and put his feet on the ground. He was ready to remove the blindfold, but he stopped when Leonida came to him, tears sparkling in her eyes. Fear grabbed at Sage's heart.

"What has delayed you in greeting your husband?" Sage asked, clasping his fingers on her shoulders. He studied her expression and the tears forming in her eyes.

Then he looked past her and saw that Runner sat

beside Pure Blossom, staring gloomily down at her.
Pure Blossom was not stirring, and Sage knew that if
she had been aware of his return, she would have at
least turned her eyes to him and greeted him with a
smile.

"It is my sister?" Sage asked, easing his hands from
Leonida's shoulders. "She has weakened?"

Leonida nodded, sniffling. "Very much so," she
murmured, then gave Kit Carson a quick glance when
he began shouting to Sage about still being blindfolded
and tied.

"Damn it, Sage, what are you doing?" he said angrily. "You promised to remove the blindfold and un-
tie me. Don't tell me that you've changed your mind."

Sage moved away from Leonida and quickly tended
to Kit Carson, then walked away from him in long
strides, his thoughts now only on his sister. When he
reached Pure Blossom and knelt beside her, his heart
cried out his anguish to every nerve ending in his body.
She had lapsed into a coma.

Fighting back tears, knowing that it was womanly
to show such emotions, Sage lifted Pure Blossom into
his arms and began rocking her back and forth, his
eyes filled with grief.

Kit Carson stepped to Sage's side. "I see that your
sister is quite ill," he said, his voice drawn. He looked
at her more closely and placed a hand on her brow.
The heat of her flesh was like hot coals scorching him.
He looked up at Sage with worried eyes. "It is my
belief that your sister has come down with the prairie
fever that is now sweeping the Indian tribes. Sage,
because she has never been strong in the first place,
she hasn't got a chance in hell in recovering."

Leonida stifled a sob behind her hand and held Runner close as he snuggled against her leg, clinging to her.

"Had I not been forced to come after you, I would have been here for my sister," Sage grumbled, fire in his eyes as he stared down at Kit Carson.

"You weren't forced to do anything," Kit defended himself. "Abducting me will gain you nothing except perhaps being hung because of it."

Sage continued rocking Pure Blossom back and forth in his arms. He knew this was not the time or place to discuss the issues with Kit Carson, but since it had already begun, so be it. What he had to say would not take long. It had just been important to say it in the presence of his people so they would know the terms of the agreement that he hoped to achieve with Kit Carson.

"There will be no hangings," Sage said quietly, yet with feeling. "Not even will my people place a noose around your neck. You will not be harmed at all. You will be released along with the white captives if you promise to return to Fort Defiance and tell them that you see it best not to interfere any further in our lives, so that the Navaho can ride free along land that has been theirs since before the white people even knew it existed. Promise that you will see to it that my people—even those that you have now as captives—will not be herded to a reservation."

"You know that you are asking the impossible of me," Kit said, sighing heavily. "I have no final say in these matters. I take my orders from the Great White Chief in Washington, who dictates all things to the white people, even Kit Carson."

"You are wrong," Sage grumbled. "The Great White Chief values your word, as well as your life. If you speak for the Navaho favorably, he will listen."

"Only if he wishes to," Kit said solemnly. "When it comes to Indians, scarcely does he ever favor them over the comforts of the white settlers."

When Pure Blossom began chanting and talking out of her head, Sage felt guilty for having argued in her presence. He glared at Kit, then walked away from him, Leonida at his side.

"I never thought that it might be prairie fever," Leonida said, gazing at Pure Blossom, whose face was beet-red. "Until today she scarcely had a fever. Now? It came on her so quickly."

Sage took Pure Blossom to her blankets, laid her on one and wrapped her in another one.

He turned to Leonida and took her hands in his. "Our medicine man must sing over my sister," he said thickly. "But first a house of bent saplings and leaves must be built quickly for her, to keep her out of the weather."

He put a hand on Leonida's cheek, reveling as always in the softness of her flesh. "At the same time I will see that you have a house of your own," he said. "We may be here for some time. I cannot leave this place while Pure Blossom is this ill."

Leonida swallowed hard, for Kit Carson's words that Pure Blossom would not be recovering had burned into her heart. This would be her final resting place.

She glanced down at Runner, who once again kept vigil at Pure Blossom's side. It gave her a queasy feeling to think that he might come down with the same dreaded disease, yet she felt confident that he wouldn't. He had been around Pure Blossom both night and day for as long as she had been ill, and neither he nor anyone else of the village showed signs of contracting the disease.

Leonida watched Sage ordering his men to build the

houses, then watched him as he took Kit Carson aside and began discussing again about the fate of his people.

She peered into the deepening shadows of night, hoping that no one had followed Sage and Kit to this camp of Navaho.

26

Like outcast spirits, who wait,
And see, through Heaven's gate,
Angels within it.
—THACKERAY

Pure Blossom's wigwam had been put together quickly.
A fire now burned in the fire pit in the center of the
dwelling, and smoke spiraled upward and spread out-
ward like dancing, swaying ghosts.

Pure Blossom lay unconscious on thick pallets beside the fire. Leonida and Sage sat on opposite sides
of her, awaiting the arrival of the medicine man, the
"singer."

Sage had already paid him many horses to conduct
the ceremony. He had spent a great deal of time learning what to do, so he had to be paid well.

Outside, everyone stood around a nearby fire, ward-
ing off the chill of the night with blankets snuggled
around their shoulders. Sage had dispensed with worrying that a fire might attract enemies, and a great fire
leapt toward the sky.

The Navaho's enemies were many, but their worst
enemy at present might be the prairie fever. Fires were
needed not only for warmth, but for cooking nourish-
ing food. Sage's people needed both the fires and the
warm food to keep them healthy during the long nights
of plummeting temperatures. And Sage would go no
farther than this valley now that his sister had worsened.

Leonida placed another cool, damp cloth on Pure

Blossom's brow in an effort to get her temperature down. She was glad that Runner was fast asleep in the wigwam built for her and Sage. Now that it was suspected that Pure Blossom had prairie fever, everyone who had come in contact with her had a chance of coming down with the awful disease. It seemed to strike those whose resistance was low, and Leonida hoped that no one else in the village, except perhaps those who were old and ailing already, would contract it. It seemed now that all along, when Pure Blossom's health had been clearly failing, she had been coming down with prairie fever. Her worsening health had not been caused by her disabilities. After some time, she became so weak that it was much easier for the fever to claim her in its fiery intensity.

Suddenly the air was filled with the pulsing beats of a drum. Leonida turned quickly around, and her gaze fell on an elderly man who wore a long, flowing robe without any beads or design. His hair, drawn back from his face, hung in one long, gray braid down his straight back. Although his face was furrowed with wrinkles, he was a handsome Navaho, his dark eyes gentle and kind as he gazed back at Leonida. She did not know his name, but everyone referred to him only as the singer.

As he came farther into the wigwam, Leonida took the damp cloth from Pure Blossom's brow and went to the other side of the structure. The singer stood over Pure Blossom, looking sadly down at her. Slowly he moved to his knees beside the pallet of furs, his bone-thin hands drawing the blankets down away from her, exposing her thin, fever-racked, naked body to his wizened eyes.

Scarcely breathing, Leonida watched the medicine

man put himself in what seemed to be a trance as his
hands trembled over Pure Blossom's body.

Outside, the drum pulsed into the night, many
women singing along with it.

Inside the wigwam of the sick, the singer continued
to run his hands over Pure Blossom's body, himself
now breaking into song, the song of the mountains, a
holy song to the Navaho.

> The Chief of Mountains, and beyond it,
> In life unending, and beyond it,
> In Joy unchanging, and beyond it,
>   Yea, now arrived home, behold me.

He paused, drew the blanket back over Pure Blossom, up to her chin, then sang again. His hands
seemed to be moving in sign language, while he sang
the words aloud.

> Seated at home behold me,
> Seated amid the rainbow;
> Seated at home, the Holy Place!
> Yea, seated at home behold me.
> The Chief of Mountains, and beyond it,
> Yea, seated at home behold me,
> In life unending, and beyond it,
> In Joy Unchanging, and beyond it,
> Yea, seated at home behold me.

The deep resonance and feelings of the medicine
man as he sang his prayer songs touched Leonida
deeply. She fought back the urge to cry, fearful that it
might break the spell of the singer. He seemed magi-
cal, as though capable of bringing Pure Blossom out
of her coma, yet Leonida had seen others who had
drifted off into the same sort of unconscious state.
Sadly, none of them had ever survived. Not even the

most skilled physicians had been able to discover the mysteries of comas.

As for the Navaho, the singer conducted the ritual of his healing ceremony to compensate for some power which was attempting to destroy their harmony. They believed that they must live in harmony with nature and that when their people became ill it was not because of a germ, but because they had fallen out of that harmony.

Leonida silently scoffed at this belief, knowing that Pure Blossom was not the cause of her own debilitating ailment. In truth, nature had wronged *her* as far back as when she had been carried within her mother's womb and her frail body had begun to take its shape.

But Leonida continued to stand stiffly beside Sage, accepting this Navaho healing ritual as something she must get used to, since she was now an integral part of Navaho life. She watched with much interest as the singer spread a white buckskin on the floor of the wigwam and, slowly and evenly, covered the buckskin with pure white sand. The creation of sand paintings by the singer was an important part of the ceremony.

Then the medicine man began singing again as he sifted colored earth and yellow pollen through his fingers onto the sand to make a bright, sacred picture. His fingers were skillful, and Leonida, who loved art and poetry, saw a great deal of beauty in the formations of the figures and designs on the sand. She knew that because of the sacredness of the depiction, it must be completed, used, and destroyed within a twelve-hour period.

The singer continued to construct the elaborate sand paintings designed to cure the patient, now saying prayers to Changing Woman, the most important Navaho god. She was the one who did good things and tried to help people. Her husband, the Sun, wasn't always so helpful, and the singer made prayers asking the Sun to do good instead of evil.

The ceremony to win the help of the gods lasted far into the night, the steady rhythm of the medicine songs pulsing and groups of singers outside on opposite sides of the fire vying with one another in endurance. Like the central pile of burning logs, the songs flared unextinguished until the stars faded.

At dawn, the singer ceased his songs and prayers. He gazed down at his painting, then destroyed it.

Leonida was leaning against Sage, completely drained of energy as the singer left Pure Blossom's wigwam. Dutiful wife that she was, Leonida had endured the long night of standing with Sage during the curing ceremony.

She gazed sleepily down at Pure Blossom, anguished to see that Sage's sister was no better than before. She still lay unmoving, in a sound sleep.

Leonida looked at the entrance flap of the wigwam, and realized that the singers had finally ceased. Everything was quiet in this temporary village. Even the pulse of the drums had faded away.

Sage knelt down beside his sister and put his hand on her brow. With a sudden smile he looked up at Leonida. "Her face is cool to my hand!" he said, his voice breaking with joy. "The singer has brought her back, on the road to recovery."

Leonida wanted to share his enthusiasm, yet she feared the worst—that even though the fever had broken, it had already done too much damage to Pure Blossom's frail body for her to become healthy and vital again.

She knelt beside Sage and placed a gentle hand on

his cheek. "Darling, that's wonderful," she murmured, forcing a smile. "That's so wonderful."

Sage gazed down at Pure Blossom again, then leaned over her and drew her up into his powerful arms. "Pure Blossom," he whispered into her ear. "It is I, your brother. Did you hear the songs and prayers? They were for you. They were to cure you. Come back to me, little sister. The world would be a lonely place without you."

Leonida heard his pleas. She wiped tears from her eyes, watching Sage put his sister back down on the pallet of furs and gently draw the blankets over her again.

Sage turned to Leonida. He placed a hand at the nape of her neck and drew her lips to his. He brushed a kiss across her lips, then helped her up from the floor. "It is time for us to rest," he said. He led her to the door. "Others will take our places beside my sister while we rest and fill our bodies with nourishment."

"Right now going to sleep is all that sounds good to me," Leonida said, clinging to Sage's side as they walked out into the brightening light of morning. "If I ate, I don't think I would even taste it, I am so tired."

"We will sleep, then eat," Sage murmured, guiding her toward their small wigwam.

Runner, who had given in to sleep long ago, raced out of the wigwam, wiping his eyes. "How's Pure Blossom?" he asked.

"She is better," Sage said, patting his head.

Leonida bent down and put her hands on Runner's tiny waist. "Sage and I must get some rest," she softly explained. "Go to Sally. She will give you some breakfast. Stay with her while Sage and I sleep."

Runner gazed up into Leonida's eyes somberly, then

he flung his arms around her neck and gave her a fierce hug. "I love you," he whispered, then broke away and took off in a mad dash toward Sally, who was just accepting food from some of the Navaho women who had cooked it over the open fire all night.

Leonida and Sage went inside the small temporary dwelling. Runner had not known how to keep a fire going, and Leonida was glad. She did not want any light in the wigwam to disturb her rest. She did not want any heat next to her skin except that which radiated from her husband's flesh. Even though she was so tired, she knew that if Sage asked, she would willingly join him in lovemaking.

But Sage didn't say anything about making love, nor did he approach her sexually. In the shadows of the small dwelling he stretched out on his stomach, and the wigwam was soon filled with his easy, measured breathing.

Seeing that he had not removed his moccasins, Leonida took it upon herself to do that so he could be more comfortable. Once they were set aside, she caressed his feet lovingly for a moment, and then she removed her clothes and stretched out beside him on the thick pallet of blankets.

Snuggling close, she felt the lethargy of sleep quickly claim her. Soon she was wandering through a wonderland in a dream—a land of flowers dotted the landscape, their fragrance filling the air like some rich French perfume. Birds were in abundance, soaring through the air, singing. Small animals scampered here and there, the squirrels the feistiest as their tails whipped nervously up and down, supporting them as they jumped from tree to tree like monkeys.

In this dream there was no sadness. Leonida experienced only pure happiness, to a degree that she had never known before. Sage rode into view on a snow-white stallion, stopping only long enough to whisk her up onto the horse with him. Sitting on his lap, facing him, Leonida clung to him and tossed her head back. Her hair billowed in the wind behind her.

Sage's mouth went to the hollow of her throat and he kissed her. He held the reins with one hand and with the other opened her blouse to him. His mouth covered her breast, sucking the nipple to tautness. As his horse galloped onward, seemingly of its own volition, Sage and Leonida began making love. Then Leonida was wrenched awake by someone speaking Sage's name outside the wigwam.

Her husband awakened with a start.

"Someone is calling for you outside the wigwam," Leonida said, scurrying into her skirt and blouse. "Oh, Sage, what if they have come about Pure Blossom?"

Sage gave her an uncertain look, then hurried to the door and went outside. The afternoon was waning into evening. He found a middle-aged Navaho maiden there, looking up at him with troubled eyes.

"What is it?" he said, putting a hand on her shoulder. "Why have you awakened your chief?"

The maiden's eyes wavered as she stared up at him, clasping and unclasping her hands nervously. "It is your sister," she finally said, her voice breaking. "She is making death rattles in her throat."

Sage broke into a mad run and rushed breathlessly into Pure Blossom's makeshift wigwam.

Leonida followed, just as breathless. She watched Sage kneel over his sister and peer down at her, his hands at her face.

Leonida gasped when she heard the strange, gurgling sounds coming from Pure Blossom's lungs as she struggled for every breath. She had heard those sounds before—

—just before her mother had died.

She swallowed the urge to cry out when she saw Pure Blossom's eyes open wide, fixed in a stare, one eye looking in one direction, the other looking in another.

Sage's heart seemed to stop as he looked down at his sister, his whole body filled with a great choking sensation as he listened to the sounds coming from the depths of her lungs.

And her eyes.

They were open, yet surely not seeing.

If she could see, she would look at him.

And she didn't.

Her eyes were strangely unblinking and fixed.

In a momentary trance, not moving or touching, only feeling a devastation more deadly than ever before in his life, Sage had done nothing but stare at his sister. Without even yet thinking, he picked her up into his arms and laid his cheek against hers, finding it cold to the touch.

Then suddenly he realized that she was no longer breathing.

She had just died in his arms.

"*A-i-i-i-*," he cried, holding her near and dear to his heart as he rocked her slowly back and forth.

Leonida went to him, but did not extend a hand toward him, knowing that at this moment he knew nothing but sorrow and that she could not lift it from him—not until he accepted what had just happened.

Sage rocked Pure Blossom for a while longer, then gently placed her back onto the pallet of furs. With trembling fingers he closed her eyes and covered her with a blanket.

Leonida knelt beside him and took one of his hands in hers as he began a soft chant. Outside, where no one yet knew of Pure Blossom's death, there were the normal sounds of a day's end. Someone had set up a loom. She could hear the thump thump thump of the weaver pounding down the thread in the loom.

A child laughed in the distance.

Someone was chopping wood.

A faraway turtledove seemed to be mocking the death inside this makeshift hogan.

27

A little while in the shine of the sun, we were
   twined together.
Joined lips forgot how the shadows fall when the day
   is done,
And when love is not.

—ERNEST DOWSON

The moon was hidden behind dark clouds, and in the distance lightning forked in lurid streaks across the heavens. Sage held Leonida's hand as they stood on a butte above the Navaho camp. Below them in thick, visible shadow, people moved, horses stamped, and smoke rose from tiny fires.

"Why does one's life have to be so fraught with pain?" Sage said, his voice hollow. "From birth, the struggle begins with one's emotions. Is there anyone, anywhere, who has not been beset with personal tragedies over and over again? There is not one among my people. That is the truth." He turned his dark eyes to Leonida. "Is it this way for the white people also? Are their daily struggles as deeply felt as the Navaho's?"

Leonida moved into his embrace and hugged him. "My darling, I can only speak for myself, and yes, I feel my losses deeply," she murmured. "First my mother died, and then my father. It was not easy to accept that lot in life, that of being alone, without parents to love and to confide in."

She leaned away from him and gazed up at him. "You changed so much for me," she said softly. "You

gave me new purpose in life. I don't feel alone anymore. My darling, let me help you with this pain . . .
with this emptiness that you are now feeling. There is
no need for either of us ever to be lonely again. And
as for your sister's death, yes, it is a tragedy. But the
pain will lessen as each day passes. It is with a voice
of experience that I speak.''

"My woman, you speak with much wisdom and
feelings,'' he said. ''It is good that I have found such
a woman to be my wife. You see, it is not only my
sister's death that lies heavy on my heart. It is everything—this escape to a new land, the abduction of Kit
Carson, and the fact that I have to bury my sister far
from land that she has known since childhood.''

He turned and gazed down at his camp again. ''I
feel as though I am a child again, with the unsure
future of an Indian, *all* Indians,'' he said solemnly.
''Although I am a chief, my powers are few. One by
one they have been taken from me. Even now, while
my sister awaits her burial ceremony at sunrise tomorrow, I feel perhaps even less than a man.''

Leonida paled and gasped. She gazed up at him, his
tortured voice paining her as though someone were
sticking knives into her heart. She suddenly felt so
helpless. How could she reach beyond his anguish and
bring him back to her?

Seeing this defeated side of him frightened her. The
only way she knew of making him forget his troubles
was making love to him, and now did not seem the
time to do this. Lovemaking at this time might even
be sacrilegious in the eyes of the Navaho.

Sage turned to her. ''Let us return to our dwelling,''
he said, taking her hand. ''It has been long since I last
ate. Even if I have no way to feed my soul at this time,
at least my body can take nourishment.''

Leonida stood on tiptoe and brushed a kiss across his lips. "Tomorrow will be hard, but after that, let us look forward, to our future, and all that we will be sharing," she said, beseeching him with wide, imploring eyes. "There is much to look forward to, my love. Your new village, and . . . and perhaps even a child? Would not that be grand, Sage? To have a child that we truly could call our own?"

Sage did not answer her right away. He gazed down at her with a lifeless expression, then placed one of her hands over his heart. "It is with every heartbeat that I wish for a child in your image," he said. "Yet I do not see it as wise at this time. As you have seen, so much stands in the way of our happiness. It is not good to bring a child into this world of questionable future. Runner will be our child. Is he not enough?"

Leonida was stunned to realize that he was not eagerly anticipating becoming a father. She had thought that all Indian warriors, especially chiefs, wished for a son to carry on their lineage. That Sage had actually accepted Runner as that son amazed her. Surely he said this because at this moment, in grieving over his sister, he was not thinking straight.

Although Leonida loved Runner with all her heart, she did not want her only child to be someone else's.

Solemnly, she walked alongside Sage as they made their way down the hillside. Suddenly she felt empty. She placed a hand over her abdomen, shivering at the thought of her womb being barren forever.

Another thought came to her. She glanced over at Sage, wondering what he would do if she became pregnant anyhow? They had done nothing to prevent pregnancy. Possibly she could be pregnant even now. Surely if she was, he would not turn his back on the child. Perhaps a child born of their love might even save him from this destructive void that was reaching through him like a sore, spreading its venom from cell to cell, killing him slowly.

When they reached the campsite, Sage stopped and looked for a moment on Pure Blossom's dwelling. It was circled outside by those who had loved her. Inside the singer was singing his dead song, a prayer to the soul of the dearly departed.

Sage wrenched his eyes away and walked quickly from Leonida and into their small dwelling. She stared after him for a moment, trying to understand why he was treating her this way. Grieving over a loved one made a person do many things that they regretted later. She knew that for a fact. She recalled not wanting anyone to get near her when her mother had passed away. Getting through the funeral had been the hardest thing in her life. It had seemed a social event for all of her parents' friends and relatives. When they had gathered near the casket, where her mother lay so stone-white and cold, and chattered and laughed together, it had been more than she could bear. She had taken it upon herself to order everyone from the house, leaving her father aghast.

When her father had died, she had stood at the back of the room, controlling her urges to scold those who laughed, smoked, and talked over her father's lifeless body. By then she was older and she had learned the art of restraint.

Putting herself in Sage's place, Leonida hurried into the wigwam. She stopped and gasped. Sage was obviously just as stunned as she at what lay in a circle around the fire.

Then she thought back again about the food that had been brought to her parents' house when her mother had died. Everyone had outdone themselves making the most delicious food ever for the grieving family. At the time she had felt that it was wrong to eat the food; she felt as though they were having a picnic at the expense of her mother. But her father had explained that it was traditional for friends, neighbors, and relatives to bring food to the family of the deceased, as a way to give their condolences.

It seemed that the Navaho were practicing a white people's tradition, for never had she seen such piles of food. Although their crops had been destroyed and their animals slain or abducted, the Navaho had taken from their stores of food that which they wanted to prepare for their chief and family. The smells were delectable as they wafted into her nostrils. Her stomach growled, and she could actually feel her mouth watering. Then she remembered how long it had been since she had eaten.

She glanced over at Sage. She knew that he had gone much longer without food than she had. He even looked pale and gaunt from hunger. She had to see to it that he took advantage of the generous offerings from his people.

"Would you look at the food?" she said, grabbing one of Sage's hands and moving him toward it. She gazed up at him. "I'm starved. Aren't you? I don't think I can get a wink of sleep if I don't eat something."

Sage eyed the food, actually weak from having gone so long without eating. If he thought back, he could not really remember the last time he had taken nourishment.

In fact, his eyes were blurring from the lack of food in his body. And although he did not like to think of eating during his time of mourning, he knew that he must. He must stay strong for his people, in order to lead them.

Sage allowed Leonida to guide him down onto a cushion of blankets beside the fire and the food. He gladly accepted a tray that she fixed for him, eyeing it hungrily. He waited for her to fill her own wooden plate with food for herself. When she finally sat down next to him, with corn fritters, sliced peaches, pine-needle tea, and various other offerings, and started plucking the different morsels up with her fingers, he dove in. Soon his plate was empty, almost without even a blink of his eyes.

Leonida giggled at how quickly he had emptied his plate. She set her own plate aside and refilled his. "Your people are wonderful cooks," she murmured. "I hope one day to learn all of the secrets of Navaho wives, so that I can always have a delicious meal waiting for you."

Sage put a hand on her wrist, urging her to set the plate down on the floor of the wigwam. "My wife, my stomach has been warmed by food," he said huskily. "But now my heart needs the same sort of nourishment." He drew her into his embrace, his mouth moving toward hers. "My wife, love me tonight. Help lift my burdens at least for a while."

"I'm always here for you, darling," she whispered, twining her arms around his neck. She glanced toward the closed entrance flap. "But what about Runner? He should be coming home anytime now. We can't allow him to find us making love. He will learn soon enough the desires of the heart."

"Runner is staying with Adam tonight," he said, combing his fingers through her long and flowing hair. "When he asked, I thought it best. I thought perhaps

I might not be able to sleep, with the sadness of tomorrow pressing down on my heart.''

"Darling," Leonida whispered, taking nibbles of his lower lip, "let our lovemaking be a potion for your grief. Let it heal you. Pure Blossom would not want you to grieve so over her death. She wanted nothing more of life than to see that you were happy. Darling, you *were* her life, her reason for getting up in the morning. You were her every heartbeat. Through you, my love, she still lives.''

"You speak with the wise heart of a Navaho elder," Sage said, smiling down at her as he framed her face between his hands. "Your words have touched my very soul. I love you. Oh, how I love you.''

His mouth bore down upon hers. He gently took her wrists and pulled her away from the fire and food, spreading her out beneath him, where blankets and soft pelts were laid across the floor.

He kissed her for a moment longer, then slowly, almost meditatively, removed her clothes. After she was splendidly naked before him, Sage stood up and began undressing, but stopped when she came to him and moved his hands away. She removed his clothes herself, her eyes locked with his.

"Forget everything tonight, my darling, except our passion for each other," Leonida murmured, tossing the last of his garments aside. "Tonight, my darling, give yourself up to the pleasure. I love you. Let me show you how much.''

Smiling up at Sage, she took his hands and led him down over her as she lay down on her back. Their lips met in a frenzied kiss, and when she opened her legs to him, locking them around his waist, he began his eager thrusts within her.

"I love you," she whispered as he slipped down to

suckle one of her breasts. She twined her fingers through his thick black hair as pleasure spread through her body.

"Darling, darling . . ." she whispered in a husky voice she did not recognize as hers.

Once again his steel arms enfolded her, and with one insistent thrust he was in her again, magnificently filling her. She rolled her head back and forth, her body seeming to be one massive heartbeat, throbbing from her head to her toes with building excitement and anticipation.

Sage buried his fingers in Leonida's hair and held her face still, his lips finding hers in a gentle kiss. He felt her hunger in the hard, seeking pressure of her lips. He was almost beyond coherent thought as the wild splendor spread its fire through him, the flames licking at his insides.

The passion was cresting.

He was soaring, flying higher and higher.

He moved himself more slowly within her, then faster, with quick and demanding thrusts.

Soon his body turned to liquid fire, and he grew dizzy with the passions exploding within him. He clung to Leonida as his body spasmed into hers.

She cried out against his lips as she gave herself over to the bliss of the moment, feeling him pressing endlessly deeper as he plunged again and again into her.

And then they lay cuddled together, breathless. Sage stroked her back. "Tonight we perhaps made a child?" he whispered against her cheeks.

Leonida's eyes widened and her breath slowed. "Darling, the way you said that makes me think you would wish it to be so," she said, leaning away from him so that she could see him clearly. "A short while ago you spoke against having a child. What has changed your mind?"

"My wife," Sage said, brushing a kiss across her lips. "You are the reason. You should never be denied anything as precious as having a child. And, my beautiful Leonida, you have ways of convincing your husband that the future is not all that bleak after all. Perhaps a child would heal many of my deep-seeded wounds, caused by the injustices of the world. A child is an innocent thing. A newborn child gives one the feeling of a rebirth for all things. Our child, Leonida. Our child would do this for this Navaho chieftain."

"Then I pray that I can tell you soon that I am with child," Leonida whispered, her lips trembling against his as she kissed him.

"I would wish for a daughter first," Sage whispered against her lips. "She will be called Pure Blossom. My sister would be alive, always, in our child."

"That is such a beautiful thought," Leonida sighed. "I shall whisper it to Pure Blossom tomorrow while I help prepare her for her burial."

Sage hugged her tightly to him. "You are so very special," he said, his voice breaking. "So very, very special."

28

The trees and bushes round the place
Seemed midnight at noonday—
                    —JOHN CLARE

The next morning everything was solemn again between Sage and Leonida as they ate their early-morning
meal. Leonida understood Sage's silence as he sat staring into the flames of the fire, after scarcely touching
his food. Soon they would be placing his beloved sister
in the ground, far from the place where their ancestors
had been buried.

This too seemed to tear at Sage's insides. Resentment toward the white man burned within him like a
fire spreading. Suddenly he turned to Leonida. "There
is much to be asked of you today," he said.

Leonida's eyebrows rose questioningly. She set her
wooden platter aside, her own food half-eaten. "What
do you mean?" she murmured. "What are you going
to ask me to do?"

"Last night you spoke of helping prepare my sister
for burial," Sage said, gently placing a hand to her
cheek. "My wife, I must ask more of you than that. I
must ask you to prepare my sister for burial alone."

"Alone?" she gasped. She had dreaded even as-
sisting the other women, yet she felt that it was required of her because the dead was Sage's sister. "Why
must I do this alone? Everyone loved Pure Blossom.
There will be many of your women who will want to
care for her."

"As time goes on, there will be many customs of my people that you will learn," Sage said thickly. He caressed her chin with his thumb, then moved his hand away from her face. "Today you will learn one of the most important customs of the Navaho."

"And that is?" Leonida prodded, yet she dreaded hearing the answer. The thought of being alone with Pure Blossom, readying her body for burial, frightened her.

And how was she to know what to do? It would be bad enough to be with Pure Blossom now, seeing her so stone-cold in death and remembering how vital she had been even with her affliction. But to take on the duties of readying her for her grave?

Yet how could she say no to her husband?

"The Navaho people are very hesitant to touch a dead person, and outsiders, non-Navaho, have always been recruited to prepare the dead and to remove the corpses from their dwellings," he explained, his eyelids heavy as he gazed at her.

"But how could that be possible?" Leonida asked softly. "The Navaho live a secluded life, away from the others."

"It has not always been that way," Sage said bitterly. "I recall the neighboring Pueblo, who when I was a child were always ready to come to the aid of their friends, the Navaho. And although so many Kiowa were our enemy, there were some friendly bands with whom we exchanged favors."

Sage doubled his hand into a tight fist at his side. "But now there are none we can call friends or allies," he said in a hiss. "The white people have seen to that. Those who once allied themselves with the Navaho are now scattered like blowing grains of sand in all directions of this earth. The customs of the Navaho must change because of this.''

His eyes softened and he took her hand in his, squeezing it lovingly. "But today there is one among us who can help as my sister is prepared to travel to the Country of the Ghosts, the destination of human beings after death. You, my wife, are the one we will depend on today. Can you do this for your husband and his people?''

Leonida swallowed hard and forced a smile. "Yes, I will do this for you,'' she said, flinging herself into his arms and hugging him tightly. She still dreading her task with all her might, but if this could help lighten his burden, then so be it. She *must* do it. Yet a thought struck her that made her pull away from Sage.

"But I don't know what to do,'' she blurted, timidly looking up at him. "How can I do this if I am not shown?''

"You will not be shown, but you will be instructed by Gay Heart, a close friend of Pure Blossom's,'' he said, his voice breaking. "She will tell you what to do. Everything.''

"Oh, I see,'' Leonida said, though she still did not feel any better about it. The responsibility frightened her, for what if she did something wrong? Would this affect the burial rites? Would this change the course of Pure Blossom's journey to the "Country of the Ghosts''?

Her thoughts were catapulted back in time, to the day before her mother's funeral. Although Leonida had not been very old, she had been forced to accompany her father to the mortuary. Her knees had trembled as she stood at his side while he made the burial arrangements and chose the casket. It had been so morbid to her, she had become ill, choking back the urge to retch as her father ushered her quickly out of the dark and gloomy mortuary.

She shivered at the memory of standing aside and watching as her mother was prepared for her final resting place in the casket. Several women had fussed over her mother in her bedroom while preparing her for her casket. Earlier, the women had chosen the dress that she would wear. It was black and sequined, nothing at all like her mother would ever have had in her wardrobe.

Leonida had shuddered as they combed her mother's hair into a tight bun atop her head. She had been proud of her long, flowing golden hair.

But it was the makeup on her mother's face that made Leonida want to shout at the women to get away from her. With all the makeup they put on her porcelain-white face, these women made her mother look like a circus clown instead of the sweet and soft-spoken person she had always been.

Remembering these things made it easier for Leonida to accept the responsibility of Pure Blossom's appearance. She would let no one make her look like a clown. She would make sure that Pure Blossom was not a mockery of the way she had been in true life, so sweet and giving, so loved.

"There is someone else that I must approach about Pure Blossom's burial," Sage said, his jaw tightening, his eyes suddenly filled with tormented anger.

"Who?" Leonida asked, moving to her feet along with Sage. As he dressed himself in his dark velveteen breeches, and a velveteen shirt to match, Leonida also dressed in a garment devoid of bright colors and frills. It was a full-skirted gingham dress with a high collar and long sleeves. As she waited for Sage to respond, she brushed her hair until it lay across her shoulders and down her back in glistening, golden waves.

Sage bent over and pulled on a knee-high buckskin moccasin. "Kit Carson is aware of the Navaho's tradition as well," he said, pulling on his other moccasin. "I must go to him. I must seek his help. If he agrees, then tonight, as the sun sets, we will make bargains between us that will best suit us both."

"You're not going to ask him to help with the ceremony?" Leonida gasped. She went to him and put a hand on his arm. "Sage, surely you wouldn't."

"I thought about this hard and long into the night," Sage murmured, gently resting his hands on her shoulders. "Kit Carson has known the Navaho many moons. He once was a friend. Perhaps drawing him into the ceremony of the Navaho might bring friendship between us again, not only between me and Kit Carson but between him and my people, as a whole."

"But he has said, time and again, that he cannot make decisions that will affect the welfare of your people without the direct order from the president," she said, her voice guarded. She was not sure just how much the Navaho men accepted their wives' debating their decisions. Until now Sage had seemed open enough with her to make her believe that she could be as open with him.

"He has more powers over decisions than he allows anyone to think," Sage said, smiling smugly. "If he helps with the burial before he knows that I am ready to set him and the captives free as payment for his help, then he will prove to me that he is worthy of my chancing to trust him again."

"What are you going to ask him to do at the

ceremony?'' Leonida asked softly, doubting her husband's logic for the first time since she had met him. This man, this Kit Carson, was not to be trusted ever again.

"He will be asked to remove Pure Blossom's body from her dwelling,'' he said, his voice drawn. "He will carry her to her final resting place and lay her there. By doing so, he will align himself with the Navaho again. And while doing this, he will be aware of the full meaning of his sacrifice. He will expect to receive his freedom. He will expect to see the Navaho as friends then, instead of enemies. He will follow his heart then to do what is right by them.''

"I hope you are right,'' Leonida said, more under her breath than aloud.

He lifted her chin so that her eyes met his. "Let me explain the belief of the Navaho burial ritual to you,'' he said softly. "Then as you witness it, you will understand. After you have prepared Pure Blossom for burial, her body will not be taken out the doorway, but through a hole broken in the north wall. The wigwam will then be abandoned and never entered again by any Navaho. Pure Blossom will be carried to a high, commanding bluff that overlooks the river. Such a serene place of burial is desired because of its solemn dignity.''

He stopped and cleared his throat. Talking about the burial of his sister pained him deeply. "She will be buried several feet deep in the burying ground which the Navaho refers to as the "grave habitation,'' he continued. "She will be buried in a sandy place where excavation is easy. My sister's soul will have to undertake a long journey before it reaches its destination. Somewhere along the way her spirit will stop and drink at a large hole in the ground, after which it will shrink and pass on to the 'Country of the Ghosts,' where it will be fed with spirit food and drink. After this act of communion with the spirit world, her spirit may not ever return.''

Sage drew Leonida into his embrace. He stroked her waist-length hair. ''All Navaho people possess two spirits, a greater and a lesser,'' he said. ''During one's illness, the lesser soul is spirited away by the denizens of ghost land. It is my belief that my sister's spirit is of the greater, and that her soul waits to be released from her frail, twisted body, then to be a thing of beauty in the hereafter.''

''I would like to think that also,'' Leonida said, gazing up at him with tears in her eyes.

''I must go and speak with Kit Carson,'' Sage said, easing Leonida from his arms. ''My sister awaits your arrival.'' He leaned a soft kiss to her lips. ''My sister will somehow know your obedience and kindness to her. I will thank you for her.''

He started to walk away, then turned and smiled down at Leonida. ''On entering the spiritual sphere, my sister will be treading in the footsteps of heroic beings who have preceded her, who have vanquished the forces of death and what the white people call 'hell,' thusly stripped of their terror,'' he said, his voice warm with feeling. ''One day we, too, will travel the same path and we will embrace my sister again.''

Leonida wiped tears from her eyes as he left the wigwam. Then she herself left, turning toward Pure Blossom's dwelling. The Navaho were gathered around the house, demonstrating their grief in various ways. As Leonida stepped inside, she found the singer standing near the corpse, chanting softly, and then occasionally singing his dead songs, his prayer to Pure Blossom's soul.

A young Navaho maiden, pretty and petite, with midnight-dark eyes and hair and gentle facial features, was obediently kneeling down beside Pure Blossom, a milk-white doeskin dress draped over her arms, a roll of birch-bark resting on the floor beside her.

Leonida went and knelt beside the woman, knowing that this must be Gay Heart. They spoke only when Leonida needed further instructions as to how she should prepare Pure Blossom for her burial. First Leonida smoothed the blanket away from Pure Blossom. Her naked body was already turning a strange color, similar to ice frozen firmly on a river.

A basin of water with a cloth, and suds from a yucca plant floating at the top, was set on the floor beside Pure Blossom. Leonida did as she was told. She began washing Pure Blossom, giving her body the aroma of the yucca.

When that was done, Leonida took the beautiful dress that was offered her. She gently put the dress on Pure Blossom and then she attached several ornaments to the clothes and placed silver bracelets on her wrists and a beaded necklace around her neck.

Having seen how Pure Blossom took such pride in her floor-length black hair, Leonida took much time in brushing it, then braiding it in one long braid, bringing the end of the braid to rest between Pure Blossom's hands.

"She is beautiful," Gay Heart whispered, looking down adoringly. She then turned a soft smile to Leonida. "She must now be wrapped in a roll of birch bark. This will preserve her body at least until her spirit has taken its last steps into the Country of the Ghosts."

Leonida smiled weakly at the maiden, then accepted

the roll of birch bark in her arms. She gazed at Pure Blossom a moment longer, taking her last look at her beloved friend. Then, swallowing a lump that was building in her throat, she managed to get the birch bark under Pure Blossom and slowly wrapped it around her.

When this was done, the singer left the wigwam and announced that it was time for the short walk to the chosen burial ground.

As Leonida turned to leave the wigwam, she stopped with a start when she saw Kit Carson entering.

"You've agreed to do this for Sage?" Leonida whispered, stunned by his decision, yet feeling relieved. Perhaps Sage and Kit Carson had come to an understanding—one that benefited both Kit and the Navaho.

"Does it seem so astonishing that I would?" he whispered back. He placed a gentle hand on her cheek. "Pretty lady, I have done this many times before for the Navaho. The only difference is that this time I do it in the capacity of captive. Yet because of my admiration for Sage, I could not refuse him."

"Thank you for your kindness," Leonida said, taking his hand from her cheek and gently lowering it to his side. "I also wish your generosity could be offered under different circumstances. Why couldn't you have been as generous about everything else that the Navaho believe in? Like their need for freedom."

Her chin held high, Leonida moved past him into the heat of the morning. She went to Sage's side and watched Navaho warriors tear the birch bark away, opening the wall at the north side of the house, making it large enough for Kit Carson to carry Pure Blossom through. The chanting and singing continued, the voice of the singer the most prominent of all, echoing into the heavens with the remorseful songs.

Soon Kit appeared at the readied hole. Carrying the wrapped body in his arms, he stepped through the hole, then walked on past the congregation, going where Sage had directed him earlier to go. The people followed him up a hillside, Sage, Leonida, and the singer at the lead. The walk was dusty, the sun hot, the heat pulsing.

When the crest of the hill was reached, a shade tree was pointed out. Beneath it the grave had already been dug. Pure Blossom was laid into the opened arms of the earth.

Kit stepped back and stood beside Sage and Leonida. Gifts were placed in the grave with her. Leonida had not known of this custom, and badly wanted to give Pure Blossom something of herself. Her hand drifted to the squash blossom necklace that rested around her neck. Sage had repaired its clasp. Her fingers trembled as she unclasped it, filled with remembrances of the moment Pure Blossom had given it to her. Pure Blossom would be proud of this gift, for while she was alive she had known how precious it was to Leonida.

Leonida knelt down and placed the squash blossom necklace with Pure Blossom's other gifts of love.

A warm hand in hers drew her back to her feet. She gazed up into Sage's loving eyes, seeing pride in them, letting her know that he approved of the gift.

The ceremony lasted a short while longer as songs continued to be lifted into the heavens. And then the crowd began slowly dispersing. Sage went to the grave and knelt down on both knees. He began scooping the dirt over Pure Blossom's wrapped body and the many gifts that lay in the grave with her.

Leonida put a hand to her mouth, stifling her wonder when Kit went and knelt on the opposite side of the grave and helped Sage fill it with the dirt.

Sage and Kit stopped for a moment, their eyes meeting momentarily. Then they both smiled and continued with the chore at hand.

Leonida sighed. For the first time in weeks she had hope that things were going to work out after all.

29

Yes, this is Love, the steadfast and the true,
The immortal glory which have never set.
                                    —CHARLES SWAIN

Leonida served Sage and Kit Carson corn soup and pine-needle tea, then sat down beside Sage with her own platter of food. Though the two men began eating in silence, her own appetite had waned with apprehension of what lay ahead. Runner was still with Adam, as Leonida had encouraged in order to keep him out of range of the possible heated arguments that might arise between Sage and Kit.

Unable to eat, Leonida set her wooden bowl aside, then grew even more tense when Sage set his bowl down beside him, his soup half-eaten. She looked guardedly over at Kit Carson as he also set his bowl aside, having scarcely touched his food.

"It is with much gratitude that I thank you for your part in my sister's burial services," Sage said, drawing his knees part way up to his chest and crossing his legs at the ankles. He placed a hand on each of his knees, his back stiff. "For your kindness, I wish to speak with you of your freedom."

"Pure Blossom was sweet, kind and innocent," Kit said. "I was glad to assist in her burial." He drew his knees up before him as well and hugged them with his arms. "I now listen to what you have to say with an open mind and a friendly heart," he said, nodding at Sage.

"Our friendship goes back in time many moons," Sage said, his face a mask of control. "It is because of this, and because of what you did for my sister, that I am allowing you to leave. You are no longer a captive. Nor are the white women and children. But, Kit Carson, hear my warning well. This Navaho chieftain, and his people who are loyal to him, will never be enslaved on a reservation. I take my people far, far away, where no white man can find or harm them. It is best that when you leave, you do not turn your eyes in this direction again, for if you or your pony soldiers ever come near my people again, this Navaho chieftain will become your bitter enemy forever."

"I listen to you with mixed emotions," Kit said. "You speak of freedom in one heartbeat, and in the next you speak the word 'enemy.' "

"Only because I have found that when dealing with *any* white man, one must not ever be too confident that friendship will last long between them," Sage said flatly. He folded his arms across his chest. "Is that not so, Kit Carson? Have you not turned your back on Sage now more than once, to make room in Navaholand for more white people settlers?"

"Only in the name of progress," Kit said, his eyes wavering.

"Progress," Sage said in a hiss. "That word cuts deep into my soul. Does not that word mean in the English tongue 'a gradual betterment'? Whose? Of course it is always the white man's, not the Navaho's. It is called progress in the white man's culture if the Navaho are forced into a white man's prison cleverly named reservation."

Sage placed a fist over his heart. "Kit Carson, this chieftain thinks of progress for *his* people," he said. He then leaned over, staring angrily at Kit. "This chieftain warns you never to get in the way of the Navaho's progress again," he said. "Do you understand?"

Kit squirmed uneasily on the mat beneath him. He ran his fingers through his thick golden hair and cleared his throat nervously.

Then he put his hands on his knees again, straightening his back and squaring his shoulders. "Your words are firm, as are your convictions," he said. "I promise you, Sage, that I will do everything in my power to see that you are left alone, so that you are able to build a good life again with your people. I will tell the President my feelings for you and your people, and that I believe you should not be forced onto a reservation. I am certain myself that you had no part in the raids on the settlers."

Then Kit paused. "Yet there was that attack on the stagecoach," he said solemnly. "That was an act of terrorism. Some of the white pony soldiers were wounded. You even have with you many white captives. That is something the President won't be able to forget so easily."

"And I would not expect him to," Sage said matter-of-factly. "I regret having wounded several pony soldiers. But no harm has come to the captive women and children. They have become among us as though Navaho themselves. They have been fed well. They have been kept warm with Navaho blankets and fires. They have slept comfortably alongside the Navaho. You can take *that* back to your President. Tell him to ask any of those who have lived among the Navaho these past weeks if they have any complaints, other than not having been given the right to leave."

"There was one casualty among the women, isn't that so?" Kit asked, forking an eyebrow.

"Yes, there was one among the women who passed away," Leonida said quickly. "Trevor Harrison's mother, Carole. But she died of natural causes. Even if she had been at the fort, she would still be dead. She had a lung ailment. Her days were numbered when she entered the stagecoach. You cannot blame Sage for that."

"I was not sure of the circumstances," Kit said humbly. "I will take Trevor back with me to Fort Defiance. I will make sure he is placed with relatives."

"That is not necessary. Trevor is now called Runner," Sage said proudly. "My wife and I have taken him in, as though he was borne of us. He is now our son in every way."

"You have adopted him?" Kit said, gasping. He leaned forward, frowning. "I'm sorry. I still must take him back with me. He will be better off with relatives."

Desperation seized Leonida's insides. "You can't have him," she said in a rush. "I mean to say, he has no living relatives. Before she died, Carole asked me to raise him as if he were my own child. I gave my word that I would. And, Kit, I never break a promise to anyone."

For a moment there was a strained silence, then Kit nodded. "I am sure you will make a good mother," he said in an unconvincing voice. "But there is the fact that you are now married to Sage. The child will have no means to acquire an education." He cleared his throat. "And, Leonida, he will be raised to learn the customs of the Navaho, instead of—"

"I am already teaching him how to read and write," Leonida interrupted. There was now at least a measure of peace between Sage and Kit. She wished to get these discussions over with and get Kit on his way before something was said that would cause Sage to change his mind.

"And to live with the Navaho, one must learn their customs," Leonida continued. "He is adapting well. And he is happy. Isn't that all that matters?"

Kit kneaded his chin, then nodded. "The child has suffered a great loss," he said. "And if you have the ability to lift him up from his grieving and be happy, so be it. Who am I to argue against something that is obviously right for the child?"

"My wife is very right for the child," Sage said. His voice and his smile were soft as he cast a quick glance toward Leonida.

Then his eyes narrowed as he turned his conversation back to the business at hand. "You have said that you will plead the Navaho cause with your President," he said. "That is good and I am grateful. But there is one more thing that we have not discussed."

"And that is?" Kit said, leaning forward.

"Those Navaho who came down from the mountain and surrendered to the soldiers," Sage said smoothly. "A part of the terms of my releasing you is that you promise to release those of my people who foolishly joined you to go to the reservation."

Kit's jaw tightened. He straightened his back and placed his hands on his knees again. "You have already promised my release," he said, his voice drawn. "You said nothing then of further terms of my release."

"It is being said now," Sage said flatly.

Kit inhaled a deep breath. "I'm sorry, Sage," he said softly. "That's impossible. Those Navaho surrendered. They did it willingly. This is something that cannot be reversed. It is by the order of the President that they are going to the reservation. It is not an easy task changing the President's mind. I will be waging perhaps a private war between myself and the President when I go and argue *your* case. Let us leave it at that, Sage, or all might be lost and I may be forced to hunt you down again.''

Kit paused. ''Think of those of your people who stood devotedly by you,'' he then said. ''They deserve to have a chance. I am giving them *and* you a chance to escape to a new land. Let me and the captives go now without requiring promises of me that I cannot keep.''

Sage gave this much thought. He was unhappy about getting only half of that which he had demanded from Kit Carson, yet he knew that what Kit had said was true. If Sage insisted on the release of those Navaho who had turned their back on their chief, he might be endangering the rest of his beloved, strongly devoted people. It did not seem a risk worth taking.

''Go,'' he said, rising to his feet. ''You are free to leave. Take the captives with you.''

Leonida rose slowly to her feet, relief flooding through her.

Kit got to his feet and went to Sage. He looked questioningly into Sage's dark eyes, then without further thought embraced Sage affectionately. ''My friend,'' he said. ''It is good to be able to call you that again.''

Sage returned the hug, then stepped away. ''Friendships last as long as trust is maintained between two people,'' he said. ''I will go now and speak to my warriors about your return to your people. Many will escort you and the women and children. Horses will be loaned you until you reach your people.''

''That is very considerate of you,'' Kit said. ''Thank you, Sage. I truly appreciate it.''

Sage turned and left.

Leonida went to Kit. "Thank you for everything," she said, then without hesitation gave him a hug. "Thank you for understanding what freedom means to Sage and his people."

"I have always understood the meaning of freedom for all Indians," Kit said. "Most of my adult life has been spent trying to make wrongs right between the white and Indian communities. Of late, though, it has become almost impossible. There are so many settlers rushing west for land and a new way of life. The Indians are in the way. Navaholand is now populated more with people who have white skin than those with red. Washington wanted it this way." He shrugged. "I'm one man and I take my orders from Washington. What else can I say?"

Leonida clutched his arm strongly. "Please do all that you can to assure Sage's freedom," she begged. "He deserves no less and you know it."

"All that I can say is that I will try my damnedest," Kit said. He gazed into her eyes. "What am I to tell Harold when I get back to the fort?"

Leonida flinched and drew her hand back to herself. The sudden mention of Harold caught her off guard. "Harold?" she murmured. "Lord, I had completely forgotten about him." She ran her fingers through her hair nervously, then lifted her chin proudly. "Tell him the truth, Kit. Tell him that I am now married to Sage. It isn't fair to let him think that he might still have a chance with me."

"How did this marriage come about?" Kit asked, clasping his hands behind him. "You were among those taken captive, were you not?"

"Yes, I was," Leonida said. "But not intentionally. Sage had no idea I was on that stagecoach."

"What difference did it make if he did or not know?" Kit further questioned.

"You see, we had met before," she said, blushing. "We had been attracted to one another before the stagecoach holdup. When we were thrown together as we were traveling toward his stronghold, our true feelings for one another surfaced. We were married shortly after we reached his stronghold."

"Even though you were spoken for by Harold?" Kit asked, sighing.

"Perhaps Harold still regarded me possessively," Leonida softly explained. "But I did not feel the same toward him, ever. My father arranged the marriage. As you saw, I was on the stagecoach leaving Harold. That was explanation enough to him, I thought, as to why. I could never marry a man like him. I don't even know now why I ever allowed my father to persuade me that it might work between myself and that . . . and that cad."

"I see," Kit said, then put a hand gently on her shoulder. "I shall make Harold understand things." He cleared his throat nervously. "I wish you much happiness, yet I don't see how it can be achieved living the life of an Indian."

"As Sage's wife, I could not be happier," Leonida murmured. "Whatever obstacles get in the way, Sage and I will work them out together."

Runner burst into the wigwam, crying. Leonida caught him up into her arms as he made a lunge for her.

"What's the matter, sweetie?" she asked, brushing tears from his cheeks.

"Adam is leaving," Runner wailed. "He can't leave. He's my best friend!"

Leonida felt trapped, not knowing what to say that

might alleviate his pain. He had already lost his mother. And now his best friend was leaving him? To a small child, a best friend was something like a lifeline. They depended on each other for sharing their secrets and for so many more things.

And she was afraid that his next words would be— to allow him to go with Adam, to return to the ways of the white world instead of living like an Indian!

"You should be happy instead of sad that Adam and his mother are able to return now to their loved ones," Leonida tried to explain. "Don't you know that Adam's father is worried sick over him? If anything happened to you, Sage and I would hardly be able to bear it. It is the same with Adam. His father will be so happy when he has his son back with him. Adam will be as happy to be with his father. And Adam's mother. You want her to be happy, don't you? She's going to be reunited with her husband. That is like if I had been gone for a long time and I was finally able to return to Sage. Can't you see? It is the same for Adam and his mother and father."

Kit smiled from Leonida to Runner, then left the wigwam.

Runner sniffed and gazed up at Leonida. "Will I ever see him again?" he asked in his soft little voice.

"I'm certain of it," Leonida said, relieved that he, as usual, was adapting quickly to change. "In fact, I will see to it, my darling Runner, that one day you two will play again together. It might be several years before this can be achieved, but, sweetie, you *will* see Adam again."

Runner snaked his tiny arms around Leonida's neck and hugged her. "I love you," he said, then wriggled free of her arms. "I've got to go and tell Adam that we will see one another again. That will make him so happy!''

Leonida smiled, inhaled a relieved breath and gave a small prayer of thank-you to her Lord, then left the wigwam. When she got outside, she stood watching for a moment as the women and children packed up things that the Indian women had given them as gifts of remembrance. Tears came to her eyes as she watched these women of different skin colors hug one another, some crying, truly hating to leave one another.

Then Sally came to Leonida and embraced her, tears streaming down her cheeks. "I was so wrong about so many things," she murmured. "Forgive me?"

"Forgiven," Leonida said, returning the embrace. "This isn't a final good-bye. I've promised Runner that he will play with Adam again. I'm not certain how, or when, but I will see that my promise is kept to that youngster."

"I will look forward to the day we meet again," Sally said, hugging Leonida again. Then she fell in step with the other women as they began walking toward the horses assigned to them, their children riding in the same saddle with their parents.

Leonida rushed to Sage's side. Runner came and clung to Leonida. His eyes were wide and he was biting his lower lip to keep from crying as he waved a last time to Adam.

Kit turned and saluted Sage, winked at Leonida, then urged his horse into a soft trot through the camp, the women and children behind them, the Navaho warriors riding alongside, in groups of threes.

Soon the horses' hooves could no longer be heard. The Navaho women stood silently craning their necks to get a last look, and then returned to their chores of cooking, washing clothes, and putting wood on their campfires.

"Well, that's that," Leonida said, sighing. She smiled up at Sage. "It's going to work out, darling. I know it is."

Sage did not respond. His jaw was tight and he was staring into the distance. Leonida had to wonder if he was already regretting his decision to let Kit Carson go. Sage had to know that without Kit, he no longer had his trump card.

30

I am desolate and sick of an old passion,
Yea, hungry for the lips of my desire.
—ERNEST DOWSON

The journey to Fort Defiance had been a long and grueling one for Kit Carson. Halfway there, he began to feel ill, yet he could not put his finger on what was wrong. Slowly his energy drained from him and he needed to stop more often than he wished to catch a wink of sleep. He was needing more rest than had ever been required of him before.

He was sitting in Harold's office listlessly as they discussed the events of the past few weeks. Kit scarcely heard what Harold said, and his temples were pounding.

Harold sat behind his desk. He noticed Kit's lethargy, yet thought it was because of the long journey and the imprisonment that he had endured.

"When it was discovered that you had been abducted from the camp, the men went immediately in search of you," Harold said, leaning forward and resting his elbows on the desktop. "When they couldn't find you, they thought it was best to travel on to Fort Defiance, since they themselves feared an attack by renegades. They had no idea it was just one man that took you away."

"Sage is not just one man," Kit said, cold perspiration lacing his brow. "He's got more fortitude and courage than ten men. I can't help but admire him."

"You said that he took you to his temporary camp," Harold said, his eyes narrowing. "Tell me where that is."

"Telling you that won't help you find him," Kit said, evading Harold's demand. "By the time you get to the campsite, Sage would already have reached his destination, and from what he has told me, no one but Sage has ever been there. Give it up, Harold. You've got more to worry about than one man and his few warriors."

"That's true," Harold said, his voice even and smooth. "Leonida. You said that she was in the stagecoach that had been hijacked. Well, damn it, you've returned the women and children and Leonida was not among them. I'm sure *you* know the reason why. I couldn't get any of the women to give me any answers about Leonida. They just ignored me when I asked them. So, Kit, it's up to you to let me know what's happened to Leonida."

Kit looked carefully over at Harold. "Are you certain you want to know?" he asked.

"How many times must I tell you?" Harold said, his voice rising in frustration. "Tell me, damn it. Now."

Kit shrugged. "Alright, I'll tell you," he said. "But you aren't going to like it one damn bit." He paused, then blurted. "She's married to Sage. She's his wife. And Carole Harrison's son, Trevor? He's staying with Leonida and Sage, being raised as their son in the tradition of the Navaho."

Harold's eyes widened. "How can that be?" he stammered. "She was my betrothed. And how could you allow the boy to stay—"

Kit interrupted. "Don't ask me to explain anything else about any of that," Kit said in an agitated grumble. "All that I can say is that I've given my word to Sage that I'm going to do everything within my power to see that he's not bothered anymore. He's going to be given a chance at freedom again. As long as they are far away from land that is wanted by the government for the settlers, why should we *want* to bother him?"

Kit took a handkerchief from his rear breeches pocket and wiped the perspiration from his brow. When his finger touched his flesh, he flinched, realizing that he had a fever.

His thoughts returned to Pure Blossom's burial. He had announced to the Navaho that her body had been ravaged by prairie fever. At that very moment he himself had been exposed. He knew that, since he was so tired and drained of energy from the heat on those long days of travel and from pushing himself beyond his endurance, his resistance to disease had been diminished.

Kit looked over at Harold, and foreboding grabbed him in his gut. Only during the stage when the person with prairie fever had a temperature was it contagious.

At this moment he was exposing Harold.

He pushed his chair back so quickly that it fell backward and crashed onto the floor. Lightheadedness overcame him, and he had to grab the desk to keep from falling to the floor.

"Good Lord, man, what's the matter?" Harold gasped, rising quickly from his chair. He went around and, placing an arm around Kit, attempted to lead him to another chair, but Kit brushed him away.

"Get away from me," Kit said, his throat suddenly feeling parched.

"What?" Harold said. He took a step back. "What is this all about?"

Still gripping the desk hard, Kit looked at Harold. "Forget Sage and Leonida for a second and take a good look at me," he said, his voice breaking. "What do you see?"

"I see a man in dire need of medical attention," Harold said, inching away from Kit.

"I'd say you are right," Kit mumbled, his knees trembling as he rose slowly from the desk. "I've got prairie fever. I would imagine you don't truly have to take precautions to stay away from me, after all. You've already touched me. You have been exposed to my breath. I would wager that you will start to feel poorly even as soon as tonight. Slowly you will feel drained of energy, and then comes the fever. Yes, Harold, I'd say we'll be sharing the same room in the infirmary here at the fort."

Harold paid little heed to what Kit was saying. He was unable to forget his obsession with Leonida. With Kit too ill to know what was going on, Harold would have free rein to do as he damn well pleased. He would go against Kit's recommendations and find Sage's new stronghold, no matter how long it took. He would take his most valuable men, who could withstand the punishment of many days' travel.

A loud thumping sound drew Harold back to the present. "Good Lord," he gasped. Kit was unconscious on the floor. Not wanting to touch him, afraid of further exposure, Harold ran from the office. Outside, he was glad to find some of his soldiers loitering beside the building, talking and smoking fat cigars.

"Kit Carson has fainted dead away in my office," Harold shouted, waving his hands frantically. He did not give the soldiers a hint of what was wrong with Kit, not wanting to frighten them. "Two of you. Go and get him. Take him to the infirmary. And be quick about it. He's sick as hell.''

The men hesitated. They began backing away from Harold.

Harold's eyes narrowed angrily as he reached out and grabbed two of the soldiers by the arms. "Get in there, you yellow-bellied cowards," he hissed. "Get Kit to the doctor so he can be looked after."

The two men rushed away.

Harold went storming around the barracks, shaking men out of their bunks and wrenching others away from their poker games.

After they were all standing at attention out in the middle of the courtyard, Harold began pacing back and forth, glowering at them. Occasionally he looked toward the infirmary windows, hoping that Kit was still too ill to hear his orders. Kit was the only one standing in the way of his determination to find Sage and—ultimately—Leonida.

He would not accept the fact that she had been running from him in the stagecoach the day it had been attacked. All she needed was a little convincing! And Harold knew ways of convincing that would turn her no to yes.

"Men, we've a job to do," he shouted, clasping his hands behind him as he continued pacing. "Since neither you nor Kit was able to capture Sage and his runaway Navaho, it's time to try again."

He glanced at the fenced-in Navaho, waiting for their long walk to New Mexico. He had to leave enough able-bodied men to escort them, and he had to leave enough soldiers to protect the fort.

"Those who traveled with Kit Carson while searching for Sage, step out of line and prepare yourselves to escort the captive Navaho to New Mexico," he ordered.

He began walking stiffly before the men, tapping one and then another on the shoulder. "You men that I'm choosing will travel with me," he said flatly. "The remainder will stay behind and guard the fort."

After a short while Harold was on his horse ready to travel, his assigned soldiers lined up on horses behind him, other horses packed well with provisions for the many days' journey. He looked over his shoulder as the Navaho captives began walking in the opposite direction, their heads hung, children wailing and clinging to their mothers. He ignored their frailty and the fact that they were being forced to go all the way to New Mexico on foot. He did not have horses to waste on them. As far as he was concerned, the more who died while making the long trek to the reservation, the fewer would have to be fed and cared for once there.

Wheeling his horse around, Harold rode away at a hard gallop, his soldiers dutifully following. He saluted a young officer who was standing guard outside the wide gate of the fort. Then he gazed straight ahead, a smug look on his face.

Soon Leonida would be his again, and Sage would be hanging from a tree, a noose around his red neck.

It was just turning dusk when Harold saw several horsemen up ahead, obviously unaware of him and his soldiers. They were riding hard into the pale light in the same direction that Harold was traveling, the noise of their horses' hooves surely drowning out that made by his soldiers' mounts.

Harold motioned with his hand to advance quickly on the horsemen, who were close enough now that he could tell they were Indians. His heart pounded within his chest at the thought that Sage might possibly be among them, yet it did not seem reasonable that he would not be with his people—and Leonida.

"Then who?" he asked, idly scratching his brow with one hand while the other gripped the horse's reins tightly.

When he overtook the four Indians, Harold's eyes widened and a smile broadened on his lips. His soldiers surrounded the Indians, their rifles aimed at them. Harold moved away from the soldiers and drew up beside one of the Indians. "Well, if it ain't my lucky day," he said, chuckling. "It's none other than Chief Four Fingers."

The Kiowa looked guardedly at the soldiers, one by one, and then glared at Harold. "Is Four Fingers your reason for traveling with an entourage of soldiers?" he said in broken English. "Or is it someone else? You would not think it luck that you find Four Fingers unless you wish to use Four Fingers' services."

"Exactly," Harold said, squaring his shoulders. He put a hand on Four Fingers' arm. "You know this land like the palm of your hand. I want you to take me to Sage's new stronghold."

"Four Fingers knows nothing of Sage's new stronghold," Four Fingers grumbled. "Four Fingers no longer cares. Nor should you."

"Well, I do care," Harold growled. "I care plenty. Now do as you are told or you'll get shot on the spot. Take your pick. A bullet or my thanks once we've found Sage."

Chief Four Fingers glared at Harold, then nodded. "I will do this thing if you promise my freedom after the deed is done," he said, tired of bargaining over and over again for his freedom.

"You have it," Harold said, nodding. He gave Chief

Four Fingers' warriors a troubled glance. "How about them? Will they cooperate? Or should we shoot them?"

"These are my most devoted warriors," Four Fingers said, looking guardedly from side to side at the rifles now aimed mainly at his men. "Lower your rifles. They will ride with us, *if* you will also promise them their freedom once Sage has been found."

Harold nodded again. "Agreed," he said. "They'll be given their walking papers along with you. I have no need for you Kiowa after that." He smiled slowly. "Not after I have my woman with me again."

"The white woman is your reason for hunting down Sage?" Four Fingers said, arching his eyebrows.

"You've guessed it," Harold said, laughing softly.

Chief Four Fingers smiled. "She has beguiled many men, I see," he said.

"Just don't you get any ideas about taking her for yourself," Harold warned, then wheeled his horse around and rejoined his soldiers.

Harold ordered his men to disarm the Kiowa, then shouted at the Kiowa chief. "Take off, Four Fingers," he said. "Lead the way. But don't try anything. Your back is an easy enough target."

Leonida smoothed a blanket up over Runner after her bedtime stories sent him into a peaceful sleep.

"He sleeps soundly," Sage said, coming to Leonida's side. He took one of her hands and drew her against him, gazing down at her. The firelight gave her skin a golden, satiny glow. "Woman, are you ready to warm my blankets?"

The moon was high. The breeze was soft and smelled sweetly, for a pine forest stretched out behind the Navaho's night camp. Leonida smiled up at Sage and ran her fingers through his thick, black hair, his headband having been placed with his rifle beside his spread blankets.

"I'd like to take a walk," Leonida murmured. "I'm too restless to sleep."

"What bothers you, my wife?" Sage said, releasing her from the circle of his arms, then putting one of them around her waist again as she began walking beside him away from the campsite.

"Although Kit Carson gave his word that he would do everything within his power to assure your continued freedom, I fear that he will become powerless against those who are above him in authority," Leonida said, frowning up at Sage. "And Harold? Lord, when he finds out that I've married you, he'll be angry enough to bite nails in half."

"He will get over it," Sage said.

"He is not the sort to give up all that easily," Leonida further worried aloud, stepping over a branch that had fallen from a tree, blocking their path. "I'm afraid he'll come looking for us, Sage. He'll bring many soldiers. What if he finds us?"

"We are many days ride ahead of him," Sage reassured her. He stopped and turned, putting his hands on her shoulders and stopping her. "We will soon be at my new stronghold. Once we are there, no one can find us, especially the white pony soldiers."

"They found your other stronghold," Leonida murmured, gazing up at him with worried eyes.

"Only because Four Fingers guided them there," Sage said in a low growl. "Four Fingers is no longer seeking vengeance. He has gone his way, we have gone ours. He knows not of the location of my new stronghold. We will arrive there safely and live there without fear of being discovered. I have chosen well, my wife.

Do not show lack of faith in your husband now, when it is most important.''

''I'm sorry,'' Leonida said, flinging herself into his arms. ''I didn't mean to show lack of faith in you again. It's just that I don't trust anyone else. Especially Four Fingers. Does a man like him ever forget his hunger for vengeance?'' She paused and leaned away from him, gazing into his eyes again. ''And what of Harold? I fear that he will search for me to the ends of the earth, if necessary. I fear his anger, Sage.''

Sage moved his hands to the nape of her neck and drew her lips to his. ''Like I said, my wife, have faith in your chieftain husband,'' he said softly. He pressed his mouth against her lips and gave her a heated kiss as he pushed her down onto the ground, her back cushioned by a deep bed of soft pine needles.

Leonida's arms clung around his neck as his eager fingers lifted her skirt, then sought that damp feathering of hair at the juncture of her thighs.

She spread her legs wide, opening herself to him, unaware that he had shoved his breeches down below his knees. He entered her now with one strong, smooth thrust. He was buried deep, his hips thrusting hard.

Sage slid his mouth from her lips. ''Tonight forget everything but your husband,'' he whispered against her ear, the heat of his breath causing a tingling sensation to race up and down her spine. ''Ride with me to the moon, where we will swing in its half cradle tonight among the stars.''

''My darling, take me there quickly,'' Leonida whispered back, breathless as desire spread deliciously through her. She sought his lips and kissed him urgently, her fingers splayed across his hips, urging him endlessly deeper within her.

Sage pulled the tail of her blouse free from the waist

of her skirt, then his fingers crept inside it. He moaned against her lips when he found her nipples taut, her breasts as soft as a rose petal against his palms. Then he abandoned her lips and bent low, lifting one of her breasts to his mouth.

His lips closed over a nipple, his tongue flicking around it, drawing a long and sensual moan from deeply within Leonida. He felt the fires of passion spreading through him, tremors of pleasure cascading down his back when one of her hands circled around his manhood as he paused in his thrusts for only a moment.

Withdrawing himself from inside her, he reveled in the touch of her fingers on him and marveled at how she knew the skills so well to pleasure him in this way. He moved his hips in rhythm with her fingers, sucking in a wild breath as he felt the rush of pleasure which meant that he was coming too close to the ultimate of wild splendor. He urged her hand away from him, cupped her throbbing center with his hand, then entered her again with one hard thrust.

Placing his hands beneath her buttocks, he lifted her more tightly against him, making it easier for him to take powerful strokes, filling her more deeply.

Leonida twined her fingers through his hair and pulled his lips down against hers, touching his tongue to hers through her parted lips. Again his hands found the soft swells of her breasts and gently kneaded them. She arched toward him, over and over again. With a groan he met the thrust of her soft body against his.

Then his breath caught and held as he stilled his strokes within her. Their lips parted. He lay his cheek against hers, then resumed his thrusts. The flood of pleasure swept raggedly through him. His loins gave off a great shuddering. He wrapped her within his arms and held her close as their bodies jolted and quivered together, then subsided, exhausted, against each other.

Feeling as though they were the only two people in the universe, Leonida kissed him, and her hands stroked his perspiration-laced skin, making him groan huskily as she closed her fingers around his shrunken shaft.

Sage rolled away from her and stretched out on his back on the cushion of pine needles. He closed his eyes and became lost to rapture as his wife loved him again in ways wonderful to him. He felt content that tomorrow they would be sharing the same sort of bliss in the privacy of the hogan that he would already have built for her in their new stronghold, a place that he had rightfully named ''paradise.''

31

Why so dull and mute, young sinner?
Pr'y thee, why so mute?
—Sir John Suckling

Harold was beginning to doubt the importance of finding Leonida. Perhaps he was even doubting his sanity for having come out in this damnable heat. The sun was beating down from the heavens this day like a death ray.

He squirmed in his saddle and licked his parched lips. He squinted into the haze that was dancing along the sand that stretched out before the soldiers.

Harold gazed over at Chief Four Fingers, wondering if the Kiowa chief was leading him on a wild goose chase. It was unnatural to place trust in an Indian. The Navaho had been allowed to set up their tents just outside the fort to sell their wares, and look at how they repaid this kindness. Sage had attacked a stagecoach and had taken captives, Leonida among them. Surely he had used some kind of questionable tactics to persuade Leonida to marry him.

Yes, he thought to himself. She *was* worth traveling through this damnable heat over. He would not give up the search until he had her with him again.

Harold thrust his heels into the flanks of his horse and rode up beside Four Fingers. "How much longer are we going to have to travel across this desert?" he shouted, wiping a bead of perspiration from his brow with the back of his hand. "Surely this isn't the way to Sage's new stronghold. The women wouldn't last one hour had they been forced to travel in this heat."

"This is not the way he would have traveled with his people," Four Fingers said, glowering at Harold. "But it is the way Four Fingers travels to get to the other side of those mountains that you see in the distance, where I think Sage has taken his people. It is uncharted land. It is land I scarcely know myself. That was where I had planned to go eventually to hide away from the likes of you. It seems I did not go there soon enough."

A big ball of sagebrush came tumbling by in the hot breeze, its sagelike odor wafting through the air behind it. A lizard, with its large, beaded eyes and flashing tongue, darted by, soon burrowing its way deep into the depths of the sand, apparently seeking a cooler hideaway until the moon replaced the sun in the sky.

"I'm not like that lizard," Harold grumbled. "I'm forced to endure this damned heat. How much longer, Four Fingers? Give me an estimate of how long it's going to be before we can leave this desert."

"By nightfall you will be sleeping on grass beneath trees," Four Fingers said matter-of-factly. Then he nudged his horse with his moccasined heels and rode away from Harold, edging in between his Kiowa companions.

Four Fingers leaned over, close to his warrior. "He is a weak man," he said, grinning. "Neither he nor his soldiers will last the rest of the day in this heat. By nightfall we will be riding free again. We will then see if Sage *is* making his new stronghold in those mountains yonder. If so, we will take it away from him. We will enter the camp under cover of night and one by one kill the Navaho while they are sleeping."

His eyes narrowed. "One among them will be

spared," he said. "I *will* have the woman with hair the color of corn silk. She will bear my children."

"And what if the child has hair the color of wheat?" one of his warriors dared to say.

"Golden hair . . . black?" Four Fingers said, shrugging. "During these times when the number of the Kiowa is lessening, does it truly matter the color of the hair? That the child has Kiowa blood flowing through its veins is all that matters."

Harold did not like seeing the Indians chatting among themselves. He feared that plans of escaping were possibly being discussed. He snapped his reins and rode up to the Kiowa.

"I didn't say that you could gossip like women while on this journey to find Sage," Harold said with a feral snarl. "Just keep riding. Do you hear?"

A shiver rode up Harold's spine when Four Fingers gave him a savage glare, yet he shrugged it off. He hardly had to worry about his safety when the Indians had no weapons, and he and his soldiers had so many.

He rode onward, flanked on each side by a Kiowa, while the soldiers rode up to stay close behind them. A movement in the distance, through the dancing haze of the heat, drew Harold's keen attention. He leaned over his saddle horn and cupped a hand over his eyes, trying to shield them from the sun. He strained to see what had drawn his attention, but he could see only the blur of the heat as it shimmered across the sand.

"It must've been a damn mirage," Harold whispered to himself, shuddering at the thought of not surviving this heat. Thinking he saw things might be the beginnings of heatstroke.

He glanced over at Four Fingers, knowing that the Kiowa chief would welcome seeing his white pony soldier companions drop one by one, like flies, from their saddles, from heat exhaustion. The way Harold's clothes seemed to be pressing in on him, like heated gloves clutching him from his shoulders down, he felt that he could hardly stand another minute of wearing the damnable uniform. The deep blue color of his uniform was drawing the sun to it like a magnet. He was even beginning to feel lightheaded.

Again he saw movement in the distance. He squinted his eyes, afraid to accept that what he was seeing was a mirage, for surely after hallucinating came unconsciousness.

Trembling and afraid, he stared into the distance with more determination. He almost shouted with relief when he saw that it was no mirage after all, but many horsemen riding toward him.

Suddenly he shuddered, realizing that there was no reason at all to be happy about seeing men on horseback out in the middle of the desert. He and his men had no cover if they were attacked, and scarcely any energy left for the fight that was due. The heat had drained them of their energy.

"Who is that?" Harold cried, giving Four Fingers a harried look. "Can you tell? Who's approaching us?"

Chief Four Fingers drew up quickly, forcing his horse to a sudden stop.

Everyone followed his lead.

Harold leaned closer to Four Fingers. "Why did you stop?" he shouted, sweat pouring from his brow and stinging his eyes as it rolled across them.

"Renegades!" Four Fingers said, fear etched on his usually stoic face. "It is Navaho renegades. These renegades are the ones responsible for the massacres and killings of the white settlers. They are responsible

for my band of Kiowa being so few in number. They
kill without reason or feelings. They are heartless.''

"Good Lord," Harold said, panicking. He looked
in all directions but saw no route of escape. If he and
his men turned and ran, the Navaho would soon catch
up with them. If they met them head on, they would
have no chance of surviving. From the looks of it, the
Navaho renegades outnumbered this entourage of soldiers and prisoners three to one.

He saw that he had only one order to give. ''Dismount and get your horses on their sides,'' he shouted.
''Use them as cover. Defend yourselves as best as you
can.''

In a scramble his men forced the horses to the
ground. The soldiers, as well as the Kiowa, knelt down
behind them. The Kiowa were given weapons again,
for now they were all fighting for their lives together.

Harold gulped hard and steadied his aim, his fingers
trembling on the trigger as the Navaho came dashing
toward them. Tears came to his eyes, for he knew that
soon he would be meeting his Maker and he was afraid
that he would be turned away, to go where all sinners
had to go.

He had one last fleeting thought of Leonida, his
heart thumping wildly as an arrow pierced his chest
and he discovered too late the difference between Sage
and these bloodthirsty renegades.

One by one the soldiers fell, followed by the Kiowa
warriors. Four Fingers clutched at the arrow buried
deep in his chest and looked wild-eyed at the renegade
who lowered his knife to remove the Kiowa's scalp.

Kit Carson awakened with a start. He rose up on an
elbow, finding his nightshirt drenched with perspiration. He glanced at the nightstand beside his bed,

where a candle wick floating in the melted wax still
burned. His nose wrinkled at the scent of medication
from several half-empty bottles on the table.

Then he was aware of something else—a woman on
the other side of his bed, her hand now cool against
his brow.

He turned to her, eyes wide. "Sally?" he said.
"Good lord, Sally, how long have I been here like
this? My recollections are vague about everything right
now."

"You've been slightly out of your head with a raging
fever," Sally explained softly. "But now it's gone.
Your flesh is finally cool. You asked how long you have
been so ill? I've even lost track of time. I have hardly
left your bedside. It was a way to say thank-you for
everything that you've done, not only for me and Adam
but also for Leonida and Sage."

Kit's eyes widened and he bolted quickly to a sitting
position, knocking Sally's hand clumsily away.
"God," he said. "Sage!"

He gave Sally a quick look. "I left orders for Sage
to be left alone," he said, frowning. "I hope Harold
heeded them." He nodded toward the door. "Sally,
go and tell Harold that my fever has broken and that I
am lucid again. I need to talk with him. It's urgent."

"Sir, Harold's been gone almost as long as you've
been raging with fever," she murmured. "He took a
good portion of the soldiers with him. It is rumored
that he might be going to look for Sage. I must admit,
this was another reason I stayed so steadfastly at your
bedside. I desperately wanted to get you well again.
You are the only one who can stop Harold. But still,
Kit, you are not well enough to ride, even if your fever
has broken. You must be so weak."

Kit's face reddened with rage, his eyes narrowed,

and his nostrils flared. "That goddamn idiot," he said, swinging his legs over the side of the bed. "That bastard! Doesn't he know a direct order when he hears it? What does he think he's doing, refusing to listen to reason about the Navaho? But I must remember—it's not the Navaho who made him leave the fort in a frenzy. It's Leonida. He just won't let go."

Sally rushed to her feet and went to the other side of the bed, gasping when Kit tried to stand, then fell back onto the bed as his knees gave way.

"Kit, you're too weak," Sally said, going to him and trying to steady him as he again determinedly placed his feet firmly on the floor. "You can't go anywhere in this condition."

"Nothing's stopping me," Kit growled. He brushed her helping hand away, smiling grimly when he finally succeeded at standing on his own. "I'm going after Harold. If I have to search up one side of this land and down the other, I'm going to find the scoundrel. If I have to be tied into the saddle to continue the search, damn it then, so be it. I gave Sage my word. No one is going to make me a liar."

"Kit, let me send for a soldier," Sally said, wringing her hands nervously. "Tell him where to go. Please don't try to do this yourself. You are already weak. The sun will kill you."

"Hand me my clothes," Kit said, leaning his full weight against the bedpost at the end of the bed. "Then leave. I'll manage just fine after that."

Sally scrambled around the room and gathered up his clothes, gave them to him, and left in a flurry.

Kit dressed shakily, yanked on his knee-high boots, slapped his guns and holster around his waist, then flopped a hat on his head.

He grabbed his rifle and sauntered from the room,

weak but yet holding on by sheer will. He welcomed some bread and cheese that Sally gave him as he walked without stopping toward the door. Eating these, he went out in the courtyard.

Soon he had enough men rounded up to travel. He left scarcely enough there to protect the fort, yet he saw no other choice in the matter.

Sally and the women filled all of the saddlebags with enough food to last several days and hung large canteens of water over the saddle horns of the saddle.

Kit mounted, gasping for breath with the effort. He shook off a moment of light-headedness and settled himself in the saddle, then saluted the soldiers who were being left behind and left.

Among this entourage of soldiers was a Navaho scout who was paid well for his services to the army. He knew this land, surely as well as Sage, Chief Four Fingers, and all renegades. If anyone could find Harold and the soldiers, he could.

The Indian scout led the soldiers, and Kit forced himself to sit square in the saddle, even though waves of weakness kept washing over him.

Hours passed. Day turned to night. They stopped to eat and get a few winks of sleep.

Early the next day they traveled on. The morning came in muted pinks, oranges, and grays. The desert stretched out before Kit in the hazy light.

He did not question the scout about traveling now in the desert. He seemed to be an expert at tracking as well as scouting and to know where he was going.

As the sun rose to high noon beating down upon Kit, dizzying him, he thought he saw something ahead through the haze of heat, something stretched out along the sand, unmoving.

Suddenly the scout raised a hand for everyone to

stop. He rode back and edged his horse closer to Kit's. "Death lies in the sand ahead," he said in a monotone.

"Do you think it's . . . ?" Kit began, but the scout interrupted him.

"I will ride ahead and see, or you can accompany me there," the scout said.

"I've come this far," Kit said. "I may as well go the extra mile."

Somberly, cautiously, the entourage moved onward. When they arrived at the death scene, Kit turned away and held his head low, retching. He closed his eyes, yet he could not keep the picture of what he had just seen from surfacing in his mind's eye.

Harold, scalped.

Chief Four Fingers, scalped.

All of the others, scalped.

"No one survived the massacre, soldiers and Kiowa alike," Lieutenant Nelson said somberly as he rode to Kit's side. "Who do you think did it? Could Sage have done this to stop Harold and the Kiowa from finding his new stronghold?"

Kit removed a handkerchief from his back breeches pocket. He gave his brow a nervous swipe and turned his horse around so that he would not have to see the dead bodies again, with the flies buzzing over them and the lizards scampering around in the sand close by.

Kit glanced up into the heavens at the buzzards circling in the sky. He shivered, then glared at the soldier. "I've known Sage for many years," he said flatly. "The man that I have always known and admired could never be responsible for this heartless act. So don't let me ever hear you suggest that he was again. This is the work of renegades, surely the same ones who've been slaughtering innocent settlers. It seems we should've concentrated more on finding them instead of running the Navaho from their land.''

Kit gave Harold only another fleeting glance, then turned quickly away. ''Lieutenant Nelson, those men must be returned to the fort for proper burial,'' he said somberly. ''See to it.''

He swung his horse around and rode away, his head hanging low.

32

Serenely in the sunshine as before,
Without the sense of that which I forbore.
—ELIZABETH BARRETT BROWNING

Like a desert mirage, the canyon spread an emerald counterpane among the arid vastness. Irrigated by springs that swelled to a river, the valley bloomed with lofty cottonwoods and willows. In the distance, twin sandstone pinnacles rose into the sky.

Sage reined in beside Leonida's horse and reached for Runner, bringing him over onto his lap and smiling at his wife. "This is your new home," he said proudly. "Was not it worth waiting for?"

"It is so lovely," Leonida sighed. "It is so perfect."

The music of the river could be heard as it rippled beneath limestone cliffs. Lizards and chipmunks scampered to and fro, the inhabitants of this paradise.

"Look at the little animals," Runner squealed as a chipmunk dashed toward Sage's horse, then stopped to peer up at humans, obviously for the first time. "Can I have him? Can he be my pet?"

Sage laughed throatily as he slipped Runner from his lap onto the ground near the chipmunk, surprised when the animal did not run away. "I started to say that I doubted if it would let you come near," he said. "But it seems, Runner, that you may have found a friend."

"It apparently doesn't know to fear humans,"

Leonida said, watching Runner bend to the ground and scoop the chipmunk up into his hands.

When Runner held the animal close to his face, the chipmunk emitted a strange, soft barking sound, yet still did not try to escape. It locked eyes with Runner, fast friends, it did seem.

Her back aching, Leonida placed her hands at her waist, stretched, and groaned.

Sage saw her discomfort and slid quickly from his saddle and helped her to the ground. "The ride was long and hard," he said. "But it was necessary. I still do not altogether trust Kit Carson. I especially don't trust Harold Porter. Once he hears that you are my wife, he will hate me with a vengeance. He will stop at nothing, I am sure, to see me dead."

"I wish I had never met that man," Leonida said, moving into Sage's embrace. Over her shoulder she was watching everyone dismount. She could tell that, as she was, they were all in awe of this place that was now to be their home.

She eased out of Sage's arms and with him watched the activity of the people. The men were unloading supplies from their horses. The women were herding the smaller children into the shade, telling them to stay out of the way while the hogans were being built. The older children began scampering around, searching for the proper trees from which bark would be taken to cover the hogans. The men were inspecting the trees, from which the frames of the hogans would be made.

"I must join the men in preparing the wood and bark for the hogans," Sage said, turning apologetically to Leonida. He frowned, noticing how pale she looked, with dark rings beneath her eyes. And he had not failed to see her keeping herself from retching these past couple of days. He wondered what she could have eaten to cause her to be ill. They had eaten the same food, and he had felt nothing akin to nausea. He would not allow himself to think that she was in her first stages of prairie fever. That possibility pained him too deeply.

"You rest beneath the trees with the children," Sage flatly ordered Leonida.

"While the other women do my part?" she said, gasping at the thought. "Never."

She worked her fingers through her hair, combing out the tangles from the windy ride on the horse. She ran her fingers down the front of her skirt, smoothing out the wrinkles from sitting in the saddle so long.

"The saddle was so very uncomfortable," she complained. "So hard. So narrow."

"I will soon remedy that," Sage said. "Soon you will have your own saddle, one that will fit your every contour."

"I appreciate the thought, darling, but I hope I never need to ride a horse ever again."

"Horses are also rode for pleasure," Sage said, smiling down at her.

Leonida flinched when another wave of nausea swam through her. Cold perspiration covered her arms and face as she fought back the urge to retch again. Now she was almost certain that she was pregnant. She smiled sheepishly up at Sage; she had not yet told him.

She was going to tell him tonight.

"There it was again," Sage growled, gently gripping her shoulders with his fingers. "For a moment you looked ill again. You should not work with the women. You must rest."

Leonida placed a hand on her abdomen, thinking that perhaps he was right. She had seen death claim two of her best friends. Her mother had suffered two miscarriages. Leonida did not want to experience the same loss. She wanted this baby. She wanted to share this child with Sage and Runner. They would be such a happy family.

"All right," Leonida said. "I won't help build the hogans. But I will help prepare the food for everyone. I am certainly strong enough to cook."

Her willingness to give up the fight to help with the manual labor so easily surprised Sage. He raised an eyebrow as he lowered his hands from her and lifted her chin up so that she was forced to look him square in the eye.

"Do you have anything to tell me?" he asked.

"Like what?" Leonida said, her eyes innocently wide, yet wondering if he suspected already the miraculous changes happening within her body.

"You backed away from an argument too easily," Sage said. "That is not like you. Tell me why. Is it because you are more ill than you allow me to see? I must know if you are. I will have the singer sing over you, to make you well."

Leonida stiffened at the thought of being "sung" over, having seen how little it had helped Pure Blossom. The thought of her possibly ever needing a true doctor filled her with foreboding. And when she started with her labor pains, what if a doctor was needed to help with the birthing? That, as well as her worry about losing the child, frightened her.

"Darling, I'm fine," Leonida reassured. She was thankful for Runner's interference when he began tugging on her skirt, gazing up at her with that sweet pleading that she had grown to know so well.

"What is it, sweetie?" Leonida asked, giving Sage a sidewise glance as he turned and walked away, headed for his Navaho warriors, who were already busy chopping and digging, many of the women working alongside them.

"Can I make a cage for my animal?" Runner asked, hugging the little chipmunk to his chest. "I'm afraid he'll run away."

Leonida knelt down on a knee before him. "Runner, let's not put him in a cage," she murmured. "That would be cruel." She placed a gentle hand to his smooth cheek. "You've seen how the Navaho have been threatened by imprisonment at a reservation, haven't you?"

"Yes," Runner said, tilting his head to one side.

"And you've seen how they have fled to a new land, to keep from having to go to live on the reservation?" Leonida continued.

"Yes . . ." Runner murmured.

"Well, darling, it's almost the same with this tiny animal," Leonida said, gazing down at the chipmunk that sat trustingly in Runner's hand. "He would not want to be caged any more than the Navaho do."

"But if I let him go, he'll run away," Runner whined.

"If that's what he wants, then you should let him," Leonida said, patting Runner on the head. "If he wants to be a friend to you, he won't go far."

Runner gazed down at the chipmunk, then at his Navaho friends skipping and playing, and then down again at his animal friend.

Leonida saw that Runner was being torn with choices; she knew he wanted to join his friends at play, yet he feared losing his animal friend if he set it free.

"Runner, you know what's best," she said.

"Yes, I know," Runner mumbled, then opened his arms and hands and allowed the chipmunk to scamper free. "He didn't want to be friends after all."

Leonida pulled Runner into her arms and gave him a gentle hug. "Go and play with your human friends," she teased, playfully smacking his little bottom. "Perhaps your chipmunk will return soon."

Runner nodded and rushed away, quickly joining his friends. Leonida watched, proud of this young man who was being raised as her son. She knew that Carole would be just as proud.

Placing her hands at the small of her back, she stood up and watched Runner awhile longer. Then her gaze moved to Sage. She smiled to herself, loving him so much, and wanting so much for him. But her smile faded when she thought about the news that Kit Carson had taken to Harold. He was not the sort of man who took to being scorned so easily.

Forcing him from her mind since she wanted to enjoy having finally arrived where her husband's stronghold was to be established, Leonida hurried toward the women, who were building a great outdoor fire and taking food supplies from their travel bags to prepare the evening meal. She knew that everyone was already tired from the long journey, but by nightfall they would be not only worn out but starved as well. She wanted to be there to assist in at least this small way.

The day passed quickly as the busy hands built one forked stick hogan after another on a terrace of land overlooking the river, some referring to them as *atchideezahis*, pointed houses. The frames were covered with bark, the adobe clay baked as hard as a brick to be applied later, when there was more time to see to the perfection of each. Gay Heart had explained to Leonida how this would be done—that the clay would be wet and then plastered over the bark, making a thick-walled house that would be warm in the winter and cool in the summer.

As with the hogans on the mountain, all of the doors faced east to greet the rising Father Sun.

The afternoon was waning now. The sun was low, the shadowed sides of the cliffs becoming deep pools of violet seeping out across the land. The sunset was bringing the drab clay bluffs to life. A soft breeze was making the cottonwood leaves sing and whisper. The horses were grazing close by, munching on the watercress that fringed the bank of the stream.

Shaded by a cottonwood, Leonida sliced the flatbread that she had made from wheat flour, as cabbage, beans, corn, and squash simmered over the fire in the center of what was quickly looking like a village.

As the people dispersed after the long day's work to go to the river to be refreshed, Leonida gazed slowly around. The word "Paradise" did describe this place well, she thought. A rich, deep green was usually not a part of the desert landscape, but Sage had known the art of finding it, for there it was, a perfect shelter for his people in the deep canyon. In this strip of green could be grown the three sister crops, corn, squash, and beans, and whatever else the people's hearts desired. They could finally plant their revered peach seeds that they had saved after eating the last of the peaches from the other stronghold. In time even sheep would be acquired and would multiply in the wide green pastures.

Sage knelt down beside her, his stomach rumbling as he got a whiff of the food cooking over the fire. He accepted the piece of bread that Leonida handed to him.

Then he turned and admired the handiwork of his people. "And so the new Navaho village takes shape," he said proudly. He gazed at Leonida. "Is not it all a fine piece of work done by my people?"

Leonida looked at the many hogans standing like tall, pointed tents, sorting out with her eyes the one that Sage had labored so hard over through the long, hot hours of the day. "They are beautiful," she said, sighing. She looked up at Sage. "I'm so glad we're finally here. I hope we have no more problems, Sage. It would be wonderful to awaken each morning without fearing what the day brings us. I want this so much for you. You deserve it. Your people deserve it."

"I have no choice but to believe that Kit Carson is a man of his word and will see to it that we are left in peace," Sage said. He turned and smiled as his people began gathering around the outdoor fire, their platters already being filled with the delectable-smelling food.

He turned to Leonida and offered her a hand. She got to her feet, then picked up her large platter of sliced bread to add to the feast. After setting this among the other bowls of steaming food, she searched for Runner. When she found him asleep beneath a tree, the chipmunk scampering around him, sniffing, her heart went out to the child. Runner had worn himself out playing. And his new playmate had returned.

She decided against waking Runner up just yet. The food would be there into the long, shadowed hours of night. There were no signs now that the people were tired. They were enjoying themselves, a celebration seemingly in its first stages.

Now certain that she was eating for two, Leonida sat beside Sage and ate ravenously. All day she had refrained from picking at the food that she had helped prepare. She knew that she must begin now to watch what she ate, and how much. She did not want to become so large that it would be difficult for her to have her baby. Especially out here, where the birthing of her child depended so much on her and how she prepared herself for it.

She gave Sage a glance, smiling. She could hardly wait to tell him her suspicions. Would it not add to the joy that was showing on his face as he kept looking around at his people, who were finally enjoying life, with hopes aplenty for the future?

Sage felt her eyes on him. He turned and studied her expression, seeing something about it that seemed different. She was harboring a pleasant secret, one that he hoped she would share with him. "You look as though you have something to say to Sage, yet not," he finally said. He placed a hand on her cheek, smiling as she leaned her face into his palm. "Do you wish to tell me what it is, or does your husband have to continue wondering?"

Leonida glanced around her, then moved closer to Sage. "Not now," she whispered. "Later. I promise I will tell you later."

"Is it about Runner?" Sage prodded. "Did you see? The chipmunk has returned and is waiting for Runner to awaken, to play with him."

"Yes, I saw the chipmunk," Leonida said, smiling up at him. "But, no, what I have to tell you is not about Runner."

Sage took Leonida's empty platter and set it down beside his own. He grabbed her hand and urged her to her feet, and laughingly began leading her away from the merriment. It had become more pronounced, with singing and dancing, the thump-thump of a drum setting the beat.

"Where are you taking me?" Leonida asked, her hair billowing out in golden streamers.

"Where we can talk with the moon and the stars," Sage said, now running in a soft trot, Leonida following his lead. "They will not spread your secret after you tell it to me."

Leonida ran hand in hand with him until they reached the banks of the river, far from the hogans towering above. It was a private place where all that could be heard were the night sounds of crickets and frogs, and where the lightning bugs' miniature lanterns glowed mysteriously in the dark. It was a place of fragrant pines and wildflowers and of sweet, warm breezes.

Sage put his hands on Leonida's waist and turned her around to face him, then held her close, their bodies straining together. "Now tell me," Sage said huskily, bending to brush a teasing kiss across her lips. "What is your secret? Do you know that it is not good to keep a secret from your husband?"

"Perhaps not," Leonida said, shrugging teasingly herself. She trembled with ecstasy and gasped with pleasure as he gathered her skirt up into his hands, bunching it up past her thighs, holding it there with one hand, while his other cupped the center of her desire and thrust a finger within her.

"Tell your husband," Sage said, caressing her bud of pleasure, then thrusting his finger within her again, slowly, then faster and faster, dizzying her with the splendor that was building within her.

"How can I be expected to remember what it was that I had to tell you if you continue making me mindless?" Leonida said breathlessly. She lay her cheek on Sage's powerful chest and twined her arms around his neck as he gently pushed her to the ground. Her skirt hiked up now, and Sage's breeches lowered, he entered her and began his eager thrusts.

"The secret matters not to me any longer," he said, his passion rising, his body fluid with fire. "Being with you like this is all there is at this moment. You are the reason I breathe, eat, and even exist. Love me, my wife. Love me."

"You are my everything," Leonida whispered back, his pulsing, satin hardness pressing deeper. "And the child will make everything so perfect."

Sage did not miss a stroke as he took in what she had said. At first he thought she was talking about Runner, but when he reflected for a moment, he realized that she had said that the child *would* make everything perfect. He stopped abruptly, his eyes wide. "Child?" he said, his heart thumping. "What child do you refer to?"

Leonida giggled. She reached for one of his hands and placed it on her tummy. "That child," she said softly. "The one growing within the walls of my womb. Our child, Sage. Yours and mine."

The blissfulness of the announcement momentarily rendered him silent. Then he pulled her against him and gave her an excited hug. "We will be true parents this time," he said. "The child will be borne of our love. It is something so wonderful it is hard to imagine."

"It is wonderful," Leonida said, placing her hands on his face and drawing his lips down upon hers. She gave him a sweet kiss, and when he thrust himself within her again, this time he gave her a slow and leisurely kind of loving, and her gasps of pleasure became long, soft whimpers.

33

Doom takes to part us, leaves thy heart in mine
With pulses that beat double.
—ELIZABETH BARRETT BROWNING

Several Months Later

A fire was burning low in the fire pit. A large black pot hanging over it gave off delicious fragrances of onion, carrots, and various other vegetables cooking with chunks of rabbit mixed in to make a stew.

Outside the hogan, corn, the silks just showing against the sky, was aplenty in the large, communal garden. The seedling peach trees that had been set out in the fertile valley close to the village were sprouting from the soil, the promise of fruit now a reality.

It was early morning. The fire was welcome to Leonida, for the night had been cooler than usual. She was sitting on a mat beside the fire, Runner squatting in front of her with his back to her. She was brushing his hair with a sheaf of straw after having shampooed it with yucca-root suds.

"Ouch," Runner complained. "You pulled my hair."

"I'm being as careful as I can," Leonida murmured. "Just sit still for a moment longer and then you can go and join your friends at play."

"Please hurry," Runner whined. "I don't want to play with my friends. I want to go and look for Chips. She's been gone for days and days."

"Your chipmunk has just gone away long enough to have her babies, and then she'll come back and be your friend again," Leonida said softly. "And while we're talking about your chipmunk, don't you think it's best to change her name to something more lady-like now that you know she's a she? Chips sounds too boyish to me."

"I like the name Chips," Runner said stubbornly. He shrugged. "Anyhow, she doesn't know the difference. She's used to being called Chips. Another name might confuse her."

Leonida smiled. "Perhaps you're right," she said, laying her brush aside. She pulled Runner's shoulder-length hair back and tied it in a *Chongo*.

Then she turned him around to face her. "There. It's done," she said. "You can go now. But don't go far looking for Chips. I cannot tell you often enough about those dangerous cliffs."

Runner nodded and bounced to his feet. When he started to rush away from Leonida, she grabbed his hand and stopped him.

When he turned around, frowning, she gazed up at him. "Did you hear me clearly enough about not going far?" she said flatly.

"Yes, ma'am," Runner said, looking soberly down at her. Then his gaze shifted, stopping at the swell of her stomach as it pressed tightly against the inside of her cotton skirt. He fell to his knees and looked up at her for approval. Every day he listened at her stomach to see if he could hear the baby's movements.

Leonida was always touched by his interest. She placed a hand at the back of his head and smiled down at him as he scarcely breathed, his eyes curiously wide.

She was well aware of her baby moving around inside her, for her ribs got an occasional kick.

She had to believe that she was going to have a boy. Surely a girl would not be as active or as strong. She recalled one day when she had rested a bowl on her round mound. Suddenly the child kicked so hard inside her, it knocked the bowl to the floor. Another time she had felt the perfect shape of a knee or an elbow. Those times she would cherish in her storehouse of memories forever.

"Do you hear anything?" Leonida murmured. "You'd better watch out," she then teased. "You'll get kicked."

Runner giggled.

She moved her hand away from his head as he leaned away from her. "I could hear some strange sort of sounds today," he marveled.

"Yes, the baby is quite active this morning," Leonida said, splaying her own fingers over the large ball of her stomach. "It's a wonderful feeling. I know the child is healthy."

"Will it be a brother or a sister?" Runner asked for at least the hundredth time.

"Well, I hope it's a boy," she said, her eyes twinkling. "I wouldn't want a daughter of mine running around with such a name as Chips."

"You still say I will have a part in naming the child?" Runner asked, his eyes anxiously wide.

"We are a family, aren't we?" Leonida said, placing a gentle hand on his cheek, now tanned almost as copper as the Navaho's. With his dark eyes and raven hair, he did look more Navaho than white. "We will have a family council. We will listen to each other's suggestions. The choice will be a mutual one."

Runner gave her a beaming smile, then left the hogan in a mad dash.

Her afternoon meal simmering in the pot, her three-room hogan spotlessly clean, Leonida decided to go outside and sit in the shade while she awaited Sage's return. He had left before she rose from their bed, saying that he was making something special for her.

But he had warned her that it was something that she could not use until after the birth of the child.

She was wondering what it could be, thrilled at the thought that he was making her a special gift. Yet didn't he know that it was enough—just to have him?

Feeling so content, Leonida went to the pile of blankets that lay against the wall. Tears pooled in her eyes when her gaze fell on the blanket that Pure Blossom had made for her wedding to Harold. Sage had allowed her to keep it after she had told him that Pure Blossom wished it.

Lifting it, she draped it over her arms, then waddled to her basket in which was stored her basket-making paraphernalia. Carrying these things, she went outside the hogan. After spreading the blanket on the ground, she got as comfortable as it was possible to be in her condition and began working again on a basket, her agile fingers weaving willow stems and yucca leaves together.

She would weave for a while, then rest and gaze around her, eagerly watching for Sage's return. She nodded a quiet hello to those who walked past her, some women carrying basket water bottles pitched with *jicara*, pinyon gum from the river, another bearing an *olla*, or water jug, balancing her awkward burden atop her head. Some women were chasing after children, others were busy at the large communal outdoor fire, where food was always kept over the fire for those who did not want to heat up their hogans too much.

Some women bent over their grinding bins, making cornmeal by rubbing dry corn between handstones and slanted slabs, or *metates*. The differing textures of stones produced various degrees of fineness.

Across the way several women sat outside their hogans, weaving on their looms. Some were using blanket looms, upright frames four or five feet wide and equally as high, with which the women made blankets and shawls. Some were using belt looms, the sort that maintained tension with a leather strap that circled the waist.

Beyond the hogans lay a varied and wonderfully beautiful land. Mesas of brightly colored rocks jutted up from flat valleys covered with soft gray-green sagebrush. Deep canyons formed gashes in the high plateaus, and steep gullies snaked through the flat bottomland.

Travel anywhere for long in a straight line was impossible. She had learned that in this place of mystery and beauty the long way around was always the shortest.

In the far distance she could see great pine-covered mountain ranges cutting across the country. Clumps of juniper and pinyon pines added their dusty green to the landscape, and over it all was the most brilliant of blue skies.

"My wife, the air is dry and sparkling today, is it not?" Sage said, suddenly there beside her, carrying a beautiful saddle.

"Yes, quite," Leonida said, scarcely audible. She laid her half-made basket aside on the blanket, and slowly pushed herself up from the ground, her eyes never leaving the saddle.

"You like?" Sage said, holding the saddle out for her closer inspection.

"It's lovely," Leonida said, smiling up at him yet disappointed. She had thought that he was going to present her with his special gift today. Instead it seemed that he had been working on something for himself.

Then she felt guilty for being selfish. She truly would rather him have something than herself.

"The saddle will look beautiful on your chestnut stallion," she quickly blurted.

"I did not make it for use on my horse," Sage said, studying the saddle himself, proud of his handiwork.

Then he nudged it closer to her. "It is your gift that I told you about," he said, smiling broadly. "It is a high-cantled Navaho saddle seat of slung leather over which you will throw a dyed goatskin for travel. As I promised, this was made so that your travels on horse can be more comfortable. Do you like it?"

Stunned by such a manly gift instead of something delicate and feminine, perhaps made out of flowers into a pretty wreath to hang inside her hogan, Leonida was momentarily speechless. Then knowing the hours it had taken to make the saddle, and knowing the love that had gone into it, she reached out and ran her hands over the leather. "It's so soft and smooth," she murmured. She started to take it from him, but he stopped her.

"It is too heavy for you to lift now, while you are with child," he said. "But after the child is born, you can lift it onto a horse and ride beside me. I will show you hidden places that will take your breath away."

"I truly can hardly wait," Leonida said, looking

wide-eyed up at him. "It's been so long since I've gone anywhere but our hogan."

Then her gaze shifted downward. She placed her hands on her tummy, smiling. "But I mustn't complain. One day soon our child will also see the wonders of our paradise," she murmured.

Runner came dashing toward them. Sage set the saddle on the ground and met Runner's approach on bent knee. Sage's eyes widened when he discovered what Runner was holding in his hands.

Leonida gasped and knelt down beside Sage as Runner came up to them and showed them his prizes.

"I found Chips," he said excitedly. "And Chip's babies. Look at them. Count them. There are four of them."

Leonida blanched. "Darling," she said, staring down at the tiny things, no larger than a spool of thread. "You shouldn't have taken the babies from their mother. She'll be unhappy, Runner. Shame on you."

Then her eyes widened when Chips came ambling along. When she reached Runner, she settled down on his moccasined foot, as content as she could be.

"See?" Runner exclaimed loudly. "She is glad to share with me."

"Perhaps because she has no choice? Is not this something you are forcing on her?" Sage said, patting Runner on the head. "Now take them back where you found them. Leave them there so Chips can feed and care for them. My son, they are not your responsibility. I do not even think you want them to be. They require being fed many times during the day *and* night."

"Darling, she has her family now, as you have yours," Leonida said softly. "Let them go and enjoy life as a family, and Runner, don't look for them again. It is in their best interest to live their lives separate from yours.''

Runner sighed, then nodded.

Sage picked Chips up and placed her among her babies in Runner's outstretched hands. "Take them to their home, Runner," he said in a flat command. "It *is* best for them."

"Oh, all right," Runner said. Then he turned and walked briskly away.

"He has so much to learn about life," Leonida said as Sage helped her back to her feet. She put her hands on the small of her back and groaned.

She peered down at the saddle again, then smiled over at Sage. "Thank you, darling, for the gift," she murmured. "I will use it proudly."

The sound of a horse approaching the hogans from behind drew Leonida and Sage around at the same time. Sage shielded his eyes with his hands, then stiffened. It was Spotted Feather. Sage had been awaiting his scout's return after having sent him away many sunrises ago to investigate the land around them, to see if any intruders were near, and to go on to Fort Defiance.

Sage had made the saddle for Leonida not only because of his devotion to her but also because he had needed to keep his fingers busy to make the days pass more quickly until the scout returned with answers that the chief so badly wanted.

Spotted Feather wheeled his horse to a stop and dismounted. Leading his horse behind him, he went to Sage.

"What news have you brought me?" Sage said, going to clutch Spotted Feather's shoulders.

"The news will give you cause for different emotions,'' Spotted Feather said, his gaze stoic. ''Some is good. Some is bad.''

Sage's jaw tightened. ''Tell me the bad news first,'' he said. ''Then good news will be even more appreciated.''

''Our Navaho people that surrendered to the white pony soldiers were forced on 'the long walk' across three hundred miles of barren wastelands and are now on a reservation, confined at Bosque Redondo, in New Mexico, far from their beloved homeland,'' Spotted Feather said bitterly. ''They are made to live among unfriendly Mescaleros. Where they live now is a flat, colorless region, and they are being forced to eat alien food and to drink bitter water which makes them ill. They are a most miserable people and are constantly pleading with their captors to be allowed to go home.''

A sick feeling swirled in Sage's stomach. ''And how do you know this?'' he said, his throat tight.

''I cleverly hid away in the bunkhouse at the fort and listened to conversations between the white pony soldiers about our people,'' he said thickly. ''They laughed at our people, mocking them for being Indian.''

There was a strained silence. Leonida looked up at Sage, feeling bad. The Navaho were a proud and courageous people. How could anyone mock them?

But of course, she knew who would. Ignorant, pitiful fools.

Filled with a deep sadness, bitter and disheartened, Sage wanted to go and release his imprisoned people, but he knew that his efforts would be for naught. They had chosen the road on which they wanted to travel, knowing that at the end of this road they would not find anything akin to happiness.

Sage and his other, most devoted people had chosen theirs. He would not risk the lives of those who had shown their devotion to him and go and release those few who had not trusted his judgment.

"Tell me the good news," Sage said, ending further talk of the imprisoned Navaho. "What news have you brought that will please me?"

Spotted Feather's eyes brightened, as though he felt relieved not to have to discuss further those who had chosen reservation life. "As far as the eye can see, and as far as my horse traveled, there is no one who will spoil our newly found peace," he said proudly. "And I have news of Kit Carson and General Harold Porter."

"What of Kit Carson?" Sage implored.

"He won a battle with prairie fever and is now far away, at another frontier outpost," Spotted Feather said.

Leonida's breath quickened. "What about Harold?" she asked, feeling Sage's eyes on her.

"He is no longer among the living," Spotted Feather said smugly. "Nor is Chief Four Fingers. Seems they had formed a partnership of sorts. They were searching for our new stronghold when they were cut down by a renegade band of Indians, perhaps Navaho, perhaps Kiowa. There were no survivors to point an accusing finger to those who are guilty of the crime. Kit Carson found their remains in the dessert. Everyone had been killed by arrows and then scalped."

A tide of light-headedness overwhelmed Leonida. She paled and reached for Sage's arm, for which to steady herself. "Dead?" she gasped. "Scalped? Good Lord. I terribly disliked Harold. But I would never wish that on him, or anyone."

"It is best that he is dead," Spotted Feather said.

"The white leader, Harold, was intent on finding you, Leonida. And Sage. He would have never given up the search. Never."

Thinking of the welfare of the baby, Sage swept an arm around Leonida's waist. He nodded to Spotted Feather, then walked Leonida into their hogan. There he eased her down onto a blanket. "Do not mourn the man," he grumbled. "He was nothing, my woman. Nothing."

Leonida reached her hands up to Sage's face. "Oh, darling, I'm not mourning him," she said, her voice breaking. "But I can't help but be sad. I pity Harold for having turned into such a tyrant. He made his own life a living hell."

Sage understood her feelings. The goodness in her caused her to react this way over his needless death. He took her hands and drew her to him and gently hugged her.

"If you must cry, cry," he said softly. "It might be best to wash this man from your heart and mind forever. Then fill your thoughts with something more pleasant." He placed a hand over her tummy. "Has our child kicked much today?"

His question brought Leonida back to her senses. Tears for Harold were not necessary. She should be relieved that he was no longer a threat to her family, her future, and Sage's people.

Leonida pulled Sage's head down, pressing his ear gently against her stomach. "Listen through the fabric of my skirt, darling," she murmured. "Can you hear the strange noises as I am feeling them? That's our child, Sage. Our child! It is as real now as it will be when we hold him in our arms."

Sage listened, then rose, his eyes shining. "Him?"

he said, laughing softly. ''Do you realize you referred to our child as boy child?''

Leonida giggled. She twined her arms around Sage's neck and brought his mouth toward her lips. ''So I did,'' she whispered, kissing him sweetly.

34

We loved with a love that was more than love.
—EDGAR ALLAN POE

Five Years Later

Leonida was sitting inside her hogan, finishing a woven basket with finely split yucca leaves. She held one leaf in her teeth as she looped another around the rim. Fresh green leaves provided the design against a background of sun-bleached white ones. She had learned the art of making lovely baskets to perfection. This was a diamond-patterned creation, perhaps her loveliest yet.

Pausing, she gazed over at her two sons—Runner and Thunder Hawk, touched by how ten-year-old Runner took such pains teaching Thunder Hawk how to read and write, having himself honed these skills from Leonida's teachings. She had no books. Everything that she and Runner were using as tools for teaching was either of sand, paints, or beadwork. Runner was painting numbers on stretched canvas at present, and Thunder Hawk's wide dark eyes took it all in.

Sage came into the dwelling after having council with his warriors. He sat down beside Leonida and also gazed at his sons, pride swelling within him. Runner had never been jealous that his little brother was Navaho like his father, perhaps because Runner looked Navaho in many ways himself now.

Sage reached for Leonida and drew her to his side. Together they looked over at their bright-eyed daughter, who was strapped to a hard-back cradleboard. She had been propped against the wall of the hogan, where she could look around while Leonida was hard at work.

"Pure Blossom is learning today also?" Sage said, laughing softly. "Look how she looks at you. She has been watching you make your basket. She will be as skilled as you, my wife, when she matures enough to use her fingers."

"She's been the sweetest thing today," Leonida said, laying her basketwork aside. She went to the cradleboard and began untying the thongs that held her daughter in place. When Pure Blossom was free, Leonida scooped her up and held her out for Sage.

Sage took his daughter, who was dressed in a fringed doeskin gown. "Is she not even more beautiful than the stars?" he exclaimed, smiling broadly.

Leonida stroked the eight-month-old baby's hair, thick and black already. "Yes, she is ever so beautiful," she murmured. "I'm so glad that she has Navaho features. It is only right that she does since she bears your sister's name."

"My sister would have received much joy from the children," Sage said solemnly, gazing from child to child. "She so loved children. She was such a child at heart herself. So innocent. So lovable. She never seemed to be aware of her afflictions. She accepted them without question."

"You still miss her, don't you?" Leonida said, taking Pure Blossom back as Sage handed the child to her.

"As you also miss her," Sage said, smiling over at Leonida.

The baby began fussing, and it quickly turned into full-blown crying. Leonida rocked her back and forth in her arms. She gave Sage a glance. "Darling, take the boys out for a while, while I feed Pure Blossom."

Sage gathered his sons up into his strong arms, and even though Runner was much too big, carried them outside on his shoulders, leaving Leonida and Pure Blossom alone, to relish these moments as mother and daughter.

Leonida pulled her drawstring blouse down from her shoulders, releasing her milk-filled breasts. Laying Pure Blossom in the crook of her left arm, resting her child's tiny head there, she lifted her breast and placed the nipple inside Pure Blossom's tiny mouth. She watched her child taking nourishment. Pure Blossom's tiny hands kneaded the breast, and all the while the baby made soft, contented noises as she looked trustingly up at Leonida.

With her free hand, Leonida played with Pure Blossom's dark hair, trying to curl its ends, laughing when she found, as before, how impossible it was to do anything with her daughter's stiff, dark locks. It was made for braiding. And that was as it should be, since her daughter had all of her father's features.

Gazing into the baby's dark eyes, fringed by thick lashes, she could see her beloved husband's eyes. No one could look at the high cheekbones and the lovely smooth, copper skin and deny whose child she was. She *was* her father, except in the delicate lines of her face, and the tiny, perfectly shaped lips and her delicately pretty nose.

Leonida ran her finger over the bridge of her daughter's nose. "Just perhaps you have *one* of my features," she whispered, smiling.

Becoming tense, Leonida shifted her attention from her daughter when she heard the sound of horses outside the hogan. She gazed at the door, wondering who had just arrived. She doubted that she would ever relax when she heard someone arriving at the stronghold.

She tried to force her thoughts back to her daughter, but she could not help but glance toward the door. She would hear someone talking, and then Sage responding, yet no matter how hard she listened, she couldn't hear what they were saying!

"It seems like an animated conversation," she whispered to herself, becoming even more wary.

Knowing that Pure Blossom should have had her fill from this breast, she lifted her to rest against her bosom and began softly patting her back, glad when the child gave out a healthy burp. Then she placed Pure Blossom's tiny lips to her other breast.

Leonida's eyes widened when Sage came back into the hogan, the children no longer with him.

"The young braves are all right," Sage said, seeing her anxious look as she looked past him. "They are playing with the others."

"Who came to the stronghold?" Leonida asked.

"Scouts," Sage said, his eyes troubled. "They brought news of Kit Carson, and news that I do not know to trust."

"What sort of news?" Leonida said, glancing down when she no longer felt her daughter's lips moving on her breast and discovering that she was asleep. She slipped Pure Blossom away from the breast, and Sage took her and placed her on a deep pile of blankets in her crib, covering her then with a soft doeskin pelt.

"And what about Kit Carson?" Leonida prodded, pulling her blouse back up in place and retying the drawstring.

"After leaving Fort Defiance, Kit became Superintendent of Indian Affairs for the Colorado Territory," Sage said, settling down on the blanket beside Leonida. He stared blankly into the flames of the fire. "He was not there long."

"Oh? He was assigned elsewhere?" Leonida asked, noticing some sort of book slipped into the waistband of Sage's dark breeches. She was puzzled, having never seen Sage with any books before, and wondering where he might have gotten it.

"Kit Carson was assigned to the Land of the Dead, it seems," Sage mumbled. He looked slowly over at Leonida. "The great pathfinder is dead."

"How terrible," she murmured, torn with conflicting feelings about his death. She was both sorrowful that such a man as he was gone and worried that because of his death, Sage and his people would no longer have a protector.

Sage slipped the small book out from the waist of his breeches and gave it to Leonida. "This is a gift from Kit Carson to you," he said.

Wide-eyed, Leonida accepted the booklet, stunned that Kit would think enough of her to remember her in such a way. Yet in the short time she had known him, he had learned of her love of reading and storytelling. As she read the title of the book, she realized that she was not the only one who loved to tell a story. This book was Kit Carson's memoirs, titled *Dear Old Kit*, published in 1856.

"What a wonderful thing to have," she murmured,

thumbing through it. "From what I know about Kit, he knew not how to read or write. He must have dictated this to someone."

She closed it and held it to her chest. "This is such a treasure, darling," she said, sighing. "One day soon let me read it to you?"

"That would please me," Sage said, then frowned nervously. "But that reading cannot be done soon. I have other plans that must be carried out, although I somewhat fear them."

Leonida scooted closer to Sage. She took his hand in hers. "Darling, you're frightening me," she murmured. "Tell me what you're talking about."

Sage placed a gentle hand on her cheek, then took both of her hands in his. "I did not mean to worry you," he said. "And so much of the news that has been brought to me should make me rejoice. But I can never trust the word of the white man."

He paused, then continued, "It is the year 1868, a year when the white man's president, Ulysses S. Grant, has begun enforcing this concept of no longer negotiating with Indian tribes as independent, sovereign nations of people as a whole. He is now assigning most to reservations, where they can be treated as wards of the United States government," he said, his voice drawn. "This policy will inadvertently institute cultural genocide on the Indian people. The Indians will cease to exist in their natural form and will be remade to conform to the cultural patterns introduced by the white invaders. President Grant is changing most Indians into white emulators, yet . . ."

Sage paused again. He eased his hands from Leonida's and rose to his feet, slowly pacing back and forth.

Fearing what else Sage had to say, Leonida rose quickly to her feet and put a hand on her husband's arm, stopping him. She gazed up into his midnight dark eyes. "Yet what?" she said, her voice stiff.

Sage lifted a hand to her hair and wove his fingers through her shoulder-length tresses, looking down at her with heavy lids. "Yet my scouts have brought news to me about *our* people, the Navaho who had been imprisoned in New Mexico," he said thickly. "The United States government has signed a treaty with them, allowing their return to their homeland, yet cleverly assigning them a huge area of our homeland which no one else really wants. It is my duty to go and see if this is true. If it is, I must invite my people to come to our new stronghold, where no one wants for anything. They do not have to accept the poor land they have been assigned. We can share equally with those who wish to accompany me and my warriors back here."

Fear suddenly grabbed at Leonida's heart. Now she knew why Sage had hesitated at being glad over this news. "This could be a trick to draw you from the stronghold," she said, her voice breaking. She moved onto her knees before Sage, imploring him with anxious, fearful eyes. "Darling, Kit Carson is dead. Without him, can you truly trust to return to Fort Defiance? Perhaps what was told your scouts is all made up, to lure you from your stronghold."

"I have thought of that and, yes, I do fear it," Sage said, taking her hands and holding them to his chest. "But when my scouts were discovered hiding near the fort and invited inside, with promises that they would not be incarcerated, and were given this information, it did seem real enough." He glanced down at Kit Carson's book, then up into Leonida's eyes again. "And there is the book. Kit had left it there for you, should the soldiers ever see you again. They were considerate enough to send it with the scouts to give to you. Does not that seem a sincere gesture?"

Leonida gazed down at the book, then back up at Sage. "It would seem so," she murmured. "Yet it could be a part of the trick, darling. Please don't go. Why risk everything for those people who turned their backs on you? Why?"

"Because they have been forced to live a life of degradation long enough," Sage mumbled. "This land they have been assigned to may not be fertile enough to raise crops. They might starve."

He shook his head slowly back and forth. "Yet I still cannot understand why the white leader would imprison one Indian and let the other go, except perhaps to see them die slowly because they do not have enough food due to the land being too poor to raise it."

He frowned down at Leonida. "That has to be the answer," he growled. "So you see, my wife? I must go and do what I can to help my people. It is time for me to forget the past and their lack of faith in their leader. It is time to give them a new purpose in life and cause to see how wrong they were ever to walk away from what I had promised had they stayed."

"I know that you must," she murmured, flinging herself into his arms, hugging him tightly, as though it might be the last time. "I never doubted that you would."

She closed her eyes, trying to blot out doubts that

she would have to carry with her the whole time he would be gone, yet unable to. She doubted she would ever learn to trust her husband's safety on her own.

35

Quietly you walk your ways,
Steadfast duty fills the days.
—EDWARD ROWLAND SILLS

Sitting before a crackling fire in her adobe home, Leonida was busy peeling "paper" bread from her stone fireplace griddle, which had been Pure Blossom's most treasured possession, handed down from generation to generation. Leonida had been taught that paper bread was a treat, usually reserved for festive occasions. She was preparing for her husband's return, knowing that he would be home again soon. And when he returned with those of his people who had been parted from their loved ones so long—ah, but would not there be a grand celebration?

Smiling assuredly, telling herself over and over again that Sage would return safely, that the soldiers had not tricked him, Leonida carefully folded her paper bread in quarters, then began making another piece of the Navaho delicacy. She carefully spread with her hand a thin batter of blue corn meal on the smoking-hot griddle, allowed it then to bake a few seconds, then lifted it off. Pure Blossom had told her that years of practice were needed before one could smear the batter without burning fingers. Leonida was proud that for her that was not true. She had no scarring on her fingers from being awkward while cooking.

Besides preparing her "paper bread," she was cooking a thin corn gruel in a pot on the fire. For the last two evenings Leonida had hoped that Sage would arrive in time to partake of the evening meal with his family. The children had missed him. Even little Pure Blossom had been more fussy, which meant to Leonida that her daughter was missing the stronger arms of her father. As Leonida felt so much more protected while within her husband's arms, surely also her daughter had instincts enough to feel the same.

Thinking that she had enough paper bread prepared, Leonida began cleaning up the mess she had made, keeping an ear out for sounds at the door of her hogan. She was ever listening for the sound of many horses' hooves, eager to rush out and fling herself into her husband's arms if it were he.

She sighed. Still all that she heard were the children's voices as they played close by with a group of other young braves. It did her heart good to hear her children enjoying themselves in this world that was fraught with questionable deeds and heartache. Before she had moved to Fort Defiance she had never even thought about the plight of the Indians. She was just like everyone else—not thinking about the Indians at all. They were far, far away from where she lived, a part of the wilderness, desert, and mountains.

Never in a million years had she thought she would meet and fall in love with a handsome Navaho chief and marry him, becoming a part *of* the Indian community herself, taking on their same problems, pain, and injustices.

Sudden shouts outside the hogan made Leonida suck in a deep breath. She then heard the sound of horses in the distance.

"Sage," she whispered, placing her hands at her throat. "He's home. Oh, thank the Lord, he's home."

Aflutter with excitement, Leonida went to the crib

and checked on Pure Blossom. She turned and started toward the door, then stopped and gazed down at herself. "I'm a sight!" she groaned, seeing the flour smeared on her colorful skirt. Her hands went to her hair, finding it mussed up from her long hours of cooking.

"I can't let him see me like this," she fretted.

She peered at the door, her heart thumping. "But I can't take the time to clean myself up," she said aloud. "I'm too anxious to see him."

Not thinking anymore about her appearance, Leonida rushed out of the hogan, her fingers working with her hair, trying to make it more presentable. She could see Sage now. He was only a short distance away, riding straight and tall in his Navaho saddle, yet his expression was not that of a happy man.

Leonida's footsteps faltered when she saw what might be the reason for her husband's grave attitude. She was mentally counting the men, women, and children who were sharing rides with Sage's warriors. There weren't nearly as many of his people returning as she had thought there would be.

Fear gripped Leonida's insides. Yet she was sure that not that many had died on the long walk to Mexico. How could it have been that many?

Her thoughts stopped short and her eyes grew wide and disbelieving when she caught sight of at least ten sheep and the same number of goats trailing behind the returning Navaho, being herded along by two young braves.

Runner and Thunder Hawk came running up to Leonida, each grabbing one of her hands. "Daddy is home," Thunder Hawk squealed, peering up at Leonida with his wide eyes.

"Yes, Daddy is home," Leonida said, feeling torn.

She was concerned about the number of people returning to the stronghold, yet surprised and happy about the sheep and goats. The animals would be a blessing. The people's yarn had been all but used up. They had hungered for mutton and goat's milk. And soon they would be blessed with many more sheep and goats.

She turned her eyes back to Runner, wondering why he was so quiet.

Then she found out. His thoughts were on someone besides his daddy.

"I wonder if he got to talk to Adam," Runner said, now more than half as tall as Leonida. He peered ahead. "I wish I could have gone with Father. It would have been good to see Adam again." He shifted his eyes, gazing up at Leonida. "I miss him even though I haven't seen him for five winters. I wonder if he misses me also?"

Leonida hurried her pace as the horses came closer and closer. "I'm sure Adam has missed you as much," she reassured him. "He has probably even sent a message to you with your father. He's probably as practiced in his skills of writing as you are."

Runner suddenly broke free and began running hard and fast toward Sage, waving at him and shouting a greeting in Navaho. The path leading to the returning Navaho was now filled with the people of the stronghold, yet there was no singing. Everyone seemed as solemn as Sage, apprehensive as they stopped to wait for the entourage to come to them.

Even Leonida stopped and waited. She picked Thunder Hawk up into her arms, her heart thumping wildly as Sage's eyes met hers in a silent hello. She watched as he stopped his horse and reached for Runner, pulling him up into the saddle with him, then proceeded onward. Runner smiled proudly as he sat as straight and square-shouldered as his father in his father's fancy Navaho saddle.

Leonida's pulse raced, so wanting to be on that saddle with her husband, yet she stood quietly by, still waiting. Sage's bridle jangled, and his chestnut stallion pranced, his head held high, the round silver conchas on the bridle flashing in the sun.

And then Sage finally reached Leonida. He pulled the reins up tight, then lifted Runner down. Sage slid easily from his saddle and went to Leonida, hugging her and Thunder Hawk in one quick embrace.

Runner came up to Sage and cleared his throat, to get his attention. "Father, did you get to see Adam and talk with him?" Runner asked quickly. "Did he by chance pen me a letter?"

"Adam is no longer living at Fort Defiance," Sage said, his smile fading at the mention of Fort Defiance and his memory of what he had found upon arriving there. There had been some amount of treachery in having him come to Fort Defiance for his people. At least he had been allowed the freedom to return to his stronghold. What saddened him was that once again more than half of those waiting for him at Fort Defiance had refused to return with him.

To have done this once had been, in time, forgivable. But twice? Those who did not return with him had torn pieces of his heart a second time, and this he would never forget—or forgive.

"Adam is gone?" Runner said a second time, finally getting his father's attention. "Where to, Father?"

"His father was assigned to another fort far away," Sage said, turning to nod at those who had dismounted and were walking past him toward their loved ones, who awaited them in twos and threes a few feet away.

"I'll never get to see him again," Adam said, lowering his eyes to the ground.

Seeing Sage cast worried glances all around him, as though he had dreaded this return home instead of looking forward to it, Leonida placed a hand on Runner's shoulder and drew him to her side, leaving Sage to do his duty to his people.

Leonida's eyes followed Sage as he went to the large crowd who were intensely hugging and talking to those who had returned, while some others stood by with tears streaming from their eyes.

Slipping Thunder Hawk from her arms, Leonida bent down and gathered both of her sons close around her as Sage raised his hands, and a muted hush fell among his people.

Everyone turned their eyes on him. His warriors led their horses on around, and held their reins tightly as they stood alongside the others. Leonida saw within the warriors' eyes the same expression that Sage held in his.

"Disappointment met my return to Fort Defiance," Sage said, his voice drawn. "The total freedom I thought was our people's was not there. There were restrictions made on this thing the white pony soldier leaders called 'freedom.' The great white leader has decided to make the Navaho once again self-sufficient on land that was once ours, but only if we agreed to live within a reservation, with strict boundaries on all four sides, within which the Navaho are to stay."

Leonida scarcely breathed, realizing now that Sage's people had returned from their imprisonment in New Mexico only to enter into another, no different except that it was on land familiar to them.

Their way of life would never be the same, it seemed.

Sage continued speaking after a brief pause while the young braves took the sheep and goats on past them to the stronghold.

"As you will notice, we now have sheep and goats," Sage said moodily. "These were gifts from Kit Carson. In papers that are called a 'will,' he remembered Sage and his people. He willed these animals to us so that we could once again become a vital people in all ways."

He paused again, then continued. "As you will also notice, few of our people returned to live among us at the stronghold," he said thickly. "They had choices to make. Those who did not return to the stronghold chose once again a life separate from ours. They could not resist what the white men offered them if they agreed to stay confined to a reservation. Nor may you be able to resist going to live on the reservation once you hear what their offerings were to bribe our people into bending to the will of the white man again. They have issued those families who choose reservation life over ours at least fifteen thousand sheep and goats, and five hundred head of beef cattle, and many hundreds of pounds of maize."

Many gasps rose from the crowd of Navaho, causing Sage's heart to skip a beat and his eyes to narrow. "Listen further, my people," he shouted, raising a fist in the air. "The Navaho who live on the reservation must relinquish any right to occupy lands outside this reservation. And even though the Navaho retain hunting rights on unoccupied lands outside the boundaries of the reservation, that is an empty offering, for most of that land not occupied by white people now is desert and worthless."

Sage gazed over at Leonida, then went to her. She rose next to him, and his arm moved protectively around her waist, while Thunder Hawk moved to Leonida's side, clinging, and Runner moved to Sage's side, standing straight and tall in his shadow.

"The white man treaty makers knew clearly the nature of the land allotted the Navaho," Sage said, his voice drained of feeling. "And hear me well, my beloved people. All unauthorized people are to be excluded from the assigned reservation land and from the offerings of the white people. We are unauthorized people. We must be content now to stay in our canyon and live from this land that we have claimed as ours. The gifts from Kit Carson will soon multiply. We need not the white man's treaty, or his so-called freedom. We have our own freedoms. Our own treaties amongst ourselves! We are one, united, as one heartbeat! Let us never hunger for more than that."

Then he paused again, his gaze shifting from Navaho to Navaho. "But if there be one among you who wishes to join those on the reservation, you are free to go," he said guardedly. "Go now, or never."

There was no response.

No one even seemed to bat an eye, much less step forward to tell Sage that they wished to leave the stronghold and his devoted command.

Sage fought back the tears that were stinging his eyes, proud that he had finally achieved a loyal following. It touched his heart so much that he wanted to move among his people and give them all a generous hug.

But he knew that he must refrain from showing his gratitude outwardly. He feared that it would diminish his nobility somehow. As time went on, he would show his gratitude in ways that would be more worthwhile.

"Then so be it," he said, lifting his chin proudly. "Now let us move on to our stronghold. We have cause to celebrate. We are a people united. We are the blessed ones."

Leonida clung to Sage's side as they walked among his people toward the cluster of hogans a short distance away, where the smoke from the cook fires curled peacefully skyward.

36

So shall we not part at the end of the day,
Who have loved and lingered a little while,
Join lips with a sigh, a smile . . .
—ERNEST DOWSON

Both wanting to put all connections of the past with
the white pony soldiers behind them and feeling
threatened by the spirits of his enemies, Sage and his
warriors held a week-long curing ceremony to help
them rediscover their true selves, threading throughout
it the relationship and trust and respect among his
Navaho clan. The ceremony was also meant to free
Sage and his warriors of anxieties by ''killing'' off
their enemy spirits, gaining strength from a juniper
stick given added power by attached eagle and turkey
feathers.

It was now the last day of the ceremony, a time for
its lighter side—a time of dancing, singing, laughter,
and feasting.

Leonida sat among the women, close to the large
outdoor communal cook fire, where many delicacies
were steaming, wafting delicious aromas into the
night air. She was clapping her hands in time with
the music while the young braves of the village performed a dance, their breechclouts flapping in the
wind as they lifted and stamped their feet in the dust.

Sage came and sat down beside Leonida. When
she gazed over at him, she could see what she had
hoped to see ever since she had met him: peace.
Within his midnight-dark eyes she could see con-

tentment, happiness, and tranquillity. The ceremony had lifted all of the troubles and burdens from his heart.

She became overwhelmed with happiness herself, knowing that he was no longer carrying around with him all of the sadness and heartaches of his people. They had been cast away into the wind, hopefully gone forever.

Sage put an arm around Leonida's waist and drew her to lean close against his side. His throaty laughter drew her out of her deep thoughts. "What is amusing you?" she asked softly.

"Thunder Hawk," Sage said, motioning toward him with a nod. "See how he dances skillfully among those who are much older? He is as agile as a bobcat. Just watch him. Does he not make you so proud?"

"Yes, very," Leonida said, reaching for Sage's hand, gently grasping it. She glanced over at Runner, whose attention seemed to have been drawn from dancing to a pretty young maiden.

Leonida nudged Sage with her elbow. "Look at Runner," she said, giggling as the pretty girl grabbed her son's hand and ran off with him, taking him to a group of other children who were more interested in playing games than dancing. "Who is she? She is a beautiful child."

"That is Gentle Fawn," Sage said, his eyes also admiring the young thing, who wore a pale blue velveteen skirt and a matching velveteen blouse, with turquoise jewelry at both her throat and her wrists. Her raven-black hair was worn in one long braid down her back, and she had dotted smudges of bloodroot on her cheeks to make her look older.

They watched Runner for a moment longer, then

both rose to their feet when they heard Pure Blossom crying from inside their hogan. Arm in arm, they went inside. Sage lifted Pure Blossom into his arms, as Leonida sat down on a soft cushion of blankets beside the fire.

"Soon she will not be feeding from your breast, but joining her family to eat meals," Sage said, putting the babe into Leonida's waiting arms. "Look at how fat her arms and legs are. And look at her face. With your milk she has blossomed into someone very pretty."

"Yes, she is pretty, and it won't be long until she is singled out by a certain young man to join her in fun and games," Leonida said, laughing softly as she put Pure Blossom's lips to her breast. She watched her daughter feeding for a few moments, then gazed over at Sage with a soft smile. "Everything is so wonderful now, darling. I am so very happy."

"Life among the Navaho is not a simple thing," Sage said, placing a hand on her cheek, this thumb caressing her beneath her chin. "But it is a challenge most welcomed by my wife? Yes?"

Leonida leaned into his hand. "I wouldn't have it any other way," she murmured.

Sage bent low over Leonida and cupped her free breast, then placed his lips over the nipple. He flicked his tongue around the nipple yet did not suckle from it, leaving that honor to their child. After Pure Blossom was finished nursing, having grown old enough to get her nourishment elsewhere, then he would claim his wife's breasts as his own again, the source of much pleasure for him.

"She's asleep," Leonida whispered, laughing softly. "That was the fastest dinner my daughter has ever drunk. For the moment I guess she prefers sleep over milk.''

"That is good," Sage said, his voice now husky with desire for his wife. "She can sleep. We can make love.''

Sage lifted the child from Leonida's arms and took her back to her crib, gently placing her on her cushion of blankets. He pulled another blanket over her, then turned to Leonida, his eyes filled with hunger for her.

Leonida rose to her feet and went to Sage, melting into his arms. She gazed up at him. "What about the boys?'' she whispered, her heart throbbing with need of her husband. "What if they decide to come home sooner than we expect them to?''

Sage held her within his muscular arms, his head bent low, his breath hot on her lips. "Do you not hear the laughter and music?'' he said, teasingly brushing a kiss across her lips. "As long as there are games and fun to share with others, both of our sons will not even think about home. Do not fret so, pretty wife. This time is ours alone. Let us take advantage of it.''

Leonida's stomach growled hungrily as the aroma of food drifted into the hogan through the door. "Handsome husband, are you not hungry?'' she whispered, sucking a wild breath of rapture as he smoothed his hands between them and cupped both of her breasts, kneading them.

"Let us not speak of food," Sage said. "Let us not speak of anything. The moments are wasting away in talk.''

Suddenly he grabbed her up into his arms and carried her toward their bedroom, lifting her high enough to kiss her. Leonida twined her arms around his neck,

thrilling inside as though it was their first time together. All of her senses were yearning for what lay
ahead—the promise of boundless pleasure.

Stretching her out on her back on the soft cushion
of their bed, Sage was already aware of the tingling
heat pressing in on his loins, surges of warmth flooding through him at the promise of what he was going
to share once again with his wife.

Her pulse racing, Leonida stretched her arms above
her head as Sage removed her blouse. Once it was
tossed aside, she lifted her hips so that he could quickly
remove her skirt. She shivered with pleasure from her
head to her toes as he knelt down over her and began
worshiping her flesh with his mouth and tongue. She
closed her eyes and enjoyed the euphoria building
within her as he found and pleasured her most sensual
places. Yet she was glad when he rose from her, realizing that she was too near to going over the edge
into ecstasy.

Sage understood her bidding as she ever so gently
shoved him away from her. He also was near to the
exploding point, and he had not yet filled her with his
throbbing hardness.

Moving over her, Sage's eyes burned with passion
as he looked down at her. ''Darling, I've missed you
so these past several days,'' she murmured. She
framed his face with her hands and drew his lips to
hers. ''But it was worth it, to see you so at peace with
yourself.''

Sage's mouth seared hers, her lips quivering and
passionate against his. Her breasts strained against his
fingers as he cupped them within the palms of his
hands. Desire gripped her when he thrust himself into
her softly yielding folds. She felt a tremor from deep
within, and she moaned against his lips as he began

his rhythmic strokes, her hips rising to meet his quickening thrusts.

Leonida's throat arched backward as he slipped his mouth down from her lips, across the vulnerable hollow of her throat, and then fastened gently on her breast, yet still not suckling from it. He kneaded them gently, feeling how warm and full they were. When a droplet of milk spilled from one of the nipples, Sage stilled his movements within her and gazed from the milk up into Leonida's eyes.

Aware of what had happened, Leonida shifted her gaze downward and swept the milk droplet onto the tip of her finger, then smiled up at Sage as she moved the finger towards his mouth.

"Taste of my milk," she murmured. When he hesitated, she placed the finger against his lower lip, the milk rolling onto it. "It's all right, darling. Please? Tell me how it tastes?"

Sage ran his tongue over his bottom lip and tasted the milk, then smiled down at her. "Sweet," he said softly. "It tastes as sweet as my wife smells."

In a blaze of urgency he claimed her lips again with his mouth, emitting a thick, husky groan as Leonida lifted her legs and locked them around him, drawing him even more deeply into her. Wrapping her within his powerful arms, he pressed deeper and deeper. It was as though a great fire was burning within, agony and bliss as his passion spread through his whole body, now fluid with the burning, fierce heat of wild splendor.

Leonida clung to him, overcome by the almost unbearable sweet pain of bliss, the excitement building within her like the deep rumblings of a volcano shortly before it erupts.

When she reached that ultimate splendor, she drew in her breath sharply and gave a little cry. Sage's head now rested on her bosom as he groaned in pleasure and his hips moved in a frenzy, thrusting over and over again into her.

Too soon it was over. Breathing hard, Sage rolled away from Leonida. He turned on his side toward her and gently cupped her cheek. "You are even more beautiful now that you have carried two children in your womb," he said. "And that seems impossible, for that day I first saw you I felt as though you were perhaps a vision of my imagination, yet never in my midnight dreams had I seen anyone as lovely or as sweet. My wife, you are what my midnight dreams are now made of. So you see? I never part from you even when I sleep."

"In my early teens I tried to envision the man of my dreams," Leonida murmured. "I could never find in my mind's eye exactly what I wanted in a man. It always seemed a blur. Now I know why. I was meant to fall in love with an Indian, and as you know, in my culture that is something that is not accepted. To most, it is even forbidden. So I could not envision marrying a man that would be forbidden to me."

She locked her arms around his neck and drew him close. "My darling, you are far more than what I could have ever envisioned in my childhood fantasies," she whispered. "You are not only handsome, but your heart is good toward everyone. Kit Carson knew that to be so. That is why, in the end, he tried to compensate for the wrong he did you, by giving your people the goats and sheep. He knew that they would soon multiply."

"The pathfinder was a great man," Sage said, leaning away from Leonida. He twined his fingers through his dark hair and pushed it farther back from his brow. "It is unfortunate that somewhere along the way he listened more to the white leaders than to his heart."

Loud, excited squeals from the outer room drew Sage and Leonida from their bed. Dressing quickly and breathlessly, they had just fastened their last buttons when both of their sons burst into the room.

"Chips is back," Runner said, holding the tiny chipmunk out for Sage and Leonida to see. "See? She has returned to me after all these years. She remembers me."

"But one of her legs is gone," Thunder Hawk said gloomily, pointing to where the missing limb should be. "A hawk, it is responsible."

Leonida sighed sadly when she took the chipmunk into her hands and examined it. "She has surely taken a beating while gone from you," she murmured. She held the chipmunk to her bosom. "You poor thing."

"It is unfortunate that the chipmunk has been injured," Sage said, picking up a son in each of his arms and carrying them to the outer room, with Leonida at his side petting the chipmunk on her brown crown of a head. "But you should feel blessed that she was able to return at all, if that was what she wanted to do."

"Her babies are all grown up and gone," Runner said sadly.

"As one day you will grow up and go out on your own away from your parents," Leonida said, dreading the thought of his ever leaving her.

Sage set both boys on blankets close to the fire. He patted them each on the head, then went and put an arm around Leonida as she bent to set Chips free. She smiled down at Runner as the chipmunk scampered quickly onto Runner's lap, as though afraid ever to leave his protection again.

"Seems she won't be leaving you," Leonida said, laughing softly.

Sage took Leonida by the hand. "I think it's time to join the celebration again," he said, walking her toward the door. "The aroma of the food is drawing me to it. Come and show me the food that was prepared over *our* fire. It will be the best of all."

Leonida looked over her shoulder before going on outside. "Come on, boys," she said. "Let's sit together as a family while we eat."

"What about Pure Blossom?" Thunder Hawk said as he came bouncing toward Leonida. "She is family. Should she not join us also? It seems to be taking her so long to grow up enough to be like me and Runner."

Sage laughed throatily as he swept Thunder Hawk into his arms and left the hogan. "She will never be like you and Runner," he said, balancing Thunder Hawk on his shoulder as they walked toward the tantalizing smell of the food. "In many ways she will be different."

"But she will join us soon to eat with us," Leonida interjected. "Perhaps in a month or two."

She gazed down at Runner as he came to her side, serious as he still petted his chipmunk. He had so many qualities of his father, all good. He was compassionate, brave, and intelligent. She had to believe that one day he would make as great a leader as Sage.

Then she cast a worried glance at Thunder Hawk. She could not fear the future in that her two children might end up competing for leadership, causing brothers to become enemies.

She shook her head to clear her mind of such thoughts. Tonight was so far from that future, and tonight everything seemed perfect, ah, so wonderfully perfect.

Dear Reader,

I hope you enjoyed *Savage Nights*. Those of you who are collecting my Indian romance novels, and want to hear more about them and my entire backlist of books, can send for my latest newsletter, autographed bookmark, and fan club information, by writing to:

Cassie Edwards
6709 North Country Club Road
Mattoon, IL 61938

For an assured response, please include a stamped, self-addressed, legal-sized envelope with your letter. And you can visit my Web site at www.cassieedwards.com.

Thank you for supporting my Indian series. I love researching and writing about our beloved Native Americans, our country's true first people.

Always,

Cassie Edwards

CASSIE EDWARDS

SAVAGE INTRIGUE

To be a Dakota Indian in 1862 Minnesota is to live in constant fear of lynching and hanging. Even a white doctor known for treating Native Americans is viciously murdered, leaving his daughter, Sheleen, to fight off his attacker and flee for her life.

Rescued in the remote woods by Chief Midnight Wolf, Sheleen feels she has found her true home at last. In his bronzed, muscular arms, she will no longer feel alone. But Sheleen still has challenges to face, and a secret that must be revealed. Before she can know the ecstasy of complete fulfillment, she will have to resolve this...*Savage Intrigue*.

ISBN 10: 0-8439-5536-8
ISBN 13: 978-0-8439-5536-1 $6.99 US/$8.99 CAN

CASSIE EDWARDS

Savage RAGE

To Hannah Kody, the Kansas Territory is her escape, a chance to ride horses with the wind in her hair and taste true freedom, all while acting as her brother's failing eyes. His ranch will fall into the wrong hands— those of his shifty foreman—without her.

Yet those limitless plains hold more than freedom; they are also the home of Strong Wolf and the Patawatomi people he will one day lead. Hannah soon feels *he* is her destiny. Together they might save the land they both love from ruin. Together, they might flee from sorrow and betrayal to a place of pure joy and pure love.

ISBN 10: 0-8439-5884-7
ISBN 13: 978-0-8439-5884-3 $4.99 US/$6.99 CAN

To order a book or to request a catalog call:
1-800-481-9191
This book is also available at your local bookstore, or you can check out our Web site **www.dorchesterpub.com** where you can look up your favorite authors, read excerpts, or glance at our discussion forum to see what people have to say about your favorite books.

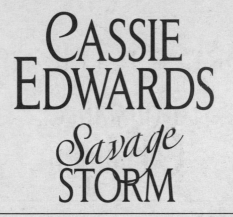

CASSIE EDWARDS
Savage STORM

Born among the settlers, but raised by the Navaho, Runner's destiny is to become their leader. He is enraged when railroads begin rolling into the Arizona Territory, breaking promises made to the Navaho and destroying their precious land.

The copper hair and probing gray eyes of Stephanie Helton do nothing to improve circumstances. Runner's desire for her defies reason. The choice between Stephanie's tender kisses and his people's plight threatens either to break his heart or to make it soar to the heights of love, even through a...*Savage Storm*.

ISBN 10: 0-8439-5885-5
ISBN 13: 978-0-8439-5885-0

$4.99 US/$6.99 CAN

To order a book or to request a catalog call:
1-800-481-9191
This book is also available at your local bookstore, or you can check out our Web site **www.dorchesterpub.com** where you can look up your favorite authors, read excerpts, or glance at our discussion forum to see what people have to say about your favorite books.

LORD OF THE NILE

Constance O'Banyon

From the destruction of Roman battlefields to the delights of Egypt's bedrooms, he's seen it all. But as two ships cross in the dangerous currents of Alexandria, Ramtat catches sight of the most intriguing woman he's ever beheld. A tamer of wild beasts, the mysterious beauty is as fiery as the burning sands of her homeland, lush as a desert oasis. With kiss following sultry kiss, their desire knows no limits. Slave girl or princess, her identity can be unlocked by the emerald-eyed cobra charm that dangles between her breasts, but only her love matters to the...*Lord of the Nile*.

ISBN 10: 0-8439-5821-9
ISBN 13: 978-0-8439-5821-8 $6.99 US/$8.99 CAN

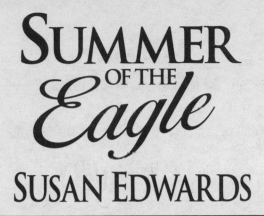

SUMMER OF THE *Eagle*

SUSAN EDWARDS

Blaze is an outcast. The most powerful healer in her tribe, she uses her impossible abilities only for good, but even that has alienated her fellow Sioux. She herself fears some of the things she can do.

But the winds of destiny are rising, sweeping Blaze toward freedom and others of her kind. There is darkness in her visions, but also a man: a tall, buckskin-clad stranger with golden-brown hair and eyes as green as the leaves on the trees. Though he is nothing like her, his eyes promise understanding, kindness, and a love that will be hers and hers alone.